SPIN THE BOTTLE

The explosion of a revolver shot split the air, followed by a shrill scream from a woman and the sound of running feet. The deadly gunshot silenced Gus, the piano, and all other noises except the sound of people scrambling for cover. Fargo ran to the door and looked inside. There were only two men standing; they swayed, glaring daggers at each other.

The combatant to Fargo's left snarled, "Draw, damn you!" Fargo considered what would be best for him to do. He didn't want to shoot anybody if he didn't have to, and he sure as the devil didn't want these two throwing lead at each other in a crowded barroom.

He could think of only one way to arrange this. Silently he entered the room, making sure the door didn't squeak on its hinges, and reached for a bottle standing on a table. Taking careful aim, he wound up, then let the bottle fly, targeting the gunman's head.

It took only seconds. The sound of the bottle hurtling through the air barely registered on the occupants of the room before it hit its subject with a sickening crunch. Fargo winced and drew his Colt, just in case. The man folded up like a concertina and hit the floor with a thud.

THE
TRAILSMAN
#221

CALIFORNIA
CRUSADER

by

Jon Sharpe

A SIGNET BOOK

SIGNET
Published by New American Library, a division of
Penguin Putnam Inc., 375 Hudson Street,
New York, New York 10014, U.S.A.
Penguin Books Ltd, 27 Wrights Lane,
London W8 5TZ, England
Penguin Books Australia Ltd,
Ringwood, Victoria, Australia
Penguin Books Canada Ltd, 10 Alcorn Avenue,
Toronto, Ontario, Canada M4V 3B2
Penguin Books (N.Z.) Ltd, 182–190 Wairau Road,
Auckland 10, New Zealand

Penguin Books Ltd, Registered Offices:
Harmondsworth, Middlesex, England

First published by Signet, an imprint of New American Library,
a division of Penguin Putnam Inc.

First Printing, March 2000
10 9 8 7 6 5 4 3 2 1

The first chapter of this book originally appeared in *Montana Gun Sharps*,
the two hundred twentieth volume in this series.

Ⓞ REGISTERED TRADEMARK—MARCA REGISTRADA

Printed in the United States of America

PUBLISHER'S NOTE
This is a work of fiction. Names, characters, places and incidents are either
the product of the author's imagination or are used fictitiously, and any
resemblance to actual persons, living or dead, business establishments,
events, or locales is entirely coincidental.

The Trailsman

Beginnings . . . they bend the tree and they mark the man. Skye Fargo was born when he was eighteen. Terror was his midwife, vengeance his first cry. Killing spawned Skye Fargo, ruthless, cold-blooded murder. Out of the acrid smoke of gunpowder still hanging in the air, he rose, cried out a promise never forgotten.

The Trailsman they began to call him all across the West: searcher, scout, hunter, the man who could see where others only looked, his skills for hire but not his soul, the man who lived each day to the fullest, yet trailed each tomorrow. Skye Fargo, the Trailsman, and the seeker who could take the wilderness of a land and the wanting of a woman and make them his own.

1860—California, where the word of God falls upon godless ears, and where a fast draw and hot lead are the only sure paths to redemption. . . .

1

A feeling of contentment crept over Skye Fargo as he and his big pinto stallion rose slowly through the tall pine, fir, and incense cedar trees. He inhaled the balsamic scent of the forest and was glad the army didn't need his services again any time soon. This was beautiful country. He'd seen it before, but he'd sure like to explore it some more.

Curly fronds of new ferns appeared almost primeval to his appreciative eye, growing in clumps beneath the trees. Small yellow and purple flowers poked their heads through what looked like hundreds of years' worth of fallen leaves and conifer needles. The thick mulch muted the sound of the Ovaro's hooves, making the impression of otherworldliness almost palpable.

As if to remind Skye Fargo that he lived on this earth with the rest of God's creatures, red squirrels scolded him from tree trunks and birds chirped lustily at one another from branches. He startled a deer, which turned and bolted off through the trees. If he didn't know better, he might just believe himself to be the first human being ever to travel through these woods.

He did know better, however. Indians had lived

here for generations, leaving Mother Nature's handiwork pretty much as they'd found it. Then the Spaniards had come and subjugated the Indians, using the land to graze huge herds of cattle. Indians and Spaniards were no longer the only humans living here now, though. Fargo considered that something of a shame.

California. Land of sunshine and gold. Fargo appreciated the sunshine; indeed, he lifted his bearded face and allowed the sun's rays to soak into his skin, basking in the heat like a lizard. He wished nobody had ever discovered gold here, because the pristine beauty of this magnificent place wouldn't last long once the white men got to trampling it underfoot. Hell, they already had, in spots. California had been declared a state a scant year afer gold was discovered.

He sighed, wishing the white man, in his pursuit of civilization, didn't always cut such a swath of destruction wherever he went. But that was the nature of the beast, he reckoned, and who was he to argue?

A discordant sound smote his ears, and he frowned. If there was one thing that could bring a fellow back to earth with a thump and remind him he wasn't alone on it, it was hearing the racket generated by a human squabble. Who the hell was that, shouting and arguing and spoiling the stillness of the day? He sighed again, heavily. He couldn't seem to get away from trouble, no matter how hard he tried.

Here he'd been thinking he'd make a peaceful visit to Gus Perkins in Barley Flats, as long as he was in California on army business, and not have to deal with anything more difficult than deciding which of Gus's sporting girls to bed. He should have known better. Peace and Skye Fargo didn't often find themselves in the same place at the same time for very long.

He listened awhile longer. The noises were becoming more distinct. "Shoot, there's a woman involved," he muttered to his horse. "And she sounds scared."

The Ovaro jingled the bit as if he were suitably outraged.

He pondered his options. They became fewer when he heard the woman shout, "No! No, you vicious fiend! Stop that!"

"Aw, hell." He frowned and nudged his horse to the right, through a stand of towering fir trees, in the direction of the strife.

Whoever the voices belonged to, they were making such a din that they didn't hear Fargo's approach. When he rode past a clump of mesquite bushes into a clearing, he viewed an interesting spectacle.

Four men, drunk as he'd suspected, surrounded a lone woman. The men were laughing. The woman wasn't. Rather, she was berating the men in no-uncertain terms and stamping her foot as if she meant it. Fargo folded his hands over the saddle horn and watched for a moment, entertained. A mule cropped grass at the other end of the clearing. Since it held a sidesaddle and heavily laden saddlebags, Fargo assumed it had been the woman's means of transportation before the contretemps began.

"Whooo," slurred one of the men—miners, from the looks of them. "Ain't she a hellcat, though, Pete?"

"Don't you dare swear in my presence, you abandoned wretch!"

The woman, whose face was bright pink with rage, wasn't an altogether bad-looking article—or wouldn't be if she ever calmed down again. Her clothing was kind of prudish, though. She wore a black dress, high-necked and prim. Her hair might be kind of pretty if she didn't have it braided and wrapped up in such an uninviting way. It looked sort of reddish, although that might be a trick of the light filtering through the surrounding trees. Her high-topped shoes were laced to within an inch of their lives. So was she, for that matter. Her bonnet had been snatched by one of the miners, who dangled it by its ribbons between dirty fingers. The woman made occasional grabs for it, but the miner avoided her swipes, staggering backward as he did so, laughing as if he hadn't had such sport in a long time.

"Come on, now, ma'am. We're only playin' with ya a little bit. We don't mean ya no harm."

"No harm?" the woman shrieked. "No *harm*? Why, you drunken louts!"

Fargo shook his head when the woman managed to get hold of her bonnet and started a tugging match with the miner who still held the ribbons.

"Listen, lady," another miner said. "We was just re-laxin' here in the shade when you come up to us. We didn't do nothin' to you."

"I was *lost*," the woman cried. "I needed *help*! And what did I find? Four men who are lost to all decency!"

"That ain't fair, ma'am," the man said. He seemed the most judicious, if not the most sober, of the four miners. "We didn't expect no lady to interrupt us. We was just havin' ourselves a little celebrash—cele-bray—party."

"We was happy to help you," said another. "But you started in on us, tellin' us how dishgushtin' we was."

4

They had a point, if they were speaking the truth. No fellow appreciated being lit into for excessive drinking by an interfering female, and a stranger to boot. Nevertheless, Skye Fargo knew where his duty lay. The woman was crying now. He judged her tears were more from anger than from fright.

Fargo plucked his Colt out of his holster and, thus armed, he urged the Ovaro forward. In order to get everybody's attention, he gave one short, sharp whistle through his teeth.

The woman clapped her hands to her ears. The miners, less stable on their pins than she, tried to spin around. Two of them fell over for their efforts.

The one who'd held the bonnet said, "Shoot, who's that?"

The judicious one, from his new position on his butt in the clearing, shook his head to clear it. The other two men only gaped at him, their mouths hanging open, their bleary eyes blinking, as if they were trying to focus them.

"I think you four ought to say you're sorry and clear out of here now. The lady doesn't appreciate your attentions."

The woman dropped her hands from her ears. They immediately formed fists, which she propped on her hips in a belligerent pose. "I should say I don't!"

One of the men moved. Fargo didn't know if the move was voluntary or if it was the whiskey making him sway, but he wasn't taking chances. He cocked the Colt. "Don't try anything."

"I—I ain't doin' nothin'," said the man and he staggered back.

Fargo shook his head and peered at the woman. "I don't think they meant you any real harm, ma'am."

"No?" The woman glared at her former tormentors. One of her hands left its perch on her hip to brush a few strands of hair out of her eyes.

She shook her finger at the four men, who stared at her with varying expressions on their faces, the primary one of which was befuddlement. "Shame on you all. *Shame* on you!"

Not one of the men dared speak in the face of her reproaching finger. She folded the finger up into a fist and propped it on her hip again. "I suppose it was the evil of the devil's brew doing the harm for them," she said scornfully.

Skye Fargo didn't sneer at her. He knew that whiskey did bad things to men when they drank too much of it, but he wouldn't personally stigmatize it as evil, or as coming from the devil. He liked a good snort of bourbon occasionally himself. Because he felt sort of sorry for the woman, he said, "Probably. They don't seem to be really bad fellows."

She sucked in about a bushel of air and let it out gradually. Fargo blinked, because when she did it, he realized she had quite a bosom on her. Too bad she didn't seem like the sort to share it with a lonely traveler.

She eyed the four men and her expression turned sympathetic. "Poor misguided souls."

Although he wouldn't go as far as all that, Fargo said, "Right. So, do you need some help, ma'am? I heard you say you were lost."

One of the miners bobbed his head. "She shed she was losht."

The woman shuddered. "Not as lost as the four of you, I fear."

She went to her mule and flipped open a saddle

bag. When she came back, her hands were full of tracts which she began to distribute to the four men. "Here. When you sober up, I want you to read these. Perhaps this experience was ordained by God to guide you into the light."

"Th' light?" The bonnet-holding miner blinked fuzzily a couple of times.

"The light of Jesus Christ, my good man." The woman's smile could only be described as radiant. "He will lead you from the paths of wickedness and onto the narrow path of righteousness. *He* will guide you away from the lures of liquor and sin. *He* will purify your life!"

Fargo didn't know about those poor fools, but he didn't want to be led away from the lures of liquor and sin. Before she got too wound up, he said, "Uh, ma'am, if you want me to help you get to wherever you're going, maybe we ought to start before the light fades."

One of the miners gave him a grateful smile. "Yeah. Good idear."

The woman didn't appreciate Fargo's interruption. She frowned up at him. "One moment, if you will, sir. These men need my help. They are the reason I'm here." She shook a tract at him.

"We are?" The four men gaped at her.

Since none of the miners seemed to be in the mood for violence, Fargo holstered his Colt, although he didn't drop his guard.

"Indeed you are. I came to California to spread the light." The woman finished handing out her tracts, dusted her hands together, and beamed at the four miners as if she'd done an important day's work. "There. Now I'm going to go to Barley Flats, my dear sirs, and should any one of you feel the need to talk to someone about asking God's divine grace into your heart in order to cleanse your life, please look me up. My name is Miss Genevieve Wiley, and I shall be happy to pray with you."

"P—pray?" The judicious miner goggled.

"Indeed, my good fellow." She clutched her hands together at her waist and got an evangelistic light in her eyes that Fargo feared boded ill for the rest of his trip to Barley Flats. "In fact, I do believe the four of you—" She shot Fargo a glance and decided, with a nod and a smile, to include him. "That is to say, the *five* of you—could use some of God's grace to rain down upon you right this minute."

"Uh, ma'am—"

She held up a hand to forestall Fargo's further comments. "No, my blessed, heaven-sent rescuer—"

"Resh-cuer?" The bonnet-holding miner, who hadn't tried to rise, turned over, cradled his head on his folded arms, and shut his eyes.

The judicious miner muttered, "Heav'n shent?"

"Yes. My gallant, heaven-sent rescuer and the four of you deserve some prayers." She held her arms up to the heavens, shut her eyes, and started in. "Our precious Heavenly Father, please take these sinners into Your divine care. Lead them away from the path of wickedness, and show them the light of Your blessed mercy."

She looked like she was in some kind of ecstasy. Fargo had usually seen that expression on women's faces under different circumstances. He wondered if it was blasphemous to think of them now.

Miss Wiley paused in her oratory, opened her eyes, and seeing that her audience hadn't even bothered to bow their heads, much less close their eyes prayerfully, she frowned. Fargo hoped she wouldn't lay into them again.

She didn't. Evidently deciding it wasn't worth the energy it would take to penetrate the fuzzy brains of a quartet of drunken miners, she concluded quickly. "Please care for them and keep them in Thy mercy. In the name of Your Son, Jesus Christ, Amen."

"Amen," Fargo muttered.

"Amen," mumbled the judicious miner.

"Amen," slurred another one.

The bonnet-holder sent a sonorous snore up to heaven.

2

you both always felt about each other, she didn't want
to be seen in his loving embrace...

"It's so fortunate for me that you're going to Barley
Flats too, Mr. Fargo."

The smile Genevieve Wiley gave Skye Fargo made
him wish it were on the face of a different kind of
woman—the kind who enjoyed the sorts of entertain-
ments and relaxations he did.

"Yeah."

If he had a choice between riding through the spectacular mountain scenery of California with a missionary, or riding through it alone with his horse,
he'd take the latter any day. Unfortunately, he perceived no choice in this instance. He'd butted in, and
now he was stuck.

"It was part of God's blessed design that you come
upon me in my hour of need, Mr. Fargo, and I honor
Him for that." Her little gloved hands held the reins
fairly well. At least she didn't jerk at the mule's
mouth when she steered.

He considered asking her why God's blessed design had stuck her in that clearing with four drunk
miners to begin with, but didn't. She'd probably say
His ways were mysterious and unclear to mortal
men. As far as Fargo was concerned, that was the ex-

cuse folks always fell back on when they didn't want to be bothered thinking for themselves.

"I've been a missionary for several years now, and I've seen it happen over and over again. The good Lord provides just when one believes all hope is gone."

"That so?" Skye Fargo had seldom been at a loss for words, but he couldn't think of many to heave back at Miss Genevieve Wiley at the moment. It didn't seem to matter, because she was doing all right without his help.

"Indeed," she continued. "My beloved father—my earthly father, not my Heavenly One—used to tell me, 'Genevieve, believe in God's infinite mercy, and all will be well.'"

Miss Wiley heaved a big, happy sigh. Fargo wished she wouldn't do that. She had a shape a man could easily fall in lust with, as well as the brightest greenish brown eyes he'd ever seen. She even had a smattering of freckles across her nose. The longer he remained in Miss Genevieve Wiley's company, the more he wished she wasn't a missionary.

"Isn't this a glorious land, Mr. Fargo? Unspoiled, untamed, yet with God's magnificent bounty just waiting to be revealed."

"Uh, yeah." Fargo wished they weren't so far from Barley Flats. Being in Miss Wiley's company made him itch to reveal her personal magnificent bounty.

"How long do you expect it will take us to get there?"

"A day or two more, I should think."

"My goodness." She looked slightly daunted.

She'd managed to shake out her bonnet and it didn't seem too badly spoiled, although Fargo suspected its brim would never quite recover from the battle it had been through. He said, "Barley Flats is in the White Mountains, near the eastern border of California."

It was a hell of a place, too, according to Gus, who'd written Fargo a letter about it. Wild and free and full of the sorts of amusements Fargo liked, although its citizens seemed to favor killing each other a good deal too much for his taste. Whatever its penchant for murder, Gus thought Barley Flats was a swell town. Fargo imagined Gus was right.

He also expected Miss Wiley would find plenty of sinners to save there. Although Fargo's own opinion of missionaries was lukewarm at best, he sort of hoped she wouldn't be discouraged when she discovered she'd undertaken too huge a job for so small a female, no matter how big her heart.

"I've heard it's a rough place," she said thoughtfully.

"So have I."

She heaved another happy sigh. "So I'll have plenty of work to do, I suppose."

"Right."

"It seems a shame that when men set out to seek their fortunes, they leave their morals behind."

Her expression sagged for a moment into one of sadness. He squinted at her, wondering if she was really as holy as she wanted folks to believe. He had no reason to doubt her. More's the pity.

"It's a shame," she continued. "I should think that the finding of great quantities of gold and silver would bring a fellow closer to his Maker, rather than driving him further away. After all, it was God's plan that put the gold and silver into the ground, and His acquiescence that allowed man to dig it out again."

"Mmmmm."

"But such is the fallen nature of mankind." She shook her head, then brightened. "Nevertheless, I shall not shirk! I know my duty. Don't you think it's fortunate when a person discovers his or her calling in life when he or she is still spry enough to perform it, Mr. Fargo?"

Hell, Fargo expected he'd be spry enough to perform until the day he died. And he'd been blasted into his life's calling when he was too young to voice an opinion on the matter. He didn't share his expectations or his history with Miss Wiley, but opted for another noncommittal, "Mmmmm."

The sun was getting lower on the horizon, and he decided it would behoove them to find a place to camp before it set entirely. The information he'd gleaned in Modesto gave him to understand that he would have no trouble with Indians in the area. Outlaws might be another matter, and he wanted to set up a secure campsite while there was still light.

He spotted a clearing with a stream running through it some fifty yards off the trail and guided the Ovaro to his left. "That might be a good place to camp, ma'am. Stay here while I scout it out."

"Very well, Mr. Fargo."

She gave him one of her beaming smiles, and Fargo rolled his eyes as he trotted to the clearing.

The site would do, and Fargo set about preparing for the evening. Miss Wiley claimed she wasn't unhandy when it came to building campfires, so he left her to collect wood while he tended to the Ovaro and the mule.

When he'd finished with the animals, he discovered the missionary hadn't fibbed. The fire she'd built was more than adequate for supper and warmth. Not that he expected it would get very cold, since it was mid-June and the day had been hot. Nevertheless, they were in the mountains, and you never knew.

He laid out two bedrolls, using fallen pine needles as mattresses. He put extra padding under Miss Wiley's in deference to her status as a female, even if she did claim to be a missionary. Missionaries, he presumed, were willing if not eager to encounter hardships in their chosen line of work.

He left Miss Wiley to do whatever she wanted while he went into the woods in search of something to cook over the fire. Two rabbits were obliging enough to show up before he'd gone very far, so he killed them, skinned them there so as not to offend his traveling companion's sensibilities, and carried them back to camp.

She was reading beside the fire when he showed up with supper. She looked up and smiled at him. "Oh, my, what a good provider you are, Mr. Fargo."

"Yeah." He spitted their dinner and, as the fire settled into coals, set about rigging up roasting forks to balance the spits on. She continued reading. He nodded at the book. "The Bible?"

"Yes, indeed. My constant companion. Would you like for me to read aloud to you, Mr. Fargo?"

"That's all right, ma'am. Think I'll go wash up."

"The water is most refreshing."

"I'm sure it is."

Freezing cold was more like it. It came straight from the snow melting in the high Sierra Nevadas. Fargo didn't mind the cold, though. He appreciated

the convenience of the stream so close to camp and did a thorough job of washing off the trail dust.

They ate the rabbits and some tinned peaches in relative conviviality. Fargo was glad of Miss Wiley's forbearance, because he'd anticipated a sermon or two and she didn't give him even one. She made him wait to eat until she'd said a powerfully long grace, though, but he'd endured worse hardships than that in his life, so he didn't complain.

After supper, when daylight was almost gone, Miss Genevieve Wiley said, "Would you please avert your face, Mr. Fargo? I need to undress for bed."

Fargo blinked at her. "Uh, ma'am, I think it would be best to sleep in your clothes tonight. You never know what might happen overnight. I don't expect any unpleasant surprises, but, well . . ."

She frowned prettily. "What sorts of unpleasant surprises would you anticipate if you *did* expect any?"

"Remember those four fellows who had you cornered back a ways, ma'am?" He kept his tone pleasant.

"Oh." Her frown deepened. "Do you think they're going to come after me? You said yourself that they didn't seem to be truly bad men."

He kept his patience. "No, ma'am. I don't think they'll come after you. But I don't know who else might be out here, and neither do you. California's a new place, and it's grown very fast since gold was discovered. It's attracted an unruly element, and there's no law to speak of to keep it under control."

"Oh." She spent several seconds thinking. "I hate to sleep in my clothes."

Fargo was so used to sleeping in his buckskins that

he didn't have to think twice about his own overnight wear.

"But if you believe it would be prudent for me to do so, Mr. Fargo . . ."

He did, and showed her so by nodding.

"Very well."

Fargo was sitting on a log, cradling a tin mug of boiled coffee in his hands, relaxing before he crawled into his own bedroll. He damned near swallowed it, cup and all, when Miss Genevieve Wiley sat on a log across the fire from him, lifted her skirts, and proceeded to remove her shoes and roll her stockings down right in front of his eyeballs.

Sweet Lord have mercy, she had a pair of legs on her that would do justice to any female on earth. He was goggling in earnest when she looked up from her task, saw him, and uttered a little squeak. "Mr. Fargo!"

Well, she hadn't asked him to avert his face this time. "Sorry, ma'am." It was a lie, but what did he care? Nevertheless, he turned his head and glowered into the night-dark forest.

He heard some rustling sounds from across the way, then Miss Wiley's muffled voice came to him. "You may turn around now, Mr. Fargo. I beg your pardon for not warning you before I set about to remove my—you know."

Apparently she was too pure to speak the word "stockings" aloud. "Yeah, I know."

Damn, he wished she hadn't shown him those legs of hers. He considered her shape in the nature of a mockery, and was feeling grumpy when he finally crawled between his blankets, settled his head on his saddle, and made sure his Colt revolver, Arkansas

toothpick, and Henry rifle were handy. He stared up into the starlit night sky for about ten seconds before his mind drifted, his eyes closed, and sleep claimed him.

3

Skye Fargo had lived in the wild for a long time. He'd earned his reputation as the Trailsman honestly and had honed his senses to be vigilant even as he slept. Therefore, when he heard a twig snap beneath the tread of a foot—animal or human, he knew not—he was awake and alert instantly.

He'd positioned his own bedroll so that he had a clear view of the entire camp and nothing could sneak up behind him. The fire had burned down low, but in the near blackness he perceived a hulking shadow creeping toward Genevieve Wiley's bedroll.

So it was a white man. No Indian worth his salt would saunter about in the open like that. Fargo presumed as well that even California Indians, who didn't have to be as fierce as some tribes because of their easy pickings, would have learned the art of silent stalking in childhood. He heaved a muffled sigh, wishing he could get at least one good night's sleep since he expected the next two days on the trail with his missionary were going to be stressful.

But such was not to be. As quietly as a wraith—Fargo, too, had learned silence early in life—he picked up his Colt. A quick assessment of the interloper and the surrounding woods indicated to Fargo that the man was alone.

Whoever that fellow was, he'd made his way to Miss Wiley's bedroll and was bending over her, obviously assuming that Fargo was asleep. Which proved again that he'd not had proper training in the frontier skills. He wasn't going to last long at this rate.

Fargo made not the least little noise when he walked up behind the man, who was reaching for Miss Wiley, and knocked him on the head with the butt of his Colt. The man grunted and fell over sideways.

Miss Genevieve Wiley screamed. Fargo, while not pleased by the ungodly noise, was not surprised either.

As he bent over and disarmed the man, who lay on the ground groaning, he said through gritted teeth, "It's all right, ma'am. He won't hurt you."

"Who is it?" Miss Wiley was frantic. "What happened? Oh, dear Lord, Mr. Fargo, what happened?" She sat up, holding her blanket to her chin.

"I don't know who it is, ma'am. He crept into camp and was leaning over to touch you when I knocked him down."

"Merciful heavens!"

Feeling particularly savage—Fargo hated having his sleep interrupted by clumsy villains—he yanked this specimen to his feet, dragged him a few yards, and slammed him up against a tree. The man grunted and groaned pitiably. Fargo didn't feel sorry for him in the least, but shook him until his head rattled and his eyes opened.

"Who the hell are you, and what the hell do you think you're doing, sneaking into our camp like that?"

"Mr. Fargo!" Miss Genevieve Wiley clearly didn't approve of Fargo's vocabulary.

Too bad. He snarled, "Shut up, Miss Wiley."

She gasped.

He turned to the intruder and repeated, "Who are you?"

The man shook his head on his own this time, trying to clear it. He croaked, "Leave go of me. I didn't mean no harm."

"Right. You're going to get shot one of these days if you keep sneaking into folks' camps. In fact, I might just shoot you now and save the world the trouble." He wouldn't, of course, but he was mad and it felt good to make the threat.

"No! Mr. Fargo, please don't shoot him!"

Dammit, if there was one thing Fargo didn't need right now, it was a bleeding-heart missionary telling him not to kill this bastard. He scowled at Miss Wiley, who had managed to get out of her bedroll and now stood hugging herself, shivering in her bare feet, and looking at him with huge frightened eyes. She ran up to him and grabbed hold of his shirt, which wasn't fair because he couldn't shake her off without letting go of the villain—and he wasn't about to do that.

"You mustn't shoot him, Mr. Fargo! Please don't shoot him. Shooting him would be—would be—would be horrid!"

He glowered at her hand clutching his shirtsleeve. "Why would it be horrid? What do you think he was planning to do to *you*?"

Releasing his sleeve, she flapped her mouth a couple of times uselessly. "Was he going to do something to me?"

She transferred her big-eyed stare from him to the

outlaw, who muttered, "No, I wasn't doing to do nothing to you, ma'am."

"There, you see, Mr. Fargo? He wasn't going to do anything to me." She smiled triumphantly.

Fargo sighed clear down to his toes. "Listen, Miss Wiley. Whether he was or he wasn't, he sneaked into our camp. Folks don't do that if they aren't bent on mischief. A fellow always signals the camp before he shows up in it. It's good manners. Now, maybe I won't kill him, but I sure as hell am not going to let him go so he can finish whatever it was he started."

She frowned at him, but didn't argue. "Very well, but please mind your language."

"Right." Disgusted, Fargo yanked the man, a burly fellow with an unshaven face, over to another tree, a smaller one with low-growing branches which might prove to be useful. "I'll just tie you up here, and tomorrow morning I'll decide what to do to you."

"I think you busted my head."

"That's a hell of a lot less than I wanted to do."

"Mr. Fargo!"

"Right. Don't swear."

After he'd tied the man's wrists together, Fargo snapped, "Where's your horse?"

The man looked up at him, a defiant expression on his face, but when Fargo bunched up his fist and showed it to him, he blurted out, "Over there. The other end of the clearing." He nodded his head to his right, a gesture that seemed to hurt him, because he squeezed his eyes shut and moaned.

So Fargo brought the man's horse into the camp, hobbled it next to the Ovaro and the mule, unsaddled it, threw a blanket over it, and let it be. Then he built up the fire so he could have a better look at their

21

nighttime visitor. There was a big knot on the side of his skull where Fargo's Colt had smacked him, and the skin was broken.

Miss Wiley, spotting the blood, squeaked. Fargo braced himself, anticipating what would come next. He was right.

She ran over to the bound man, inspected his wound, and cried indignantly, "Oh, my goodness, Mr. Fargo, look what you did to this poor creature!"

"Maybe I should have let him do what he wanted to do to you instead?"

She turned and scowled at him. "I don't believe he was going to do anything at all to me, and you needn't be sarcastic. I am going to bandage this poor sinner's head."

"Fine. Do whatever you want to do to him—except turn him loose."

"I shan't turn him loose." Going to her bedroll, she sat and struggled into her stockings and shoes.

Fargo watched her do it because she had nice legs, and he hoped his scrutiny would annoy her. She looked up once, glowered ferociously, which only tickled him, and didn't say a word. Her prickliness under the circumstances actually struck Fargo as kind of funny, and his bad mood lifted.

Miss Wiley tramped to the river to wet some bandages she'd removed from her saddlebag, then went to the intruder and bent over him. The man had his eyes pinched tightly together in pain. He deserved at least that, no matter what Miss Wiley thought. He watched her working the man over, speaking softly to him—probably reciting sermons and prayers—and felt almost sorry for the guy. He'd bet anything that the fellow wished he'd chosen some other camp to invade.

He waited until Miss Wiley had finished administering her prayers and unguents, bundled the man up against the cold with a blanket—Fargo resented that—and got herself back into her bedroll before he himself returned to bed. His senses were alert, but he perceived no lurking danger, so he allowed himself to sleep after a while.

Nothing further happened to disturb his rest.

Shortly before the sun rose the following morning, he awoke. He had the animals attended to and the coffee boiling in time to salute the dawn with a jolt of the bitter liquid. There were some bacon slices and corn cakes sizzling in a pan as well, and the aromas of the clean mountain air, cooking food, and fresh coffee blended into a medley Fargo would remember for the rest of his days. He loved the wilderness. With a sigh, he recalled that this was California, not the wilderness, and that he wasn't alone in it.

Neither Miss Wiley, who was a mere lump under her blankets, nor the interloper, who was slumped over asleep in what looked like a mighty uncomfortable position, had awakened yet. Fargo watched the dawn break with a reverence for nature in his soul that undoubtedly matched that of Miss Wiley's for God.

A stirring and a muffled whimper from the tree brought his attention from the glorious new day to the man he'd whacked last night. The right side of his face was covered by a purple bruise from the blow Fargo had delivered.

"Water," the man croaked. "I need water."

"Yeah? I need a couple hundred dollars and a willing woman. So What?"

The man groaned again.

Fargo discovered Miss Wiley was also awake when she cried, "Mr. Fargo!"

Shoot. He frowned at her bedroll and discovered her sitting up and rubbing her eyes. When she stopped doing that, she frowned back at him.

"That's no way to behave, Mr. Fargo."

He didn't bother to agree or disagree, but jerked his head toward the bound man. "You take him some water then."

She sniffed, sounding superior and self-righteous. "Very well. I shall." She did, spilling a good deal of it down the man's front, which wouldn't hurt him any.

Fargo watched, resigned to his fate but unsure about what to do with the bound man. He reckoned he'd let him go, unarmed. Hell, there were no authorities to take him to, and what few there were didn't care about a criminal until after he'd killed somebody.

He didn't wait for Miss Wiley to finish her morning grace before he ate his breakfast, a blasphemy that earned him a disapproving glare from his traveling companion.

Once she'd quit blathering over the chow, Miss Wiley fed the intruding bastard two of the corn cakes, a hunk of bacon, and a tin cupful—her cup, not Fargo's—of coffee for breakfast. After that, she walked up to Fargo and stood scowling at him as he strapped saddlebags over the Ovaro's broad back.

"Well?" she said after several seconds, "What are you going to do with that poor man?"

That poor man? Fargo could hardly stand it. He turned and glowered down at her. For such a small

24

woman, she sure was a large pain in the ass. "I'm going to let him go, Miss Wiley."

That took the starch out of her sails. She opened her mouth and blinked several times, out of words for once. Fargo wished he could have that effect on her more often. He elaborated. "I'm going to pack up here, load you on your mule, make sure that man doesn't have any other weapons on him anywhere, and let him go."

"Oh."

"You gotta leave me a gun, dammit!" the man whined.

Fargo eyed the intruder coldly. "The hell I do."

"Mr. Fargo!"

"He started it," Fargo growled, offended that she'd reprimand him and not a fellow who was obviously a scoundrel.

She sniffed.

As they resumed their trip to Barley Flats, leaving behind the man who had violated their camp—after Fargo had explained exactly what he could expect if he tried to follow them—Fargo knew it was going to be a long trip.

4

It was a *very* long trip.

Miss Genevieve Wiley wasted no time setting in to lecturing Skye Fargo on the glories of forgiveness and how a soft answer turneth away wrath and how vengeance was the Lord's, not his. In other words, she thought he'd been too hard on their overnight visitor. Fargo tried his best not to listen.

He had a little help about three in the afternoon of their second day together, when two masked and armed bandits rode out from behind the covering trees. Fargo sighed heavily.

Miss Wiley screeched. Hell of a lot of good that did.

"Hold your hands up," one of the villains growled.

"Stand and deliver," the other one, a poet, evidently, said. Fargo was mildly entertained.

"Deliver what?" he asked politely.

Miss Wiley said, "Do something! For heaven's sake, *do* something!"

He glanced at her sideways. "The last time we got held up, you wanted me to let him go. Make up your mind."

She huffed.

"Don't get smart with me, cuss," the first villain advised. "Throw down your guns."

Fargo shrugged. "Whatever you say."

"Do it slow," the poet added.

So he did. With slow, deliberate moves, Fargo lifted his Colt from its holster and dropped it on the ground. Then, again slowly and deliberately, he unfastened the strap of his saddle scabbard and lifted his Henry rifle out of it. He shifted the rifle to his other hand and leaned sideways over the Ovaro, ostensibly to place the Henry on the ground. At the same time, he gently pulled his razor-sharp Arkansas toothpick from the sheath strapped to his calf.

He heard what he'd been expecting: the sound of a hammer being pulled back on two guns. So, the two didn't plan on leaving witnesses. Fargo wasn't surprised, although he wasn't happy about it.

Quick as lightning, he straightened in his saddle, firing the rifle and whipping the toothpick forward. The knife hit its target only a second after the bullet. The countenances of both bandits registered shock before death wiped all expression from their faces forever. They dropped over backward as their horses danced. One man ended on his back with his right boot heel in a stirrup. The other bounced crazily around in his saddle as his horse jittered.

Miss Wiley screamed.

"Shut up," Fargo snapped. He was out of his saddle in an instant and flat on his face, surveying the woods for any other would-be evildoers. There were none. With a savage oath, he rose to his feet and went to the two dead men. What a woeful waste of human life. Fargo wished the two were still alive so he could scold them for being such fools.

To the accompaniment of Genevieve Wiley's hysterical questions and sobs, he calmed the outlaws' horses and lowered the men's bodies to the ground. Then he unmasked them—they were both unprepossessing samples of humankind—and proceeded to inspect the men's belongings, searching mainly for identification. Even outlaws had families, after all.

But he found only a very small leather pouch containing an even smaller amount of gold dust on the first one, and a fairly nice, gold-plated pocket watch on the poet. The pickings seemed pitifully small to Fargo, who thought a man's rewards ought to match the effort he put into achieving them. Hell, these two could have clerked at a dry-goods store with less effort, made more money, and they'd have still been alive to spend what they'd earned.

Oh, well. Fargo tried never to second-guess his fellow travelers on this road to perdition. He did, however, finally get sick of listening to Miss Wiley fussing. He stood and turned to her. "If you want to do something useful, get down off your horse and help me with these two." He didn't say it gently because he was tired of her constant carping and preaching.

His suggestion brought her up short. "Help you do what? What can I do?"

"You can help me drag them aside, for one thing."

"Me? Help you drag two corpses aside? Where?"

He squinted up at her. "What's the matter, Miss Wiley? Didn't God ever tell you that a person has to do more than gab in this lifetime?" Because she was a lady, and he wasn't generally mean to ladies, he softened his tone. "After we lay them out, you can pray over them, all right?"

"Lay them out?" She finally quit staring at him and dismounted. She walked stiff-legged over to Fargo's side. He supposed she wasn't used to riding a mule over long distances. When she reached him, she looked down at the two dead men with a grimace of distaste on her face, her nose wrinkled. "Aren't you going to bury them?"

"No, ma'am."

She jerked her head to look up at him. "Oh, but Mr. Fargo, you must!"

"No, ma'am. It's not my job to bury these two. They were going to kill me and rob the both of us and who knows what else? You being a good-looking female and all, they might have got other ideas after they shot me and took our loot."

He had to give her credit. She didn't blush. She looked like she might haul off and slug him, but she didn't blush.

"Nonsense," she said crisply.

"It's not nonsense. Now help me here."

She did—probably because she couldn't think of a good reason not to, except that she didn't want to touch a dead man. Fargo appreciated her sensibilities, but she was in a raw country now, and a person had to be prepared for lots of things, some of which were bound to be even more distasteful than this. Life wasn't all prayers and sermons in California, and it was past time she realized it.

She was out of breath and puffing when they got the men deposited side by side under a tree, with their arms folded over their chests.

It wasn't respectful enough for Miss Genevieve Wiley. After she caught her breath, she started in on him again. "I still think you ought to bury them, Mr. Fargo. It's the Christian thing to do."

He eyed her with disfavor. "You're the one who's so

dead set on doing the Christian thing, Miss Wiley. If you think they ought to be buried, you do it."

"Me? Bury them?" She gazed at him with those huge hazel eyes of hers. Then she looked at the dead men. Then she turned toward the dead men's horses. "I, ah, don't see any shovels anywhere."

He nodded. "Exactly. They might have a tin spoon in their saddlebags. I haven't gone through them yet."

"A spoon? A person can't dig a grave with a spoon!"

"Right. So what say you quit bellyaching, and we look through their saddlebags and get on our way to Barley Flats. If there's any law there, we'll tell them exactly where to find these two. The law can pick them up and bury them if it wants to." If, of course, the corpses were still there. For all Fargo knew, a grizzly bear would find them easy pickings and tasty as all get-out. He didn't say so to Miss Wiley.

She didn't like it, but she acquiesced at last. Thank God. He didn't find much in the men's saddlebags, although he did discover their names. Skye Fargo and Miss Genevieve Wiley had been accosted by Phineas Bragg and Theodore Edward Hall. Fargo shook his head and felt kind of empty inside as he contemplated the circumstances that had probably brought the men to California, and what straits they must have come to in order for them to attempt brigandage.

"A man makes his own choices," he muttered in order to quell any sympathetic stirrings in his soul. Hell, he might have been laid out dead right now instead of them if they'd succeeded in their robbery attempt, and it was better this way.

"I beg your pardon?"

Ever since she'd shut up about burying their attackers, Miss Wiley had kept her mouth closed, which had rested Fargo's ears considerably. He was sorry he'd prompted more noise from her. "Nothing. Just thinking out loud."

She sniffed.

That was all right. Better sniffs than words. "Mount up again, ma'am. We'll be on our way."

When he glanced at her, he was unhappy to see that she now sported a mulish expression on her face. He braced himself for another argument and asked, not gently, "What is it now?"

"We can't just go away and leave them without some kind of Christian ceremony."

"Jesus." His was an exclamation of disgust.

"Exactly!" Hers was an exclamation of delight that he'd finally understood her.

He glanced at the heavens and wondered what fickle fate had sent this woman to plague him. It was no use arguing with her. Hell, it would take less time to let her pray over the bastards than to try to dicker her out of it. "Go ahead. Pray."

So she did. She'd gone on for five minutes and was winding herself up for another five when he got tired of playing her game. He grabbed her bodily up off the ground, and plopped her in her saddle. She screeched, naturally, but he ignored her. "Come on. We've got to get to Barley Flats."

"You can't manhandle me that way!"

He didn't even bother contradicting her, but nudged the big pinto forward. He took the two loose horses with him and didn't turn his head to see if Miss Wiley followed.

She did.

They met with no more interruptions on their trip. Before the day was over, they'd left most of the tall trees behind them and were traveling through lush, green meadowlands. They camped that night beside a lake that had the oddest rock formations Fargo had ever seen.

"Merciful heavens," Miss Wiley said, eyeing them in wonder.

"California's full of interesting scenery," Fargo commented.

"It certainly is."

"Those rock formations are something, aren't they?"

"God's wonders are everywhere," she said piously.

"Yeah."

He caught fish for their supper that night, and cooked it himself over the fire Miss Wiley built. She was good for something, he guessed.

They arrived in Barley Flats the afternoon of the following day, and Fargo almost fell down on his knees and thanked God for it because he was so tired of Miss Wiley's proselytizing. Since she'd probably think a prayer of thanks meant he'd succumbed to her missionary zeal, he didn't. He'd sure be glad to be rid of her, though.

He halted the Ovaro in front of the Miner's Rest Hotel, a ragged wooden structure that looked as if it had been thrown up overnight and not thought about since. On the other hand, everything in Barley Flats looked as if it had been thrown up overnight. Tents, shacks, and lean-tos abounded.

"This all right, ma'am?" he asked politely, knowing it would have to do whether she liked it or not.

She eyed the building skeptically. "Well—"

Gunfire erupted from somewhere up the rutted road, and Miss Wiley had the good sense to scramble down from her mule. "It will do."

He smiled at her. It was the first time he'd had reason to smile in two days. "Good. I'll help you get your things inside and get you settled."

"Thank you very much, Mr. Fargo." She scuttled inside the building and waited for him there, peeking out from behind the door as if she expected a bullet to find her there if she wasn't careful. For all Fargo knew, she was right. According to Gus, at least a murder a day was perpetrated in Barley Flats. He didn't tarry in unstrapping her saddlebags and soon joined her in what passed for the hotel lobby. She marched up to the registration desk, and he followed, looking around with interest.

Barley Flats seemed to be a haven for the roughest element. The hotel's innards were fairly clean and presentable, but as he gazed outside he saw a regular riot of commotion. The gunfire had prompted a stampede up the street in the direction of the noise—which didn't make any sense, really. When folks started shooting at each other, Fargo generally judged it best to get out of the way, not run into the fray.

Not, plainly, the citizens of Barley Flats. There must have been a hundred bearded men out there, running, walking, or staggering—folks apparently did a lot of drinking in Barley Flats—up the street. He grinned. This was exactly the place where Gus Perkins would feel right at home. Fargo was glad Gus and Barley Flats had found each other, and he trusted Gus would introduce him to the town properly.

He turned when Miss Wiley spoke at his back. "Very well, Mr. Fargo. I have secured a room."

She didn't look awfully happy about it. Fargo didn't ask why. As he walked past the registration desk with her saddlebags over his arm, however, he noticed that the clerk had a sour expression on his face. She'd probably tried to convert him and he'd balked.

Miss Genevieve Wiley and Skye Fargo engaged in one last brangle before he was rid of her at last: over what to do with her mule. She'd neglected to consider the poor animal and wanted to argue with Fargo about whether or not she had to board him in a livery stable. He finally managed to get her to see some common sense, pointing out reasonably that the hotel wasn't equipped to care for animals. She didn't like it, but eventually she gave him two dollars for the mule's care, and he escaped, leaving her to her own devices.

He boarded both the mule and the Ovaro in the livery stable, explained the two extra horses to the liveryman, who took them in with pleasure—Fargo suspected he'd sell them—then headed for Gus's place. He'd seldom been so glad to see the last of a pretty woman as he was to see the last of Miss Genevieve Wiley.

5

Gus's Place was designated as such by a gaily painted wooden sign swaying in the breeze. That's where the gunfire had come from. Fargo found that out when he asked the hotel clerk where to find the saloon and was directed up the street. Therefore, he discovered himself heading toward trouble, just like the rest of the fools in Barley Flats. In his case, it didn't much matter, since Miss Wiley was as much trouble as most of the gunfights he'd been in. He considered it a fair exchange.

As he ambled up the dirt road, the Trailsman took a good, long look at Barley Flats, California. He'd been in boomtowns before, but not often, and this one looked like it was booming more than most. New construction stood cheek-by-jowl with the tents and hovels he'd noticed before.

Several structures looked as if they'd been started and then abandoned before completion. He grinned to himself, wondering if the builders had forsaken their work in order to look for gold.

Probably. Men were pure fools for gold. He'd be willing to wager that a builder made more solid money than most of the miners toiling in the streams and mountains of California. Every now and then he'd read about someone striking pay dirt, but Fargo expected those who got rich panning for gold were outnumbered a thousand-to-one by those who went broke doing the same thing.

He was admiring Gus's Place, which was actually a relatively nice-looking building, when a shriek pierced the air directly over his head. Looking up, he perceived a scantily clad female teetering on the edge of a windowsill. She was mighty unsteady, and he didn't especially fancy seeing her splattered all over the dirt road in front of him. He stood still and stared at her, wondering how in hell she'd gotten there, and if someone inside the room was going to pull her back inside.

It was kind of hard to tell from his vantage point, but she looked like a pretty girl, with lots of blond hair curling around pretty white shoulders and a shape that made Fargo remember all the things he liked about women. He also approved of the red-and-black corset she wore, and her black stockings held up by red garters. He did question her common sense, however. That window ledge was a mighty skinny one. Unless she had a damned good reason for being on it, he could think of lots of better ways she could pass her time.

She screamed again, only this time she used some words. "No! No, I will *not* do that, Mr. Harlan O'Bannon! And you can't make me! Not without another five dollars, dammit! You got your money's worth already!"

Somebody near Fargo mumbled, "He must'a wanted her to give him a French lesson." He sniggered when Fargo glanced at him. "Harlan, he fancies he's got hisself somethin' in his pants that any woman'd want. Most of Gus's girls don't like it, though. They'll do it if a feller pays extra."

"Oh." Fargo couldn't offhand think of anything else to say, although he appreciated the information being so freely given. He'd keep it in mind, in fact, when he met Gus's ladies, of whom, evidently, the window lass was one. He wondered what her name was so he could ask for her.

His unspoken question was answered only seconds after he hadn't asked it. Life was taking an upward turn.

"C'mon, Sheila, it'll be fun," came a slurred voice from inside the room.

Sheila disagreed. "You don't know what the hell you're talking about. Fun, my fanny!"

She had a nice fanny. Fargo could see it plainly from where he stood beneath her. The rest of her wasn't bad, either. She was round in all the right places, but not so round as to blur her finer assets. He pushed his hat farther back on his head and called up to her. "If you want to let go, ma'am, I'll be happy to catch you."

His comment seemed to startle her, because she glanced down at him and her foot slipped. She wavered sickeningly and screeched again. Shoot. That window wasn't awfully far from the ground, but if she fell she'd bust something for sure. He moved up a little. "Just let go, ma'am. I'm right here. I won't let you get hurt."

"I'll die." She sobbed. "You can't catch me!"

"Sure I can."

"Hell, Sheila," said Harlan from inside the room. "You don't haf'ta jump. I'll come get you."

Sheila shouted, "You just leave me the hell alone,

Harlan O'Bannon! I already did what you paid me for, and I'm sick of giving it away!"

The man who'd informed Fargo what the fight was about sniggered again.

"But, Sheila—" Harlan had started whining.

"No!"

Fargo said, "Just let go, ma'am. I'll catch you."

She eyed him doubtfully from her perch on the windowsill. "You promise?"

"I promise."

Her doubt seemed to waver. "You look like a big one."

"Oh, yeah, I'm plenty big." He smiled to give her courage.

His smile—and perhaps his words—had an effect. Her scared and angry expression gave way to one of curiosity. "Say, you're new to Barley Flats, aren't you?"

Fargo tipped his hat. "Yes, ma'am. And I'm already enjoying the sights." He winked to make sure she caught his meaning.

She did and giggled.

"Sheila!" Harlan growled. "Get back in here and untie me!"

Untie him? Fargo's eyebrows arched. Well, hell, maybe Sheila wasn't the girl for him after all. On the other hand, he didn't suppose the tying-up part was required.

Sheila scowled inside the room. "I will not! You can just stay there and rot, Harlan O'Bannon! I wish now that I hadn't tied you to the doorknob, because I'm like to kill myself jumping out of this window. But I'm through with you!"

"I bet she did him good before she was through

with him, too," said the Greek chorus at Fargo's side, who snickered yet again.

Now there was some encouraging news. Fargo called up, "Come on, ma'am. Just let go. I'm right here."

"Well . . ." Sheila gazed down at Fargo. Then she glanced into the room and stuck out her tongue. Looking again at Fargo, she smiled and said, "All right. Here I come!" She let go of the windowsill and jumped.

All sorts of things had been aimed at Skye Fargo during his adventurous life, and this wasn't really the first time a woman had thrown herself at him, but it was a novel experience anyway. He caught her easily, although she gained a good deal of momentum as she fell and he staggered a little under the weight of her.

Cheering erupted on the street, and Fargo realized for the first time that he and his friendly commentator weren't alone there. A herd of wild miners had gathered to watch the fun.

Sheila grabbed Fargo's hat and waved it in the air, playing to her audience. "Take a bow, sugar, and tell the good folks of Barley Flats who you are." She pointed her toes and posed in his arms, for all the world as if she'd practiced this maneuver forever.

What the hell. Fargo could play this game, too. With Sheila in his arms, he executed a bow in the direction of the miners, who cheered again and added some claps and stomps to the general clamor. "Skye Fargo, ma'am, at your service."

"Skye Fargo?" The commentator whistled under his breath. "Hell, I've heard of you."

There wasn't much Fargo could do about that. He

ignored the man and asked Sheila, "Where do you want to go now, sweetheart?"

"I work at Gus's Place, Mr. Fargo." She plopped his hat on her own blond curls and licked her lips. "And it would be my pleasure to give you a real friendly welcome to Barley Flats. You're sure a handsome one."

He grinned back. "Thanks, Sheila. I'll be happy to take you up on that offer, but I've got to say hello to Gus first. We're old friends."

"You would be." She pouted and sighed. When she did that, her bosom pressed against his chest. It was quite a bosom, and Fargo hoped Gus wouldn't take long in greeting an old friend, because he'd like to take care of business with Sheila as soon as he could. Living with Miss Genevieve Wiley, being forced to listen to her, and being compelled by gentlemanliness not to touch her, had taken its toll. He could hardly wait to have a friendly tumble with a more kindly disposed female, especially one that looked and felt like Sheila.

With a wave to his audience and a good-natured grin, he went up to the batwing doors and backed inside the saloon. The miners cheered and whooped.

All in all, he'd had less cordial greetings upon his arrival in strange towns.

Her name was Sheila Lewis, and she led Fargo to the bathhouse in the back of Gus's Place shortly after Gus had greeted him. Fargo had told Gus where to find the two bodies in the mountains.

"I'll send a couple of men up there to haul 'em back," Gus said. "If they're still there."

"Thanks, Gus."

Sheila grabbed his arm, and Gus grinned.

"This one's mine now, Gus. You can have him later."

With a chuckle, Gus waved them away. "Have a good time. I'll see ya later, Skye."

"I'm gonna give you the best bath you ever had, big man," she promised Fargo with a wink.

"She will, Skye," Gus affirmed, nodding cheerfully. "Sheila, she's the best gal I got."

Fargo was glad to hear it. She'd slipped a wrap over her corset while he chatted with Gus. He now watched her hips as she went before him, and his groin tightened in anticipation. She was quite a hunk of female flesh, Sheila was, and he looked forward to being bathed by her.

A steaming tub was already prepared in the bathhouse. Sheila went over and tested the water, then looked over her shoulder and smiled at him. "All right, sweetie pie, take 'em off."

"Happy to oblige." Fargo stripped off his holster and set it on a table beside the tub. Since he never completely let down his guard, he made sure his Colt was within easy grabbing distance.

Sheila came over and fingered his shirt. "Let me help."

"Any time, sweetheart."

By the time Sheila had maneuvered his shirt off, his boots and stockings off, and his trousers down, Fargo was ready for lots of things.

"Lord above, but you're big!" Sheila was stroking his stiffened manhood as she spoke, and Fargo shut his eyes with pleasure. "But I promised you a bath, and I keep my promises."

He was disappointed when she released him, but he didn't repine since she seemed eager to please him.

"Step in," she cooed, fingering the steaming water.

He did, and she poured something that smelled sweet into the water. Fargo wasn't sure he wanted to smell like a flower, but he expected Sheila knew what she was doing. He sank back against the wooden back of the tub with a deep sigh. "This feels good."

"It'll feel better in a minute, honey."

Fargo heard the rustle of fabric against fabric and opened his eyes. They opened wider when he realized the rustling noises were coming from the clothes Sheila was shedding. She winked at him. "I like to give a good, personal bath, sweetie."

His throat had closed up on him, and he could only nod and grunt. Lordy, but she was a sight for his sore eyes. She'd already shucked her wrap, and now she was working on the ribbons tying her corset together. She dropped it and wore nothing but a camisole and drawers, both lacy numbers that didn't hide much. She soon peeled the remaining camouflage away and stood before him, naked as the day she was born, all pink and white and pretty, the hair at the juncture of her thighs a little darker than the blond hair on her head.

Fargo blinked at the perfection of her natural assets as she walked to the tub. She had heavy breasts, but they didn't sag. Rather, they seemed to be pointing straight at him, their rosy nibs puckered and hard already. Her hips rolled with her walk, and her thighs, all milky and white, about had him drooling.

"I'll just get me the soap right here," she said, pausing to lean over, giving him a spectacular view of her round, pink buttocks. She glanced at him over her shoulder, and he knew she knew the effect she was having on him. He swallowed when she grabbed a bar of soap and turned, giving him a good once-over with her pretty blue eyes. "You sure are a sight, Mr. Skye Fargo."

"So are you." He'd begun to croak, and he was starting to ache with the need in his groin.

She laughed low in her throat, reminding him of a purring cat. "I like you a lot, Skye. A whole lot."

He had to swallow again before he could say, "Likewise."

She started on his back, rubbing the soothing, sweet-smelling soap into his muscular shoulders and back, and he almost sank into the water and drowned himself when he felt her breasts on his back, rotating the suds in a way he'd never experienced before. "I like the way you lather up a man, Sheila."

"I like doing it. Dip down a little bit, honey, to get the soap off, and I'm going to start on your legs. Beginning with the toes."

She did, one by one, bringing damned near every single one of her assets into play, including her tongue and teeth. By the time she'd worked her way up to his iron-hard manhood, he was about done for. Beyond speech, he only moaned his pleasure as she worked on him.

"I think it's time for me to get in there with you," she said when he was just about ready to explode.

He managed to crick his eyes open. "You do?"

"Yep."

So she did. First one long, gorgeous leg went into the tub, then the other one. And then, since she had a leg on either side of his hips, she very gently, and with a good deal of hissing pleasure, lowered herself onto his shaft, impaling herself with his long, hard rod. She was as hot and wet as the bathtub by that time, and she slid him in and out in a slick rhythm that was about the greatest pleasure he'd ever felt.

"It's okay, honey," she panted into his ear. "You can come any time. There'll be plenty of time for me later." And she bit him on the ear she'd just spoken into. With one last deep thrust, his release came in spasms that left him limp and exhausted.

"That's the way," Sheila purred. "That's just the way."

Skye felt a little bit as if he hadn't performed his manful duty until Sheila started nibbling on his neck. Then, when she rubbed her beautiful, full breasts against his chest, gave him one of her deep, velvety, erotic chuckles, and he felt himself begin to stiffen inside her, he decided he was up to this.

And he was. In fact, he was up to a lot more.

"Oh, Skye, that feels so good!" Sheila's hips lifted to accommodate his plunging shaft. Her back arched, and her breasts thrust at him.

He grinned. "Feels good to me, too, honey." As he pumped into Sheila's tight passage, he was feeling damned good, as a matter of fact. This was their second go-round, and he was looking forward to at least another two or three—with a pause in between to recruit his resources with the food Gus had sent up along with some good bourbon.

"You're real good at this."

She wiggled her bottom and tightened around him, and he almost lost control. He growled, lowered himself on her, and rolled over so she was splayed on top of him. He had a perfect view that way.

Sheila knew what to do with herself in that position, too, and she proceeded to demonstrate. Her breasts bounced deliciously as she rode him. When he squeezed them, then raised himself so that he could tease her nipples with his tongue, she threw her head back and groaned. He dropped back and began to rub the nub between her thighs with his finger as he watched her writhe above him.

"Oh, Skye, I can feel it. I'm going to come again!"

He felt her tighten around his shaft, saw her give an eloquent shudder, and he exploded, filling her with his essence. Her convulsive climax milked him dry, and she collapsed on top of him like a spent balloon, only much more supple and soft. He sighed and relaxed completely. Now this, he decided, was the way to live. He'd never understand why some folks—like Miss Genevieve Wiley, for instance—despised their own sensual natures, when they could gain so much pure pleasure from sensuality.

Sheila purred on top of him. He stroked her from her shoulder blades to her soft, dimpled bottom, and on down as far as he could reach. Her skin was like damp silk under his rough hands. She was built for the man-pleasing business, and Skye could only be glad she'd taken to it with such gusto.

A soft breeze filtered in through the open window. The room they were in was on the second floor of Gus's saloon. Gus had directed Sheila to take him to the best room. Chintz curtains fluttered in on the breeze, and a thick Turkish carpet covered the floor. The sheets were even clean.

"Repent, sinners!"

The sound was faint, and it took Fargo a minute to distinguish the words.

Then it came again.

"Repent, sinners! Let not your flesh be weak, but turn to the Lord."

Sheila was dozing comfortably on top of him when realization finally filtered through his sated brain. His eyes popped open. He frowned. Sheila's eyes opened lazily.

"What's the matter?" Her words were fuzzy. She was sated, too.

"I'm not sure."

She mumbled a protest when he gently moved her from on top of him to his side. The breeze felt colder without her warmth there to soak it up. He had a feeling he was going to regret what he was about to do, but he did it anyway.

With a grunt, he rose from the bed, padded softly to the window, and glanced outside. Then he groaned.

Sheila had propped herself on an elbow when he turned to answer her. She made a gorgeous picture there, all soft and pink and feminine. She was a hell of a lot more gorgeous than what he'd just seen on the street below.

"It's nothing, really," he told Sheila.

"Then come on back to bed, sweetie." She patted the sheet beside her invitingly.

He took the invitation. Better that than to suffer the sight he'd just witnessed outside. Even as he crawled back in bed and took Sheila in his arms, he had a sinking feeling in his gut that his association with Miss Genevieve Wiley hadn't yet concluded.

She was there. Right outside. On the street corner. Thumping her Bible and beseeching the sotted miners of Barley Flats, California, to abandon their wicked ways and turn to her brand of the Gospel. And the miners to whom she was preaching didn't look as if they appreciated her message one little bit.

He moaned when Sheila slid down until she knelt between his legs. As she took his shaft in her two little hands and began to lick it hard, he decided he'd think about Miss Wiley later.

6

After their bath and their go-round in bed, Fargo and Sheila slept for a long time. When he awakened, he was as hungry as a bear who had just come out from hibernation. Fortunately, Gus was downstairs waiting for him.

"How's about some chow, Skye?"

"Best idea I've heard in a long time, Gus." Except, that is, for the several Sheila had recently proposed. Nevertheless, he was happy to accompany Gus to dinner.

They dined at the Gold Nugget, a chophouse next door to Gus's Place. As they walked over, Miss Wiley was still at it, waving her Bible and haranguing the mob.

After the waiter brought their food—two huge steaming platters full of steak, onions, and potatoes, Gus asked, "So, did Sheila show you a good time?"

Gus winked at him, stuck another big bite of juicy steak into his mouth, and chewed enthusiastically.

Skye Fargo smiled. "She sure did." He sighed lazily.

"She's a honey, all right." Gus pulled some small pebbles from his pocket. "Here, Skye. Look at these."

Fargo whistled softly under his breath. "Holy

Moses, Gus, is it smart to carry that much gold around with you?"

Gus's belly laugh warned Fargo that his comment had amused him. "Hell, Skye, this here ain't real gold."

"Really?" Fargo picked up a big nugget and held it up so that it caught the light pouring in from the window. "It looks like gold to me."

Gus nodded cheerfully. "Ain't it the truth? That there's pyrite. What folks hereabout call fool's gold, because it fools a lot of people into thinking it's real."

"I'll be. Is there a lot of it around here?"

"Yup. Here. Take some of 'em. They're kind of fun for keepsakes." He handed Fargo several more chunks of pyrite to go with the one he still held.

Fargo laughed and slipped the fool's gold into a little leather pouch. "This'll give me something to show the soldiers at the fort when I go back."

As the meal continued, Fargo told Gus about his trip to Barley Flats with his traveling companion. Gus laughed. "I don't know, Skye. I don't think many of the fellers here in town are going to thank you for bringing her here."

"I don't expect they will. But I couldn't very well ignore her troubles, could I?"

"I don't suppose so." Gus downed half a mug of beer. "It won't do 'em no harm to have somebody preach at 'em anyway. There's too much killin' going on here in Barley Flats."

As if to prove it, gunfire erupted outside. A high-pitched, all-too-familiar scream pierced the air, and Fargo grunted. "Aw, hell, that sounds like her again. I suppose I'd better see what's going on out there."

Gus snorted and downed more beer. "I'll go out

and help you, Skye. The fellows all know me. Besides, you might need me to protect you from that hellcat missionary."

Both men laughed as they left their half-eaten meals on the table and strode outside. Sure enough, Miss Genevieve Wiley was standing with her hands pressed to her cheeks, staring down at a body bleeding at her feet. Fargo made a quick survey of the street, perceived no lurking danger, and he and Gus walked over to her.

She looked up at him, her hazel eyes big and frightened. "Mr. Fargo! I've never been so glad to see anyone in my life!"

"What happened, Miss Wiley?"

"I don't know. I heard a loud noise, and then that man cried out and fell down. He's—he's bleeding." She suddenly swayed, and Skye caught her before she could faint, making a tidy bundle in his arms.

Gus knelt beside the fallen man and rolled him over. He grunted. "Hmmm. Joe Hamilton. A couple of folks thought he was a claim-jumper. I expect he was, and probably worse, since he's been spendin' money like a drunken sailor lately. Everybody figured the only way he'd ever get money was to steal it. That's probably what this was about."

Miss Wiley had been sucking in and releasing huge breaths of air, thereby pressing her bosom against Fargo's chest invitingly. She whispered, "C—claim-jumping. What's that?"

Gus looked up and smiled at her. "It's when somebody takes over somebody else's gold claim without his permission, ma'am. Sometimes a feller will just move claim markers. Sometimes they'll go farther than that."

"Farther? What do you mean?"

Glancing at her, and at Skye, Gus said, "Well, ma'am, sometimes men get to shootin' at each other when there's gold involved, y'know."

"Oh. How dreadful."

Her voice was weak, and she didn't look as if she understood yet, but Fargo decided it was time for her to move some. He was beginning to react to her body pressed against his, and that would probably shock her as much as seeing somebody shot in front of her. "Here, Miss Wiley, are you steadier now?"

"I—I think so." She wobbled a little bit when he released her, but Fargo didn't think she'd fall over. "My goodness, what a violent place Barley Flats is."

"It is that, ma'am," Gus said cheerfully. He rose and looked at the crowd that had gathered. "Better pick him up and take him to the doc's place, boys. He's still breathin'."

"He is?" A tall man standing at the back of the throng sounded annoyed.

Gus nodded and stepped aside as the tall fellow strode purposefully up to the fallen man.

"Well, he ain't going to be breathing much longer," the man said. Then he drew a long Smith & Wesson revolver from his waistband and shot the man on the ground between the eyes.

Miss Wiley screamed again. Fargo almost didn't blame her this time. He caught her before she hit the dirt as she fainted.

Several of the men standing around grabbed the shooter and wrestled him to the ground. "Here now, Harry," said one of them. "You know you can't go around shooting people like that."

"Dammit!" cried Harry. "He stole my claim!"

51

"He didn't steal it," another man objected. "You lost it to him in a fair game of poker."

"It wasn't fair, either," protested Harry. "He cheated. I swear he had an ace up his sleeve."

"Well, we'll have to look into it," Gus told the men. "You know the rules, Harry. If we decide you was out of line, we'll have to hang you."

Harry glowered at Gus, then at the body on the ground. "Hell, I reckon I know it, Gus, and I expect it'd be worth it to swing for the pleasure of killing that bastard. I know he cheated me, though."

Fargo would have scratched his head in amazement at the strange ethics prevailing in the gold-mining community if his arms weren't full of Genevieve Wiley.

Gus, who seemed to be as near to authority as Barley Flats had, said, "Take the body to the undertaker's, boys, and then we'll have us a little trial in the saloon for Harry here."

Everyone seemed to be amenable to Gus's suggestion, so they proceeded to carry out his instructions. Fargo watched with interest, still holding Miss Wiley in his arms. "I guess I'd better take her to her hotel, Gus. I'll be back shortly."

"I'll have the waiter at the Gold Nugget send the rest of our dinners over to the saloon, Skye. Sorry for the trouble."

Fargo shrugged. "Not your fault, Gus." He appreciated Gus's suggestion, though, because he was still hungry. Out of the corner of his eye, he caught a glimpse of someone who looked familiar, and he turned as fast as he could, but his agility was hampered by Miss Wiley. He squinted, but the man he thought he'd seen had vanished between two build-ings.

Gus, who'd been watching him, asked, "What is it, Skye?"

Fargo continued to stare at the alleyway, contem-plating whether or not he should dump Miss Wiley and investigate, but decided against it. "Nothing, I guess. Thought I saw somebody I'd met before."

Gus eyed him keenly. "Don't look to me as if your association was pleasant."

Fargo laughed. "It wasn't. If that's the man I thought it was, he snuck into our camp a couple of nights ago and tried to get at Miss Wiley."

"Whew! Don't know as I'd care to tangle with a Bible-beater myself." Gus grinned.

Fargo returned his grin with one of his own. "Don't know as I'd blame you. She's not as obliging as Sheila, let me tell you."

Gus guffawed as he turned to go back to his saloon to prepare for the trial. Fargo wondered who'd act as judge, and bet with himself that it would be Gus.

Miss Wiley came to before he'd carried her up the stairs, for which Fargo was grateful. He was not, how-ever, happy when she screeched in his ear. He set her down as soon as she began to struggle.

"What are you doing to me?"

He hadn't even got her propped upright before she started beating on his chest with her fists. He caught them in his hands and held her away from him. "I was trying to get you upstairs to your room, dammit."

"Don't swear at me!" She yanked her hands so hard, Fargo feared she might wrench her shoulders.

He pressed his lips together to keep from uttering

another curse. He said tightly, "You fainted out there on the street. I was just trying to see you to your room so you could rest."

"I don't believe you!"

He rolled his eyes. "Now there's a fine Christian attitude for you. I should think you'd thank me for not leaving you there in a heap on the dirt."

She began to waver in her attack, although she still pulled on her hands, trying to wrest them away from him. Her eyes narrowed, and she looked at him hard. "Is that really what happened, Mr. Fargo?"

He nodded. "You folded up like a fan when that fellow came over and shot the other one between the eyes. If you don't believe me, ask anybody. Looked to me like the whole town was out there watching."

Her nose wrinkled, and he saw her swallow. "Oh. Yes, I do believe I remember that now." She shuddered.

Fargo figured he'd performed more than his duty by Miss Wiley by this time, but chivalry made him ask, "Can you make it to your room on your own, ma'am?"

She tugged her skirt down from where it had bunched up around her comely thighs. "Yes, I believe so. Thank you." Her thanks sounded grudging.

He didn't expect much more, really, since his help had been offered grudgingly. "Think nothing of it." He turned to go back to Gus's when he stopped and looked back at her. There was probably nothing to his uneasiness, but he thought it would be only fair to warn her, just in case he hadn't been mistaken out there on the street. "Uh, ma'am?"

She'd started climbing the stairs, clutching the bannister as if her knees were shaky. Turning, she frowned down at him. No surprise there. "Yes, Mr. Fargo?"

He tried not to resent her frown. "I thought I'd better tell you that I think I saw that man out there."

"What man? Please be clear, Mr. Fargo. I've had a difficult day, and I'm not up to untangling nonsense."

Criminy, she was something else, wasn't she? Fargo sucked in about a bushel of air and let it out slowly. "The man who invaded our camp on the trail and tried to get you. I thought I saw him outside."

She gazed at him in perplexity for a moment, then understanding struck. "Oh!"

Now why, Skye wondered, did she have that briefly seen look of satisfaction on her face? It was gone now, and he wondered if he'd been mistaken. There was no reason he could perceive for her to feel good because a man who'd tried to assault her had followed her to Barley Flats. He shook his head. He was probably wrong about her expression. Unless, of course, she aimed to save the bastard's soul.

"Thank you for the warning, Mr. Fargo," she said a moment later. "I appreciate your concern."

"It's nothing, ma'am." He tipped his hat, turned, and decided that thinking about Miss Genevieve Wiley was a stupid pastime when he had half a good steak and a trial waiting for him at Gus's Place.

7

Fargo won his bet with himself about the judge at the trial of Harry—whose last name turned out to be Finnerty; it was Gus who presided as judge. He dusted off a table and shoved it across the room until it almost touched a far wall, placed a chair behind it against the wall, and sat himself down. Fargo was surprised to see how judicial he looked.

Gus used his gun as a gavel, and he rapped it sharply on the table as soon as he was ready to begin the proceedings. Fargo was impressed at the immediate silence that descended on the gathering. It didn't take the citizens of Barley Flats very long at all to pick twelve men to act as jurors.

Since California had been admitted to the Union several years before, Fargo imagined the jurors were supposed to be citizens of the United States of America. But jurisprudence in Barley Flats wasn't his concern, and he didn't question the right a Swede, a Mexican, a Spaniard, and a Chinaman had to sit in judgment of Harry with a bunch of men from back East. Harry didn't protest either, and Fargo assumed Harry knew more about justice in Barley Flats than he did.

He was grateful that Gus didn't prohibit the sale of

liquor while the trial was going forward. Fargo chewed on the rest of his steak and downed a mug of beer as he watched.

As soon as the jury was impaneled, and all twelve men swore with all appropriate gravity to perform their duty, Gus rasped, "All right, boys, we've got to decide whether or not Harry here was justified in shooting Joe Hamilton dead."

"I was," Harry declared stoutly.

Scattered laughter erupted in the courtroom, and Gus rapped his gun gavel again, and gave everyone a good glare. They quieted immediately. Gus cleared his throat and continued. "I know you think so, Harry, but that's for the jury to decide."

"*Sí*," said the Mexican on the jury, nodding.

Gus eyed the Mexican shrewdly. "You speak American good enough to understand what's goin' on, Miguel?"

"*Sí*," The Mexican said again.

"All right. I reckon the rest of you can understand enough to get by on."

The casualness of the situation might have tickled Fargo more if a man's life didn't depend on the outcome of the trial. Finished eating, he pushed his chair back, leaned against the wall, chewed on a toothpick, and watched, fascinated.

"You got anybody representing you, Harry?" Gus asked, his tone benevolent. "Bill Fisher's a lawyer. Want him to help you out some?"

"Naw. Besides, I think Bill's dead drunk."

Fargo glanced around and saw that the makeshift courtroom was packed with men drinking beer and whiskey, watching the proceedings with evident interest. Gus looked around his courtroom, too, spotting a man with his head resting on his arms, sending snores to the ceiling, and nodded. "Want to wait till he wakes up?"

"Naw. I don't need nobody. I can say what happened as good as anyone, I reckon."

Gus nodded. "All right, then, why don't you tell us why you think Joe deserved to be shot?"

"He stole my claim."

"You said that before, Harry. But you need to tell us why you think so. Sam Wiggins said you lost your claim in a poker game, fair and square."

"It was a rigged game, dammit," Harry said hotly.

"No cussin', Harry. We're in court now."

A mumble of approval went up in the room.

"Sorry," muttered Harry. Fargo was surprised that he actually appeared embarrassed.

"It's all right, Harry. Just don't forget again."

Harry nodded.

"So how come you think Joe rigged the game?" Gus's mild blue eyes twinkled like stars. He obviously enjoyed his role as judge.

"'Cause no deck of cards ever made has five aces in it, dammit." Realizing he'd slipped again, Harry muttered, "Sorry, Gus."

Gus nodded his forgiveness. "If you saw all five of them aces, why didn't you say something then and there? If you'd' a shot him then, nobody would have said anything at all."

"Well . . ."

The proceedings didn't take very long. Several men came forward to attest to Joe Hamilton's lack of moral fiber. A couple of others said they'd seen him cheating at cards more than once. One fellow swore that Joe Hamilton had stolen his donkey, but his testimony was generally discounted when it was pointed out that the donkey had been found several miles to the south of Barley Flats, sporting with a wild horse.

In the end, Harry went free, although Gus warned him to be more careful in the future.

"It's lucky for you nobody liked Joe Hamilton." Gus spoke sternly, and Harry hung his head. "You go around shootin' a man folks like, and the verdict's likely to be different next time. You remember that, Harry. You scared the pants off that missionary lady, too, and it ain't proper to go around scaring ladies. There ain't very many ladies around here."

Fargo grinned.

"Yessir," Harry mumbled, properly humbled. "I'm sorry."

Gus nodded sharply. "All right. Just you remember that. Now, I'll have to fine you something for disturbin' the peace, but I guess there won't be no hangin' today."

There were shuffles and murmurs in the courthouse saloon. Fargo couldn't tell if the men were glad to be spared building a scaffold, or if they were sorry they were being denied the spectacle of a hanging.

Gus banged his gun on the table again, said, "Fifty dollars. You can pay up when you got the money, Harry. I'll write it down in the court log book."

"Thanks, Gus." Harry sucked in a big breath. "And I want to thank everybody else. I'll spring for a round." He looked up quickly. "That is, I'll pay when I got the money, Gus. You know I'm good for it."

Gus sighed, shoved his makeshift judge's table away, and rose from his judicial bench. "I know it, Harry. All right. I'll add a round for the house onto your fine in the court book." Gus walked to the bar, went behind it, and bent over a table there. He looked like he was writing something.

A cheer went up, and Fargo imagined that if Harry ever killed anybody else, the victim had better be a saint, or Harry'd get away with it again. Not that Fargo cared. The event had been intriguing from beginning to end, and he appreciated the entertainment.

In fact, his whole day had been good. He'd finally gotten rid of Genevieve Wiley, he'd had a swell time with Sheila, he'd eaten a good dinner with Gus, and witnessed a California trial by jury. More or less.

With a contented sigh, he decided the rest of his evening could be spent playing some friendly games of poker in Gus's Place, drinking good bourbon, and maybe having a nice chat with another amiable woman. Gus had some pretty ones working for him. Sheila might be the best, but how would Fargo know that for sure if he didn't sample them all?

First, though, he wanted to satisfy his curiosity about something. Gus came over to finish his own steak, and Fargo pulled out a chair for him. "Interesting trial, Gus."

Gus laughed. "I reckon we're a little crude here in California, Skye, but at least Barley Flats has got some kind of law. Lots of places don't."

"So I've heard. I'm curious about that court log book of yours. Can I see it?"

"Sure." Gus got up and bellowed, "Gloria!"

A gloriously rounded woman with shining black hair and huge blue eyes sang back, "Right here, Gus!"

Gus winked at Skye. "Gloria, she's the best gal I got."

"I thought Sheila was the best."

Gus laughed again. "She is. So's Gloria. Depends

which one you got at any given time. They're all the best."

"I see." Fargo laughed, too.

"Bring me the logbook, Gloria, sweetheart," Gus called.

"Sure thing, Gus!"

Gloria swished up a few minutes later, her hips swaying deliciously. She eyed Fargo with what looked to him like greedy interest, although he acknowledged to himself that he might be reading too much into her smile. He smiled back and nodded.

"Gloria, this here's Skye Fargo, an old friend of mine."

"Happy to meet you, Gloria."

"I'm happy to meet *you*, Mr. Fargo. Sheila's told us a lot about you." She winked at him. "A lot of really good things."

"That's nice of her."

"Take a look, Skye. It's all writ down in there."

Gus plopped a huge and official-looking ledger book on the table. Gloria pulled up a chair and sat next to him.

"Skye here's interested in how we keep records in Barley Flats," Gus said around a mouthful of cold steak and potatoes.

"Is he? Well, maybe I can show him." Gloria leaned over the ledger book, her low-cut gown revealing a set of breasts that had Fargo salivating. "See here, Mr. Fargo? This is where Gus made a record of Harry's fine." She pointed at an entry with a blood red fingernail. "And here's where he bought a round for the house. You can see Gus wrote the fine down as 'Citations and Assessments,' and the drinks as 'Incidentals.' He keeps track that way."

"Er, yeah, I see." He was having a hard time wrenching his gaze away from Gloria's bosom. It was damned near spilling out of her dress. He cleared his throat and looked at Gus, who was enjoying the sight of Gloria every bit as much as Fargo was.

Fargo spent the rest of the evening at the poker tables. He won twenty dollars, then lost twenty-five, and then won another fifteen, so he was well satisfied when he went upstairs with Gloria. He was even more satisfied an hour later when he left Gloria to go back to his room at the Miner's Rest Hotel.

The night sky was black as tar, although there were plenty of lanterns hanging around to light his way. He hadn't drunk so much bourbon that he was stumbling, but he was pleasantly fuzzy. It took him, therefore, a moment to register the fact that a woman who bore a striking resemblance to Genevieve Wiley was hastening down the boardwalk on the other side of the street.

Fargo stopped and squinted at the woman, who had a cloak pulled tightly around her shoulders and seemed to be scurrying about in a very surreptitious manner. As he watched, she darted between two buildings and disappeared. He blinked and stared harder, trying to discern her form in the shadowy darkness.

Then he rubbed his eyes, sure he was merely seeing things. Why in the name of glory would Miss Genevieve Wiley, missionary, be sneaking around in a rough town like Barley Flats at this time of night? She wasn't going to preach a sermon in the back alley, was she?

He considered hollering across the street in an attempt to scare her out from between the buildings—

after all, maybe she was in some kind of trouble—and decided against it. He was in no condition to be dealing with Miss Wiley if that had indeed been her. Besides, everything he knew about her had led him to the conclusion that if she got herself into some kind of trouble, she could shriek loud enough to wake the dead. Surely somebody would come to her aid if she needed it.

Fargo continued on his way to the hotel room, climbed the stairs with little difficulty, and went on to his room.

He slept like a baby and had pleasant dreams.

8

"Dammit, Gus, I swear to God I had my poke right there, and when I went back, it was gone!"

Gus scratched his head. Fargo sat at the bar, nursing a cup of strong black coffee. He didn't feel too bad, considering his alcohol intake the night before, but he couldn't quite face breakfast yet. He watched the upset miner with moderate interest. Sounded to Fargo as if he'd been robbed.

"You sure you didn't spend it last night, Farley?" Gus looked at the miner kindly. "You was kinda drunk, you know."

"I know." Farley frowned. "But I wasn't *that* drunk. Hell, I know better than to drink up my poke. I panned that dust myself, dammit. It was hard work, and I was gonna send it home to my ma in Virginia."

Gus shook his head. "I'm right sorry, Farley. Was your room broke into?"

Farley shook his head, puzzled. "It didn't look like it, but I know I locked it. Hell, nobody leaves his room unlocked in Barley Flats."

"True, true." Gus was silent for a minute. Farley looked depressed. "Uh, you ain't been keeping company with a female, have you, Farley?"

Farley blinked, startled. "A female? Where's a man

gonna find him a female in Barley Flats, Gus? 'Cept the ones here in your place, but they work here. They don't hang around with none of us miners unless we pay 'em."

Gus nodded. "I reckon so. Just a thought, was all."

"Well, if you hear anything, let me know. All right, Gus?"

"Sure thing, son. I hope your poke turns up."

"Yeah. Me, too." Farley headed toward the door of the saloon, his entire posture declaring his state of dejection.

"Too bad," Fargo commented, watching Farley push through the batwings.

"Yeah. I don't like it when men get to stealin' from each other that way. It's one thing to jump a claim, but it's taking things too far to rob a man's own room."

Fargo hadn't apportioned crimes in that particular way before, and he wasn't sure he understood.

Evidently, Gus read the question on his face, because he continued. "I mean, all these men have come out here to California to find gold, so they sometimes get a little carried away when they're dealing with staking claims. There's lots of arguin' that goes on by the river, and sometimes the best of them can't figure out the exact barriers and borders around claims. But when a man's done his job and got his gold, most folks don't touch it. They might envy it, but they don't try to steal it. That's flat-out meanness, and most of these men ain't mean."

Fargo must have still appeared skeptical, because Gus laughed. "Oh, all right, Skye, I reckon these men are as mean as any, but most of 'em have too much respect for the work that goes in to working a claim to want to deprive a friend of his earnings. Hell, it ain't everybody that ever sees color at all, much less makes a sizable poke. And everybody in town knew Farley was going to send that money home to Virginia. His ma's sick."

A tall redheaded woman in a Chinese silk wrapper caught his eye as she walked down the staircase. Fargo watched her with true appreciation. She was quite a sight. Her ginger hair caught sunbeams streaking through the windows, her shiny blue robe set off her fiery hair to perfection, and her skin was as white as milk.

Gus nodded at the woman. "That there's Myrtle, Skye. She's the best gal I got."

Fargo tore his attention away from Myrtle and grinned at Gus, who grinned back. "The best, is she?"

"The best for mornings," Gus answered, laughing. "Sheila and Gloria, they like to sleep in. Myrtle, she's up with the birds, and just as eager to get pecking. So to speak."

"H'lo, Gus," Myrtle said. Her voice was husky and low, and it sent shivers down Fargo's back. She watched him with eyes that were as brown as chocolate, as warm as toast, and as sweet as honey. "You must be Skye Fargo. Sheila and Gloria told me about you." She sat next to him, crossed her legs, and allowed her silk robe to fall aside so Fargo had a good look at her lovely, long legs.

He cleared his throat, and wished he could do the same for his head. "Yes, ma'am. Gus tells me your name's Myrtle."

"That it is. Like the flower."

When she put a hand on his arm and leaned slightly in toward him, his manhood reacted instantly. "I heard you were drinking last night, Mr. Fargo. I've

66

got a sure cure for a big head after a night of drinking."

"You do?" He blinked stupidly.

"I sure do." She gave him a wink and turned to Gus. "Don't I, Gus?"

"She sure does, Skye. Myrtle's cure is good for about anything that ails a man. I recommend it."

Who was he to argue? He tossed a coin on the counter. "You two talked me into it."

With a low laugh that reverberated through Fargo's body like massaging fingers, Myrtle slid off the bar stool and took his arm. He got up, too, gazing raptly at Myrtle's robe, which had not merely revealed her legs, but had parted in the front to uncover most of her right breast.

He'd just taken her arm to lead her to the staircase when the front doors of the saloon burst open, and two men rushed in. Myrtle squeaked and pulled her robe together, and Fargo turned to see what was going on.

"Gus!" cried one man. "Did you hear what happened to Jack?"

Gus frowned at the newcomer. "Jack? No. What's the matter?"

"He's dead."

Both men skidded to a stop in front of the bar and stood there, panting and looking like their news horrified them in the telling as much as it did Gus in the hearing. Gus's eyes goggled. "Jack? Dead? What the hell happened?"

Myrtle squeaked again, and she looked as if the news had rattled her. "Who's Jack?" Fargo asked.

Gus looked at him. Fargo didn't like to see the genuine grief in his eyes. "Jack Billings. He was everybody's friend, Skye. I expect he was the best-liked man in Barley Flats." He turned back to the messenger. "What the hell happened, Louie?"

Louie, the man who'd shouted the news, exchanged a glance with the man who'd run into the saloon with him. Both men shook their heads. "Nobody knows. We found him this morning, shot in the chest."

The other man nodded. "He was late coming to the river, and I went up to see what was keeping him. He—he—" The man had to pause and breathe deeply several times. "He'd been dead for a few hours. And his cabin was ransacked. His stake was gone."

"I don't like this. That makes Jack and Farley both who got robbed overnight." Gus glanced from Louie and his friend to Fargo. "I don't suppose you'd be willing to look into this, would you, Skye? I'm sure Myrtle will be happy to oblige you later."

When Fargo glanced at Myrtle again, she was crying. He guessed that decided the matter for him. "Don't cry, honey. I'll try to find out what happened."

She sniffled. "Thank you. I—we—all of us girls liked Jack a lot. Hell, everybody liked Jack. He was a nice man." Myrtle turned and rushed up the stairs, her blue silk robe fluttering out behind her.

With a sigh of regret that his morning wasn't going to get off to as sweet a start as he'd hoped, he returned to the bar where Gus was still talking to Louie and his friend. The two men nodded at him. Gus said, "Can you wait a minute, Skye? I'm going to get Henry to watch the bar for me, and I'll go with you to Jack's place."

"Sure, Gus. Take your time." He introduced himself to Louie and the other man, whose name was Saul.

It was a somber procession that left Gus's Place and walked down the rough dirt road. The day was crystal clear, the sky blue and empty. There wasn't a cloud in it, and not a breath of wind stirred.

After they left the boardwalk, they continued until they got to a ramshackle cabin sitting back from the road several yards, separated from the rest of the world by a tumbled down wooden fence. Fargo noted with interest that somebody had planted roses along the fence. They weren't particularly well tended, but they were blooming like crazy, their flame red flowers perfuming the air.

Fargo nodded toward the roses. "Did Jack plant those?"

"Yeah. He liked his flowers, Jack did." Saul had to wipe his eyes. "He brung flowers to everybody in town when they was sick."

"He made good soup, too. He shared everything. You know what I mean?"

Louie looked beseechingly at Fargo, who nodded. "Yeah." Shoot, he'd never even met Jack, and he liked him, too. He felt sorry for the folks in Barley Flats, because he didn't expect anybody'd be taking Jack's place in their hearts any time soon.

The door of the cabin stood open, and a gaggle of miners stood around looking unhappy, their heads bare, their hats in their hands. They turned when they heard Fargo, Gus, Louie, and Saul trekking up the flagged pathway to the door. Several of them murmured a greeting.

Gus said, "This here's Skye Fargo, boys. He's going to take a look and see if he can figure out what happened. Skye, he's had experience with this sort of thing."

Fargo nodded an acknowledgment and slipped between a couple of the miners and into the house. He removed his hat, looked around, and muttered, "Whew! Somebody sure wanted something, by the looks of it."

The place had been completely ransacked, and not gently. Furniture had been upended and tossed around, drawers hung out of the one cabinet in the room, and the rugs were rumpled up. Jack's body was sprawled on his unmade bed. He was fully clothed, and a big red-brown stain spread from the hole in his chest and had soaked the bed. It looked to Fargo as though he'd surprised someone and had gotten shot for it.

He walked to the bed and stared down at the body. "Anybody know who he was with last night?"

Several of the bystanders murmured. One of them said, "He was at the saloon until late."

"He was playing poker with Kanaka, wasn't he?"

"Kanaka?" Several men turned and searched the crowd.

A dark-skinned Indian stepped forward, looking sick. He stammered, "W—we was playin'. Yeah."

"You left together, didn't you?" Gus's eyes narrowed.

Kanaka held up a hand. "Yes, but we separated right outside your saloon, Gus. Honest."

Fargo gathered that Kanaka was known as an upright man, as nobody denied his allegation.

Gus said, "You two left a little after midnight, close as I can recall. That what you remember, Kanaka?"

The man nodded. He looked almost too shaky to talk. Fargo didn't press the issue, but glanced around the room, wishing all these men hadn't stormed in and cluttered up the scene of the crime. Nothing he could do about it now.

Gus asked, "Can you tell what happened, Skye?"

"Not really." He added, "Looks like maybe he surprised someone going through his cabin and got shot for his efforts."

"Like me. Only I didn't find the bastard doin' it."

When he looked up, Fargo saw that Farley had joined the group. "Maybe so," he said.

"You got robbed too, Farley?"

"I did. Somebody broke into my room and stole my poke."

Louie looked shocked. "Jeeze."

"They didn't tear up the place, though. Not like this."

Louie turned to Gus, as if he expected an answer from that source. "Who'd do something like this?" He swept out a hand.

"Wish I knew, Louie," said Gus.

When Louie faced the room, the rest of the men shook their heads, as if they wished they knew, too. Fargo noted with interest that they all looked as if this particular piece of violence had shocked and appalled them. It was as if they could understand spontaneous outbursts, but this sort of planned burglary and murder seemed too cold-blooded and calculated to them.

"If you'd all clear out of the room, I'll take a look around," he offered. "I don't expect to find much. If there were any boot tracks or anything, they've probably been stomped out by this time."

A couple of the men looked at the floor, seeming to regret whatever stomping they'd done. Fargo said, "There probably weren't many. Whoever did this, it looks like he's had practice."

"You mean you think it's somebody who steals for a living?"

The question had been asked by a boy who didn't look much older than sixteen or seventeen. With a nod, Fargo said, "I think so." He gave a thought to the men who'd stopped him and Miss Wiley in the mountains and amended his thought. "Unless it was somebody who was just plain desperate."

But that didn't sound right to him. There was something sinister about this mess in Jack's cabin. He shook off his dismal mood. "Why don't a couple of you men take Jack here to the undertaker while I look around."

Gus supervised the removal of the body, then came back and went through Jack's things with Fargo. They didn't find a clue as to who might have perpetrated the evil deed. Nor did they find a single, solitary speck of gold dust or any of the nuggets Jack had panned out of the river.

"This ain't right, Skye. Jack, he always had some gold around. He generally didn't keep a whole lot here. Banked with Wells Fargo, like most of the men do. It ain't smart to keep much loose gold handy, but Jack should have had something in his trousers or in his hidey-hole." Gus gestured at two of the floorboards that had been lifted and left lying on a braided rug. The hole was as empty as the sky outside.

"How many people knew about his hidey-hole?"

Gus scratched his chin. "Pretty much every man in Barley Flats has some secret hiding place. Not all of them's in the same place, but it's no use pretendin' men don't hide their pokes. It only makes sense."

"But you didn't know Jack's was there?" Fargo pointed at the floorboards.

Shaking his head, Gus murmured, "No." He looked up. "Shoot, Skye, this is terrible. Two men robbed and one murdered overnight. Barley Flats is a rough town and we're used to men shootin' each other, but not like this. This is—well, it's terrible."

"Yeah. You're right." He looked around and felt sort of helpless. "Wish I could tell you something, but I haven't found a single thing that might point to the killer."

Gus heaved a big sigh. "I reckon if anybody could find a clue, it's you, Skye. Let's go to the Gold Nugget and get us some breakfast. I'll get some of the boys to clean this place up. I know Jack had family back in Louisiana. I expect his kin will want his leavings."

Fargo agreed to breakfast and Gus's plans. Hardly a word was spoken as they ate flapjacks and ham and drank more coffee at the café. Fargo didn't even have the heart to visit Myrtle afterward.

9

"Repent! The Lord wants you! Forsake your wicked ways and come to Jesus!"

"Aw, hell."

Gus looked at Fargo across the table, and for the first time since the two men had sat down, smiled. "That your missionary out there yellin', Skye?"

"She's not *my* missionary." Fargo drank some too-hot coffee and scalded his tongue.

"You brung her."

"Don't keep reminding me."

"Repent, I say!"

Gus chuckled. "I'd say she's got her work cut out for her here in Barley Flats."

"I'd say you're right." Fargo was beginning to feel he hadn't done anyone any favors by rescuing Miss Genevieve Wiley from her four drunken friends the other day.

"Say, Skye," Gus said, after swallowing another bite of flapjack, "do you s'pose she'd be willing to say a few words over Jack's coffin when we bury him? I expect the boys'd like that. Maybe it'd make them a little easier on your friend out there if she was to do somebody some good."

"I reckon we could ask her. You're right. It would

give her something to do besides irritate the good citizens of Barley Flats."

Gus shrugged. "I don't know about the *good* part anymore."

Fargo grunted around a mouthful of ham. "If you want me to, I'll ask her when we're through."

Nodding, Gus shoveled another bite of flapjack into his mouth.

So, after they'd paid their bill, the two men moseyed out of the Gold Nugget. Miss Wiley had drawn a crowd. She was haranguing them with obvious fervor and, if Fargo was any judge, a good deal of glee. He'd seldom met anyone who liked a job more than Miss Wiley liked hers. Probably because it made her feel superior. He tried to stifle his opinion as he walked up to her.

It took her a minute to see him in the crowd. When she did, she didn't look pleased. He frowned at her. She frowned back.

He decided he'd try to start out polite, no matter how their confrontation ended up. "Morning, Miss Wiley."

"Good morning, Mr. Fargo." She sounded as stiff as she looked.

"Gus and I have a question for you."

"Oh?"

Gus, evidently worried that the two of them were going to start scrapping, stepped in front of Fargo. "Yes, ma'am. Skye and me, we wondered if you'd do us the kindness of saying some words over the coffin of Jack Billings, who was killed last night."

Her eyes grew wide. "Good heavens! He was *killed*?"

"Yes'm," said Gus.

Fargo thought there was something odd about her reaction, although he couldn't put his finger on exactly what it was. "The men in Barley Flats were fond of him, Miss Wiley, and they want to bury him right."

She cleared her throat. "I see." She hesitated for a moment, then gave a brisk nod. "Very well. I shall be happy to recite some holy words over the poor man's last resting place. I'm sure the good Lord would want me to do at least that." As if she couldn't help herself, she added, "Although I'm sure He would have wanted Mr. Billings to have lived a good Christian life more than He'll appreciate Christian words having been said over his corpse."

"Dammit, Miss Wiley, how do *you* know Jack Billings wasn't a good Christian? From all I've ever heard about him, he was a good neighbor and a generous friend. Doesn't that count for anything?" Fargo knew he'd erred as soon as Miss Wiley registered his opening curse. But, damn it all, who was *she* to be condemning people for not being Christians when she didn't even know them?

Perhaps fortunately, he didn't ask that question, and she didn't bother answering his first one. Instead, she turned to Gus. "When will the funeral be, Mr. Perkins?"

"I'll talk to the undertaker. It'll probably be this afternoon. I'll let you know as soon as we have a firm time. Maybe Skye here can take you to our Boot Hill then."

Fargo glared at Gus, who winked back. Miss Wiley drew herself up to her full height and said in a voice as cold as ice, "Fine. I shall see you then, Mr. Fargo." She turned on her heel, lifted her Bible, and was about to start spewing hellfire and damnation again, when he interrupted her.

"Wait a minute, ma'am."

She whirled around and glowered at Fargo. "What is it, Mr. Fargo?"

"Just curious, is all. Why did you choose this particular corner, if you don't mind me asking?"

"Why?" She looked around. The spot from which she had chosen to preach was directly across from Gus's Place and the Gold Nugget Chop House, up several yards from the Miner's Rest Hotel, and in front of the Barley Flats Assay Office and the Wells Fargo Barley Flats bank branch. Fargo wasn't surprised when she said, "It's convenient."

Which was true. It was also the best place from which to view miners carrying out their various business enterprises. Fargo imagined that anyone who entered Gus's Place looking pleased with himself would also be noticeable. Not to mention men who entered the assayer's office and the bank. Any astute confidence trickster could spot his—or her— mark with ease from that location.

He shook his head. What a stupid notion. Hell's bells, Miss Wiley was about as likely to be a confidence trickster as he was himself. And he was more honest than most men. He just had a headache. That's all that was the matter with him.

Miss Wiley did a good job at Jack's funeral. Fargo had to hand it to her. She didn't get too carried away with trying to make all the men gathered around the grave feel guilty about being alive and men. Rather, she recited a rather sweet prayer, did the "Ashes to ashes, dust to dust" thing, and led a hymn. He was impressed rather than annoyed, which he considered a distinct improvement in his relationship with Miss Wiley.

She was happy when several of the men donated some gold dust and nuggets to her when the service ended, and most of them mumbled their thanks. She assured the men that their donations would be put to God's work.

After the funeral, Fargo decided to go back to Gus's Place and see if Myrtle was still available for a little stimulating massage.

She wasn't. He was disappointed.

"Sorry, Skye," Gus said sympathetically. "But Myrtle, you know, she's the best gal I got, and she's always busy. Why don't you sit down and play a game of cards. I'm sure she'll be free—that is, she'll be *available*—soon."

He was wrong about that. No sooner had Fargo sat down and been dealt a poker hand—and a good one, at that—than a sharp scream tore through the saloon. Every man in the place dropped what he was holding and leaped to his feet. Gus ran out from behind the bar.

"What the hell was that?" one of the men at Fargo's table asked.

"It sounded like Myrtle." Gus looked worried.

Fargo drew his Colt and started for the stairs, when a door on the second floor flew open and Myrtle, struggling and screeching because she was being gripped painfully by a big, burly man, flew out of the room. Fargo's eyes narrowed. The man holding her captive was the very one who'd sneaked into his and Miss Wiley's camp several nights before.

The man spotted Fargo and gave him a wicked grin. "We meet again, Mr. Fargo."

"Yeah." Fargo was worried about Myrtle. "What the hell are you doing to that woman?"

"I'm using her as a shield. That should be obvious to anybody."

"He—he's the man who killed Jack." Myrtle's voice shook like a leaf in a gale.

"I did not!" the man snarled indignantly.

"Damn," muttered Gus, who was standing behind Fargo.

"How do you know he killed Jack?" Fargo asked.

"I found some of Jack's things in his clothes."

"Ask her why she was goin' through my clothes, why don't you?" growled the burly man. "It ain't like I wasn't going to pay her. She had no business goin' through my things."

"I wasn't going through them!" Myrtle cried indignantly. "Your pants fell off the chair and all that stuff fell out. I was picking it up for you!"

"Right. Well, it don't matter, because I'm using you for insurance, and I'm going to leave Barley Flats right now. You're coming with me."

"Let her go, and nobody will hurt you," Gus pleaded.

Myrtle's captor laughed evilly. "Now why do you suppose I don't believe you, old man?"

"Let them go, Gus," Fargo muttered. "I'll get her back—safe, I hope."

Gus looked at Fargo. "I hope to hell you can do it, Skye. Myrtle, she's a good girl."

Fargo gave him a little grin. "I know. She's the best."

Gus didn't grin back. "They're all like my own daughters, Skye."

Fargo knew Gus was telling the truth. The barkeep's heart was damned near as big as he was, and there were tears in his blue eyes.

"All right," Gus told the villain. "Take Myrtle and go. But if you hurt a hair on her head—"

"I won't. She's my only ticket out of here."

That was true. The entire barroom full of miners watched as the burly man slowly inched toward the door, using Myrtle as a shield. Myrtle's big brown eyes held a world of fear, and Fargo tried to give her some strong and silent encouragement with his own eyes. He didn't know how much good it did her, but it made him feel better.

No one in the saloon stirred until she and her captor were outside. Then there was a general scramble toward the door, but Gus brought everyone to a halt with a holler.

"Hold it! Everybody stay right where you are. The only man who's going outside until I say so is Skye Fargo. If you all run out there, that man will kill her for sure."

The men seemed to perceive the sense in Gus's warning, because the stampede stopped. Shortly afterward, the silence was broken by the clatter of hoofbeats as a horse tore up the road. Fargo raced to the door and saw the outlaw, with Myrtle perched in front of him, galloping away. Folks on the street stopped to stare. He noticed Miss Wiley, her mouth agape, staring after the retreating horse with an expression of shock on her face.

"What's going on?" she screeched as Fargo

rushed outside to get his Ovaro from the livery stable.

He didn't have time to stop and chat, so he didn't answer, but kept going to the livery stable. He was saddling the big pinto stallion, bringing along an extra blanket—he figured he'd either wrap Myrtle's dead body in it, or cover her for warmth if she was alive—when he realized Miss Wiley had followed him. Her persistence irked him, and he scowled at her. "I don't have time to talk right now, Miss Wiley."

"But what happened? Where was that man going?"

"How the hell do I know? But he's got Myrtle, and I'm going to get her back."

"Oh, dear Lord." She pressed her hands to her cheeks. "Please don't hurt him, Mr. Fargo!"

He mounted and gazed down on her incredulously. "Don't hurt *him*? What about *her*? *She's* the one in trouble here."

"Oh, of course. Of course, I meant that too."

She didn't, either. Fargo knew it as well as he knew his own name. However, there was no time to puzzle over Miss Wiley's skewed priorities, which seemed to extend forgiveness to sinners and not a care to anybody else. He rode the Ovaro out of the livery stable and up the road as if all the demons of hell were chasing them.

He had no trouble following the tracks of the outlaw and the captive sporting girl. For the first part of his pursuit, he could almost keep track of their path by the gaping souls he passed, all of whom seemed to be staring up the beaten road and chattering with each other. As the Ovaro thundered past groups of miners, he heard snatches of conversations, thrown up to his ears along with the dust and grit of fast travel.

"—was Myrtle, by damn!"

"What the hell . . .?"

"—don't look like she wants—"

"—he don't hurt her—"

Soon, signs of civilization—and even those of the mining community—grew thinner and thinner, and the countryside got rougher. The trail became more difficult to follow, although the Trailsman, an expert at this sort of thing, didn't have much trouble with it. At least the villain hadn't discarded Myrtle anywhere, which was encouraging.

Nevertheless, he was feeling pretty grim by the time he crested a hill and saw, far below, the mounted man approaching a small river that bubbled out from a stand of cedar and pine trees. It looked as if Myrtle had started struggling, and Fargo hoped she wouldn't keep it up. The only reason she'd been safe so far was because the man needed her.

The big pinto had started down the hill when the villain looked back over his shoulder and saw that he was being pursued. Fargo was too far away to hear whatever foul curses the man uttered, but he heard Myrtle's scream when the louse thrust her from the saddle without slowing down. Then he kicked his horse up even faster, and the animal splashed into the river and scrambled out on the other side.

Fargo winced when he saw the girl hit the earth. It was a long way down from a horse racing at a full-tilt gallop. Fargo had his Henry out of its scabbard in an instant, but he was too far away, and the scoundrel was riding too fast for him to draw a steady bead on him. Instead, he hurried to where Myrtle lay, unmoving, in a clump of brush.

10

Saving Myrtle's life was far more important than catching the escaping outlaw, and Fargo knew it, even though he wished he could do both. Since there was only one of him, he reckoned the hardcase would have to wait until later.

As for Myrtle, her body was draped at an uncomfortable angle in the bushes which, fortunately, weren't full of thorny stickers. Thank God for central California flora. It wasn't nearly as prickly as the flora found in dryer parts of the state.

Fargo raced over to her, and had dismounted before the Ovaro came to a complete stop. He heard her moaning, and hoped that was a good sign. At least she wasn't dead.

"Myrtle!" he cried as he ran over to her.

Her eyelids flickered and her eyes were dazed and unfocused when she tried to find him. "Wh—what happened?" She whimpered, and her eyes drifted shut again.

"Careful now. Don't try to move." Very gently, Skye began a survey of her limbs, trying to determine if anything was broken. "Where does it hurt, Myrtle?"

"Everywhere."

She gasped in pain when he pressed her shoulder.

"Don't try to move. Just take it easy. I want to see if anything's broken."

She subsided with a moan. Poor thing. She was going to be a mass of bruises, but so far he hadn't detected any broken bones.

"Take it easy, Myrtle. I'm going to try to bend your right leg. If it hurts too much, give a holler, all right?"

Evidently not trusting herself to talk, she merely nodded. Fargo very carefully lifted her right foot, which had lost its shoe somewhere in her wild ride, and bent the leg at the knee. She sucked in a breath, but didn't cry out. He considered that a good sign. "All right, honey, now let's try the left one."

She nodded again, weakly. The left leg bent, too, and Fargo released the breath he'd been holding. He carefully moved both of her feet to assess the state of her ankles. Neither appeared to be broken or severely sprained. She was surely going to be sore as hell, but there weren't any bones broken. If she hadn't sustained a concussion, her prognosis looked good to him.

"Can you open your eyes, sweetheart? I know it hurts."

"I—I think so." She did, and groaned piteously. "Oh, God, I hurt. I think my head's busted."

"Let's find out. Take it easy now. Take a look at my hand and tell me how many fingers I'm holding up."

She gazed fuzzily at his hand and said slowly, "Two, unless I'm seeing double."

He chuckled. "No, I've got two fingers up. What about now?" He closed his hand into a fist.

"Um, none?"

"Right as rain. I think you're going to be all right,

sweetie, but I don't think we'd better do any traveling until you've rested up some."

She closed her eyes again and whispered, "Good idea."

"You're as gritty as they come, Myrtle," he told her approvingly. "Now, I'm going to lift you up. It'll probably hurt, but you need to get off of those bushes and out of the sun. I'll carry you into that stand of trees over there, and fix you up a little bed with my saddle blanket. We can rest there for as long as you need to, and I'll fix you some willow-bark tea. That'll help with the aches and pains."

"Thanks." Her voice was weak, but she seemed impelled to ask, "What about Gus? He'll be so worried."

"I know, honey. He's the one who sent me after you. He knows we'll both be coming back, one way or another."

She squinted at him as he lifted her. "One way or another? You mean you told him you'd bring me back, alive or dead?"

"Right," he said with a broad smile. "And I aim to see that it's alive."

Her eyes drifted shut again, and she murmured, "Thank God." Then she put her arms around Fargo's shoulders and allowed him to carry her through the stream and into the trees.

With a whistle, Fargo summoned the Ovaro, who followed them through the water. "I'm going to set you down under this tree, Myrtle. There's some leaves there, so it's probably not too hard, but I'll get you fixed up more comfortably in a minute."

"Take your time," she whispered. "I'm in no hurry."

"I'll bet you're not." He had to hand it to her. She must be as sore as the devil, yet she wasn't griping.

He had a fairly comfortable bed rigged up for her in a few minutes, and laid her down on it, covering her with the blanket he'd brought along. Then he built a fire under the tree, got a pot from his saddlebag, and began to boil water.

"This tea I'm going to fix tastes bitter, Myrtle, but it's good for what ails you. The Indians use willow bark all the time."

She whimpered something he didn't catch. He brewed up the tea, making sure it was strong enough to get up and walk by itself, stirred some of his sugar supply into it, and brought the tin cup over to the blanket. She heard him coming, and cracked one eye open.

"I don't suppose you have any brandy to pour into that tea, do you?"

He grinned down at her. "Not just now. Drink this first, and we'll see if it stays down. If you don't have a concussion—and I don't think you do—you can have some brandy after you drink the tea."

She groaned as she struggled to a sitting position. "Oh, God, I feel like hell."

"I bet you do."

Nevertheless, she drank the tea. Fargo had to help her at first, holding the cup for her, but she managed to hold on to it herself by the time she drained the cup, grimacing the entire time. "Lord, that tastes bad."

"I know it does. Do you think it's going to stay down?"

She paused for a minute, assessing the state of her stomach. "I think so."

"How do you feel?" he asked, watching her closely.

"A little better." She didn't sound sure of herself or of her diagnosis, either.

"I think we'd better plan on staying here for at least another few hours. The more you rest, the better off you'll be."

She eyed him unhappily, and tried to wriggle herself into a more comfortable position, grunting in pain. "I don't suppose you thought to bring any laudanum or morphia with you, did you?"

He grinned at her. "I might have done something like that. And I think it would be a good idea for you to take some before I get to cleaning your scratches."

"You're gonna wash them?"

He nodded. "With soap and water." At the worried expression on her face, he reassured her, "I'll wait until the laudanum takes effect first."

She shut her eyes and groaned, "Thank God."

After he dosed her with several drops of laudanum in water, he heated up some water, helped her disrobe—which was a task he enjoyed a lot, since Myrtle was built along splendid lines—and washed her wounds carefully.

When he was through, he smiled at her. "There. I don't think you need any stitches. They're mostly just scrapes."

"I'm glad of that. If I feel this bad without stitches, I can't even imagine how I'd feel if you took a needle and thread to me."

"You're going to be fine."

He helped her into one of his shirts, because it was looser and would be more comfortable than her whalebone and stays. "Thanks, Skye," she whispered, obviously at the end of her endurance.

"Just lie down now, Myrtle. I think you'll feel better when you sleep some."

"I hope to God I do."

Shortly afterward, under the influence of her ordeal, the willow-bark tea, and the laudanum, she dropped into an exhausted slumber. By the time she awoke, the sun had set, and Fargo had some fish cooking over the fire he'd built. He'd made some corn cakes to eat with the fish, and had even scavenged some wild berries.

When he heard her stirring, he left his supper preparations and went to check on her. "Don't try to move too fast," he told her. "Take it easy."

She muttered something under her breath and then said, "Don't worry. I couldn't move fast if my feet were on fire." With a grunt, she managed to push herself to those feet and stood, swaying, in the firelight. "By God, I think I'm going to live."

He reached her before her knees gave out, and steadied her with a laugh. "I think you will too, but you're still going to have to take it easy for a while."

"You're telling me."

She was full of gumption, and Fargo liked her for it and for her humor, which was remarkably good considering the adventure she'd been through. They ate fish and corn cakes, and he made her drink some strong coffee laced with a little bit of laudanum to lessen the aches from all her bruises.

"We'll stay here tonight, and tomorrow, if you feel up to it, we'll get on back to Barley Flats."

She nodded her assent. "Sounds good to me. I sure don't feel up to riding today."

"Didn't think so. Want any more coffee?"

"No thanks."

Fargo fixed up a bed for himself across the fire from Myrtle. She eyed it skeptically. "You have to sleep that far away from me for some reason I don't know about?"

He looked up quickly from his preparations. "What do you mean, Myrtle?"

"I mean," said she, "that I don't much fancy sleeping alone. And it'll be a whole lot warmer and more comfortable if we sleep together."

He swallowed. "Um, I'm not sure I take your meaning."

She rolled her eyes. "Come on now, Skye Fargo. I know good and well you're not slow. I want you to make love to me, for God's sake. Is that so hard to understand?"

Actually, it was. He tried to think of a tactful way to say so. "Um, but aren't you too sore for that sort of thing?"

"No."

That was concise. And, since he didn't think it would be polite to argue with an invalid, Fargo picked up his bedroll and moseyed to her side of the fire. "Guess I'll take your word for it."

She patted the blanket beside her. "Good. You just park your big, handsome self down here, sweetie pie, and we'll see if we can't make the both of us feel better."

"Always happy to oblige a pretty woman," he said, and flipped his own blanket out to overlap with hers. With quick, deft movements, he undressed.

"Whoa, you're even more breathtaking than I figured you'd be," Myrtle said with real appreciation as she looked at Fargo's lean, muscular frame. "Sheila and Gloria told me about you, but I wanted to see for myself."

"You're exactly as beautiful as I figured you'd be." He looked down at her, appreciating the way her hair caught the fading firelight and seemed to sparkle. "Need help getting out of that shirt, sweetheart."

"Oh, I think I can manage." She did, and leaned back on her elbow, showing Fargo everything she had to offer, which was a lot. She had long, beautiful legs, gloriously rounded thighs, and hips with a lush triangle of red-brown curls between her legs, a softly rounded belly, and the most perfect breasts he'd seen in a long while. Her nipples were dusky and already pebbled and looked like they were begging him to do something interesting with them.

He caught his breath when she stretched and smiled at him, and his manhood started to harden immediately.

"I feel better already," she said in a soft purr.

"So do I."

He didn't need another invitation, and sat next to her and took her in his arms. Her skin was warm and supple, and was as smooth as glass. "You just lie back, honey, and don't try to do too much."

"Sounds like a good plan to me." She said in a husky voice.

So that she wouldn't strain herself, he took the lead. He hoped to feel every single gorgeous inch of her body, and as his mouth covered hers and her tongue began to mate with his, he decided he was really glad he'd gone out alone to rescue Myrtle. It would be too much to expect her to share her favors with more than one man, and this was exactly the way he'd planned on spending the evening anyway—with a gorgeous and willing woman.

She was more than willing. She responded to his touch as if he had stoked a fire, pressing herself into him and feeling his muscles with skillful hands and fingers. When she reached for his rod, he groaned. Her hand lightly caressed him until he was writhing with pleasure. He returned the favor, fondling the curls between her thighs and finding the nub of her pleasure.

"You're sure this isn't too much for you?" He hoped to hell her answer would be no, because he was as hard as a rock and it might just kill him to stop now.

"If you dare even think about quitting, I'll shoot you dead, Skye Fargo."

That settled that, he reckoned. He continued his survey of her body, enjoying every second, as she continued to explore every hot, silky inch of his iron.

"Ahhh. That feels so good."

He continued to pleasure her with his thumb as he thrust his fingers in and out of her inner cavern, and she met every thrust with an arch of her hips, never stopping her own ministrations. It wasn't long before he felt her inner muscles begin to quiver. Then, with a little cry she was convulsing underneath him. Because he couldn't wait any longer, he drew himself over her and, with a deep thrust, plunged his manhood into her tight passage, taking full advantage of her contracting muscles and arching hips. With a couple of furious, hard plunges, he joined her in sweet release.

With a heavy sigh, he lowered himself, trying not to smother her body with his. He was almost too exhausted to be surprised when she muttered, "Get the hell on top of me. I'm not ready to let you go yet."

It took all his energy to push himself up so he could look down at her. "You're sure?" Lord, she was beautiful, with her flame red hair spread out beneath her head, her lips rosy and swollen with his kisses, and her eyes, heavy-lidded and sleepy, and an expression of sated bliss on her face.

"I'm sure." To prove it, she hooked her arms around his back and tugged him down on top of her.

Who was he to argue? A couple of hours later, he woke up long enough to pull a blanket over the two of them. By that time they were sleeping side by side, and Myrtle had thrown a leg over his own. He patted her tenderly, and sighed back into sleep.

11

Myrtle was moving pretty slowly the next morning, although she claimed she felt fine. "After last night, I can face anything," she told Fargo when he handed her a cup of coffee. "You're even better than I thought you'd be."

"Likewise." He grinned at her across a replenished fire, over which he was cooking more fish and corn cakes. "You're quite a woman, Myrtle."

She groaned, shoved the blanket down, and gave him a full view of her many spectacular assets. "Got a comb anywhere, Skye?"

He had to swallow before he could get his voice to work. Myrtle looked *very* good this morning, considering she had livid blue bruises all over her body. Not to mention all the cuts and scratches. He tried to concentrate on her injuries so as to tame his manhood into some kind of proper conduct. It didn't help much. He was as hot as a live coal and as hard as a pistol barrel when he carried the comb over to her. "Want me to comb it for you?"

She smiled at him. "I think that sounds like a great idea."

An hour or so later, they were heading back to Barley Flats. Fargo was feeling relaxed and very, very happy. Myrtle was humming a merry tune.

"Repent, I say! Repent of your greedy, wicked ways!"

Fargo frowned when he heard that oh-so-familiar rant as he guided the Ovaro down Barley Flats's one dirt road. He glanced toward the Wells Fargo Bank building, the only building in Barley Flats that looked perfectly solid.

There she was, thumping her Bible, and exhorting the poor men who struggled in the river for gold to forsake their evil ways and do what she wanted them to do. It didn't seem fair to Fargo. Those men were only trying to make their ways through life, just like the rest of mankind. He didn't think they deserved to be sent to hell over it. "Nuts. I thought maybe she'd have given up by this time."

Myrtle, who was straddling the saddle in front of him, looked at the female street preacher and said, "Who is she?"

"Miss Genevieve Wiley. I helped her out on my way to Barley Flats, and she's been hollering at the miners here ever since."

Myrtle giggled. "Well, you can't get lucky all the time, I reckon. I expect you should pray that most of the women you rescue are more like me than they are like her."

He gave her a squeeze. "You can say that again."

As Miss Wiley continued to holler up a storm, Fargo and Myrtle walked toward Gus's Place, attracting a throng by the time they got to the batwing door. When he carried her inside, the saloon erupted into cheers. Gus hurried over to them.

"Myrtle! Thank God you're all right!"

"Thanks to Skye Fargo," she purred, smiling prettily at her audience.

"The son of a gun dumped her at the river." Fargo got angry, remembering. "He just threw her off his horse. Didn't even slow down."

"Bastard!" grunted Gus. Several other men in the room voiced their outrage as well.

"It wasn't any fun. Until later." Myrtle winked at Gus, who eyed Fargo and laughed.

"I'll bet."

"Why don't I take Myrtle upstairs, Gus, and then you can tell me what's been happening around here."

"Good idea. There's something going on, that's for sure. I'm sure that devil who took off with Myrtle never came back here yesterday, but there were more robberies overnight."

Over Myrtle's languidly draped body, Fargo frowned. "That doesn't sound right, Gus. Unless the man had a companion in crime. But he was alone when he came to your place, wasn't he?"

"Yup. All by his lonesome."

Fargo stood there thinking for a minute, with Myrtle in his arms. Then he shrugged. "I reckon you can tell me about it after I get Myrtle settled."

Gus led the applause when Fargo started up the stairs. Myrtle waved at the men and posed, and Fargo wondered if Gus picked all his women for their showmanship qualities.

"Will you come back here and see me again before you leave Barley Flats?" she asked, batting her gorgeous eyes at him.

He tipped his hat. "You can bet on it, Myrtle." She

blew him a kiss, and he left her with a wink to go back downstairs and talk to Gus.

Gus met him at the foot of the stairs with a glass of bourbon and a smile. "Thanks for going after her, Skye."

The two men sat at a table near the bar. Fargo tilted his glass at Gus. "Here's mud in your eye." It was good bourbon, and it felt like silk going down. He sighed with contentment. "So, tell me what's happened, Gus. You say there's another thief working in Barley Flats?"

"There sure is. Whoever it is got into a couple of tents last night when the men were here in the saloon and took both men's pokes. Just like he done with poor Jack, only nobody got killed last night."

Fargo sipped more bourbon. "It's a mercy nobody else got killed, at any rate."

"Yeah, but nobody likes thinking they can't leave their rooms without taking their gold with them. Hell, Skye, that stuff's heavy. And, while most of these men try to keep as much of their take in the Wells Fargo Bank as they can, they can't always get there. It ain't fair. Most of these men are barely making ends meet. And as rough as Barley Flats is, most of the men who work in the river and the mines have more respect for other people's property than that."

Fargo nodded sympathetically. "Have you done anything to try to find out who's doing the stealing?"

"Not so far. Until last night, we thought it was a freak happening—you know, that the bastard who took Myrtle had done the stealin' and wouldn't try to come back to town after he was found out."

"But you were wrong."

"We sure were. I reckon either another thief's come

to town, or that man had an accomplice we don't know about."

Fargo tipped his glass at Gus. "Have you noticed any strangers in town?"

Gus gave him a look he should have expected, and he held up a hand to thwart a reprimand. "I know, I know. All the men in town are strangers."

"That's about it. Hell, there ain't a man in California who was born here, unless it's a Spaniard or an Indian. The rest of us are from somewhere else, and most folks don't stay any longer than it takes them to go broke. Then they're headed back to Vermont or Kentucky or wherever they come from with their tails between their legs and terrible stories about the horrors of California gold camps."

Fargo chuckled. "Sounds about right to me."

"The only folks makin' money are the bankers and saloon keepers—oh, a few of the miners made a fortune in gold at first, but most of the river gold was panned out a couple of years after that first nugget was discovered."

Fargo sighed and sipped bourbon. "Yeah. But folks don't like to give up their dreams, I reckon."

"I reckon." Gus frowned, stuck his finger into a puddle of water on the table, and began making designs with the water. "I don't like it, Skye. I don't like it that somebody's robbin' folks in the night. It's not the way crime's carried out in Barley Flats."

Fargo cocked his head and narrowed his eyes. "I didn't know that there was a right way to commit crimes, Gus."

Gus chuckled. "Well, you know what I mean. Most of the crimes are murders and such-like. Men get drunk and get mad and shoot each other. We don't have much of this stealin' stuff going on."

"What about the man who jumped that other man's claim?"

Gus shrugged. "Oh, well, sure. We get claim-jumping every now and then, but that's about it. And that Joe Hamilton was a bad apple to begin with. Most of the folks around here don't steal other folks' pokes."

"They do now." Fargo drained his glass and shuddered when the burn hit his stomach.

Gus looked keenly at Fargo. "But you know, Skye, if you was to keep a lookout, you might be able to find out who's doing the taking."

"Me?" Fargo didn't know that he liked that idea. His main aim in visiting Gus in Barley Flats was to get himself some recreation—a few poker games, a few pretty girls, some drinking—he didn't particularly want to work.

"You're the best man I know," Gus said simply. "Hell, I'll pay you. You don't have to guard our town for free."

"It's not the money, Gus. I just don't know . . ." His words petered out. He hated to disappoint an old friend. He also, however, hated to work when he wanted to be playing. Hell, he worked hard when he worked. He liked to play hard when he played. He didn't care to overlap the two.

On the other hand, Gus's guileless blue eyes looked so pleading, and Fargo liked Sheila and Gloria and Myrtle so well that he hated to think some rotten thief was running blithely through Barley Flats, plucking purses as he went, with no one to stop him. He heaved a gusty sigh. "All right, Gus. I'll take a look around tonight. I'm only one man, though. If I don't catch the crook, don't blame me too much."

Gus beamed at him. "Wouldn't think of it, Skye. Thanks a lot." He turned in his chair and gestured to someone Fargo couldn't see from where he sat.

When he did see, he blinked. He might have known Gus was beckoning to a woman. And one whose wares Fargo hadn't yet sampled.

"This here's Joella, Skye. Joella, this here's Skye Fargo."

Fargo removed his hat politely. "Good afternoon, Joella."

She blushed prettily. "Good afternoon, Mr. Fargo."

"My God, ain't the two of you formal, though?" Gus laughed heartily. "You show this man a good time, sweetheart, because he's gonna be helping us out."

Joella, a tiny brunette with huge brown eyes, looked up at Fargo with awe on her expressive face. "He's already helped out. He rescued Myrtle, didn't he? And he caught Sheila when she fell out of the window."

That's not quite the way Fargo remembered the episode, but he didn't say so. Good Lord, her eyes were all but worshiping him. What the hell. He didn't want to let the woman down. He rose and held out a hand. "Happy to know you, Joella. Care for a drink?"

"I'd rather do something else, Mr. Fargo." She blushed again, rosily, and lowered her eyes.

Gus went off into a gale of guffaws. "Hell, your reputation gets any bigger, and there's gonna have to be two of you to take care of all the females fallin' at your feet, Skye."

Fargo eyed Gus without favor. Then his attention

turned to Joella. She was quite a little honey, small but amazingly well proportioned. Her dark hair was glossy in the lantern light, and her skin had a lush olive hue. Her dress was short enough for him to get a good view of her shapely ankles, and he had no reason to doubt that the rest of her would be as appealing as the parts he could see.

Aw, hell, why not? Barley Flats wouldn't need his detective services until after the sun set. He could while away a couple of hours with Joella, have dinner with Gus, and be fit as a fiddle to take up his observations along about nine.

So, to the accompaniment of the tinny piano music coming from the corner of Gus's Place, and the faint rantings of "Repent, ye sinners!" floating over the tobacco smoke from outdoors, Skye Fargo and Joella made their way upstairs.

Although Gus hadn't said so yet, it took Fargo no time at all to conclude that Joella was the best gal Gus had.

═══ 12 ═══

"What if we don't want to repent?"

Fargo stopped and grinned at the drama unfolding before him when he stepped out of Gus's Place, intending to go to the Gold Nugget for a bite of dinner before he started his evening patrol of Barley Flats's one main street. Miss Wiley didn't like the question the miner had asked her. Her annoyance was written large on her face.

She shook her Bible at the man—a boy, really—who was grinning like an imp. "I know you think you're being funny, young man, but if you'll pause to consider for a moment, you'll understand that your eternal salvation is no laughing matter."

"But I thought I was facing eternal damnation, not salvation," the lad said, trying to sound innocent.

Miss Wiley huffed. "There you go, young man. You see? You're jesting. But the Lord's love is nothing to jest about. Would you rather burn in hell or live eternally with our blessed Father in a heaven so glorious you can't even imagine it?"

"Well . . . I don't know, lady. It seems to me that the road to hell is the fun one. According to you, I'd have to give up all my recreations if I wanted to go to heaven, and you can't give me any firm proof that it even exists. I mean, what if I gave up all my fun, and there wasn't no heaven at all? What then?"

Miss Wiley shook her head sadly. "Alas that you should think so, my boy. For it's the devil speaking through you. If you'll only pause and reflect about how transitory the pleasures of this life are, you'll see that I'm right. When you consider the possibility that you'll spend eternity burning in agony, I'm sure life's fleeting joys are but a drop in the mighty ocean."

The boy looked mighty skeptical. "I don't know, lady. Seems to me you're making a big deal out of something that ain't so bad."

Fargo had to agree with the boy on that one. After his round with Miss Joella, he wasn't about to give up earthly delights for somebody else's notion of what heaven was supposed to be. Anyway, he didn't expect Miss Genevieve Wiley knew what she was talking about. Oh, he had no doubt she was sincere in her vision of heaven, but Fargo seriously doubted that she knew a blessed thing about earthly delights.

Because he kind of liked her in spite of her many irritating qualities, and because he also felt a certain responsibility, both to her and to the miners in Barley Flats—after all, he'd brought her here—he walked up to her before she could tackle the youngster again. "How-do, Miss Wiley. I see you're still holding down this particular street corner."

She glared at him malevolently, which didn't seem right to him. After all, she was supposed to love everybody, wasn't she?

"I am spreading the word of our blessed Savior, Mr. Fargo."

Fargo glanced at the boy, who was still grinning. "Yeah, and having a whole lot of luck at it, too, I see."

She sniffed. "You aren't one bit funny, Mr. Fargo."

"I'm sure that's true. Say, Miss Wiley, how about I buy you a nice steak for supper?"

She gave a little start of surprise. Then her eyes narrowed, and she squinted at him suspiciously. "Why are you being nice to me all of a sudden?"

"There's nothing sudden about it. I've always been nice to you, ma'am. I rescued you from a bunch of drunks, saved you from ravishment, and brought you to Barley Flats."

She harrumphed indignantly.

"It seems to me that it's you who haven't been very nice to me," Fargo went on. "You keep insisting that I'm going to hell, which I don't take awfully kindly, considering all I've done for you."

The young miner who had been conversing with her earlier watched Miss Wiley and Fargo with avid interest. She noticed his observation, frowned, and turned her back on him. He only grinned harder. When she faced Fargo again, she tilted her head to an angle that he recognized as defensive. "I beg your pardon," she said stiffly. "I didn't mean to give the impression that I don't approve of you."

His own eyes opened wide. "Hell's bells, Miss Wiley, but you've been standing on this corner for a week now, telling every man in Barley Flats that he's damned to eternal perdition. If that doesn't indicate disapproval, I don't know what does."

"Oh, dear."

Fargo was amazed when he saw tears pool in her big hazel eyes. He was sorry he'd upset her, but honest to God, she didn't really think she'd been behaving kindly, did she? He held out a hand. It was meant to be a friendly gesture, but she shrank away from him. "Come on, Miss Wiley. Let's have a bite to eat together and make up our differences. I'll buy you dinner."

She squinted up at him. For a second, Fargo thought he saw a look of greed in her pretty face.

"You'll pay?" Her voice was a little sharper than it had been.

But then a tear slipped from her eye and slid down her cheek. Fargo felt awful.

"Thank you, Mr. Fargo. That's very kind of you."

It was very kind of him, actually, considering how little he was looking forward to a sermon over dinner, but he didn't say so. Instead, he gave a small bow and replied, "It will be my great pleasure, Miss Wiley."

She put her little hand in his, tucked her Bible into her pocket, and walked across the street with him. The waiter at the Gold Nugget looked alarmed when the big man and the little woman entered the chophouse. Fargo suspected the man had been treated to at least one of Miss Wiley's redemptive harangues in the past several days. Nevertheless, he led her to a table, and even pulled out a chair for her to sit on before he took his own seat.

"It doesn't sound as if you've been having a very successful stay in Barley Flats, Miss Wiley."

She looked at him across the table, her eyes cautious. "My experience here has been—varied," she said after a significant pause. "It's not been all bad."

"I'm glad to hear it."

In deference to his dining companion, and because he didn't really like to drink when he had work to do, Fargo asked for coffee instead of beer when the waiter came over to take their orders. He ordered a steak, and Miss Wiley did likewise. "Although I know I'll not be able to eat it all," she grumbled. "They serve such large portions."

"I'll finish it for you," Fargo offered generously.

"Thank you very much." Her tone was dry, and she frowned at him over her coffee cup.

The waiter brought their plates, and Fargo waited until Miss Wiley had bowed her head and prayed for several seconds over the chow. He was polite enough not to start any arguments during the first part of their meal. In fact, he offered her a compliment.

"You did a good job at that funeral the other day, Miss Wiley."

"Thank you, Mr. Fargo." She gave him a doleful smile. "I only hope the poor man we laid to rest is in the arms of the Lord right now."

"Yeah. Me, too." He chewed some steak and only gazed at Miss Wiley serenely when she shot him a suspicious glance.

After a few minutes of chewing and silence, she put down her knife and fork and began fingering her coffee cup. She looked nervous to Fargo, although he acknowledged that his viewpoint might be skewed. He wasn't used to people like Miss Wiley, and hoped he never would be.

"Who was that man you chased yesterday, Mr. Fargo?" she asked suddenly.

"The man I chased? Oh, yeah. The one who kidnapped Myrtle. I don't know his name. They say he's the one who killed Jack Billings."

Her back stiffened. "*He* killed Mr. Billings? How does anybody know that?"

Fargo lifted his shoulders. "Myrtle—the girl he kidnapped—saw some of Jack's things in his clothes."

"Oh." Miss Wiley looked terribly disapproving.

Fargo discovered he wasn't surprised. "And I suppose she had a good reason to recognize them."

"I expect she did," Fargo said with what he hoped was a wicked grin. He had the satisfaction of seeing her straight back stiffen even more.

Miss Wiley bit viciously into a piece of steak and chewed on it as if it were Fargo she were chewing on.

"Listen, Miss Wiley," he said, keeping it friendly, "not everybody's called to do the same sorts of jobs in this life. You got called in one direction. I reckon Myrtle got called in another."

With careful deliberation, Miss Wiley set her knife and fork down again. "Do you *dare*," she said slowly, "to compare me with that—that—strumpet?"

"Strumpet? Well, now, I don't know that she's a—"

"She is, too! Any woman who demeans herself by selling her body to lustful men is a strumpet, Mr. Fargo, whether you like it or not!"

"If you say so, Miss Wiley."

"It's the truth! Anyway, I'm sure you're mistaken about that poor man."

"How did Billings's stuff get into his pockets?"

"I'm sure I don't know. Perhaps he found the items somewhere."

Fargo snorted.

"And I'm also sure he only took that—that—*Myrtle*—for protection. Otherwise, I'm sure the ghastly men in Barley Flats would have hanged him from the nearest tree, whether he'd killed Mr. Billings or not." She jammed a bite of steak into her mouth and chewed ferociously.

Fargo eyed her with a good deal of interest. "You're mighty sure of yourself, ma'am. That fellow had

Jack's belongings on him. It seems awfully coinciden-tal that he'd have just found them somewhere."

"Perhaps. But theft and murder are two entirely dif-ferent things, Mr. Fargo. Theft is a crime, I'm sure, but it's nowhere near as horrid a sin as murder."

"I suppose so." He didn't understand her. Not one bit. Vague suspicions that had niggled at him before stormed to the front of his brain again. Looking at her, a fellow would never suspect that she was anything but a straitlaced Christian missionary. But so many things didn't seem to add up in Fargo's mind that he decided to ask some questions. "Say, Miss Wiley, why are you so dead-set on defending that man? After all, he tried to get at you in our camp."

"I sincerely doubt that." She sounded scornful.

"And he's at least a thief, if not a downright killer."

"I doubt that, too."

"Why? Hell, he invaded our camp in the middle of the night. He was caught red-handed with some of Jack Billings's things. What is he to you, anyway? Do you know him from somewhere?"

"Good heavens, no! What a ridiculous thing to ask."

He didn't pursue the matter, though, mostly be-cause if he pushed too hard he knew damned well she'd start in sermonizing at him, and he didn't want to hear it. He guided the conversation along more peaceable lines, and they parted almost amicably when the meal was over.

"Thank you very much, Mr. Fargo. It was nice of you to invite me to dine with you."

"You're welcome, Miss Wiley. Glad you enjoyed it."

She nodded and headed to the hotel where, Fargo

imagined, she aimed to freshen up before she went back to her street corner and began her evening shift.

"Wait up, Miss Wiley. I've got to visit my room in the hotel, too."

She turned and gave him a tight smile. "Oh? I thought you spent your evenings in the saloon, Mr. Fargo. Drinking and gambling and getting up to heaven alone knows what other deviltry."

He winked at her. "You mean bedding the nice ladies there?"

"Mr. Fargo!"

"You asked."

"I did not."

"That's right. You accused, you didn't ask."

If her lips pinched up any tighter, they'd look like a couple of raisins. She didn't say another word to him, but only stormed along at his side. Fargo imagined she wished him to the devil, but would never say so.

She offered him one last furious frown before she trotted up the stairs to her room. He followed at a more leisurely pace. In his room, he fetched his Henry, checked it, loaded it, and laid it on the bed. Then he did the same with his Colt revolver. If he did run into trouble tonight, he wanted to be prepared.

13

The evening was quite pleasant. Fargo could get used to the weather in California without much trouble. Maybe when he got too old to ramble, he'd move out here, build himself a little house, and settle down. The Ovaro would like that fine, and Fargo—

He realized what he was contemplating and laughed out loud. As if he'd ever be happy squatting in one place for longer than a few days!

Still, Barley Flats was set in some mighty pretty country. A soft breeze blew, and the fragrances of lilacs and honeysuckle wafted to him along with piano music from Gus's Place. The piano player, a man named Chauncy with a smile as big as the sky, played better than anyone else Fargo had ever heard. The tinkling music followed him down the boardwalk and back again, and accompanied him into alleyways and behind a couple of buildings, where he found nothing of any note.

In fact, there didn't seem to be much of illicit behavior going on in Barley Flats at all that night. Several men who'd had too much to drink wobbled from building to building, but they mostly looked like they were having a good time.

Along about midnight, a ruckus erupted. Fargo

heard it before he saw it, coming from Gus's Place along with Chauncy's pretty music. He didn't think much about it until he heard Gus's voice, raised in a shout, over the sound of a squabble.

"Cut it out, you two! If you've got a quarrel, take it outside."

"Dammit, he cheated!"

"I did not!"

"Where the hell'd the king of clubs come from?"

"From the dealer, damn you!"

A clatter of wooden furniture spurred Fargo toward Gus's Place. He didn't want folks to bust up Gus's tables and chairs. Gus hollered, "Stop that!"

The explosion of a revolver shot split the air, followed by a shrill scream from a woman and the sound of running feet. The deadly gunshot silenced the piano, Gus, and all other noises except the sound of people scrambling for cover. Fargo ran to the door and looked inside, being cautious since he didn't fancy getting shot at.

He saw that there were only two men standing, swaying, glaring daggers at each other. He didn't see Gus, who must have hit the floor behind the bar, along with everyone else in the room. He tried to find the woman who'd screamed, but couldn't.

The combatant to Fargo's left snarled, "Draw, damn you!"

The other man said, "I ain't gonna draw. You already got your gun out. It ain't fair."

"Cut it out, you two. You don't want to kill each other."

That was Gus. Fargo glanced toward the counter, and saw Gus's shiny bald pate barely sticking up from the business side of the bar.

"Dammit, Gus, he was cheating."

"I was not."

They were never going to get anywhere that way. Fargo considered what would be best for him to do. He sure as the devil didn't want those two shooting at each other in a crowded barroom.

He'd better think of something quickly, though, because the man with the gun had begun to wave it around. Both adversaries were drunk, so there'd be no reasoning with either of them.

He could think of only one way to arrange this. Silently, he entered the room, making sure the door didn't squeak on its hinges, and reached for a bottle standing on the table closest to the door. He'd played a little baseball from time to time, and found he could pitch as well as any man. Taking careful aim, he wound up, then let fly with the bottle, targeting the gunman's head. The man might be injured that way, but if the bottle hit any of his other body parts, the fool was liable to pull the trigger reflexively.

It took only seconds. The sound of the bottle hurtling through the air barely registered on the inhabitants of the room before it hit its subject with a sickening crunch. Fargo winced and drew his Colt, just in case. The man with the gun folded up like a concertina and hit the floor with a thud. The other man, his mouth hanging open, blinking stupidly, watched it happen, and didn't seem to believe his eyes. He muttered, "Charley? Charley, what the hell happened to you?"

Gus lifted himself up and heaved an enormous sigh of relief. "Thank God for your quick thinking, Skye."

Fargo nodded, but didn't let down his guard.

The man who'd been aligned against Charley

stopped staring at his fallen foe and looked up at Fargo. The change in his posture made him stagger a little bit, and he grabbed at the table to keep himself upright. "You done knocked Charley out," he said to Fargo.

"Looks like it." Fargo scanned the room. It didn't appear to him as if anyone else had malicious intentions, but he decided to wait a minute to be sure. Folks started pulling themselves to their feet.

Sheila popped up from behind an upended table near the stairs. She nodded and smiled at Fargo, then held a hand out to somebody else behind the table. "Come on up, Constance. It's all right now. Mr. Fargo took care of everything."

A small white hand came up and gripped Sheila's, and then a woman Fargo hadn't seen before emerged from behind the table. He blinked. Damned if she wasn't every bit as gorgeous as the other four in Gus's Place.

His attention was rudely recalled from the lovely lady by the voice of Charley's foe. "Why the hell did you go and do that to Charley?" He sounded peeved.

Fargo squinted at the man. "He was going to shoot you," Fargo pointed out reasonably.

"Charley? Hell, Charley'd never shoot me. I'm his best friend."

"That's enough, Homer," Gus said, coming out from behind the bar. "Why don't you take Charley to his place, and then go on home to bed."

Gus reached out to take Homer's arm, but Homer yanked it away. His precipitate gesture made him stagger and nearly fall down. Fargo decided to keep his Colt out for another little while.

"Homer!" Gus was getting annoyed. "Cut it out.

Just go on home now, and everything will be all right."

"The hell you say." Homer was glowering at Fargo, weaving on his feet, and looking as belligerent as only a drunken man can look. He had his right hand held out to his side, hovering over his holster. "Draw, you lousy polecat!"

Fargo lifted an eyebrow. "You talking to me?"

Homer didn't like that. He bellowed, "Hell, yes, I'm talkin' to you! Draw, dammit!"

"I've already drawn, Homer." Fargo pointed out what should have been evident even to Homer, trying to sound less irked than he felt. Drunks were such a pain in the ass sometimes.

Homer drew his head back and squinted hard at Fargo. "Oh. Yeah, I see. Well, then shoot, dammit!"

"This is ridiculous." Fargo shook his head, hoping he wouldn't have to pull the trigger for such a senseless reason.

"It sure is." Gus was apparently fed up with the commotion in his place, because he reached out and shoved Homer hard. Homer, already unsteady on his pins, fell over backward, banging his head against a table as he went. Gus knelt immediately and grabbed Homer's gun before Homer could do anything with it. As it happened, Homer had knocked himself out.

"Jesus. These two are a pair, all right."

Fargo holstered his Colt and went over to assess the damages. "You're right about that." He squatted beside Charley and pressed his head, which felt kind of pulpy where the bottle had connected. "He's going to have a hell of a headache come morning."

"He'd have had one anyway, what with all the drinkin' he's done tonight. Homer's going to be pretty sick, too." Gus lifted his head and scanned the room. "Hey, Bill, can you and Curtis help take these two idiots back to their cabin?"

A couple of men who'd flattened themselves out on the floor when the gunfire started, got up and walked over. "Sure, Gus. Do you think they need to see the doc?"

"Doc's drunk by this time of night," Gus said. "Just take 'em home. If they want to get their skulls bandaged in the morning, let 'em."

Neither Bill nor Curtis found fault with Gus's reasoning, so they started with Homer, Bill taking the man's feet and Curtis his arms. Fargo watched them cart the unconscious man outside, and wondered why men did crazy things to themselves. Hell, life was hard enough sober. Drunk, it didn't bear thinking of.

"Have you spotted anything interesting, Skye?"

Fargo followed Gus to the bar, where he accepted a drink of bourbon. "Not a thing. It's quiet out there tonight."

"Yeah, I expect the only excitement is happening at my place." Gus didn't sound happy about it.

Fargo grinned and tipped his glass at his friend. "You got that right. Are those two really friends?"

"They say they are," Gus said sarcastically.

Both Fargo and Gus watched as Bill and Curtis, having deposited Homer, returned to fetch Charley. Charley was the bigger of the two, and his carriers staggered a bit under his weight. Gus called out, "Come back here and I'll stand you both to a drink on the house for helpin' out."

Curtis smiled happily. "Thanks, Gus. Will do."

Fargo tossed down the rest of his bourbon. "Well, I

suppose I'd better go on out and patrol some more. For whatever good it'll do."

Gus shrugged. "Can't hurt, I reckon."

"I suppose not."

The night seemed especially black after being in the bright lights of the saloon. Fargo blinked into the pitchy darkness. Then he thought he perceived a shadowy figure creeping along on the other side of the street. He casually crossed the road, not wanting to make a fuss if whoever that was wasn't bent on mischief.

Whoever it was seemed to be trying to disappear into the shadows. Before Fargo reached the boardwalk, the figure stiffened and sidled into a doorway. If his eyesight wasn't as sharp as an eagle's, he'd not have noticed.

"I won't hurt you," he said, keeping his tone light. "Just out checking on the welfare of the community." He grinned inside at the highfalutin' sound of that.

He heard an all-too-familiar sniff. "Is that you, Mr. Fargo?"

"Miss Wiley?" Hell, he might have known. "What the devil are you doing out here at this time of night? It's way past midnight."

She stepped away from the doorway. She was fully clothed, he noticed, in a black dress and with a black shawl drawn over her head and pulled around her shoulders. She frowned up at him. No surprise there; he was accustomed to her frowns by this time. "I heard a commotion, and came outside to see what it was."

He tilted his head and peered down at her. He didn't believe her. "What kind of commotion?"

Her lips pinched together momentarily, but she apparently decided against scolding him for questioning her. "I heard gunfire. I—thought I might be of some service if anyone was hurt."

Although he could think of no good reason for his doubt, he still didn't believe her. Yet why else would she be outside after midnight in a hellhole like Barley Flats? Nobody in town was sober enough to listen to a sermon at this time of night, and she surely knew that. "It's not smart to follow gunfire, ma'am. It's best to hit the floor. Or stay in bed, if that's where you were."

She lifted her chin defiantly. "Thank you, Mr. Fargo. I shall bear your advice in mind."

"You do that. Now, I reckon I'd better see you back to the hotel. It's also not a good idea for a lady to be waltzing around town alone at night."

"I was not *waltzing* around town!"

It tickled him that she sounded so indignant. "Whatever you were doing, I'm going to take you to the hotel now, ma'am."

She sniffed again. "Very well."

So with a stiff-backed, stiff-necked Genevieve Wiley mincing along beside him, Skye Fargo walked to the hotel across the street. They'd been walking for several paces when he realized she was jingling. He squinted down at her, wondering where the sounds were coming from.

"Do you hear that?" he asked.

"Hear what?" she asked back.

"Sounds like coins jingling in a pocket or something."

"You're hearing things, Mr. Fargo." Her voice was as tart as vinegar.

He didn't say anything, but continued walking. The

jingles continued jingling. Dammit, the noise was coming from her. He stopped abruptly and grabbed her arm, which made her jerk around. The accompanying sound elevated itself from a jingle to a clank.

"All right, Miss Wiley, what's that noise? And don't tell me you don't hear it, because you're making it."

"Don't be absurd, Mr. Fargo!"

"I'm not being absurd, dammit—"

"Don't swear at me!"

"What do you have hidden on you, Miss Wiley? You'd better tell me, because I aim to find out."

"You're making a mountain out of a molehill, Mr. Fargo. I—have a derringer in my pocket, and I expect some coins have bumped against it."

He didn't like it. "You carry a gun?"

"You're the one who says this place is dangerous. I decided perhaps you were correct about that, and armed myself."

"Bullets and Bibles, eh?" He couldn't make out her expression in the dark, but was pretty sure she was about as mad at him as she'd ever been.

"All right, I'll drop it. For now."

"Thank you ever so much."

Her sarcasm tickled him. However, after he'd left her at her hotel—even walked her upstairs and made sure she'd locked herself in—the funny feeling he had about Miss Genevieve Wiley refused to abate.

14

Word came early the next morning that both Charley and Homer had been robbed overnight. Speculation ran wild as to whether they were still at Gus's or had been carried home before the beastly deed had been done. Fargo had his suspicions, especially when he learned that a bagful of coins Charley had been hoarding had been carted off.

He approached Miss Genevieve Wiley when she was in full voice, harassing the miners of Barley Flats to repent their sins and take up with the Lord. She glanced up, gave him a good hot frown, and raised her voice. "The Lord's way is the only way! Beware the earthly fleshpots and the wickedness of lustful thoughts and actions, for they lead to eternal hellfire and damnation!"

She looked directly at Fargo when she shouted that part, which made him think that perhaps she'd heard something about his activities with some of Gus's girls. He didn't let it stop him, mainly because he wanted to get to Miss Wiley before anyone else figured out her game.

"Listen, Miss Wiley, I think it's time we had us a chat."

"I'm busy, Mr. Fargo," she snapped. "This is my work. My calling. My—"

"Bullshit."

Her mouth open to spew more words at him, that one short, sharp word closed it for her. Her shock gave way to indignation almost at once, and she said, "How dare you!"

He leaned close and hissed into her ear. "I'll tell you how I dare, Miss Wiley. It's because I know damned well it's you that's been the Barley Flats thief."

Her face drained of color, and she seemed to wobble a little on her pins. "Wh—what? What did you say?"

"You heard me."

"You can't mean it."

"Want to try me?" Fargo sucked in a deep breath. "Listen, I don't want to holler it to the whole town, because I'm afraid they might do something to you. They don't cotton to folks who steal other people's things around here."

"You're being absurd!"

"You won't think it's so absurd if anyone besides me figures out you and that bastard friend of yours are involved in a theft ring. After having you holler at them for a week or more, I don't think they'll be very nice to you if they discover that bag of coins that you stole last night in your hotel room. Justice is carried out swiftly here in California, and not very kindly. I don't want to see you dangling from a rope." He added, somewhat acidly, "Although I'm not sure exactly why not."

She swallowed hard. He had to hand it to her. It didn't take her long to get over the shock of unexpected discovery. She drew herself up to her full missionary fighting stance. "You're being ridiculous, Mr. Fargo! I'm a woman of God's word. I'm a missionary, spreading the gospel of the good Lord's mercy to the benighted men of the gold camps. I'm a—"

"God dammit, you're a thief. And you're in cahoots with the man who shot Jack—"

"I keep telling you that he didn't shoot that man! He *didn't*!"

Fargo nodded. "Yeah, I expect you know a lot more about that incident than you've told so far. So, do you want to come along with me quietly so we can talk about this, or do you want me to take you to the saloon and see how much the men you've robbed like knowing you've hoodwinked them all?"

She huffed. Then she turned around. Then she stamped her foot. But at last she capitulated. Fargo expected it nearly killed her to do so, but he also expected she had no choice, because he'd discovered her dirty little secret. All sorts of things made sense to him now—why she'd been so set on defending the man whom Fargo had assumed was going to assault her. Her defense of him when it looked as if he'd killed Jack Billings. Her sneaking around Barley Flats after any respectable woman should have been in bed and asleep.

"What do you want me to do?" she asked sourly. "Are you going to turn me over to the authorities?"

Fargo thought about it. There weren't many authorities in Barley Flats. He hadn't been joking about the men in town hanging her. She'd made a real pain of herself. "First, take me to your hotel room. I suppose if we give the men back their losses they'll be easier on you."

The color returned to her cheeks in a flash. "We'd better go somewhere else."

"I figured you'd rather do that than talk about this in front of the whole town."

"You're being a beast, Mr. Fargo." She grabbed his arm and began yanking him toward the hotel. "I've never been so offended in my life, but I realize I should have expected something of this nature from you."

"Give it up, Miss Wiley," Fargo suggested dryly. "It won't work. I know you're the thief."

"Will you stop saying that!"

"No."

"Blast it, Skye Fargo, at least shut up about it in public, will you?"

Aha. This was better. Fargo grinned and followed her to the hotel.

She didn't utter another word until they got to the lobby. The clerk was napping behind the counter, and Miss Wiley dragged Fargo into a corner as far away from the registration desk as she could. There she turned around, planted her fists on her hips, and glared at him. "All right, Mr. Fargo, what are you talking about."

"It won't work, Miss Wiley. If you don't take me up to your room and show me the loot, I'm going to turn you over to Gus. He's about the only law Barley Flats has."

He thought he had her with that one, but he'd underestimated her. "You beast! I knew you were depraved, but to threaten me if I don't take you to my hotel room is beyond enough!"

Shaking his head, he muttered, "Good God. Come on, Miss Wiley, the game's up. I'll break into your

122

room if you don't take me there and show me the booty yourself."

He could almost see the gears turning in her head as she tried to think of some way out of this present crisis. After fully long enough for her to come up with and reject a dozen different plans, at least one of which probably included shooting him dead, she sagged. "Oh, very well. Come with me."

"Good idea." She started to walk away, but he grabbed her. "Hold on there. Not that I don't trust you or anything, but I'm going to keep a hand on you."

She growled something he didn't catch, which was probably just as well, but she didn't try to shake him off. That showed some sense, and Fargo honored her for it, although he still didn't trust her and was not about to let go of her.

"I'd like to know what you expect to find in my room," she muttered.

"I expect to find stolen loot, Miss Holier-Than-Thou Wiley."

She gave him one of her patented sniffs. "You're making a terrible mistake, Mr. Fargo. I had nothing to do with those thefts."

"Right, and it was your spurs jingling last night when you were creeping around town after midnight."

"Hogwash!"

But his last sarcasm shut her up. She stalked past the desk clerk without so much as a nod or a prayer, although Fargo smiled at the man. He didn't say anything about his current mission, since he truly didn't want to see Miss Wiley torn to bloody strips in front of his eyes by a herd of irate miners. And he knew damned well that if they discovered the missionary who'd been making their lives miserable was the author of their theft miseries, too, she wouldn't have a chance.

Later, Skye Fargo knew he should have taken a clue from the increased volume of Miss Wiley's voice as she fumbled in her pocket for the key. At the time, he was still too busy trying to figure out how to save her life to worry about her voice. Ever since he'd first met her, she'd been screeching at him. He didn't think anything of it when she said, "I tell you, Mr. Fargo, that you're making a big mistake. There's nothing in this room that doesn't belong to me."

"No need to shout, ma'am," Fargo told her.

"Very well," she said, her aspect grim. "On your head be it."

She shoved the door open. The Trailsman, who'd had experience with criminals several times in the past, gestured for her to precede him into the room. She did, and he followed, stopping in the door frame to look around.

The room was as prim and neat as she was. He noted that the bed was made, a few toilet articles were set out in a tidy row on the bureau across the room, and there didn't seem to be a speck of dust anywhere. She crossed to the window and turned around, folded her arms across those succulent breasts of hers, and frowned. "All right, search away." She made a gesture with her right hand, and Fargo stepped over the threshold.

He barely registered a sound from behind him, but had begun to whirl around and draw his Colt when the blow fell. Pain exploded in his head, and the world went black.

15

Fargo didn't know how long he had been stretched out on Miss Genevieve Wiley's hotel room floor, but he had a hell of a headache when he finally came around. Sitting up with care, he tenderly felt his skull. There was a lump the size of a hen's egg on the back of it, and when he examined his fingers, he saw blood.

Whoever had beaned him, and Fargo suspected it was Miss Wiley's burly friend from the forest, he'd been hiding behind the door. She'd warned him that there was trouble coming by jangling and fussing with the keys and announcing their presence, and Fargo felt like an idiot when he thought about it now.

He lifted his head and surveyed the room. The sun was barely lower in the sky than it had been when he and Miss Wiley argued in the street. He noticed that particularly, since its rays hit his eyes like knives. Shutting his eyes and groaning, he decided he could allow himself another few minutes to recover.

He'd managed to make it to the bed with his eyes closed, and was leaning against it and encouraging himself to take the next step and stand up, when his brain registered what the sounds he'd been hearing from outside signified.

"Dammit, hang 'em both!" came an angry masculine voice from underneath the window.

"Wait a minute, Charley. We ought have us a trial first." That voice of reason came from Gus.

"He shot Jack, Gus!"

"I did not!"

"Shut up, you! And she's been screeching at us all week to repent, when she's nothing but a low-down, snake-eyed thief herself."

"Don't you dare call me names!"

Trust Miss Genevieve Wiley, thought Fargo, to object to being called a name when she was in danger of being hanged. He pressed his palms to the floor and managed to get himself upright. His head felt like somebody'd stuffed a hive of bees into it.

As he stood there assessing the state of his health, he realized that Miss Wiley and her friend hadn't disarmed him. He appreciated them for their thoughtfulness. His head was almost clear, although it still hurt like a son of a bitch, by the time he'd checked his Colt and discovered they'd also left it loaded. They probably expected him to sleep for hours. By the time he came to, they'd hoped to be clear of Barley Flats. Fargo wondered what had happened and how the men out there, who obviously had the two thieves in custody, had captured them.

There was only one way to find out. He gingerly settled his hat onto his sore head, left the room, went down the stairs, and crossed the hotel lobby. The clerk was nowhere to be seen, and Fargo suspected he was outside watching the fun.

The sunshine blinded him for a minute and pain

stabbed through his head like arrows, but Fargo tried resolutely to ignore it. There was a huge crowd gathered in front of Wells Fargo Bank up the street across from Gus's Place, and Fargo headed there. The argument was continuing.

"I say we oughta just hang 'em, Gus. Hell, they've been playing us all for fools."

"Dammit, Sammy, you can't just hang folks because you don't like them. You have to hold a trial."

"To hell with a trial. You just like playing judge!"

"Now that's not true, and you know it." Gus spotted Fargo, and an expression of vast relief crossed his face. "Skye! Thank God you're here. I wondered where you'd got yourself off to. I thought you was with Constance."

Fargo only wished. "No. I was with Miss Wiley. I see you found out she's the thief."

"No!" Genevieve Wiley cried.

Fargo looked at her and shook his head. Damned if she wasn't still trying to play the role of good Christian lady. "Give it up, Miss Wiley. You make a hell of a good missionary, but you'd be a rotten martyr. Your best bet is to make a clean confession of everything, and maybe these nice folks will go easy on you."

"The hell we will!" cried an angry miner. "That damned friend of hers killed Jack!"

Fargo shot a glance at Gus and raised his arm. "Hold on, folks. I think we should at least try to get to the bottom of this."

"Yes, indeed. Thank you, Mr. Fargo!" Miss Wiley smiled at him for probably the first time in their acquaintance.

He didn't smile back. "Don't thank me yet, ma'am. I'm not sure yet if it won't be best to hang you."

Her smile vanished at once.

"Skye's right. We've got to investigate this thing," Gus chimed in.

Several grumbles arose from the crowd, but nobody offered violent opposition. They weren't gentle as they accompanied the two crooks into the saloon. Fargo walked with Gus. "How'd you find out about them? I just figured it out this morning."

Gus grinned around the pipe in his mouth. "They were too cocksure of themselves. If they'd had any sense, they'd have let the lady sneak the loot out at night, and she could have met up with her friend somewheres else. Nobody would have suspected a thing, I don't suppose. But they tried to get out together—with a sack full of stuff—plumb in the middle of the day."

Fargo nodded, which reminded him of the knot on his head. "I expect they didn't dare wait that long, because they brained me and left me in her hotel room."

"Her hotel room?" Gus lifted his eyebrows and waggled them at Fargo. "And just what was you doin' in the lady's hotel room?"

Fargo managed a wry grin. "After the trouble in your place last night, I found her sneaking around town, dressed all in black and jingling like Christmas bells. When I heard that a sack of coins had been stolen, I put two and two together, piled up some other oddities about Miss Wiley, and came up with her and that man as the Barley Flats thieves."

"Good thinking."

"Thanks. Wish I'd thought some more before I walked into her room and got conked."

Gus's chuckle made Fargo grin.

There was nothing funny about the proceedings, however. The canvas sack that had been discovered with the two miscreants was emptied onto a table in Gus's Place, along with some other items from various miners who'd been victimized. The two crooks stood by stolidly, although Fargo detected a look of intense fury on Miss Wiley's face. He suspected she was mad about having to give up her ill-gotten gains.

After various citizens of Barley Flats had laid claim to their stolen goods, the trial began. Miss Wiley's friend, whose name turned out to be Cleveland Pierce, swore fifty ways from Sunday that he hadn't killed Jack Billings. Nobody believed him.

"I swear to God, he was dead when I snuck into his cabin," Pierce said several times.

"He's telling the truth!" Miss Wiley corroborated at least as many times.

There weren't any lawyers available in Barley Flats, so Skye Fargo, the least interested party in town except for the lump on his skull, interrogated them. Gus, with his gun gavel at the ready, kept order in the court.

"You keep saying he didn't kill Jack Billings, Miss Wiley," Fargo said judiciously, "but can you give the court any proof?"

"Well, of course I can't," she said sourly. Then her gaze thinned, and something seemed to occur to her. "Wait a minute. Maybe I can." She dug into her pocket, hauled something out, and held it in her hand with her fingers folded over it.

She took a deep breath and said, "All right, I admit Cleve and I entered Mr. Billings's room that night."

Grumbles and a couple of curses rose from the assembled miners. Gus rapped his gun butt on the table, and growled, "Go on, Miss Wiley."

She pinched her lips together and continued. "But he was already dead when we entered the room. What's more, we found this, sticking out of his back." She reached into her pocket and brought forth a very distinctive knife. Wrinkling her nose, she added, "Cleve pulled it out of the man's wound."

Gus squinted at the knife. Fargo walked over and took it. He held it up. "Anybody seen this before?"

Silence flooded the room. Fargo looked around with interest. Evidently, either they'd all seen it before or no one had. He turned when Gus cleared his throat. "Gus?"

Gus sighed heavily. He looked unhappy. "Yeah. I recognize that. It's unique."

That it was. It was a long knife, with a nine-inch honed steel blade. That in itself wasn't unusual, but the knife's hilt was. It was made of scrimshaw, the ivory handle carved into intricate patterns depicting life on the ocean.

The silence lasted for a full minute. It was finally disrupted by the scrape of a chair against the floor. A second later, all hell broke loose.

"He's got a gun! Duck!"

"I don't want to shoot nobody! Get the hell out of my way! I didn't mean to kill the bastard! It was an accident!"

"It's Kanaka!"

"Kanaka killed Billings!"

A shot rang out, and smoke curled from Kanaka's gun a second before he turned and ran to the door, where he turned and fired again, wildly. Fargo grabbed Genevieve Wiley and hit the floor, his body protecting hers.

"He's getting away!"

"Go after him, fellows! He killed Jack!"

From his soft cushion on top of Genevieve, Fargo saw the batwing doors swing wildly as Kanaka made his escape. The saloon was in an uproar, and nobody seemed to know what to do next.

"Skye! Skye!"

It was Gus, and Fargo knew what that meant. Muttering, "Aw, hell," he scrambled up from the floor, bringing Miss Wiley with him by a hand around her wrist. "Here, Gus, watch her. Don't let her get away, and don't let the men have at her." He shoved her at Gus, who caught her easily.

"Will do, Skye."

"And watch her partner, too!"

Cleveland Pierce, however, was already under control, having been subdued by several miners as he broke from his chair and tried to make it to the door. He was presently at the bottom of a pile of men, and didn't look like he was going anywhere.

"He's taken care of," Gus called after Fargo, who was already out the door.

"Hold it!" Fargo shouted after Kanaka.

Kanaka whirled around and fired at Fargo. He was in a panic and his shot went wide. Fargo got the feeling he was too scared to focus on accurate trajectory. He wished he had his Henry with him, but he didn't.

131

As Kanaka fumbled with the reins of a horse tethered at a hitching rail, Fargo pulled out his Colt, took careful aim, and fired. Kanaka screamed and clutched his arm as the horse took off at a gallop, leaving him to fall to his knees in the road. The gun he'd held dropped from his useless fingers. He fumbled for it with bloody fingers, but Fargo fired another shot in the dirt next to him, and his hand whipped away again.

"Don't try it, Kanaka," Fargo told him as he approached. "I don't want to kill you."

The man's head was bowed, and tears streamed down his face. Fargo judged he was in a nervous state and probably wouldn't be much of a threat, but he'd learned long ago not to take anything for granted. Therefore, he approached with great care, kicking Kanaka's gun away as soon as he was close enough.

"You got any more weapons on you?"

Kanaka's head shook back and forth. He looked pitiful, kneeling in the dirt, clutching his bleeding arm and crying. "I didn't mean to kill him. I didn't mean to kill him."

He blubbered the same thing over and over again as Fargo lifted him to his feet and guided him down the road toward Gus's Place. Fargo didn't hold with killing men for no reason, and he didn't have any idea why Kanaka had killed Jack Billings, but he felt kind of sorry for the guy. He certainly did not seem like a hardened murderer.

A swarm of men had run out of the saloon, and now milled around in front of it, watching Fargo and Kanaka's progress up the road. Fargo couldn't make out any words in the general buzz. He hoped to God

Gus had set someone to watch Genevieve Wiley, because she was tricky as the devil, and Fargo didn't trust her to remain in the saloon without a guard watching her.

A buzz erupted as Fargo walked up with his prisoner.

"Why'd you do it, Kanaka?"

"Shoot, what'd Billings ever do to you?"

"That waren't nice, Kanaka, killin' Jack."

"I didn't mean it, fellers," Kanaka said, his head hanging. "We was playin' around with the gun and it went off. I got scared and run off. I didn't know I'd left my knife there. When them two—that missionary and that other feller—was charged with the robberies, I figgered it wouldn't go no harder on them to be charged with the killing, too." He shook his head. "It wasn't nice of me, I know."

Now that, to Fargo's way of thinking, was an understatement. He didn't say anything; he had infinite faith in the justice system prevailing in Barley Flats.

"Makes sense," one of Kanaka's interlocutors murmured.

There were several other noises of agreement from the crowd.

Fargo had begun leading Kanaka through the throng when he heard a shout from inside. His heart sank when he made out the words.

"Dammit, where'd she go?"

"Aw, hell." Thrusting Kanaka at a man whom he hoped wouldn't kill him, Fargo hotfooted it inside Gus's Place. Gus was sitting on the floor, looking stunned and rubbing a knot on his head. Cleveland Pierce was swearing a blue streak around the bandanna stuffed into his mouth and twisting at his rope-bound wrists.

It was just as Fargo had feared.

Genevieve Wiley was gone.

16

"Lordy, Skye, I'm real sorry about this." Gus said with a hangdog expression. A big white bandage was now wrapped around his head.

"Not your fault, Gus." If anything, Fargo was the sorry one. After all, it had been his misguided chivalry that had thrust Miss Genevieve Wiley into the midst of the unsuspecting citizens of Barley Flats. "I'll find her. Don't worry about that." He wasn't sure what he aimed to do with her after he found her, but his mood regarding her was no longer chivalrous. Not at all.

"She slammed me on the back of the head with my own gun, and then took that fellow's bandanna and jammed it in his mouth."

Curious, Fargo pulled the bandanna out of Cleveland Pierce's mouth.

"Goddam son of a bitch! Go get her, dammit! She's getting away!"

Fargo stuffed the gag back into Pierce's mouth and turned to Gus again. "I'll go after her, Gus. Want me to bring her back?"

"Lord, no. Just make sure she stays away from Barley Flats. She shows her face around here again, and the men'll probably shoot her."

"Has everyone got his stolen goods back?"

"I think so." Gus looked very unhappy. He glowered at Cleveland Pierce, who was still trying to spit out his gag. "We still got this bandit. Guess he'll do."

The bandanna popped out of Pierce's mouth, and the words tumbled out again. "Dammit, she's the one who thought of the scheme. It was her idea to be a missionary! She used me, dammit!"

"That doesn't surprise me a whole lot," Fargo said dryly. "She's good at that. Did she steal a horse to get out of town on?"

"I don't know."

With Fargo lending a supporting arm to Gus, who wobbled woozily, the two men went outside to assess the state of livestock in back of the saloon. None were gone. They walked to the livery stable. The liveryman had gone to join the crowd at Gus's, and Fargo noted with relief that the only animal missing was Miss Wiley's trusty mule.

"That's a relief, anyway," Gus growled.

"Yes, it is." Fargo contemplated the state of affairs for a minute. "I think I'll go after her, Gus. If she still has any stolen property, I'll see if I can get it back."

"Better get at it soon, otherwise some of the hotheads in town are liable to take off and try to find her, and I expect they wouldn't be real nice to her, even if she is a female."

Fargo, who had a great deal of respect for Genevieve Wiley's resources, female or not, shook his head. "Shoot, don't let them do that. She's liable to swindle them out of their drawers and boots. Where's the first place a person can get on a train from here?"

Gus thought a minute. "Most of the gold camps have tracks into them nowadays to haul the ore out."

"I don't think she'd necessarily know about that. What about passenger rails?"

"Marysville, I reckon."

"Right. That's the way she came from, and she didn't seem too sure of her bearings. I imagine she'll head back that way."

"Good luck, Skye." Gus's voice sounded gloomy.

Fargo understood his pessimism. Miss Genevieve Wiley had managed to trick them all—even Skye Fargo, and that was a difficult task, indeed.

Assured by Gus that things were stable in Barley Flats, Fargo saddled the Ovaro and took off. He discovered he was right about Miss Wiley's plans when he found her mule's tracks after the clutter of wagon and horse tracks thinned out a mile or so away from Barley Flats.

She was an ace confidence trickster, but she wasn't much at covering a mule trail, Fargo noted with some amusement. As irritating and unscrupulous as she was, he couldn't help but like her, at least a little bit. And he was planning to see for himself what other skills she possessed. He had a gut-deep feeling that she wasn't anywhere near as sweet and pure as she wanted folks to believe.

He spotted her when he was not more than an hour away from Barley Flats. She was making pretty good time, all things considered. He didn't ride down on her, because he didn't trust her. Rather, he skirted the path she was taking, making sure he didn't lose her trail. He wanted to encounter her in the woods, if he could, just in case she decided to start shooting. He didn't think she was much of a shot, but better to have cover than not.

She looked over her shoulder a lot, probably worried that someone from Barley Flats would come after her. Which was a reasonable fear on her part. Even though she knew as well as everyone that the law in California was loose, and even though most of her ill-gotten gains had been redistributed among those from whom she'd stolen them, and even though she'd left her partner in crime behind to swing for both of them, she also understood the human being's thirst for vengeance. Smart cookie, Miss Wiley.

Fargo wondered if that was her real name. Not that it mattered.

After a couple of more hours, she stopped looking back over her shoulder so often, since they'd begun to climb into the hills. When the cover thickened, Fargo narrowed the gap between them.

When twilight began to claim the hills, he got closer still. He could hear the clopping of her mule now and, although his own horses hooves were muffled in thick fir and pine needles, he expected she'd catch on to his presence soon. Therefore, he decided to make his move.

As silently as he could, he guided the Ovaro through the tall trees until they were well in front of Miss Wiley. He then turned the horse around, and headed straight at her with his Colt drawn. He didn't want to give her any advantage at all, since she tended to grab any advantage she could and twist it to her bidding.

He must have looked like a ghost coming out of the trees when she first spotted him. He heard her gasp from yards away, and she yanked on the mule's reins.

"The game's up, Miss Wiley," he said, keeping his voice friendly.

"Skye Fargo." Her own voice was about as far from friendly as a voice could get.

"If you have any weapons, better drop them now, sweetie. I'm not giving you a chance in hell."

Silence greeted his declaration. It stretched out for several seconds during which, Fargo was sure, Genevieve Wiley was sorting through and discarding her options with the speed of one of those Chinese abacuses they used in San Francisco. Her back was straight in defiance, and he thought she might be holding her breath.

"It's no good, Miss Wiley. Your career is over."

At last she slumped, and Fargo heard a soft, "Damn."

He could hear her teeth grinding from his saddle. He reached over and twitched the reins out of her hands. "Now, about any weapons you might be holding."

"I don't have any weapons."

"I don't believe you."

She huffed, then gave it up. "Very well. Search me if you must."

That's what he'd been hoping to do, although he'd hoped to gain her cooperation first. "All right."

Because he trusted her about as much as he'd trust a coiled rattler, he lifted her out of the saddle and plunked her on the ground in front of him. She wriggled at first, but that was from surprise. When she realized he wasn't going to hurt her, she stopped resisting.

"I'm going to tie up your hands, Miss Wiley, just in case."

"Just in case of what?"

"Just in case you get any fancy ideas. I still have a

knot on my head where you brained me earlier today."

"I didn't do that. Cleve did it."

"Right. Now why do you suppose I don't believe a single solitary thing you say?"

She sniffed. "I have no idea."

The sniff was so typical of the Genevieve Wiley Fargo knew and loathed, that he laughed. "I'll hobble you, too, in case you're of a mind to kick me."

"This is ridiculous. I'm not a dangerous person."

He stared at her for a full minute, until she began to squirm. "You're about the most dangerous person I've met in a long, long time, sweetheart."

"Don't call me sweetheart again!"

He laughed, and bound her wrists together. He tied her hands to a tree before he bound her feet, because he didn't trust her not to try to knock him over with her bound hands. He found the knife in a scabbard strapped to her calf first.

Holding it out so she could see it, he asked, "You don't call this a weapon?"

"It's not a gun," she muttered.

"True enough." He found the derringer in her skirt pocket. "What about this?"

"It's very small."

"It can also be very deadly."

He stood up and took a step away from her, looked into her eyes, and grinned. "Now comes the fun part. You're going to have to strip because I'm sure you've got more firepower tucked away somewhere. You want to do it, or do you want me to?"

She tilted her head and contemplated him. The late afternoon sun was filtering through the tree branches, making the red in her hair shine.

"Before I decide that, what do you intend to do with me?"

"Take you back to Barley Flats."

"They'll hang me there."

He shrugged again. "You stole from damned near every man in the town."

"But I didn't hurt anyone."

"They'll probably take that into consideration."

She licked her lips. "Mr. Fargo—"

"Call me Skye."

He caught the flicker of triumph in her eyes, and grinned to himself. "Skye." Her voice went low and sultry. "You may call me Genevieve."

"Thanks. Is it your name?"

Triumph gave way to irritation for a split second. "Of course it's my name!"

"Just wondering, is all."

"Skye, if I were to make a suggestion that appealed to you, do you think you might reconsider taking me back to Barley Flats? After all, I know it was wrong to steal from the miners, but they *did* get their goods back."

He crossed his arms over his chest and watched her like a hawk. "Just what kind of suggestion that you might make do you think might appeal to me?"

She lowered her eyes and looked up at him through her long lashes. She was as good at the teasing look as any sporting gal Fargo had ever met. "I know you like the ladies."

"I do indeed."

"And I know a lot of ways to please a man."

"I'll just bet you do."

"If I were to be very nice to you and show you a good time tonight, do you think you might consider letting me go? It's not as if hanging me will do anybody any good."

"Oh, I don't know. It might spare the rest of the gold camps some grief in the future."

Her lips tightened. "What if I promise to leave California?"

"I don't know, Miss Wiley. There's something about my association with you that leads me to view your promises a little skeptically."

She dropped the act. "Listen, Skye. I'm a confidence trickster. My daddy's been selling snake oil to idiots for decades, and I learned from him. I only came to California to see what kind of business I could drum up. I came from the Indian Territory, and I'll go back there if you'll let me. I swear to God, I will. Hell, you can even take me to the train and throw me on it. Just don't make be go back to Barley Flats. If the miners don't hang me, Cleve will shoot me, and I'm too damned young to die."

Fargo chuckled. "Your language hasn't improved during your stay in Barley Flats, ma'am."

"Hang my language, dammit! Will you let me live, or not?"

Fargo pinched his lower lip with his fingers, pretending to think about it. "Well, now, that's an appealing offer, Miss Wiley. I've wondered for some time what you look like under those high collars of yours."

She gave him another teasing look. "I know you have. I gave you an especially fetching look at my legs our first night together, to whet your appetite."

"Damn." Fargo laughed again. "You did that on purpose?"

"I am not a fool, Skye Fargo."

"No, you're sure not."

"So what do you think about my offer?"

"I think it's a very interesting one. And I might just take you up on it. But I'll be damned if I'm going to let you take your own clothes off. I just don't trust you."

She fluttered her eyelashes. "Not even if I let you hold a gun on me the whole time? I think taking my clothes off in front of you will be—ah—titillating."

"Titillating, huh?" His groin tightened. What the hell. "All right, Miss Wiley."

"You can call me Jenny."

"All right, Jenny. I'm going to pat you down first, and then I'll untie you."

She had no concealed weapons that Fargo could find. Since he'd come to know her well, he didn't allow his appreciation of her feminine charms to lull him into any sense of security. Rather, he watched keenly as she sashayed over to a fallen log, propped one shapely foot on it, lifted her skirt, untied her garter, and rolled her sensible cotton stocking down her leg.

There was something about watching that prim black stocking rolling over all that white, silky flesh that did funny things to Fargo's heart. Jenny knew it, too. She winked at him.

"Like that, do you?"

He saw no reason to fib. "I sure do."

"There's more to come. Lots more."

She was right. After she bared the one leg, she bared the other, just as seductively. Turning to face him, she reached for the first button on her high collar. "I'm really sick of wearing these confining clothes. They're not really my style."

"I kind of figured they weren't."

She smiled at him and continued to work on her buttons, one by one. They were tiny black buttons, and she worked them with exquisite care. "Oh? And just when did you begin to figure that?"

"Not very long ago."

"Ah." The last button came loose at the waist, and she pulled the bodice open, revealing a lacy camisole. "I see."

Fargo gulped. Her puckered nipples were pressing against the fine lawn of her camisole as if they were straining to get out. She took her time, unfastening the button at the skirt of her waist and dropping the garment into the pine needles at her feet. Then she untied the tape holding her petticoat up, and it dropped into a puddle on top of the skirt. She stood before him in drawers, camisole, and corset.

"You're really good at this," Fargo muttered. His throat was tight. So was his manhood, which was straining to get out of his trousers very much as Jenny's breasts were straining to get out of her camisole.

"I've had lots of practice."

Fargo sucked in his breath when her hands went to the pink ribbon holding her corset on over her camisole. "I can tell."

She gave him a low, seductive laugh that slithered into his ears and lodged firmly in his masculinity, which throbbed. "When I'm through here, I'll help you get out of your clothes, too."

"Good."

Her corset fell away, and the only thing standing between Skye Fargo and Genevieve Wiley's lush and lovely body was several feet of forest, a flimsy camisole, and her drawers. She slid a camisole strap off of one shapely shoulder. Then she slid the other one off. Then, with one fluid movement, she shed the garment altogether.

Fargo didn't let his guard down an instant, although he breathed a sigh when the camisole was gone. He hadn't seen the shadow of a derringer, but he wouldn't put anything past her. But there was no gun tucked anywhere that he could detect. She untied the tape to her drawers, gave them a little shove, and there she was, buck naked, superb in her own personal gifts from the Maker, a glorious female specimen.

She lifted her arms and began undoing her hair, and Fargo sucked in air clear to his toes. She did it slowly, removing pins and dropping them one by one. Then she ran her fingers through the braids until her tresses tumbled over her shoulders, a magnificent red-brown against her white skin.

Putting her hands on her hips, she struck a pose. "What do you think, Skye?"

He swallowed. Then he cleared his throat and said, "Who's thinking?"

She laughed and walked up to him. He didn't let go of the Colt. "Stay there, sweetheart."

She pouted. "Don't you trust me yet, Skye?"

"Not a whit."

He wasn't about to let lack of trust stand in the way of a good time, however. "Stay right where you are, sweetie. I want to look at you while I do this."

She did. Folding her hands in front of her and, looking as sweet and demure as a bare-assed-naked female who had just teased the life out of a man could look, she stood and watched while Fargo removed his clothes as fast as he could. Her eyes grew wide when his trousers dropped, and his rod leaped out to point at her.

"Mercy, you're big." She looked from his groin to his face, and smiled. "This is going to be fun."

"I hope so." Before he laid his Colt aside, he made a point of fetching a leather pouch out of his trousers pocket. He wasn't surprised when her gaze sharpened.

"What's that, Skye?"

He tossed the pouch in the air, caught it, and slipped it underneath his jacket spread out on a rock. With a grin, he said, "I'll show you later. I'm interested in something else right now. Stay right where you are."

With a flick of his wrist, he spread a blanket on the pine needles. "All set." He stood there with his legs apart, and watched her sway up to him and kneel in front of him. Oh, Lord. It was an effort to keep his eyes open when she slid her hands up his calves to his knees and on up his thighs until she got to his thrusting organ. Cupping him in her hands, she leaned forward and slid her tongue up the length of him. His knees almost buckled.

"I think you ought to give up missionary work, Jenny. Your talents lie elsewhere."

She chuckled and nipped at his shaft.

That was it for Fargo. With a growl, he joined her on the blanket, pressed her back onto it, and finally, after all that time, took her breasts in his hands. They were wonderful. Her nipples felt like heaven under his tongue, and when his hand caressed her satiny skin and she moaned, his sex gave a huge, hard throb. His fingers found the curls between her thighs, her legs parted at once, and she lifted up her hips. He took the invitation, dipping a finger into the wet heat of her.

"Give it to me, Skye. I've been wanting to do this ever since I first set eyes on you."

"You have?"

"Lord, yes. Oh, please, please, give it to me."

"Happy to oblige." He pressed her back and poised above her.

She surprised him by lifting her legs to his shoulders, thrusting her passage at him. With a groan, he sank into her, lowering his mouth to hers, and their tongues swirled violently as he plunged in and out.

After a minute, she lowered her legs and locked them around his back, so that they were fused in a mating dance as ageless as time. She whispered raggedly into his ear. "I want to ride you, Skye."

That was fine with him. They rolled over, and she was on top of him, riding him as he'd seldom been ridden before. She was a tiger. He wondered if her passion had been banked during the days she was pretending to be pure. If so, he was very glad to be the recipient of her eruption.

"It's coming," she gasped. "It's coming! Oh, Lord!"

He rolled them over again. Thrusting hard and fast, he drove her until she screamed and, with a final rush, convulsed around his pole. With a shout of his own, he spilled himself into her. Several hard spasms emptied him completely.

Carefully, because he didn't want to crush her, he lowered himself onto her body, making sure she couldn't get away. She seemed as spent as he was, but he wasn't taking any chances.

Except for exhausted pants, silence reigned in the forest for several minutes. After a while, Fargo whispered, "How do you feel, Jenny?"

She kissed him. "I feel wonderful, Skye. I've never had it so good."

"You're a special woman, Jenny. Too bad you and I decided to go down different roads in this life."

She sighed. "Oh, I don't know. We met anyway. I reckon life has its own way of working things out."

"I guess you're right."

After another few minutes, he said, "I don't want to bring up anything unpleasant, but we still have to eat before we turn in for the night. Do I have to tie you up, or will you behave yourself?"

He wasn't sure if the little noises she made were from amusement or offense. "If I promise to be good, will you not tie me up?"

"I don't know." Although he didn't much want to, he heaved himself to a sitting position. Lord, her body was gorgeous. He couldn't keep his hand from reaching out and smoothing over her sweat-dampened skin. He shook his head, wondering if they'd ever meet again. It had been kind of fun matching wits with her sometimes. Other times it had been a real pain. "All right. You stay right here. Don't move a muscle. I'll get some supper out of my pack and build a fire."

He also put on his clothes, although she didn't. He enjoyed the sight of her spread out before him. Good thing it was summer and the weather was warm. After he'd made sure there weren't any guns, knives, or other tools that might be used in nefarious ways lying out where she could get at them, he turned his back on her and built the fire. He kept his ears open, though.

Sure enough, as he was striking his flint, he saw a movement out of the corner of his eye and turned enough to see Jenny's hand snake under his jacket and haul out the leather pouch he'd stashed there. He turned, and was amused when she tried to hide the pouch behind her back, adopting a nonchalant expression.

"Oh, yeah, I forgot about that." He kept his tone casual.

"I didn't."

"So I see." He gestured. "Open it up. It's interesting."

"I'll bet it is."

She pulled the leather thong and peeked inside. She sure looked pretty there, sitting in the altogether, peeking into that leather pouch. He heard her gasp.

"Good heavens, Skye, that's gold in there!"

He shrugged. If she could feign nonchalance, so could he. "Sure. We just left Barley Flats. That's what men do there—find gold."

"But—but how did you get this?"

"Poker."

Her eyes were huge and avid when she lifted them to look at him. "May I pour it out onto the blanket? I promise not to take any. I don't have anywhere to hide it, anyway." She gave him a coy look. "You can search me, if you don't believe me."

He laughed. "Go ahead. There's a big nugget in there I won off a fellow who'd found it in the river. Not much gold in the river any longer, according to Gus. Guess that man was lucky. Until he met me."

"Is this the one?" She lifted the biggest nugget and stared at it. He could almost read the greed on her pretty little face.

"That's the one. Put it down now, sweetie. I like you a lot, but I don't trust you around anybody else's gold, not even mine." Especially not his.

She looked hurt. "Skye Fargo, how you talk."

"Right." He took the pouch from her, and made a point of turning his back and surreptitiously sticking it beneath his saddle on the ground. "Better get on some clothes, because supper's ready. If you want to eat, that is. If you prefer to do something else, I'll be happy to oblige."

She didn't bother to look shocked. "Maybe we can do that afterward. I'm hungry after all that exercise."

This time she didn't bother with the corset, but slipped on her chemise and skirt and called it enough. They were a congenial couple as they dined on tough jerky, cold water, and some dried apples Fargo had tucked in his saddlebags. Now that Jenny didn't have an act to live up to, they talked about everything, from her life back East to the easiest marks she'd come across.

"Generally, upright Christian gentlemen are the best," she said between gnawing on her jerky and sipping water. "They're ashamed of their carnal urges."

"Oh, you're not always a missionary?"

She shook her head. "That I reserve for dens of iniquity, because the men in the dens often feel guilty enough."

When she smiled, a dimple appeared at the side of her mouth. Fargo reached out and pressed it. "You're quite a woman, Jenny."

"Thank you, Skye." She leaned into his caress. "You're quite a man."

They made love again after supper. This time was even better than the first. Fargo almost—but didn't quite—feel a pang of remorse to think he'd probably never have this opportunity again. She was one beautiful, skillful woman.

On the other hand, it would be a pleasure not to

have to watch his back constantly any longer. He slept like a log.

She was gone in the morning. So was his leather pouch. He'd heard her, of course, but he'd not stirred a muscle, not wanting her to know it. And, in truth, she'd been more quiet than he'd have given her credit for. She even led that mule of hers out of the camp before she saddled it. He hoped she hadn't gone too far. After all, it was only a trick.

Not that she knew it. He chuckled all the way through his camp-side breakfast and the saddling of the Ovaro, and he was still laughing when he mounted the horse and turned him toward Barley Flats.

He hoped she wouldn't hate him too much when she realized the gold was false. She probably wouldn't. They'd sort of reached an understanding on their last day together. Fargo wouldn't mind meeting her again someday—as long as he had some kind of warning first so he could secure all of his belongings.

He was whistling when he and the Ovaro headed down out of the mountains. He didn't have to be back to the fort for another week. He still had a lot of gambling to do, and he and Gus hadn't quite caught up on all of their adventures yet. He was also interested in the outcome of Kanaka's trial—not to mention Cleveland Pierce's.

Besides, he still hadn't had a go-round with Constance. And he definitely wanted to do that—she was the best gal Gus had, after all.

LOOKING FORWARD!
The following is the opening
section from the next novel in the exciting
Trailsman series from Signet:

THE TRAILSMAN # 222

*Colorado, 1860—Where the allure of a woman's eyes
can be as sparkling as the glint of precious gems and
every bit as perilous as the dark chasm of an open
mineshaft. . . .*

The high-pitched cry of a woman in pain brought the
big man in buckskins to a halt. His piercing, lake blue
eyes scanned the opposite side of the busy street and
spied a small crowd in front of a millinery, a store devoted to ladies' headwear. Curiosity compelled him to
see what was going on. Always cautious, he glanced
both ways first. Denver's carriage drivers and wag-
oners were notorious for not caring who or what they
ran over. Every month over a dozen dogs and cats and
other stray animals were crushed under merciless
grinding wheels, to say nothing of the occasional hap-
less humans.

Skye Fargo didn't intend to be one of them. But just

as he strode off the boardwalk, a speeding freight wagon careened around an intersection and bore down on him with all the abandon of stampeding buffalo.

The grizzled driver, cracking his whip, bawled like a drunk on a binge, "Out of my way, you clod!"

Skye Fargo couldn't rightly say what made him do what he did next. Ordinarily, he would have bounded to safety and let the wagon go on by. But not this particular morning. Maybe it was the headache he had from too much whiskey the night before; maybe it was his irritable mood at having lost almost every last cent he had at poker; or maybe it was simple resentment. Whatever the case, his Colt materialized in his hand, trained on the onrushing driver.

The man was no fool. He hauled on the reins for all he was worth, straining backward, throwing his entire weight into it as he shouted, "Whoa, there! Whoa! Whoa! Whoa!" The big wagon ground to a lurching halt, the lead animals snorting and stomping two yards from where Fargo stood.

Fargo slowly lowered the Colt, then twirled it into his holster.

"What the hell is the matter with you, mister?" the driver hollered. "Are you lookin' to get yourself killed? Learn how to cross a street, why don't you?"

"Learn how to drive," Fargo retorted. He was strongly tempted to haul the cantankerous cuss from the driver's box but another cry drew his eyes to the fringes of the crowd. Taller than most, Fargo could see over the onlookers to the center of the commotion. And he didn't like what he saw.

Sprawled on his rump in front of a store was a portly gentleman in a white suit and matching bowler. His ruddy cheeks were puffed out in rage, his thick lips twitching like those of a wild boar about to bite. "I demand that you unhand her this instant, sir!" he fumed.

The object of his wrath was a ruffian in rumpled clothes and a floppy hat. The man, grinning lecherously, had hold of a young woman's wrists. "Settle down, missy," he sternly advised. "This doesn't involve you."

"It does so!" the woman responded. "He's my father! You had no right to knock him down!"

"If he doesn't want his head bashed in, he shouldn't go around bumping into folks." The man gave her left wrist a sharp twist and she cried out again. "Now behave yourself, or I'm liable to really get rough."

The young woman did no such thing. She was in her early twenties, a stunning beauty whose golden hair spilled over her slender shoulders in curly waves. A green dress clung to her luscious form like a second skin, accentuating the ample sweep of her bosom and her flat stomach. When she moved, the dress clung to her legs, highlighting the splendid contours of her shapely thighs. Her blue eyes flashed like lightning as she drew back a foot to kick her tormentor. "Let go of me!"

Laughing, the ruffian sidestepped her kick, then pushed her against the wall. "You take after your pa, don't you, girl? Neither of you know how to listen worth a damn."

There were upwards of twenty onlookers, but not a single one was disposed to lend the young woman a hand. Her tormentor's size probably had something to do with it. He was a big man, nearly as big as Fargo, only grimier and scruffier. In addition, a Remington rested on the man's right hip, and he had the air of someone who wouldn't hesitate to use it if provoked.

"Leave her be!" the woman's portly father railed. Propping his pudgy hands under him, he sought to rise.

"Stay where you are, chubby," the bully snapped, planting the sole of his right boot in the father's chest, knocking him to the ground. "I'll get to you in a moment."

Fargo had seen enough. He barreled through the crowd, drawing frowns of disapproval and a few oaths. When he reached the man holding the blonde, he didn't ask politely for the ruffian to release her. He didn't tap the man on the shoulder, or clear his throat to get the man's attention. Fargo simply jerked his Colt, spun the hardcase around, and brought the barrel crashing down onto the crown of the man's brown hat with enough force to bring a bull moose to its knees. The man crumpled, oozing like melted wax into a disjointed heap.

Replacing the Colt for the second time, Fargo touched his hat brim to the astounded blonde. "He won't bother you any more, ma'am."

"Thank you, kind sir," she responded. Clasping his right hand in both her warm palms, she gently squeezed. "This uncouth lout was going to kick my father's teeth in. All because my father bumped into him coming out of the store."

Fargo pegged her accent as from somewhere in the deep South. Georgia, perhaps, or Alabama. "Denver isn't Savannah. This is the frontier. Men out here are rougher than those you're used to." As she withdrew her hands, one of her fingernails lightly scraped the side of his forefinger.

"So we're finding out," the blonde said, and smiled, showing pearly, even teeth. "Goodness gracious. Where are my manners? I haven't properly introduced myself. Delicia Cadwell is my name, and I'm right pleased to make your acquaintance." She bent her knee in a playful curtsy.

"Delicia," Fargo said, rolling the name on the tip of his tongue as he would a piece of hard candy. It fit her as nicely as her dress. She was a genuine beauty, her dazzling eyes and cherry lips enough to make a man's head spin.

Her father snorted. "Harrumph! I don't suppose either of you would care to assist me to my feet? The social amenities can wait until my dignity is restored."

Fargo gripped the man's elbow and boosted him upright. Now that the hardcase had been dealt with, the crowd was dispersing, with everyone venturing on about their business.

"Allow me to add my gratitude to my daughter's. Rupert T. Cadwell, at your service." The father shook Fargo's hand with sweaty fingers as fat as sausages. "I can't thank you enough, Mr. Fargo. Not that your help was truly needed, however. Another moment, and I'd have risen up and given that cretin a clout that would have left him senseless for a week."

Given how weakly Cadwell shook his hand, Fargo doubted the man could hit anyone hard enough to give them more than a mild bruise. "Glad I could be of help." Prying his fingers loose, he nodded at Delicia. "Take care."

"What's your hurry to rush off?" she asked.

"Indeed," Rupert echoed. "We would be honored if you would permit us to show our appreciation in more tangible ways. How about twenty dollars?" he said, reaching under his white jacket.

"There's no need," Fargo declined. He needed a good, stiff drink more than money right now. Just one, to ease the dull ache in his head.

Delicia grabbed his arm. "Please let us do something. How about if we treat you to a meal? Or at least a piece of pie? There's a quaint little restaurant just down the street."

Fargo hesitated. Six or seven cups of coffee would have the same effect as a glass of rotgut. And he had skipped breakfast to conserve his meager funds. Plus he still had his hotel bill to pay, as well as the stabling fee for the Ovaro. "Fact is, I haven't eaten yet."

"Then it's settled!" Rupert declared, adjusting his bowler as he led the way. "Despite what just occurred, I must say I've taken quite a liking to this city. It has a wild aspect I find rather invigorating."

"And dangerous," Fargo amended. But he agreed. He liked Denver, too. Started only a couple of years ago by rival factions, it was now being billed as the "gateway to the Rockies" and the "San Francisco of the foothills" by the *Rocky Mountain News*, the city's one and only newspaper.

Every time Fargo passed through the territory, Denver was larger. It now boasted fifteen hotels and boardinghouses, eleven restaurants, two schools, two theaters, about thirty retail establishments, and twenty-five bars and saloons. To say nothing of its bawdy houses. Fargo could remember when town lots went for twenty dollars each; now they were ten times as much.

"Danger is part and parcel of life, is it not?" Rupert asked. "There is an element of risk in everything we do. Speaking for myself, I've learned to minimize the risks, but accept them as inevitable." He gestured grandly. "Take my latest enterprise. I knew it would expose my daughters to some small degree of peril, but did I let that stop me? I certainly did not."

"Daughters?" Fargo said.

It was Delicia who answered. "My older sister, Amity, is off by herself. We'll rejoin her later at the Grand."

Fargo was impressed. The Grand Hotel was one of the best the city boasted, as elegant as any found in St. Louis or New Orleans, and ridiculously expensive. The Cadwells had to have money to spare to afford to stay there.

The restaurant they picked bore a painted sign that proudly announced it was known as THE GRUB. Inside, most of the long tables were empty. It would be hours yet before hungry workers filed in for their midday meal. Out of habit Fargo chose a table in a far corner where he could sit with his back to the wall. He held out a chair for Delicia.

Rupert T. Cadwell sank into another with a sigh. "Quite frankly, Mr. Fargo, I'm glad you agreed. I needed to get off my feet. All morning my sweet Delicia has been dragging me from store to store so she could admire the latest dresses and bonnets. I'm worn to a frazzle."

Merry mirth tinkled from Delicia's smooth throat.

"Oh, please, Father. You protest too much. What else did you have to do?"

"True," Rupert said. "Until Amity is done, our time is our own." He folded his hands on the table. "So tell me, Mr. Fargo. If it's not improper of me to inquire, exactly what do you do for a living?"

"From time to time I scout for the army. Or work as a guide. Among other things." Fargo didn't go into detail. His personal life was none of their business.

"Scout and guide, you say?" Rupert repeated, his forehead puckering. "Then it's safe to assume you're quite knowledgeable about the mountains. You must know them inside and out, as it were."

Fargo shrugged. "Better than most, I suppose." The truth was, his wanderlust had taken him from one end of the Rockies to the other, from Canada clear down to Mexico. Few frontiersmen knew the vast region west of the Mississippi River as well as he did.

"How fortuitous," Rupert remarked, swapping looks with his daughter. "Perhaps our meeting was preordained. In the next day or two we will be in need of someone with your expertise. How much do you charge to act as a guide?"

"It depends on where you want to go," Fargo said. Further talk was interrupted by the arrival of the waitress, a middle-aged woman in a home-spun dress and long apron. Fargo ordered a double portion of eggs and bacon, a slab of ham, and two sides of toast. He also told her to keep the coffee coming "until it comes out my ears."

Rupert chuckled while studying the menu. "You have quite an appetite—a trait I share." He pursed his lips, then tilted his plump face toward the waitress. "I'd like one of your apple pies, my dear—"

"A slice of apple pie," she said, scribbling on her pad.

"No, no. A *whole* pie," Rupert said. "Along with coffee and a heaping bowl of sugar." He winked good-naturedly. "Unsweetened coffee is an affront to my taste buds."

As she departed he grinned at Delicia. "Did you see how she looked at me, Daughter? I'd say she was smitten."

Delicia sighed. "Father, please. It's getting to the point where I can't take you out in public without a leash."

Fargo and Rupert laughed. Fargo found himself liking the pair, especially Delicia. When she leaned back, her breasts thrust against her dress as if striving to burst through the silken material. He couldn't help imagining how she would look unclothed and felt himself stir below the table. "What about you?" he asked her. "You didn't order anything."

"Unlike my father, I'm not a bottomless pit. Two meals a day are more than enough for me. Not six or seven."

"Now, now," Rupert rebutted. "Don't begrudge a man his minor pleasures. Eating to excess is one of my few vices. Would you rather I drank to excess?"

Delicia reached over to stroke her father's ruddy cheek. "Stick to eating. I'd rather live with a whale than a drunk any day."

And so it went for the next hour, father and daughter bantering while Fargo listened and ate. The eggs were done to perfection, the bacon thick with fat and grease, the toast layered heavy with butter. He washed it all down with four cups of coffee, then sat back to enjoy a couple more.

Fargo learned the pair were from Atlanta, that they had arrived in Denver four days ago, and that they had been taking in the sights and doing what they kept referring to as "research". "You haven't said what you do for a living," Fargo commented at one point.

"How remiss of me," Rupert said. "Perhaps I should have given you my credentials when we first met." He produced a small card from his jacket pocket and handed it over with a flourish. Boldly imprinted upon it were the words, PROFESSOR RUPERT T. CADWELL, GEMOLOGIST EXTRAORDINAIRE. D.G., P.O.R.M., M.S. Fargo had no idea what the initials meant, and said as much.

"They stand for the degrees I've earned. In short, it means I'm a qualified gemologist. One of the foremost in this country, perhaps the entire world. It's my passion in life to travel the globe in search of rare gems and minerals."

"Like gold and silver?" Fargo asked, thinking of the hordes who had flooded into the region recently on the heels of a gold strike. Hundreds arrived every month, lured by the chance to get rich quick. Most were doomed to severe disappointment; for every fledgling prospector who struck it rich, thousands worked their fingers to the bone for naught.

"I'm more interested in rare gems," Rupert responded. "Rubies, emeralds, diamonds and the like."

"Too bad no one has found any here," Fargo idly remarked. Swallowing some coffee, he saw the father and daughter exchange another peculiar glance. Both grinned, as if at a private joke.

"If they did, it would be the find of the century," Rupert said. "Yet the prospect is not all that farfetched. Many of the geologic conditions in other regions of the world that have spawned precious gems are also found in the Rockies."

"Father—," Delicia said rather harshly.

"Never fear, my dear, I won't give our little secret away," Rupert assured her. "Besides, nothing I could divulge would allow our newfound friend to get the jump on us. He lacks my vast knowledge, my years of experience, my unflagging dedication and tireless persistence."

"And your humility," Delicia quipped.

Chortling, Rupert slapped his thigh. "Did you hear her, Mr. Fargo? My own flesh and blood! I tell you, the young have no respect for their elders anymore. All they do is give a parent sass and grief."

Just then the door swung inward with a resounding crash. Into the restaurant stalked the ruffian Fargo had pistol-whipped, along with a pair of beefy friends. They surveyed the room, then made a beeline for their table, the hardcase leading his grungy companions with his thumbs hooked boldly in his gunbelt.

The patrons gaped, unsure what to expect.

"Hold on, there," the waitress said, moving to intercept the trio. "What's the meaning of this?"

"Don't butt in if you know what's good for you," the leader growled, and rudely shoved her out of the way. "The same holds for the rest of you!" he announced, glaring about the room. "Anyone who sticks their nose in will wish they hadn't."

No one spoke. No one moved.

Squaring his shoulders, the hardcase advanced to the table. "Didn't reckon on seeing me again, I bet."

Rupert was a living portrait of indignation. "What do you want? Why do you persist in hounding us? How did you know where we were?"

The man answered the last question first. "When I came to, I asked around. Someone had seen you come in here. So I fetched a couple of my pards and came back to take up where I left off."

"Can't you let us be?" Delicia said testily. "You're the one who started it, after all."

"No, this tub of lard did," the man replied, jabbing a thumb at Rupert. Then he gingerly touched his temple. "Thanks to your pa, my head is pounding something fierce."

"Thanks to me," Fargo corrected him, swiveling so he faced all three. None of them appeared to have noticed that his right hand remained under the table. "And I can do it again if you want."

"I'd like to see you try!" the ruffian blustered. "No one gets the better of Ike Talbot twice." Talbot's hand drifted toward the butt of his Remington but he froze when he heard a distinct metallic click. Glancing down, he swallowed hard, his Adam's apple bobbing. "Is that what I think it is?"

"Try to unlimber your hardware and you'll find out," Fargo said. "I want all three of you to unbuckle your gunbelts and let them drop. Then light a shuck or I'll put windows in your skulls."

Delicia rose, saying, "Maybe it would be better if we were the ones who left. We're done eating anyway. And I'd rather avoid trouble if at all possible." Gripping her father's sleeve, she headed for the entrance.

Fargo would rather it was the other way around, but he did as she requested, covering the three cutthroats with his Colt as he backed toward the door. Delicia paid the waitress, and within moments they were squinting in the bright glare of the midmorning sun. Fargo holstered his Colt but kept one eye on the restaurant as they bore to the left and blended in among scores of bustling pedestrians.

"Why is that dreadful man so determined to do me harm?" Rupert asked. "All I did was bump into him."

"Didn't you smell his breath?" Fargo rejoined. "He's half drunk, and snake-mean. He likes to cause trouble and you've given him an excuse."

"But I apologized."

"That doesn't matter." Fargo figured the professor would never fully understand. East of the Mississippi violence was the exception, not the rule. But on the frontier, violence was woven into the fabric of everyday life. Violent men were everywhere, spawned in part by the savage wilderness they called home and in part by the savagery lurking in the depths of their own dark souls. Most easterners found it difficult to believe that there were people who *liked* to hurt others, people who could kill another human being as casually as they swatted a fly.

"I apologized," Rupert said again, more to himself than to either of them.

"You could say you're sorry from now until doomsday and it wouldn't change a thing," Fargo said. "Talbot is out for blood. Yours."

"He's a filthy beast," Delicia said in disgust.

"A rabid wolf is more like it." Fargo still watched the

restaurant. "And there are a lot more in Denver just like him."

Rupert gazed up and down the street. "Where's a constable when we need one? In Atlanta there's one every few blocks."

The professor continued to judge the frontier by civilized standards, Fargo mused. There was just one overworked marshal in Denver, but he couldn't be everywhere at once. Rumor had it there was a move afoot to have half a dozen deputies appointed but so far nothing had come of the idea, thanks to certain vested criminal interests determined to keep it from happening.

As they rounded a corner, heading in the general direction of the Grand Hotel, Fargo allowed himself to relax. Talbot and company weren't following. Still, to be on the safe side, he offered, "I'll see you all the way to your hotel."

"Why, how gallant of you." Delicia, displaying those pearly teeth of hers, hooked a slender arm in his. "You're a perfect gentleman."

"Only in public," Fargo said to test her reaction, and was pleased when she laughed lustily instead of being offended.

Leaning toward him, her breast brushing against his elbow, Delicia impishly whispered in his ear, "And how, pray tell, do you act in private?"

Professor Cadwell clucked like an irate hen. "Behave yourself, Daughter." To Fargo, he said, "You must forgive her. Their mother died when my darling daughters were quite young, and I'm afraid I've been remiss in instilling moral virtue."

"In other words," Delicia teased, "my own father thinks I'm a shameless hussy."

"Not shameless, no," Rupert said.

Ahead was an alley. Fargo was so intent on the vision of loveliness at his side that he neglected to give it the attention it deserved. It was an oversight he regretted when they started to walk past and the barrel of a revolver was roughly jammed into the base of his spine.

"Not a peep out of any of you," Ike Talbot warned.

One of Talbot's friends seized Rupert, the other grabbed Delicia. Fingers grasped the collar of Fargo's buckskin shirt and he was pulled into the alleyway after them. If any of the passersby observed what was happening, none voiced an objection.

Empty crates, refuse, and a broken wagon wheel littered the alley. Fargo was shoved against a wall, jarring his chest and chin and nearly losing his hat. Talbot relieved him of the Colt, then stepped back.

"You can turn around now, mister, and get your due."

Rupert and Delicia were next to a crate, the father's arm protectively draped over his daughter's shoulder. In front of them, fists clenched, were Talbot's partners, poised like grizzlies eager to rip and rend.

"You really didn't think I'd let you get the drop on me and not do anything about it, did you, mister?" Talbot addressed Fargo. "Once word got around, I'd never be able to show my face in Denver again."

Rupert had more grit than most would in his situation. "Your juvenile posturing is grating on my nerves, sir! Were I ten years younger, I'd thrash you within an inch of your life."

Talbot nodded at the tallest of his friends, who immediately buried a fist in the professor's stomach. Rupert doubled over, wheezing and sputtering, his eyes filling with tears and spittle dribbling over his lower lip.

"You bastards!" Delicia screeched, throwing herself at her father's attacker, her fingernails hooked to rake his face. But the man backhanded her across the cheek, slamming her into the crate.

Rage gushed through Fargo and he started to take a step, stopping when Talbot cocked the Remington. It took all of Fargo's self-control not to throw caution to the breeze and tear into him.

"I wouldn't, if'n I were you. There are three of us, remember?"

Fargo had to lure the three men closer. Sneering, he said, "Three cowards who hit women and beat older men. What else do you do to prove how tough you are? Kick puppies and spit on babies?"

Talbot's features twisted in spite. "Another word out of you and you'll be laid up for a month of Sundays."

"Big talk for someone with a yellow streak down his back." Fargo's plan to provoke them into coming closer worked better than he had counted on. For in the very next moment, Talbot hissed like a rattler, gestured at his companions, and all three rushed him.

Laughter and Misadventure
in the Middle East . . .

"More than a charming entertainment. Miss Christie has done her detective work here, too. . . . a vivid evocation of exotic places and a superbly told tale spiced with adventure and humor"
                                        —*Literary Guild*

"CLEAR, DIRECT AND ENTERTAINING."
                                        —*The New Yorker*

"Agatha Christie just couldn't write a dull book."
                                        —*St. Louis Post-Dispatch*

Jane Marple Mysteries

Hercule Poirot Mysteries

Other Agatha Christie Mysteries

Autobiography

Published by POCKET BOOKS/WASHINGTON SQUARE PRESS

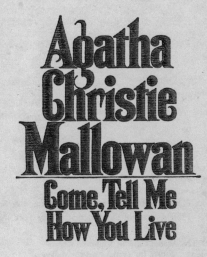

Agatha Christie Mallowan

Come, Tell Me How You Live

PUBLISHED BY POCKET BOOKS NEW YORK

POCKET BOOKS, a division of Simon & Schuster, Inc.
1230 Avenue of the Americas, New York, N.Y. 10020

ISBN: 0-671-49162-8

First Pocket Books printing October, 1977

10 9 8 7 6 5

To my husband, Max Mallowan; to the Colonel,
Bumps, Mac and Guilford, this meandering
chronicle is affectionately dedicated.

SYRIA and MESOPOTAMIA

CONTENTS

A-SITTING ON A TELL

(With apologies to Lewis Carroll)

I'll tell you everything I can
    If you will listen well:
I met an erudite young man
    A-sitting on a Tell.
"Who are you, sir?" to him I said,
    "For what is it you look?"
His answer trickled through my head
    Like bloodstains in a book.

He said: "I look for aged pots
    Of prehistoric days,
And then I measure them in lots
    And lots of different ways.
And then (like you) I start to write,
    My words are twice as long
As yours, and far more erudite.
    They prove my colleagues wrong!"

But I was thinking of a plan
    To kill a millionaire

9

And hide the body in a van
    Or some large Frigidaire.
So, having no reply to give,
    And feeling rather shy,
I cried: "Come, tell me how you live!
    And when, and where, and why?"

His accents mild were full of wit:
    "Five thousand years ago
Is really, when I think of it,
    The choicest Age I know.
And once you learn to scorn A.D.
    And you have got the knack,
Then you could come and dig with me
    And never wander back."

But I was thinking how to thrust
    Some arsenic into tea,
And could not all at once adjust
    My mind so far B.C.
I looked at him and softly sighed,
    His face was pleasant too. . . .
"Come, tell me how you live?" I cried,
    "And what it is you do?"

He said: "I hunt for objects made
    By men where'er they roam,
I photograph and catalog
    And pack and send them home.
These things we do not sell for gold
    (Nor yet, indeed, for copper!),
But place them on Museum shelves
    As only right and proper.

"I sometimes dig up amulets
    And figurines most lewd,
For in those prehistoric days
    They were extremely rude!
And that's the way we take our fun,
    'Tis not the way of wealth.

But archaeologists live long
  And have the rudest health."

I heard him then, for I had just
  Completed a design
To keep a body free from dust
  By boiling it in brine.
I thanked him much for telling me
  With so much erudition,
And said that I would go with him
  Upon an Expedition. . . .

And now, if e'er by chance I dip
  My fingers into acid,
Or smash some pottery (with slip!)
  Because I am not placid,
Or if I see a river flow
  And hear a far-off yell,
I sigh, for it reminds me so
  Of that young man I learned to know——

Whose look was mild, whose speech was slow,
Whose thoughts were in the long ago,
Whose pockets sagged with potsherds so,
Who lectured learnedly and low,
Who used long words I didn't know,
Whose eyes, with fervor all a-glow,
Upon the ground looked to and fro,
Who sought conclusively to show
That there were things I ought to know
And that with him I ought to go
  And dig upon a Tell!

FOREWORD

THIS BOOK IS an answer. It is the answer to a question that is asked me very often.

"So you dig in Syria, do you? Do tell me all about it. How do you live? In a tent?" etc., etc.

Most people, probably, do not want to know. It is just the small change of conversation. But there are, now and then, one or two people who are really interested.

It is the question, too, that Archaeology asks of the Past—*Come, tell me how you lived?*

And with picks and spades and baskets we find the answer.

"These were our cooking pots." "In this big silo we kept our grain." "With these bone needles we sewed our clothes." "These were our houses, this our bathroom, here our system of sanitation!" "Here, in this pot, are the gold ear-rings of my daughter's dowry." "Here, in this little jar, is my make-up." "All these cook-pots are of a very common type. You'll find them by the hundred. We get them from the Potter at the

*corner. Woolworth's, did you say? Is that what you call
him in your time?"*

Occasionally there is a Royal Palace, sometimes a
Temple, much more rarely a Royal burial. These things
are spectacular. They appear in newspapers in head-
lines, are lectured about, shown on screens, everybody
hears of them! Yet I think to one engaged in digging,
the real interest is in the everyday life—the life of
the potter, the farmer, the tool-maker, the expert cut-
ter of animal seals and amulets—in fact, *the butcher,
the baker, the candlestick-maker.*

A final warning, so that there will be no disappointment. This is not a profound book—it will give you
no interesting sidelights on archaeology, there will be
no beautiful descriptions of scenery, no treating of
economic problems, no racial reflections, no history.

It is, in fact, small beer—a very little book, full of
everyday doings and happenings.

Come, Tell Me
How You Live

I

PARTANT POUR LA SYRIE

IN A FEW weeks' time we are starting for Syria!

Shopping for a hot climate in autumn or winter presents certain difficulties. One's last year's summer clothes, which one has optimistically hoped will "do," do not "do" now the time has come. For one thing they appear to be (like the depressing annotations in furniture removers' lists) "Bruised, Scratched and Marked." (And also Shrunk, Faded and Peculiar!) For another —alas, alas that one has to say it!—they are too tight everywhere.

So—to the shops and the stores, and:

"Of course, Modom, we are not being asked for that kind of thing just *now!* We have some very charming little suits here—O.S. in the darker colors."

Oh, loathsome O.S.! How humiliating to be O.S.! How even more humiliating to be recognized at once as O.S.!

(Although there are better days when, wrapped in a lean long black coat with a large fur collar, a saleswoman says cheeringly:

17

"But *surely* Modom is *only* a Full Woman?")

I look at the little suits, with their dabs of unexpected fur and their pleated skirts. I explain sadly that what I want is a washing silk or cotton.

"Modom might try Our Cruising Department."

Modom tries Our Cruising Department—but without any exaggerated hopes. Cruising is still enveloped in the realms of romantic fancy. It has a touch of Arcady about it. It is girls who go cruising—girls who are slim and young and wear uncrushable linen trousers, immensely wide round the feet and skintight round the hips. It is girls who sport delightfully in Play Suits. It is girls for whom Shorts of eighteen different varieties are kept!

The lovely creature in charge of Our Cruising Department is barely sympathetic.

"Oh, no, Modom, we do not keep *out*-sizes." (Faint horror! Outsizes and Cruising? Where is the romance there?)

She adds:

"It would hardly be *suitable,* would it?"

I agree sadly that it would not be suitable.

There is still one hope. There is Our Tropical Department.

Our Tropical Department consists principally of Topees—Brown Topees, White Topees; Special Patent Topees. A little to one side, as being slightly frivolous, are Double Terais, blossoming in pinks and blues and yellows like blooms of strange tropical flowers. There is also an immense wooden horse and an assortment of jodhpurs.

But—yes—there are other things. Here is suitable wear for the wives of Empire Builders. Shantung! Plainly cut shantung coats and skirts—no girlish nonsense here—bulk is accommodated as well as scragginess! I depart into a cubicle with various styles and sizes. A few minutes later I am transformed into a Memsahib!

I have certain qualms—but stifle them. After all, it *is* cool and practical and I *can* get into it.

I turn my attention to the selection of the right kind of hat. The right kind of hat not existing in these days, I have to have it made for me. This is not so easy as it sounds.

What I want, and what I mean to have, and what I shall almost certainly not get, is a felt hat of reasonable proportions that will fit on my head. It is the kind of hat that was worn some twenty years ago for taking the dogs for a walk or playing a round of golf. Now, alas, there are only the Things one attaches to one's head—over one eye, one ear, on the nape of one's neck—as the fashion of the moment dictates—or the Double Terai, measuring at least a yard across.

I explain that I want a hat with a crown like a Double Terai and about a quarter of its brim.

"But they are made wide to protect fully from the sun, Modom."

"Yes, but where I am going there is nearly always a terrific wind, and a hat with a brim won't stay on one's head for a minute."

"We could put Modom on an elastic."

"I want a hat with a brim no larger than this that I've got on."

"Of course, Modom, with a shallow crown that would look quite well."

"*Not* a shallow crown! The hat has got To Keep On!"

Victory! We select the color—one of those new shades with the pretty names: Dirt, Rust, Mud, Pavement, Dust, etc.

A few minor purchases—purchases that I know instinctively will either be useless or land me in trouble. A Zip travelling bag, for instance. Life, nowadays is dominated and complicated by the remorseless Zip. Blouses zip up, skirts zip down, ski-ing suits zip everywhere. "Little frocks" have perfectly unnecessary bits of zipping on them just for fun.

Why? Is there anything more deadly than a Zip that turns nasty on you? It involves you in a far worse predicament than any ordinary button, clip, snap, buckle or hook and eye.

In the early days of Zips, my mother, thrilled by this delicious novelty, had a pair of corsets fashioned for her which zipped up the front. The results were unfortunate in the extreme! Not only was the original zipping-up fraught with extreme agony, but the corsets then obstinately refused to de-zip! Their removal was practically a surgical operation! And owing to my mother's delightful Victorian modesty, it seemed possible for a while that she would live in these corsets for the remainder of her life—a kind of modern Woman in the Iron Corset!

I have therefore always regarded the Zip with a wary eye. But it appears that *all* travelling bags have Zips.

"The old-fashioned fastening is quite superseded, Modom," says the salesman, regarding me with a pitying look.

"This, you see, is so simple," he says, demonstrating.

There is no doubt about its simplicity—but then, I think to myself, the bag is empty.

"Well," I say, sighing, "one must move with the times."

With some misgivings I buy the bag.

I am now the proud possessor of a Zip travelling bag, an Empire Builder's Wife's coat and skirt, and a possibly satisfactory hat.

There is still much to be done.

I pass to the Stationery Department. I buy several fountain and stylographic pens—it being my experience that, though a fountain pen in England behaves in an exemplary manner, the moment it is let loose in desert surroundings it perceives that it is at liberty to go on strike and behaves accordingly, either spouting ink indiscriminately over me, my clothes, my notebook and anything else handy, or else coyly refusing to do anything but scratch invisibly across the surface of the paper. I also buy a modest two pencils. Pencils are, fortunately, not temperamental, and though given to a knack of quiet disappearance, I have always a resource at hand. After all, what is the use of an architect if not to borrow pencils from?

Four wrist-watches is the next purchase. The desert is not kind to watches. After a few weeks there, one's watch gives up steady everyday work. Time, it says, is only a mode of thought. It then takes its choice between stopping eight or nine times a day for periods of twenty minutes, or of racing indiscriminately ahead. Sometimes it alternates coyly between the two. It finally stops altogether. One then goes on to wrist-watch No. 2, and so on. There is also a purchase of two four and six watches in readiness for that moment when my husband will say to me: "Just lend me a watch to give to the foreman, will you?"

Our Arab foremen, excellent though they are, have what might be described as a heavy hand with any kind of timepiece. Telling the time, anyway, calls for a good deal of mental strain on their part. They can be seen holding a large round moon-faced watch earnestly upside down, and gazing at it with really painful concentration while they get the answer wrong! Their winding of these treasures is energetic and so thorough that few mainsprings can stand up to the strain!

It therefore happens that by the end of the season the watches of the expedition staff have been sacrificed one by one. My two four and six watches are a means of putting off the evil day.

Packing!

There are several schools of thought as to packing. There are the people who begin packing at anything from a week or a fortnight beforehand. There are the people who throw a few things together half an hour before departure. There are the careful packers, insatiable for tissue paper! There are those who scorn tissue paper and just throw the things in and hope for the best! There are the packers who leave practically everything that they want behind! And there are the packers who take immense quantities of things that they never will need!

One thing can safely be said about an archaeological packing. It consists mainly of *books*. What books to take, what books *can* be taken, what books are there room for, what books can (with agony!) be left behind. I am firmly convinced that all archaeologists pack in the following manner: They decide on the maximum number of suitcases that a long-suffering Wagon Lit Company will permit them to take. They then fill these suitcases to the brim with books. They then, reluctantly, take out a few books, and fill in the space thus obtained with shirts, pajamas, socks, etc.

Looking into Max's room, I am under the impression that the whole cubic space is filled with books! Through a chink in the books I catch sight of Max's worried face.

"Do you think," he asks, "that I shall have room for all these?"

The answer is so obviously in the negative that it seems sheer cruelty to say it.

At 4:30 P.M. he arrives in my room and asks hopefully: "Any room in your suitcases?"

Long experience should have warned me to answer firmly "No," but I hesitate, and immediately doom falls upon me.

"If you could just get in one or two things——"

"Not *books*?"

Max looks faintly surprised and says: "Of course books—what else?"

Advancing, he rams down two immense tomes on top of the Empire Builder's Wife's suit which has been lying smugly on top of a suitcase.

I utter a cry of protest, but too late.

"Nonsense," says Max, "lots of room!" And forces down the lid, which refuses spiritedly to shut.

"It's not really full even now," says Max optimistically.

He is, fortunately, diverted at this moment by a

printed linen frock lying folded in another suitcase. "What's that?"

I reply that it is a dress.

"Interesting," says Max. "It's got fertility *motifs* all down the front."

One of the more uncomfortable things about being married to an archaeologist is their expert knowledge of the derivation of the most harmless looking patterns!

At five-thirty Max casually remarks that he'd better go out and buy a few shirts and socks and things. He returns three-quarters of an hour later, indignant because the shops all shut at six. When I say they always do, he replies that he had never noticed it before.

Now, he says, he has nothing to do but "clear up his papers."

At 11 P.M. I retire to bed, leaving Max at his desk (never to be tidied or dusted under the most dire penalties), up to the elbows in letters, bills, pamphlets, drawings of pots, innumerable potsherds, and various match-boxes, none of them containing matches, but instead odd beads of great antiquity.

At 4 A.M. he comes excitedly into the bedroom, cup of tea in hand, to announce that he has at last found that very interesting article on Anatolian finds which he had lost last July. He adds that he hopes that he hasn't woken me up.

I say that of course he has woken me up, and he'd better get me a cup of tea too!

Returning with the tea, Max says he has also found a great many bills which he thought he had paid. I, too, have had that experience. We agree that it is depressing.

At 9 A.M. I am called in as the heavy-weight to sit on Max's bulging suitcases.

"If *you* can't make them shut," says Max ungallantly, "nobody can!"

The superhuman feat is finally accomplished by the aid of sheer avoirdupois, and I return to contend with my own difficulty, which is, as prophetic vision had told me it would be, the Zip bag. Empty in Mr. Gooch's shop, it had looked simple, attractive, and labor-saving. How merrily then had the Zip run to and fro! Now, full to the brim, the closing of it is a miracle of super-human adjustment. The two edges have to be brought together with mathematical precision, and then, just as the Zip is traveling slowly across, complications set in, due to the corner of a sponge-bag. When at last it closes, I vow not to open it again until I get to Syria!

On reflection, however, this is hardly possible. What about the aforementioned sponge-bag. Am I to travel for five days unwashed? At the moment even *that* seems preferable to unzipping the Zip bag!

Yes, now the moment has come and we are really off. Quantities of important things have been left un-done: the Laundry, as usual, has let us down; the Cleaners, to Max's chagrin, have not kept their prom-ises—but what does anything matter? We are going!

Just for a moment or two it looks as though we weren't going! Max's suitcases, delusive in appearance, are beyond the powers of the taximan to lift. He and Max struggle with them, and finally, with the assistance of a passer-by, they are hoisted on to the taxi.

We drive off for Victoria.

Dear Victoria—gateway to the world beyond En-gland—how I love your continental platform. And how I love trains, anyway! Snuffing up the sulphurous smell ecstatically—so different from the faint, aloof, distantly oily smell of a boat, which always depresses my spirits with its prophecy of nauseous days to come. But a train—a big snorting, hurrying, companionable train, with its big puffing engine, sending up clouds of steam, and seeming to say impatiently: "I've got to be off, I've got to be off, I've *got* to be off!"—is a friend! It shares your mood, for you, too, are saying: "I'm going to be off, I'm going, I'm going, I'm *going* . . ."

By the door of our Pullman, friends are waiting to see us off. The usual idiotic conversations take place. Famous last words pour from my lips—instructions about dogs, about children, about forwarding letters, about sending out books, about forgotten items, "and I think you'll find it on the piano, but it *may* be on the bathroom shelf." All the things that have been said before, and do not in the least need saying again!

Max is surrounded by his relations, I by mine.

My sister says tearfully that she has a feeling that she will never see me again. I am not very much impressed, because she has felt this every time I go to the East. And what, she asks, is she to do if Rosalind gets appendicitis? There seems no reason why my fourteen-year-old daughter should get appendicitis, and all I can think of to reply is: "Don't operate on her yourself!" For my sister has a great reputation for hasty action with her scissors, attacking impartially boils, haircutting, and dressmaking—usually, I must admit, with great success.

Max and I exchange relations, and my dear mother-in-law urges me to take great care of myself, implying that I am nobly going into great personal danger.

Whistles blow, and I have a last few frenzied words with my friend and secretary. Will she do all the things I have left undone, and upbraid suitably the Laundry and the Cleaners and give a good reference to the cook and send off those books I couldn't pack, and get back my umbrella from Scotland Yard, and write appropriately to the clergyman who has discovered forty-three grammatical errors in my last book, and go through the seed-list for the garden and cross off vegetable marrows and parsnips? Yes, she will do all those things, and if any crisis occurs in the Home or the Literary World she will cable me. It doesn't matter, I say. She has a power of attorney. She can do anything she likes. She looks rather alarmed and says she shall be most careful. Another whistle! I say good-bye to my sister, and say wildly that I, too, feel I shall never see her again, and perhaps Rosalind *will* get appendicitis. Nonsense, says my sister; why should she? We climb into the Pullman, the train grunts and starts—we are OFF.

For about forty-five seconds I feel terrible, and then as Victoria Station is left behind, exultation springs up once more. We have begun the lovely, exciting journey to Syria.

There is something grand and stuck-up about a Pullman, though it is not nearly as comfortable as a corner of an ordinary first-class carriage. We always go by Pullman solely on account of Max's suitcases, which an ordinary carriage would not tolerate. Having once had registered luggage go astray, Max takes no chances with his precious books.

We arrive at Dover, to find the sea moderately calm. Nevertheless I retire to the Salon des Dames, and lie and meditate with the pessimism always induced in me by the motion of the waves. But we are soon at Calais, and the French steward produces a large blue-bloused man to deal with my luggage. "Madame will find him in the Douane," he says.

"What is his number?" I ask. The steward is immediately reproachful.

"Madame! Mais c'est le charpentier du bateau!"

I become properly abashed—to reflect a few minutes later that that is not really an answer. Why, because he is the *charpentier du bateau,* does it make it any easier to pick him out from several hundred other blue-bloused men, all shouting, *"Quatre-vingt treize?"* etc. His mere silence will not be sufficient identification. Moreover, does his being the *charpentier du bateau* enable him to pick out with unerring certainty one middle-aged Englishwoman from a whole crowd of middle-aged Englishwomen?

At this point in my reflections Max joins me, and says he has a porter for my luggage. I explain that the *charpentier du bateau* has taken mine, and Max asks why I let him. All the luggage should go together. I agree, but plead that my intellect is always weakened by sea-crossings. Max says: "Oh, well; we shall collect it all in the Douane." And we proceed to that inferno of yelling porters and to the inevitable encounter with the only type of really unpleasant Frenchwoman that exists—the Customs House Female; a being devoid of charm, of *chic,* of any feminine grace. She prods, she peers, she says, *"Pas de cigarettes?"* unbelievingly, and finally, with a reluctant grunt, she scrawls the mystic hieroglyphics in chalk on our baggage, and we pass through the barrier and out on to the platform, and so to the Simplon Orient Express and the journey across Europe.

Many, many years ago, when going to the Riviera or to Paris, I used to be fascinated by the sight of the Orient Express at Calais and longed to be travelling by it. Now it has become an old familiar friend, but the thrill has never quite died down. I am going by it! I am *in* it! I am actually in the blue coach, with the simple legend outside: CALAIS-ISTANBUL. It is, undoubtedly, my favorite train. I like its tempo, which, starting *Allegro con fuore,* swaying and rattling and hurling one from side to side in its mad haste to leave Calais and the Occident, gradually slows down in a *rallantando* as it proceeds eastwards till it becomes definitely *legato.*

In the early morning of the next day I let the blind up, and watch the dim shapes of the mountains in Switzerland, then the descent into the plains of Italy, passing by lovely Stresa and its blue lake. Then, later, into the smart station that is all we see of Venice and out again, and along by the sea to Trieste and so into Yugoslavia. The pace gets slower and slower, the stops are longer, the station clocks display conflicting times. H.E.O. is succeeded by C.E. The names of the stations are written in exciting and improbable looking letters. The engines are fat and comfortable looking, and belch forth a particularly black and evil smoke. Bills in the dining-cars are written out in perplexing currencies, and bottles of strange mineral water appear. A small Frenchman who sits opposite us at table studies his bill in silence for some minutes, then he raises his head and catches Max's eye. His voice, charged with emotion, rises plaintively: *"Le change des Wagons Lits, c'est incroyable!"* Across the aisle a dark man with a hooked nose demands to be told the amount of his bill in (*a*) francs, (*b*) lire, (*c*) dinars, (*d*) Turkish pounds, (*e*) dollars. When this has been done by the long-suffering restaurant attendant, the traveller calculates silently, and evidently a master financial brain, produces the currency most advantageous to his pocket. By this method, he explains to us, he has saved fivepence in English money!

In the morning Turkish Customs officials appear on the train. They are leisurely, and deeply interested in our baggage. Why, they ask me, have I so many pairs of shoes? It is too many. But, I reply, I have no cigarettes, because I do not smoke, so why not a few more shoes? The douanier accepts the explanation. It appears to him reasonable. What, he asks, is the powder in this little tin?

It is bug powder, I say; but find that this is not understood. He frowns and looks suspicious. He is obviously suspecting me of being a drug-smuggler. It is not powder for the teeth, he says accusingly, nor for the face; for *what*, then? Vivid pantomime by me! I scratch myself realistically, I catch the interloper. I sprinkle the woodwork. Ah, all is understood! He throws back his head and roars with laughter, repeating a Turkish word. It is for *them*, the powder! He repeats the joke to a colleague. They pass on, enjoying it very much. The Wagon Lit conductor now appears to coach us. They will come with our passports to demand how much money we have *"effectif, vous comprenez?"* I love the word *effectif*—it is so exactly descriptive of actual cash in hand. "You will have," the conductor proceeds, "exactly so much *effectif!"* He names the sum. Max objects that we have more than that. "It does not matter. To say so will cause you embarrassments. You will say you have the letter of credit or the travellers' cheques and of *effectif* so much." He adds in explanation: "They do not mind, you comprehend, *what* you have, but the answer must be *en règle*. You will say—so much."

Presently the gentleman in charge of the financial questions comes along. He writes down our answer before we actually say it. All is *en règle*. And now we are arriving at Stamboul, winding in and out through strange wooden slatted houses, with glimpses of heavy stone bastions and glimpses of sea at our right.

A maddening city, Stamboul—since when you are in it you can never see it! Only when you have left the European side and are crossing the Bosphorus to the Asian coast do you really see Stamboul. Very beautiful it is this morning—a clear, shining pale morning, with no mist, and the mosques with their minarets standing up against the sky.

"La Sainte Sophie, it is very fine," says a French gentleman.

Everybody agrees, with the regrettable exception of myself. I, alas, have never admired Sainte Sophie! An unfortunate lapse of taste; but there it is. It has always seemed definitely to me the wrong size. Ashamed of my perverted ideas, I keep silent.

Now into the waiting train at Haidar Pacha, and, when at last the train starts, breakfast—a breakfast for which one is by now quite ravenous! Then a lovely day's journey along the winding coast of the Sea of Marmora, with islands dotted about looking dim and lovely. I think for the hundredth time that I should like to own one of those islands. Strange the desire for an island of one's own! Most people suffer from it sooner or later. It symbolises in one's mind liberty, solitude, freedom from all cares. Yet actually, I suppose, it would mean not liberty but imprisonment. One's housekeeping would probably depend entirely on the mainland. One would be continually writing long lists of grocery orders for the stores, arranging for meat and bread, doing all one's housework, since few domestics would care to live on an island far from friends or cinemas, without even a bus communication with their fellow-kind. A South Sea island, I always imagined, would be different! There one would sit, idly eating the best kinds of fruit, dispensing with plates, knives, forks, washing up, and the problem of grease on the sink! Actually the only South Sea islanders I ever saw having a meal were eating platefuls of hot beef stew rolling in grease, all set on a very dirty table-cloth.

No; an island is, and should be, a dream island! On that island there is no sweeping, dusting, bedmaking, laundry, washing up, grease, food problems, lists of groceries, lamp-trimming, potato-peeling, dustbins. On the dream island there is white sand and blue sea— and a fairy house, perhaps, built between sunrise and sunset; the apple tree, the singing and the gold. . . .

At this point in my reflections, Max asks me what I am thinking about. I say, simply, "Paradise!"

Max says: "Ah, wait till you see the Jaghjagha!"

I ask if it is very beautiful; and Max says he has no idea, but it is a remarkably interesting part of the world and nobody really knows anything about it!

The train winds its way up a gorge, and we leave the sea behind us.

The next morning we reach the Cilician Gates, and look out over one of the most beautiful views I know. It is like standing on the rim of the world and looking down on the promised land, and one feels much as Moses must have felt. For here, too, there is no entering in. . . . The soft, hazy dark blue loveliness is a land one will never reach; the actual towns and villages when one gets there will be only the ordinary everyday world—not this enchanted beauty that beckons you down. . . .

The train whistles. We climb back into our compartment.

On to Alep. And from Alep to Beyrout, where our architect is to meet us and where things are to get under way, for our preliminary survey of the Habur and Jaghjagha region, which will lead to the selection of a mound suitable for excavation.

For this, like Mrs. Beeton, is the start of the whole

business. First catch your hare, says that estimable lady.

So, in our case, first find your mound. That is what we are about to do.

II

A SURVEYING TRIP

BEYROUT! BLUE SEA, a curving bay, a long coastline
of hazy blue mountains. Such is the view from the ter-
race of the Hotel. From my bedroom, which looks
inland, I see a garden of scarlet poinsettias. The room
is high, distempered white, slightly prison-like in aspect.
A modern wash-basin complete with taps and waste-
pipe strikes a dashing modern note.[1] Above the basin
and connected to the taps is a large square tank with
removable lid. Inside, it is full of stale-smelling water,
connected to the cold tap only!

The arrival of plumbing in the East is full of pitfalls.
How often does the cold tap produce hot water, and
the hot tap cold! And how well do I remember a bath
in a newly equipped "Western" bathroom where an
intimidating hot-water system produced scalding water
in terrific quantities, no cold water was obtainable, the
hot-water tap would not turn off, and the bolt of the
door had stuck!

---

[1] This was written a time before the opening of the modern
Hôtel St. George.

As I contemplate the poinsettias enthusiastically and the washing facilities distastefully, there is a knock at the door. A short, squat Armenian appears, smiling ingratiatingly. He opens his mouth, points a finger down his throat, and utters encouragingly *"Manger!"*

By this simple expedient he makes it clear to the meanest intelligence that luncheon is served in the dining-room.

There I find Max awaiting me, and our new architect, Mac, whom as yet I hardly know. In a few days' time we are to set off on a three months' camping expedition to examine the country for likely sites. With us, as guide, philosopher, and friend, is to go Hamoudi, for many years foreman at Ur, an old friend of my husband's, and who is to come with us between seasons in these autumn months.

Mac rises and greets me politely, and we sit down to a very good if slightly greasy meal. I make a few would-be amiable remarks to Mac, who blocks them effectively by replying: "Oh, yes?" "Really?" "Indeed?"

I find myself somewhat damped. An uneasy conviction sweeps over me that our young architect is going to prove one of those people who from time to time succeed in rendering me completely imbecile with shyness. I have, thank goodness, long left behind me the days when I was shy of *everyone*. I have attained, with middle age, a fair amount of poise and *savoir faire*. Every now and then I congratulate myself that all that silly business is over and done with! "I've got over it," I say to myself happily. And as surely as I think so, some unexpected individual reduces me once more to nervous idiocy.

Useless to tell myself that young Mac is probably extremely shy himself and that it is his own shyness which produces his defensive armor, the fact remains that, before his coldly superior manner, his gently raised eyebrows, his air of polite attention to words that I realize cannot possibly be worth listening to, I wilt visibly, and find myself talking what I fully realize is sheer nonsense. Towards the end of the meal Mac administers a reproof.

"Surely," he says gently in reply to a desperate statement of mine about the French Horn, "that is not so?"

He is, of course, perfectly right. It is not so.

After lunch, Max asks me what I think of Mac. I reply guardedly that he doesn't seem to talk much. That, says Max, is an excellent thing. I have no idea, he says, what it is like to be stuck in the desert with someone who never stops talking! "I chose him because he seemed a silent sort of fellow."

I admit there is something in that. Max goes on to say that he is probably shy, but will soon open up. "He's probably terrified of *you*," he adds kindly.

I consider this heartening thought, but don't feel convinced by it.

I try, however, to give myself a little mental treatment.

First of all, I say to myself, you are old enough to be Mac's mother. You are also an authoress—a well-known authoress. Why, one of your characters has even been the clue in a *Times* crossword. (High-water mark of fame!) And what is more, you are the wife of the Leader of the Expedition! Come now, if any one is to snub any one, it is *you* who will snub the young man, not the young man who will snub you.

Later, we decide to go out to tea, and I go along to Mac's room to ask him to come with us. I determine to be natural and friendly.

The room is unbelievably neat, and Mac is sitting on a folded plaid rug writing in his diary. He looks up in polite inquiry.

"Won't you come out with us and have tea?"

Mac rises.

"Thank you!"

"Afterwards, I expect you'd like to explore the town," I suggest. "It's fun poking round a new place."

Mac raises his eyebrows gently and says coldly: "Is it?"

Somewhat deflated, I lead the way to the hall where Max is waiting for us. Mac consumes a large tea in happy silence. Max is eating tea in the present, but his mind is roughly about 4000 B.C.

He comes out of his reverie with a sudden start as the last cake is eaten, and suggests that we go and see how our lorry is getting on.

We go forthwith to look at our lorry—a Ford chassis, to which a native body is being built. We have had to fall back on this as no second-hand one was to be obtained in sufficiently good condition.

The bodywork seems definitely optimistic, of the "Inshallah" nature, and the whole thing has a high and dignified appearance that is suspiciously too good to be true. Max is a little worried at the non-appearance of Hamoudi, who was to have met us in Beyrout by this date.

Mac scorns to look at the town and returns to his bedroom to sit on his rug and write in his diary. Interested speculation on my part as to what he writes in the diary.

An early awakening. At 5 A.M. our bedroom door opens, and a voice announces in Arabic: "Your foremen have come!"

Hamoudi and his two sons surge into the room with the eager charm that distinguishes them, seizing our hands, pressing them against their foreheads. "Shlon kefek?" (How is your comfort.) "Kullish zen." (Very well.) "El hamdu lillah! El hamdu lillah!" (We all praise God together!)

Shaking off the mists of sleep, we order tea, and Hamoudi and his sons squat down comfortably on the floor and proceed to exchange news with Max. The language barrier excludes me from this conversation. I have used all the Arabic I know. I long wistfully for sleep, and even wish that the Hamoudi family had postponed their greetings to a more reasonable hour. Still, I realize that to them it is the most natural thing in the world thus to arrive.

Tea dispels the mists of sleep, and Hamoudi addresses various remarks to me, which Max translates, as also my replies. All three of them beam with happiness, and I realize anew what very delightful people they are.

Preparations are now in full swing—buying of stores; engaging of a chauffeur and a cook; visits to the Service des Antiquités; a delightful lunch with M. Seyrig, the Director; and his very charming wife. Nobody could be kinder to us than they are—and, incidentally, the lunch is delicious.

Disagreeing with the Turkish Douanier's opinion that I have too many shoes, I proceed to buy more shoes! Shoes in Beyrout are a delight to buy. If your size is not available, they are made for you in a couple of days—of good leather, perfectly fitting. It must be admitted that buying shoes is a weakness of mine. I shall not dare to return home through Turkey!

We wander through the native quarters and buy interesting lengths of material—a kind of thick white silk, embroidered in golden thread or in dark blue. We buy silk *abas* to send home as presents. Max is fascinated with all the different kinds of bread. Any one with French blood in him loves good bread. Bread to a Frenchman means more than any other kind of food. I have heard an officer of the Services Spéciaux say of a colleague in a lonely frontier outpost: *"Ce pauvre garçon! Il n'a même pas de pain là bas, seulement la galette Kurde!"* with deep and heartfelt pity.

We also have long and complicated dealings with the Bank. I am struck, as always in the East, with the reluctance of banks to do any business whatever. They are polite, charming, but anxious to evade any actual transaction. *"Oui, oui!"* they murmur sympathetically. *"Ecrivez une lettre!"* And they settle down again with a sigh of relief at having postponed any action.

When action has been reluctantly forced upon them, they take revenge by a complicated system of *"les timbres."* Every document, every cheque, every transaction whatever, is held up and complicated by a demand for "les timbres." Continual small sums are disbursed. When everything is, as you think, finished, once more comes a hold-up!

"Et deux francs cinquante centimes pour les timbres, s'il vous plaît."

Still, at last transactions are completed, innumerable letters are written, incredible numbers of stamps are affixed. With a sigh of relief the Bank clerk sees a prospect of finally getting rid of us. As we leave the Bank, we hear him say firmly to another importunate client: *"Ecrivez une lettre, s'il vous plaît."*

There still remains the engaging of a cook and chauffeur.

The chauffeur problem is solved first. Hamoudi arrives, beaming, and informs us that we are in good fortune—he has secured for us an excellent chauffeur.

How, Max asks, has Hamoudi obtained this treasure?

Very simply, it appears. He was standing on the waterfront, and having had no job for some time, and being completely destitute, he will come very cheap. Thus, at once, we have effected an economy!

But is there any means of knowing whether he is a good chauffeur? Hamoudi waves such a question aside. A baker is a man who puts bread in an oven and bakes it. A chauffeur is a man who takes a car out and drives it!

Max, without any undue enthusiasm, agrees to engage Abdullah if nothing better offers, and Abdullah is summoned to an interview. He bears a remarkable resemblance to a camel, and Max says with a sigh that at any rate he seems stupid, and that is always satisfactory. I ask why, and Max says because he won't have the brains to be dishonest.

On our last afternoon in Beyrout we drive out to the Dog River, the Nahr el Kelb. Here, in a wooded gully running inland, is a café where you can drink coffee, and then wander pleasantly along a shady path.

But the real fascination of the Nahr el Kelb lies in the carved inscriptions on the rock where a pathway leads up to the pass over the Lebanon. For here, in countless wars, armies have marched and left their record. Here are Egyptian hieroglyphics—of Rameses II, and boasts made by Assyrian and Babylonian armies. There is the figure of Tiglathpileser I. Sennacherib left an inscription in 701 B.C. Alexander passed and left his record. Esarhaddon and Nebuchadrezzar have commemorated their victories and finally, linking up with antiquity, Allenby's army wrote names and initials in 1917. I never tire of looking at that carved surface of rock. Here is history made manifest. . . .

I am so far carried away as to remark enthusiastically to Mac that it is really very thrilling, and doesn't he think so?

Mac raises his polite eyebrows, and says in a completely uninterested voice that it is, of course, very interesting. . . .

The arrival and loading up of our lorry is the next excitement. The body of the lorry looks definitely top-heavy. It sways and dips, but has withal such an air of dignity—indeed of majesty—that it is promptly christened Queen Mary.

In addition to Queen Mary we hire a "taxi"—a Citröen driven by an amiable Armenian called Aristide. We engage a somewhat melancholy looking cook ('Isa), whose testimonials are so good as to be highly suspicious. And finally, the great day comes, and we set out—Max, Hamoudi, myself, Mac, Abdullah, Aristide and 'Isa—to be companions, for better, for worse, for the next three months.

Our first discovery is that Abdullah is quite the worst driver imaginable, our second is that the cook is a pretty bad cook, our third is that Aristide is a good driver but has an incredibly bad taxi!

We drive out of Beyrout along the coast road. We pass the Nahr el Kelb, and continue on with the sea on our left. We pass small clusters of white houses and entrancing little sandy bays, and small coves between rocks. I long to stop and bathe, but we have started now on the real business of life. Soon, too soon, we shall turn inland from the sea, and after that, for many months, we shall not see the sea again.

Aristide honks his horn ceaselessly in the Syrian fashion. Behind us Queen Mary is following, dipping and bending like a ship at sea with her top-heavy body-work.

We pass Byblos, and now the little clusters of white houses are few and far between. On our right is the rocky hillside.

And at last we turn off and strike inland for Homs.

There is a good hotel at Homs—a very fine hotel, Hamoudi has told us.

The grandeur of the hotel proves to be mainly in the building itself. It is spacious, with immense stone corridors. Its plumbing, alas, is not functioning very well! Its vast bedrooms contain little in the way of comfort. We look at ours respectfully, and then Max and I go out to see the town. Mac, we find, is sitting on the side of his bed, folded rug beside him, writing earnestly in his diary.

(*What* does Mac put in his diary? He displays no enthusiasm to have a look at Homs.)

Perhaps he is right, for there is not very much to see.

We have a badly cooked pseudo-European meal and retire to bed.

Yesterday we were travelling within the confines of civilization. Today, abruptly, we leave civilization behind. Within an hour or two there is no green to be seen anywhere. Everything is brown sandy waste. The tracks seem confusing. Sometimes at rare intervals we meet a lorry, that comes up suddenly out of nothingness.

It is very hot. What with the heat and the uneven-ness of the track and the badness of the taxi's springs, and the dust that you swallow and makes your face stiff and hard, I start a furious headache.

There is something frightening, and yet fascinating,

about this vast world denuded of vegetation. It is not flat like the desert between Damascus and Baghdad. Instead, you climb up and down. It feels a little as though you had become a grain of sand among the sand-castles you built on the beach as a child.

And then, after seven hours of heat and monotony and a lonely world—Palmyra!

That, I think, is the charm of Palmyra—its slender creamy beauty rising up fantastically in the middle of hot sand. It is lovely and fantastic and unbelievable, with all the theatrical implausibility of a dream. Courts and temples and ruined columns. . . .

I have never been able to decide what I really think of Palmyra. It has always for me the dream-like quality of that first vision. My aching head and eyes made it more than ever seem a feverish delusion! It isn't—it can't be—*real*.

But suddenly we are in the middle of people—a crowd of cheerful French tourists, laughing and talking and snapping cameras. We pull up in front of a handsome building—the Hotel.

Max warns me hurriedly: "You mustn't mind the smell. It takes a little getting used to."

It certainly does! The Hotel is charming inside, arranged with real taste and charm. But the smell of stale water in the bedroom is very strong.

"It's quite a healthy smell," Max assures me.

And the charming elderly gentleman, who is, I understand, the Hotel proprietor, says with great emphasis: "Mauvaise odeur, *oui!* Malsain, *non!*"

So that is settled! And, anyway, I do not care. I take aspirin and drink tea and lie down on the bed. Later, I say, I will do sight-seeing—just now I care for nothing but darkness and rest.

Inwardly I feel a little dismayed. Am I going to be a bad traveller—I, who have always enjoyed motoring?

However, I wake up an hour later, feeling perfectly restored and eager to see what can be seen.

Mac, even, for once submits to being torn from his diary.

We go out sight-seeing, and spend a delightful afternoon.

When we are at the farthest point from the Hotel we run into the party of French people. They are in distress. One of the women, who is wearing (as all are) high-heeled shoes, has torn off the heel of her shoe, and is faced with the impossibility of walking back the distance to the Hotel. They have driven out to this point, it appears, in a taxi, and the taxi has now broken down. We cast an eye over it. There appears to be but one kind of taxi in this country. This vehicle is indistinguishable from ours—the same dilapidated upholstery and general air of being tied up with string. The driver, a tall, lank Syrian, is poking in a dispirited fashion into the bonnet.

He shakes his head. The French party explain all. They have arrived here by 'plane yesterday, and will leave the same way to-morrow. This taxi they have hired for the afternoon at the Hotel, and now it has broken down. What will poor Madame do? *"Impossible de marcher, n'est ce pas, avec un soulier seulement."*

We pour out condolences, and Max gallantly offers our taxi. He will return to the Hotel and bring it out here. It can make two journeys and take us all back.

The suggestion is received with acclamations and profuse thanks, and Max sets off.

I fraternise with the French ladies, and Mac retires behind an impenetrable wall of reserve. He produces a stark "Oui" or "Non" to any conversational openings, and is soon mercifully left in peace. The French ladies profess a charming interest in our journeyings.

"Ah, Madame, vous faites le camping?"

I am fascinated by the phrase. *Le camping!* It classes our adventure definitely as a sport!

How agreeable it will be, says another lady, to do *le camping*.

Yes, I say, it will be very agreeable.

The time passes; we chat and laugh. Suddenly, to my great surprise, Queen Mary comes lurching along. Max, with an angry face, is at the wheel.

I demand why he hasn't brought the taxi?

"Because," says Max furiously, "the taxi is *here*." And he points a dramatic finger at the obdurate car, into which the lank Syrian is still optimistically peering.

There is a chorus of surprised exclamations, and I realize why the car has looked so familiar! "But," cries the French lady, "this is the car we hired at the Hotel." Nevertheless, Max explains, it is *our* taxi.

Explanations with Aristide have been painful. Neither side has appreciated the other's point of view.

"Have I not hired the taxi and you for three months?" demands Max. "And must you let it out to others behind my back in this shameful way?"

"But," says Aristide, all injured innocence, "did you not tell me that you yourself would not use it this afternoon? Naturally, then, I have the chance to make a little extra money. I arrange with a friend, and he drives this party round Palmyra. How can it injure you, since you do not want to sit in the car yourself?"

"It injures me," replies Max, "since in the first place it was not our arrangement; and in the second place the car is now in need of repair, and in all probability will not be able to proceed to-morrow!"

"As to that," says Aristide, "do not disquiet yourself. My friend and I will, if necessary, sit up all night!"

Max replies briefly that they'd better.

Sure enough, the next morning the faithful taxi awaits us in front of the door, with Aristide smiling, and still quite unconvinced of sin, at the wheel.

To-day we arrive at Der Ez Zor, on the Euphrates. It is very hot. The town smells and is not attractive. The Services Spéciaux kindly puts some rooms at our disposal, since there is no European hotel. There is an attractive view over the wide brown flow of the river. The French officer inquires tenderly after my health, and hopes I have not found motoring in the heat too much for me. "Madame Jacquot, the wife of our General, was *complètement knock out* when she arrived."

The term takes my fancy. I hope that I, in my turn, shall not be *complètement knock out* by the end of our survey!

We buy vegetables and large quantities of eggs, and with Queen Mary full to the point of breaking her springs, we set off, this time to start on the survey proper.

Busaira! Here there is a police post. It is a spot of which Max has had high hopes, since it is at the junction of the Euphrates with the Habur. Roman Circesium is on the opposite bank.

Busaira proves, however, disappointing. There are no signs of any antique settlement other than Roman, which is treated with the proper disgust. "Min ziman er Rum," says Hamoudi, shaking his head distastefully, and I echo him dutifully.

For to our point of view the Romans are hopelessly modern—children of yesterday. Our interest begins at the second millennium B.C., with the varying fortunes of the Hittites, and in particular we want to find out more about the military dynasty of Mitanni, foreign adventurers about whom little is known, but who flourished in this part of the world, and whose capital city of Washshukkanni has yet to be identified. A ruling caste of warriors, who imposed their rule on the country, and who intermarried with the Royal House of Egypt, and who were, it seems, good horsemen, since a treatise upon the care and training of horses is ascribed to a certain Kikkouli, a man of Mitanni.

And from that period backwards, of course, into the dim ages of pre-history—an age without written records, when only pots, and house plans, and amulets, ornaments, and beads, remain to give their dumb witness to the life the people lived.

Busaira, having been disappointing, we go on to Meyadin, farther south, though Max has not much hope of it. After that we will strike northward up the left bank of the Habur river.

It is at Busaira that I get my first sight of the Habur,

which has so far been only a name to me—though a name that has been repeatedly on Max's lips.

"The Habur—that's the place. Hundreds of Tells!"

He goes on: "And if we don't find what we want on the Habur, we will on the Jaghjagha!"

"What," I ask, the first time I hear the name, "is the Jaghjagha?"

The name seems to me quite fantastic!

Max says kindly that he supposes I have never heard of the Jaghjagha? A good many people haven't, he concedes.

I admit the charge and add that until he mentioned it, I had not even heard of the Habur. That does surprise him.

"Didn't you know," says Max, marvelling at my shocking ignorance, "that Tell Halaf is on the Habur?"

His voice is lowered in reverence as he speaks of that famous site of prehistoric pottery.

I shake my head and forbear to point out that if I had not happened to marry him I should probably never have heard of Tell Halaf!

I may say that explaining the places where we dig to people is always fraught with a good deal of difficulty.

My first answer is usually one word—"Syria."

"Oh!" says the average inquirer, already slightly taken aback. A frown forms on his or her forehead. "Yes, of course—Syria. . . ." Biblical memories stir. "Let me see, that's Palestine, isn't it?"

"It's next to Palestine," I say encouragingly. "You know—farther up the coast."

This doesn't really help, because Palestine, being usually connected with Bible history and the lessons on Sunday rather than a geographical situation, has associations that are purely literary and religious.

"I can't quite place it." The frown deepens. "Whereabouts do you dig—I mean near what *town?*"

"Not near any town. Near the Turkish and Iraq border."

A hopeless expression then cames across the friend's face.

"But surely you must be near *some* town!"

"Alep," I say, "is about two hundred miles away."

They sigh and give it up. Then, brightening, they ask what we eat. "Just dates, I suppose?"

When I say that we have mutton, chickens, eggs, rice, French beans, aubergines, cucumbers, oranges in season and bananas, they look at me reproachfully. "I don't call that *roughing* it," they say.

At Meyadin *le camping* begins.

A chair is set up for me, and I sit in it grandly in the midst of a large courtyard, or khan; whilst Max, Mac, Aristide, Hamoudi, and Abdullah struggle to set up our tents.

There is no doubt that I have the best of it. It is a richly entertaining spectacle. There is a strong desert wind blowing which does not help, and everybody is raw to the job. Appeals to the compassion and mercy of God rise from Abdullah, demands to be assisted by the saints from Armenian Aristide, wild yells of encouragement and laughter are offered by Hamoudi, furious imprecations come from Max. Only Mac toils in silence, though even he occasionally mutters a quiet word under his breath.

At last all is ready. The tents look a little drunken, a little out of the true, but they have arisen. We all unite in cursing the cook, who, instead of starting to prepare a meal, has been enjoying the spectacle. However, we have some useful tins, which are opened, tea is made, and now, as the sun sinks and the wind drops and a sudden chill arises, we go to bed. It is my first experience of struggling into a sleeping-bag. It takes the united efforts of Max and myself, but, once inside, I am enchantingly comfortable. I always take abroad with me one really good soft down pillow —to me it makes all the difference between comfort and misery.

I say happily to Max: "I think I like sleeping in a tent!"

Then a sudden thought occurs to me.

"You don't think, do you, that rats or mice or something will run across me in the night?"

"Sure to," says Max cheerfully and sleepily.

I am digesting this thought when sleep overtakes me, and I wake to find it is five A.M.—sunrise, and time to get up and start a new day.

The mounds in the immediate neighborhood of Meyadin prove unattractive.

"Roman!" murmurs Max disgustedly. It is his last word of contempt. Stifling any lingering feeling I may have that the Romans were an interesting people, I echo his tone, and say "Roman," and cast down a fragment of the despised pottery. "Min Ziman . . . er Rum," says Hamoudi.

In the afternoon we go to visit the American dig at Doura. It is a pleasant visit, and they are charming to us. Yet I find my interest in the finds flagging, and an increasing difficulty in listening or in taking part in the conversation.

Their account of their original difficulties in getting workmen is amusing.

Working for wages in this out-of-the-way part of the world is an idea that is entirely new. The expedition found itself faced with blank refusal or non-comprehension. In despair they appealed to the French military authorities. The response was prompt and efficient. The French arrested two hundred, or whatever the number needed was, and delivered them at work. The prisoners were amiable, in the highest good humour, and seemed to enjoy the work. They were told to return on the following day, but did not turn up. Again the French were asked to help, and once again they arrested the workmen. Again the men worked with evident satisfaction. But yet again they failed to turn up, and once again military arrest was resorted to.

Finally the matter was elucidated.

"Do you not like working for us?"

"Yes, indeed, why not? We have nothing to do at home."

"Then why do you not come every day?"

"We wish to come, but naturally we have to wait for the 'asker (soldiers) to fetch us. I can tell you, we were very indignant when they did not come to fetch us! It is their duty!"

"But we want you to work for us without the 'asker fetching you!"

"That is a very curious idea!"

At the end of a week they were paid, and that finally set the seal on their bewilderment.

Truly, they said, they could not understand the ways of foreigners!

"The French 'asker are in command here. Naturally, it is their right to fetch us, and put us in prison or send us to dig up the ground for you. But why do you give us money? What is the money *for?* It does not make sense!"

However, in the end the strange customs of the West were accepted, howbeit with head shakings and mutterings. Once a week money was paid them. But a vague grudge against the 'asker remained. The 'asker's job was to fetch them every day!

Whether true or not, this makes a good story! I only wish I could feel more intelligent. What is the matter with me? When I get back to camp my head is swimming. I take my temperature, and find that it is a hundred and two! Also, I have a pain in my middle, and feel extremely sick. I am very glad to crawl into my flea-bag and go to sleep, spurning the thought of dinner.

Max looks worried this morning and asks me how I feel. I groan and say: "Like death!" He looks more worried. He asks me if I think I am really ill?

I reassure him on that point. I have what is called in

Egypt a Gippy tummy and in Baghdad a Baghdad tummy. It is not a very amusing complaint to have when you are right out in the desert. Max cannot leave me behind alone, and in any case the inside of the tent in the day-time registers about 130! The survey must go on. I sit huddled up in the car, swaying about in a feverish dream. When we reach a mound, I get out and lie down in what shade the height of Queen Mary affords, whilst Max and Mac tramp over the mound, examining it.

Frankly, the next four days are sheer unmitigated hell! One of Hamoudi's stories seems particularly apposite—that of a Sultan's lovely wife, whom he carried off, and who bewailed to Allah night and day that she had no companions and was alone in the desert. "And at last Allah, weary of her moanings, sent her companions. He sent her the flies!"

I feel particularly venomous towards the lovely lady for incurring the wrath of Allah! All day long flies settling in clouds make it impossible to rest.

I regret bitterly that I have ever come on this expedition, but just manage not to say so.

After four days, with nothing but weak tea without milk, I suddenly revive. Life is good again. I eat a colossal meal of rice and stew of vegetables swimming in grease. It seems the most delicious thing I have ever tasted!

After it, we climb up the mound at which we have pitched our camp—Tell Suwar, on the left bank of the Habur. Here there is nothing—no village, no habitation of any kind, not even any Beduin tents.

There is a moon above, and below us the Habur winds in a great S-shaped curve. The night air smells sweet after the heat of the day.

I say: "What a lovely mound! Can't we dig here?"

Max shakes his head sadly and pronounces the word of doom.

"Roman."

"What a pity. It's such a lovely spot."

"I told you," said Max, "that the Habur was the place! Tells all along it on either side."

I have taken no interest in Tells for several days, but I am glad to find I have not missed much.

"Are you sure there isn't any of the stuff you want here?" I ask wistfully. I have taken a fancy to Tell Suwar.

"Yes, of course there is, but it's underneath. We'd have to dig right down through the Roman stuff. We can do better than that."

I sigh and murmur: "It's so still here and so peaceful—not a soul in sight."

At that moment a very old man appears from nowhere at all.

Where has he come from? He walks up the side of the mound slowly, without haste. He has a long white beard and ineffable dignity.

He salutes Max politely. "How is your comfort?" "Well. And yours?" "Well." "Praise God!" "Praise God!"

He sits down beside us. There is a long silence—that courteous silence of good manners that is so restful after Western haste.

Finally the old man inquires Max's name. Max tells it him. He considers it.

"Milwan," he repeats. "Milwan . . . How light! How bright! How beautiful!"

He sits with us a little longer. Then, as quietly as he has come, he leaves us. We never see him again.

Restored to health, I now really begin to enjoy myself. We start every morning at early dawn, examining each mound as we come to it, walking round and round it, picking up any sherds of pottery. Then we compare results on the top, and Max keeps such specimens as are useful, putting them in a little linen bag and labelling them.

There is great competition between us as to who gets the prize find of the day.

I begin to understand why archaeologists have a habit of walking with eyes downcast to the ground. Soon, I feel, I myself shall forget to look around me, or out to the horizon. I shall walk looking down at my feet as though there only any interest lies.

I am struck as often before by the fundamental difference of race. Nothing could differ more widely than the attitude of our two chauffeurs to money. Abdullah lets hardly a day pass without clamouring for an advance of salary. If he had had his way we would have had the entire amount in advance, and it would, I rather imagine, have been dissipated before a week was out. With Arab prodigality Abdullah would have splashed it about in the coffee-house. He would have cut a figure! He would have "made a reputation for himself."

Aristide, the Armenian, has displayed the greatest reluctance to have a penny for his salary paid him. "You will keep it for me, Khwaja, until the journey is finished. If I want money for some little expense I will come to you." So far he has demanded only fourpence of his salary—to purchase a pair of socks!

His chin is now adorned by a sprouting beard, which makes him look quite a Biblical figure. It is cheaper, he explains, not to shave. One saves the money one might have to spend on a razor blade. And it does not matter here in the desert.

At the end of the trip Abdullah will be penniless once more, and will doubtless be again adorning the water-front of Beyrout, waiting with Arab fatalism for the goodness of God to provide him with another job. Aristide will have the money he has earned untouched.

"And what will you do with it?" Max asks him.

"It will go towards buying a better taxi," replies Aristide.

"And when you have a better taxi?"

"Then I shall earn more and have two taxis."

I can quite easily foresee returning to Syria in twenty

years' time, and finding Aristide the immensely rich owner of a large garage, and probably living in a big house in Beyrout. And even then, I dare say, he will avoid shaving in the desert because it saves the price of a razor blade.

And yet Aristide has not been brought up by his own people. One day, as we pass some Beduin, he is hailed by them, and cries back to them, waving and shouting affectionately.

"That," he explains, "is the Anaizah tribe, of whom I am one."

"How is that?" Max asks.

And then Aristide, in his gentle, happy voice, with his quite cheerful smile, tells the story. The story of a little boy of seven, who with his family and other Armenian families was thrown by the Turks alive into a deep pit. Tar was poured on them and set alight. His father and mother and two brothers and sisters were all burnt alive. But he, who was below them all, was still alive when the Turks left, and he was found later by some of the Anaizah Arabs. They took the little boy with them and adopted him into the Anaizah tribe. He was brought up as an Arab, wandering with them over their pastures. But when he was eighteen he went into Mosul, and there demanded that papers be given him to show his nationality. He was an Armenian, not an Arab! Yet the blood brotherhood still holds, and to members of the Anaizah he still is one of them.

Hamoudi and Max are very gay together. They laugh and sing and cap stories. Sometimes I ask for a translation when the mirth is particularly hilarious. There are moments when I feel envious of the fun they are having. Mac is still separated from me by an impassable barrier. We sit together at the back of the car in silence. Any remark I make is considered gravely on its merits by Mac and disposed of accordingly. Never have I felt less of a social success! Mac, on the other hand, seems quite happy. There is about him a beautiful self-sufficiency which I cannot but admire.

Nevertheless, when, encased in my sleeping-bag at night in the privacy of our tent. I hold forth to Max on the incidents of the day, I strenuously maintain that Mac is *not* quite human!

When Mac does advance an original comment it is usually of a damping nature. Adverse criticism seems to afford him a definite gloomy satisfaction.

Am perplexed to-day by the growing uncertainty of my walking powers. In some curious way my feet don't seem to match. I am puzzled by a decided list to port. Is it, I wonder fearfully, the first symptoms of some tropical disease?

I ask Max if he has noticed that I can't walk straight.

"But you never drink," he replies. "Heaven knows," he adds reproachfully, "I've tried hard enough with you."

This introduces a second and controversial subject. Everyone struggles through life with some unfortunate disability. Mine is to be unable to appreciate either alcohol or tobacco.

If I could only bring myself to disapprove of these essential products my self-respect would be saved. But, on the contrary, I look with envy at self-possessed women flipping cigarette ash here, there, and everywhere, and creep miserably round the room at cocktail parties finding a place to hide my untasted glass.

Perseverance has not availed. For six months I religiously smoked a cigarette after lunch and after dinner, choking a little, biting fragments of tobacco, and blinking as the ascending smoke pricked my eyelid. Soon, I told myself, I should learn to like smoking. I did not learn to like it, and my performance was criticized severely as being inartistic and painful to watch. I accepted defeat.

When I married Max we enjoyed the pleasures of the table in perfect harmony, eating wisely but much too well. He was distressed to find that my appreciation of good drink—or, indeed, of any drink, was *nil*. He set to work to educate me, trying me perseveringly with clarets, burgundies, sauternes, graves, and, more desperately, with tokay, vodka, and absinthe! In the end he acknowledged defeat. My only reaction was that some tasted worse than others! With a weary sigh, Max contemplated a life in which he should be for ever condemned to the battle of obtaining water for me in a restaurant! It has added, he says, years to his life.

Hence his remarks when I enlist his sympathy for my drunken progress.

"I seem," I explain, "to be always falling over to the left."

Max says it is probably one of these very rare tropical diseases that are distinguished by just being called by somebody's name. Stephenson's disease—or Hartley's. The sort of thing, he goes on cheerfully, which will probably end with your toes falling off one by one.

I contemplate this pleasing prospect. Then it occurs to me to look at my shoes. The mystery is at once explained. The outer sole of my left foot and the inner sole of the right foot are worn right down. As I stare at them the full solution dawns on me. Since leaving Der-ez-Zor I have walked round about fifty mounds, at different levels, on the side of a steep slope, but always with the hill on my left. All that is needed is to go into reverse, and go round mounds to the right instead of the left. In due course my shoes will then be worn even.

Today we arrive at Tell Ajaja, the former Arban, a large and important Tell.

The main track from Der-ez-Zor joins in near here, so we feel now we are practically on a main road. Actually we pass three cars, all going hell-for-leather in the direction of Der-ez-Zor!

Small clusters of mud houses adorn the Tell, and various people pass the time of day with us upon the big mound. This is practically civilization. Tomorrow we shall arrive at Hasetshe, the junction of the Habur and the Jaghjagha. Then we shall be *in* civilization. It is a French military post, and an important town in this part of the world. There I shall have my first sight of the legendary and long-promised Jaghjagha river! I feel quite excited.

Our arrival at Hasetshe is full of excitement. It is an unattractive place, with streets and a few shops and a post office. We pay two ceremonious visits—one to the Military and one to the Post Office.

The French Lieutenant is most kind and helpful. He offers us hospitality, but we assure him that our tents are quite comfortable where we have pitched them by the river bank. We accept, however, an invitation to dinner on the following day. The Post Office, where we go for letters, is a longer business. The Postmaster is out, and everything is consequently locked up. However, a small boy goes in search of him, and in due course (half an hour!) he arrives, full of urbanity, bids us welcome to Hasetshe, orders coffee for us, and only after a prolonged exchange of compliments comes to the business in hand—letters.

"But there is no hurry," he says, beaming. "Come again tomorrow. I shall be delighted to entertain you."

"Tomorrow," Max says, "we have work to do. We should like our letters tonight."

Ah, but here is the coffee! We sit and sip. At long last, after polite exhortations, the Postmaster unlocks his private office and starts to search. In the generosity of his heart he urges on us additional letters addressed to other Europeans. "You had better have these," he says. "They have been here six months. No one has come for them. Yes, yes, surely they will be for you."

Politely but firmly, we refuse the correspondence of Mr. Johnson, M. Mavrogordata, and Mr. Pye. The Postmaster is disappointed.

"So few?" he says. "But come, will you not have this large one here?"

But we insist on sticking strictly to those letters and papers that bear our own names. A money order has come, as arranged, and Max now goes into the question of cashing it. This, it seems, is incredibly complicated. The Postmaster has never seen a money order before, we gather, and is very properly suspicious of it. He calls in two assistants, and the question is debated thoroughly, though with great good humor. Here is something entirely novel and delightful on which everyone can have a different opinion.

The matter is finally settled and various forms signed, when the discovery is made that there is no actual cash in the Post Office! This, the Postmaster says, can be remedied on the morrow. He will send out and collect it from the Bazaar.

We leave the Post Office somewhat exhausted, and walk back to the spot by the river which we have chosen—a little way from the dust and dirt of Hasetshe. A sad spectacle greets us. 'Isa, the cook, is sitting by the cooking-tent, his head in his hands, weeping bitterly.

What has happened?

Alas, he replies, he is disgraced. Little boys have collected round to jeer at him. His honor has gone! In a moment of inattention dogs have devoured the dinner he had prepared. There is nothing left, nothing at all but some rice.

Gloomily we eat plain rice, whilst Hamoudi, Aristide, and Abdullah reiterate to the wretched 'Isa that the principal duty of a cook is never to let his attention wander from the dinner he is cooking until the moment when that dinner is safely set before those for whom it is destined.

'Isa says that he feels he is unequal to the strain of being a cook. He has never been one before ("That explains a good deal!" says Max), and would prefer to go into a garage. Will Max give him a recommendation as a first-class driver?

Max says certainly not, as he has never seen him drive.

"But," says 'Isa, "I have wound the handle of Big
Mary on a cold morning. You have seen that?"

Max admits that he has seen that.

"Then," says 'Isa, "you can recommend me!"

III

THE HABUR AND
THE JAGHJAGHA

THESE AUTUMN DAYS are some of the most perfect I
have ever known. We get up early, soon after sunrise,
drink hot tea, and eat eggs and start off. It is cold
then, and I wear two jerseys and a big woolly coat. The
light is lovely—a very faint soft rose softens the browns
and greys. From the top of a mound one looks out
over an apparently deserted world. Mounds rise everywhere—one can see perhaps sixty if one counts. Sixty
ancient settlements, that is to say. Here, where nowadays only the tribesmen move with their brown tents,
was once a busy part of the world. Here, some five
thousand years ago, was *the* busy part of the world.
Here were the beginnings of civilization, and here,
picked up by me, this broken fragment of a clay pot,
hand made, with a design of dots and cross-hatching
in black paint, is the forerunner of the Woolworth cup
out of which this very morning I have drunk my tea. . . .

I sort through the collection of sherds which are
bulging the pockets of my coat (I have already had
to mend the lining twice), throwing away duplicate

types, and see what I can offer in competition with Mac and Hamoudi to the Master for judgment.

Now then, what have I got?

A thickish grey ware, part of the rim of a pot (valuable as showing shape), some coarse red stuff, two fragments of painted pots, hand-made and one with the dot design (the oldest Tell Halaf!), a flint knife, part of the base of a thin grey pot, several other nondescript bits of painted pottery, a little bit of obsidian.

Max makes his selection, flinging most pieces ruthlessly away, uttering appreciative grunts at others. Hamoudi has the clay wheel of a chariot, and Mac has a fragment of incised ware and a portion of a figurine.

Gathering the united collection together, Max sweeps them into a little linen bag, ties it carefully up, and labels it as usual with the name of the Tell on which it was found. This particular Tell is not marked on the map. It is christened Tel Mak in honor of Macartney who has had the first find.

So far as Mac's countenance can express anything at all, it seems to express faint gratification.

We run down the side of the Tell and climb into the car. I peel off a jersey. The sun is getting hot.

We visit two more small Tells, and at the third, which overlooks the Habur, we have lunch—hard-boiled eggs, a tin of bully beef, oranges, and extremely stale bread. Aristide makes tea on the primus. It is very hot now, and the shadows and colors have gone. All is a uniform soft pale buff.

Max says it is lucky we are doing the survey now and not in spring. I ask why? And he says, because it would be far more difficult to fine sherds when there is vegetation everywhere. All this, he says, will be green in the spring. It is, he says, the fertile Steppe. I say admiringly that that is a very grand way of putting it. Max says, well it *is* the fertile Steppe!

Today we take Mary up the right bank of the Habur to Tell Halaf, visiting Tell Ruman (sinister name, but actually not noticeably Roman) and Tell Juma on the way.

All the Tells in this region have possibilities, unlike the ones farther south. Sherds of pottery of the second and third millennium are frequent and Roman remains are scanty. There is early prehistoric painted hand-made pottery as well. The difficulty will be to choose between so many Tells. Max repeats again and again with jubilation and a complete lack of originality that this is undoubtedly the place!

Our visit to Tell Halaf has something of the reverence of a pilgrimage to a shrine! Tell Halaf is a name that has been so constantly dinned into my ears for the last few years that I can hardly believe I am actually going to see the actual spot. A very lovely spot it is, with the Habur winding round the base of it.

I recall a visit we paid to Baron von Oppenheim in Berlin when he took us to the Museum of his finds. Max and he talked excitedly for (I think) five solid hours. There was nowhere to sit down. My interest, at first acute, flagged, and finally died down completely. With lack-lustre eyes I examined the various extremely ugly statues which had come from Tell Halaf, and which in the Baron's view were contemporary with the extremely interesting pottery. Max was endeavoring to differ politely on this point without contradicting him flatly. To my dazed glance all the statues seemed strangely alike. It was only after a little while that I made the discovery that they *were* alike, since all but one were plaster reproductions.

Baron von Oppenheim stopped in his eager dissertation to say lovingly: "Ah, my beautiful Venus," and stroke the figure affectionately. Then he plunged back into discussion, and I wished sadly that I could, in the old nursery phrase, cut off my feet and turn up the ends!

We have many local conversations on the various mounds approaching Tell Halaf. All hereabouts are various legends of El Baron—mainly the incredible sums he paid out in gold. Time has exaggerated the amount of gold. Even the German government, one feels, cannot have poured out the streams of precious metal in the way tradition has it! Everywhere north of Hasetshe are small villages and signs of cultivation. Since the arrival of the French and the departure of the Turkish rule, the country is being occupied again for the first time since Roman days.

We get home late. The weather is changing, a wind starts blowing, and it is very unpleasant, dust and sand flying in one's face and making one's eyes smart. We have a pleasant dinner with the French, though it has been a difficult business smartening oneself up, or rather, I should say, cleaning oneself up, since a clean blouse for myself and clean shirts for the men is all one can do! We have an excellent dinner and spend a very pleasant evening. We return through driving rain to our tents. An unquiet night, with dogs howling and the tents flapping and straining in the wind.

Forsaking the Habur for the time being, we make an excursion today on the Jaghjagha. An immense mound quite near at hand has excited my interest, until I discover that it is an extinct volcano—the Kawkab.

Our particular objective is one Tell Hamidi, of which we have heard good accounts, but it is difficult to reach, as there is no direct track. It means taking a line across country and the crossing of innumerable little ditches and wadis. Hamoudi is in great spirits this morning. Mac is quietly gloomy, and opines that we shall never get to the mound.

It takes us seven hours of motoring—a very tiring seven hours, with the car sticking more than once and having to be dug out.

Hamoudi surpasses himself on these occasions. He always considers a car as a kind of inferior though swifter horse. In any moment of uncertainty with a wadi ahead, Hamoudi's voice rises excitedly, giving frenzied orders to Aristide.

"Quickly—quickly! Give the machine no time to refuse! Rush at it! Rush at it!"

His disgust when Max stops the car and walks ahead to examine the difficulty is extreme. He shakes his head in utter dissatisfaction.

Not so, he seems to say, should you treat a high-mettled and nervous car! Give it no time to reflect and all will be well.

After detours, checks, and the taking on of local guides, we do at last reach the goal. Very beautiful Tell Hamidi looks in the afternoon sun, and it is with a sense of achievement that the car drives proudly up the gentle incline to its summit where we look down on a marsh teeming with wild duck.

Mac is sufficiently moved to utter a remark.

"Ah," he says in a tone of gloomy satisfaction, "stagnant water, I see!"

It is hereafter to be his nickname!

Life now becomes hurried and hectic. Examination of Tells is daily more zealous. For the final selection three things are essential. First, it must be sufficiently near a village or villages to get a supply of labor. Secondly, there must be a water supply—that is to say, it must be near the Jaghjagha or the Habur, or else there must be well-water that is not too brackish. Thirdly, it must give indications of having the right stuff in it. All digging is a gamble—among seventy Tells all occupied at the same period, who is to say which one holds a building, or a deposit of tablets, or a collection of objects of special interest? A small Tell offers as good prospects as a large Tell, since the more important towns are the more likely to have been looted and destroyed in the far-distant past. Luck is the predominant factor. How often has a site been painstakingly and correctly dug, season after season, with interesting but not spectacular results, and then a shift of a few feet, and suddenly a unique find comes to light. The one real consolation is that whichever Tell we select, we are bound to find *something*.

We have made a day's excursion on the opposite
bank of the Habur to Tell Halaf again, and we have
done two days on the Jaghjagha—a much overrated
river, from the point of view of appearance—a brown
muddy stream between high banks—and have marked
down one Tell—Tell Brak—as highly promising. It is
a large mound, with traces of several periods of occupation, from early prehistoric to Assyrian times. It is
about two miles from the Jaghjagha, where there is an
Armenian settlement, and there are other villages
scattered around not very far away. It is about an
hour's drive from Hasetshe, which will be convenient
for supplies. As a drawback, there is no water at the
Tell itself, though possibly a well could be dug there.
Tell Brak goes down as a possibility.

Today we take the main track from Hasetshe north-
west to Kamichlie—another French military post, and
the frontier town between Syria and Turkey. The
track runs about midway between the Habur and the
Jaghjagha for some distance, and finally rejoins
the Jaghjagha at Kamichlie.

Since to examine all the Tells on the way and return
to Hasetshe that night would be impossible, we decide
to stay the night in Kamichlie and return the following day.

Opinions as to accommodation vary. According to
the French Lieutenant, the so-called Hotel at Kamichlie
is impossible, but impossible! *"C'este infecte, Madame!"* According to Hamoudi and Aristide it is a
fine Hotel, quite European, with *beds!* Indeed, quite
first-class!

Stifling an inner conviction that the French Lieutenant will be proved right, we set off.

The weather has cleared again after two days of
drizzling rain. It is hoped that bad weather will not
really set in before December. There are two deep
wadis between Hasetshe and Kamichlie, and if they
fill with water the road will be cut for some days. There
is only a little water in them today, and we switchback
down and up again without much difficulty—that is

to say, we in Aristide's taxi do so. Abdullah, as is his invariable custom, sweeps down in top gear, and endeavors to come up the other side in the same. He then tries to change down into second while the car is at a standstill. The engine protests and stops, and Abdullah glides gently back to the bottom of the wadi, his back wheels in mud and water. We all get out and make our contribution to the situation.

Max curses Abdullah for a damned fool, and why can't he do as he has been told a hundred times? Hamoudi upbraids him for lack of speed: "Faster, faster! You showed too much caution. Give the car no time to reflect. It would not then have refused." Aristides cries gaily: "Inshallah, we shall be out of here in ten minutes!" Mac breaks his silence to utter one of his usual depressing statements. "About the worst place he *could* get stuck. Look at the angle! We shan't get out of that for a long time." Abdullah raises his hands to heaven and utters a shrill vindication of his methods. "With such a fine car as this we might easily have sailed up in third, and then there would have been no need to change down at all, and in that way petrol would have been saved! I do everything in order to please you!"

The chorus of lamentations gives way to practical proceedings. The boards, pickaxes, and other equipment always carried for these predicaments are unshipped. Max pushes Abdullah aside and takes his place at Mary's wheel; the boards are placed in position; Mac, Hamoudi, Aristide, and Abdullah take their places ready to shove. Since Khatuns toil not in the East (an excellent idea!), I take my stand upon the bank, prepared to utter cries of encouragement and helpful advice. Max starts the engine and revs it up; clouds of blue smoke arise from the exhaust, practically asphyxiating the shovers; Max puts the car into gear and eases out the clutch; there is a terrific roar; wheels spin; the blue haze grows; out of it are heard shrill cries that Allah is excessively merciful, Mary advances a couple of feet, the clamor increases, Allah *is* very merciful. . . .

Alas, Allah is not merciful enough! The wheels lose grip and Mary sinks back. Renewed disposal of boards, renewed efforts, shouting, fountains of mud, and blue fumes. Very nearly this time!

Just a little more power is needed. The tow-rope is attached to Mary's nose and fastened to the back of the taxi. Aristide takes his place at the taxi's wheel. Everyone gets into position. Aristide displays too much zeal and lets in the clutch too soon. The tow-rope snaps. Fresh start. I am given the post of synchronizer. When I signal with the handkerchief, Aristide is to start.

Once more the maneuvers begin. Hamoudi, Abdullah and Mac prepare to shove, the two former uttering encouraging cries to the car well beforehand. Once again Max starts off. Once more fountains of mud and water arise mingled with blue smoke; the engine pants and races; the wheels start moving; I drop the handkerchief; Aristide utters a wild high scream, crosses himself, shouts Allah Kerim, and crashes in his gear. Slowly, groaning, Mary quavers forward; the tow-rope tightens; she hesitates; her back wheels spin; Max zigzags wildly; she recovers, and zigzagging to and fro up the steep bank, up she comes!

Two figures, completely drowned in mud, rush up after her, yelling happily. A third figure, also mud-stained, walks up soberly—the imperturbable Mac. He shows no signs of either discomposure or of exultation.

I look at my watch and say: "A quarter of an hour. Not too bad." Mac replies calmly: "The next wadi will probably be worse."

Decidedly, Mac is not human!

We proceed. Homoudi enlivens the road with snatches of song. He and Max are having a gay time together in front. Mac and I sit in silence behind. I am by this time reduced to gibbering idiocy when I attempt conversation. Mac bears with my idiotic remarks patiently and politely as always, according them a deliber-

ate attention they do not deserve, and replies to them
with one or other of his formulas: "Indeed?" or gently
and reprovingly, "Surely that is not so?"

Presently we arrive at the second wadi. We halt;
Max takes Abdullah's place in Mary. Aristide goes
through first without mishap. Max follows, going down
in second and changing to first as he starts up out of
the water. Mary arrives, lurching triumphantly.

"You see?" says Max to Abdullah.

Abdullah puts on his most camel-like expression.

"She would have done it this time in third," he says.
"You did not need to change."

Max tells him again that he is a damned fool, and
adds that at any rate he is to do as he is told in
future. Abdullah replies cheerfully that he always does
everything for the best.

Max abandons the argument and we proceed.

Tells are plentiful. I begin to wonder whether the
moment has not come to resume my anti-clockwise
progress round them.

We arrive at a Tell named Chagar Bazar. Dogs and
children rush out from the small cluster of houses.
Presently a striking figure is seen in flowing white robes
and a brilliant green turban. It is the local Sheikh. He
greets us with the utmost bonhomie. Max disappears
with him into the largest mud house. After a pause of
some moments the Sheikh reappears and yells: "Engineer! Where is the engineer?" Hamoudi explains that
this summons is intended for Mac. Mac goes forward.

"Ha," cries the Sheikh, "here is *leben!*" He produces a bowl of the local sour milk. "How do you
like your *leben,* engineer, thick or thin?" Mac, who is
very fond of *leben,* nods towards the water-jug the
Sheikh is holding. I see Max endeavoring to negative
the suggestion. Too late; the water is added to the
leben, and Mac drinks it off with something like relish.

"I tried to warn you," says Max later. "That water
was practically thin black mud!"

The finds on Chagar Bazar are good. . . . There is a
village, wells, other villages adjacent, and a kindly

disposed, though no doubt rapacious, Sheikh. It is put down as a possible, and we go on.

A few detours over marshy ground to reach certain Tells near the Jaghjagha at the end of the day delay us, and it is quite late when we arrive at last at Kamichlie.

With the utmost enthusiasm Aristide pulls up the car with a jerk before the first-class Hotel.

"See," he says, "is it not handsome? It is built of *stone!*"

We forbear to say that the inside of hotels is more important than the outside. Anyway, here *is* the Hotel, and whatever it is like, it has to do.

We enter, climb up a long dingy stair, and arrive in a restaurant with marble-topped tables, where there is a thick smell of paraffin, garlic, and smoke.

Max enters into negotiations with the Proprietor.

Certainly this is a Hotel. It is a Hotel with beds—real beds! He flings open the door of a room, in which four people, already asleep on beds, prove the truth of his words. There are two unoccupied beds in the room.

"There you are," he says; "and this animal here"—he kicks the nearest sleeper—"can be turned out! He is only my horse-boy."

Max makes the unreasonable request that we would like a room to ourselves. The Proprietor is doubtful. That, he says, will be enormously expensive.

Max says recklessly that he does not mind if it *is* expensive. How expensive, he asks, will it be?

The Proprietor hesitates, scratches his ear, sizes up our appearance (which, owing to mud, is not very plutocratic), and finally hazards the opinion that it will cost at least a pound for the four of us.

To his stupefaction Max agrees without bargaining.

Immediately all is activity and enthusiasm. Sleepers are aroused, servants are called. We sit down at one of the marble tables and order the best meal the house can provide.

Hamoudi charges himself with the supervision of the

sleeping accommodation. He returns some quarter of an hour later all smiles. One room is to be at the disposal of Max and myself. He and Mac will share the other. Also, "and for the good of your reputation," as he puts it, he has agreed to an additional charge of five francs for clean sheets!

The food comes; it is greasy, but hot and savoury. We eat heartily, and without more ado retire and fall on to the clean-sheeted beds. As I fall asleep, the possible question of "bugs" just stirs in my mind. Max gives it as his opinion that we are safe from bugs. This place is only recently built, and the beds are new ones of iron.

The fumes of smoke, garlic, and paraffin seep in through the restaurant next door, and there is the high chatter of Arab voices. But nothing can keep us from sleep. We sleep.

We awake, unbitten. It is later than we thought. Once again we have a full day before us. Max throws open the bedroom door and blenches slightly. The restaurant is full of the dispossessed sleepers from the two bedrooms. They lie about among the tables—there are at least a score of them. The atmosphere is very thick. Tea and eggs are brought to us, and we set off once more. Hamoudi says sadly to Max that he has talked long and earnestly to the Khwaja Macartney last night, but alas, not even now, after two months does the Khwaja Mac understand a word of Arabic!

Max asks Mac how he is getting on with Van Ess's *spoken Arabic*. Mac replies that he seems to have mislaid it.

After doing some shopping in Kamichlie, we take the road of Amuda. This is an important road—almost, one might say, a real road instead of a track. It runs parallel with the railway line, on the other side of which is Turkey.

Its surface is appalling—continual ruts and holes. We are all shaken to bits, but there is no doubt that one sees life on it. We pass several cars, and both Abdullah and Aristide have to be severely cursed for indulging in the native driver's favorite sport of trying to run down, or, at any rate, severely frighten, parties of donkeys and camels in charge of old women and boys.

"It not this track wide enough for you to pass right at the other side?" demands Max.

Abdullah turns to him excitedly.

"Am I not driving a lorry? Am I not to choose the best surface? These miserable Beduin must get out of my way, they and their wretched donkeys!"

Aristide glides softly up behind an overladen donkey, with a man and woman trudging beside it, and lets out a terrific blast of his horn. The donkey stampedes, the woman screams and rushes after it, the man shakes his fist. Aristide roars with laughter.

He in turn is cursed, but remains, as usual, serenely unrepentant.

Amuda is mainly an Armenian town, and not, may it be said, at all an attractive one. The flies there are out of all proportion, the small boys have the worst manners yet seen, everyone seems bored and yet truculent. On the whole it compares unfavorably with Kamichlie. We buy meat of a doubtful character from which flies rise in a swarm, some rather tired vegetables, and some very good freshly made bread.

Hamoudi goes off to make various inquiries. He returns as our purchases are completed, and directs us to a side road in which is a gate leading into a courtyard.

Here we are greeted by an Armenian priest—very courteous and knowing a little French. Waving his hand round the courtyard and the building at one side of it, he says that this is his house.

Yes, he would be prepared to rent it to us next spring if the "arrangements" were satisfactory. Yes, he could clear out one room, and let us have it for storing things quite soon.

Negotiations having thus been set under way, we start off for Hasetshe. There is a direct track from Amuda joining the Kamichlie road at Tell Chagar Bazar. We examine a few Tells on the way, and arrive back at our camp without incident but extremely tired.

Max asks Mac if he has suffered inconvenience from the Sheikh's filthy water. Mac replies that he has never felt better.

"I told you Mac was a find," says Max later when we are rolled up in our flea-bags. "First-class stomach! Nothing upsets him. Can eat any amount of grease and muck. And practically never opens his mouth."

"That," I say, "may be all right for *you!* You and Hamoudi never stop roaring with laughter and talking. But what about *me?*"

"I can't understand why you don't get on with him better. Do you *try?*"

"I'm always trying. He just snubs me."

Max seems to find this amusing, and chuckles a good deal.

Today sees our arrival at Amuda—our new center of activity. Mary and the taxi are parked in the Armenian priest's courtyard. A room in the house has been cleared and is at our disposal, but Hamoudi, after examination of it, recommends sleeping in the tents still! We set them up with difficulty, for there is a strong wind blowing, and it is beginning to rain. It looks as though there would be no excursions tomorrow. Twenty-four hours' rain in these parts effectually paralyzes traffic. It is fortunate that we have got a room where we can spend the day, go over our finds up to date, and where Max can write his report of the proceedings up to date.

Mac and I unload and arrange things in the room—folding-table, deck-chairs, lamps, etc. The others go off into the town to make necessary purchases.

Outside, the wind rises and the rain begins to beat down. There are broken panes in the windows and it is very cold. I look longingly at the petrol lamp.

"I wish Abdullah would come back," I say, "and we could get the heater going."

For Abdullah, devoid apparently of any intelligence,

a shocking driver, and mentally deficient in almost every respect, is nevertheless undisputed lord of those temperamental things—petrol lamps. He, and he alone, can deal with their intricacies.

Mac goes over to the heater and looks at it.

The scientific principle, he says, is quite simple. Would I like him to light it?

I say I would, and hand him a box of matches.

Mac proceeds to the task with quiet confidence. The methylated is ignited, and so on and so forth. His hands are deft and skillful, and he clearly knows what he is doing.

Time passes . . . the lamp does not light. Mac starts all over again with the methylated. . . .

After another five minutes he murmurs, more to himself than me:

"The *principle* is clear enough——"

I steal a glance at him when another five minutes have gone by. He is getting warm. He also is looking not nearly so superior. Scientific principle or no scientific principle, the petrol lamp is holding out on him. He lies on the floor and wrestles with the thing. Presently he begins to swear. . . .

A feeling that is almost affection sweeps over me. After all, our Mac *is* human. He is defeated by a petrol lamp!

Half an hour later Max and Abdullah return. Mac is scarlet in the face and the petrol lamp is unlit.

"Ah, let me do that, Khwaja!" says Abdullah. He seizes the methylated, the matches. In two minutes the petrol lamp is flaring away, although I feel tolerably certain that Abdullah has completely ignored any scientific principle there may be. . . .

"Well!" says Mac, inarticulate as usual, but conveying a good deal in that one word.

Later that night the wind rises to a gale, the rain is lashing down. Aristide runs in to say he thinks the tents are coming down. We all rush out in the rain. It dawns on me that I am now going to see the seamy side of *le camping*.

Valiantly Max and Mac and Aristide struggle with the big tent. Mac clings to the pole.

Suddenly there is a snap, the pole breaks, Mac goes down headlong into thick slimy mud.

He struggles up, completely unrecognizable. His voice rises in completely natural tones:

"D—— and —————— the ——————— ————————— ———— thing," yells Mac at last, becoming wholly human.

From that night onward Mac is one of us!

The bad weather passes, but for a day the tracks are too wet for motoring. We venture out cautiously to Tells near at hand. A possibility is Tell Hamdun—a large Tell not far from Amuda and set right on the frontier, the railway actually passing through a portion of it, so that a slice of it is in Turkey.

We are here one morning, and have brought a couple of men with us to cut a trench in the side of the Tell. The place where they are digging is cold, and I go round to the opposite side of the Tell out of the wind. The days are definitely autumnal now, and I sit on the side of the Tell huddled down in my coat.

Suddenly, out of nowhere, as usual, a horseman comes cantering up the mound. He reins his horse and shouts to me, addressing me fluently in Arabic. I understand nothing beyond the greeting, which I return politely, and say that the Khwaja is the other side of the mound. He looks puzzled, asks me another question, then suddenly throws back his head and roars with laughter.

"Ah, it is a Khatūn!" he cries. "What a mistake! It is a Khatūn to whom I speak!" and he canters round to the other side of the mound, intensely amused at the solecism he has committed in not having recognized a female at first sight!

The best days are over. Now often there are overcast skies. We have finished examining Tells. The moment has come to decide where the spades are to go in next spring.

Three Tells compete for the honor of our attention —Tell Hamdun, which is geographically in an interesting sector, our first selection, Tell Chagar Bazar; and a third, Tell Mozan. This is much the largest of the three, and a lot depends on whether there will be much Roman deposit to dig through.

Soundings must be made at all three mounds. We make a start with Tell Mozan. There is a village there, and with Hamoudi as ambassador we try and obtain workmen. The men are doubtful and suspicious.

"We do not need money," they say. "It has been a good harvest."

For this is a simple, and, I think, consequently a happy part of the world. Food is the only consideration. If the harvest is good, you are rich. For the rest of the year there is leisure and plenty, until the time comes to plough and sow once more.

"A little extra money," says Hamoudi, like the serpent of Eden, "is always welcome."

They answer simply: "But what can we buy with it? We have enough food until the harvest comes again."

And here, alas! the eternal Eve plays her part. Astute Hamoudi baits his hook. They can buy ornaments for their wives.

The wives nod their heads. This digging, they say, is a good thing!

Reluctantly the men consider the idea. There is another thing to be taken into account—Dignity. His dignity is very dear to an Arab. Is this a *dignified*, an *honorable* thing to do?

It will only be for a few days now, explains Hamoudi. They can reconsider before the spring.

So at last, with the doubtful expressions of those who embark upon a new and unprecedented venture, a dozen of the more progressive spirits step out. The more conservative elders are shaking their white beards.

At a sign from Hamoudi, picks and spades are unloaded from Mary and served out to the men. Hamoudi himself takes a pick and demonstrates.

Three trial trenches are selected at different levels

of the Tell. There is a murmur of "Inshallah!" and the picks go in.

Tell Mozan has been reluctantly erased from our list of possibles. There are several levels of Roman occupation, and though the periods we want to dig are there underneath, it would take several seasons— that is to say, more time and money than we can afford.

Today we drive to our old friend Chagar Bazar. Here the arrangements for labor are quickly made. The Sheikh is a poor man, heavily in debt, like all Arab landowners. He sees in all this some very pretty profits to be made.

"All that I have is yours, brother," he says generously to Max, the light of calculation glistening in his eye. "There need be no payment for the land. Take all I have!"

Then, as Max strides up the mound, the Sheikh bends his head to Hamoudi.

"Doubtless," he suggests, "this Khwaja is immensely rich! Is he as rich as El Baron of famous memory who paid in bags of gold?"

"Nowadays," says Hamoudi, "payment is not made in gold. Nevertheless the Khwaja is extremely generous. Moreover, in all probability the Khwaja will build a house here—a house of such beauty and grandeur that it will be mentioned far and wide. What prestige will that house of the excavation not confer upon the Sheikh? All the district will say: "The foreign Khwajas chose this spot to build and dig because of its proximity to the holiness of the Sheikh, a man who has been to Mecca and whom all revere."

The idea of the house pleases the Sheikh. He looks thoughtfully up at the mound.

"I shall lose all the crops that I am about to sow on the mound there. A heavy loss—a very heavy loss!"

"But surely," says Hamoudi, "the ground would be plowed and the seed sowed before now?"

"There have been delays," says the Sheikh. "I am about to do it."

"Have you ever had any crops there? Surely not. Who would plow a hill when there are plains all round?"

The Sheikh says firmly: "The crops I shall lose will be a heavy loss. But what of it? It is a sacrifice I shall gladly make so as to please the Government. If I am ruined, what does it matter?"

And looking decidedly cheerful he goes back into his house.

An old woman comes up to Hamoudi, leading a boy of twelve by the hand.

"Has the Khwaja medicine?"

"He has some medicines—yes?"

"Will he give me medicine for my son here?"

"What is the matter with your son?"

It is hardly necessary to ask. The imbecile face is only too clear.

"He has not his proper senses."

Hamoudi shakes his head sadly, but says he will ask the Khwaja.

The men have started digging trenches. Hamoudi, the woman and the boy come up to Max.

Max looks at the boy and turns gently to the woman.

"The boy is as he is by the will of Allah," he says. "There is no medicine I can give you for the boy."

The woman sighs—I think a tear runs down her cheek. Then she says in a matter-of-fact voice:

"Then, Khwaja, will you give me some poison, for it is better he should not live?"

Max says gently that he cannot do that either.

She stares at him uncomprehendingly, then shakes her head angrily and goes away with the boy.

I wander up to the top of the mound where Macartney is busy with his survey. An Arab boy, full of importance, is staggering about with the pole. Mac, still unwilling to risk a word of Arabic, expresses his wishes by semaphoric gestures which do not always produce the desired result. Aristide, always obliging, comes to help.

I look all round me. To the north there is the line

of the Turkish hills, with a glittering spot which is
Mardin. West, south, and east there is only the
fertile steppe, which in spring will be green and starred
with flowers. Tells are dotted all over the landscape.
Here and there are Beduin tents in brown clusters.
Though there are villages on many of the Tells, you
cannot see them—in any case they are only a few
mud huts. Everything seems peaceful and remote from
man and the ways of civilization. I like Chagar Bazar,
and hope that he shall choose it. I would like to live
in a house built here. If we dig at Hamdun we shall
presumably live in Amuda. . . . Oh, no, I want *this*
Tell!

Evening comes. Max is pleased with the results. We
will come again tomorrow and continue the soundings.
This Tell, he believes, has been unoccupied since the
fifteenth century B.C., except for some intrusive Roman
and Islamic burials. There is excellent painted pottery
of the early Arpachiyah Tell Halaf type.

The Sheikh escorts us genially to the car.

"All that I have is yours, brother," he urges again.
"However poor it makes me!"

"How happy I shall be," says Max politely, "if it
falls to my lot to enrich you by digging here. Compensation will be paid as agreed with the French
authorities for any loss of crops, your men will be
paid good wages, land will be leased from you to
build a house, and, moreover, at the end of the season
a handsome present will be made to you personally."

"Ah," cries the Sheikh in high good humor, "I need
nothing! What is this talk of payment between
brothers?"

We depart on this altruistic note.

Two cold and wintry days spent at Tell Hamdun.
The results are reasonably good, but the fact that
part of the Tell is in Turkey is against it. The decision
seems clear for Chagar Bazar, with an additional con-
cession for Tell Brak, which could be combined with
the Chagar dig in a second season.

Now it only remains to get on with the arrangements for the spring. There is a suitable site to be chosen at Chagar for the house; there is the leasing of the house in Amuda for the time while the Chagar house is being built: there is the agreement to be drawn up with the Sheikh, and, most urgent, there is another money-order waiting at Hasetshe, which we must fetch without delay in case the wadis fill and the road is cut.

Hamoudi has been throwing money about rather grandly in Amuda lately, mindful of our "reputations." The spending of money seems a point of honor with Arabs—that is to say, the practice of entertaining notables in the coffee-house! To appear mean is a terrible dishonor. On the other hand, Hamoudi beats down remorselessly the charges of old women who bring milk and other old women who do our washing for what seems an incredibly small sum.

Max and I set off for Hasetshe in Mary, hoping for the best, though the sky is overcast and there is a faint drizzle of rain. We reach there without adventure, although the rain is now falling, and we wonder if we shall ever get back.

To our despair, when we get to the Post Office the Postmaster is out. No one knows where he is, but boys are dispatched in all directions to hunt for him.

The rain begins to fall in earnest. Max looks anxious, and says we shall never do it unless we can start back soon. We wait anxiously while the rain continues.

Suddenly the Postmaster appears, walking along in a leisurely fashion with a basket of eggs.

He greets us with pleasure and surprise. Max cuts short the usual politeness with an urgent plea for haste. We shall be cut off, he says.

"But why not?" says the Postmaster. "You will then have to remain here many days, which will be a pleasure to me personally. Hasetshe is a most agreeable town. Stay with us a long time," he urges hospitably.

Max renews his impassioned demand for haste. The Postmaster slowly unlocks drawers and searches in a desultory fashion, whilst still urging on us the desirability of making a long stay.

Curious, he says, that he cannot find this important envelope. He remembers it arriving, and he has said to himself: "One day the Khwaja will arrive for this." Therefore he has placed it in a place of safety, but where now can that place be? A clerk arrives to help, and the search is continued. Finally the letter is unearthed, and we go through the usual difficulty of obtaining cash. As before, this has to be collected from the Bazaar.

And still the rain falls! At last we have what we want. Max takes the precaution of buying bread and chocolate in case we spend a night or two *en route,* and we re-enter Mary and dash off at full speed. We negotiate the first wadi successfully, but at the second an ominous sight meets our eyes. The postal bus has stuck in it, and behind the postal bus is a line of cars waiting.

Everyone is down in the wadi—digging, fixing boards, yelling encouragement.

Max says despairingly: "We're here for the night."

It is a grim thought. I have spent many nights in the desert in cars, but never with enjoyment. One wakes cold and cramped, with pains all over.

However, this time we are lucky. The bus comes lumbering out with a roar, the other cars follow, and we come over at last. It is just in time—the water is rising rapidly.

Our journey back on the Amuda track is nightmarish in quality—one long continuous skid. Twice at least Mary turns completely around and faces determinedly in the direction of Hasetshe in spite of the chains on the wheels. This continuous skidding is a very peculiar feeling. Solid earth is not solid earth any longer. It has a fantastic nightmare quality.

We arrive after dark, and the household rushes out with cries of welcome, holding up lanterns.

I tumble out of Mary and slither my way to the door of our room. It is difficult to walk, because the mud has the peculiar quality of attaching itself to your feet in vast flat pancakes so heavy that you can hardly lift them.

Nobody, it appears, has expected to see us return, and the congratulations and El hamdu lillahs are vociferous.

The pancakes on my feet make me laugh. It is so exactly the sort of feeling you have in a dream.

Hamoudi laughs too, and says to Max: "It is good to have the Khatūn with us. All things make her laugh!"

Everything is now arranged. There has been a solemn meeting between Max, the Sheikh, and the French military officer of the Services Spéciaux in charge of the district. The rental of the land, the compensation, the obligations of each party—all is set down in black and white. The Sheikh alternates between saying that everything that he has is Max's and suggesting that about a thousand pounds in gold would be a fitting sum for him to receive!

He finally leaves, a much disappointed man, having evidently entertained the wildest dreams of affluence. He is consoled, however, by one clause of the contract, which provides that the house built for the Expedition shall, when the Expedition has finished with it, revert to him. His eyes brighten, and his vast red henna-dyed beard wags appreciatively.

"C'est tout de même un brave homme," says the French Capitaine when the Sheikh has finally departed. He shrugs his shoulders. "Il n'a pas le sou comme tout ces gens là!"

The negotiations for the renting of the Amuda house are complicated by the fact—which has only recently come to light—that instead of its being one house, as we imagined, it seems to be six! And as the six houses are inhabited by eleven families, the complications increase! The Armenian priest is merely the spokesman for all the varied householders!

An agreement is finally arrived at. On a definite date

the "houses" are to be vacant, and the interior treated
with two coats of whitewash!

So now all is settled. There is now the return journey to the coast to arrange. The cars will attempt to
reach Aleppo by way of Ras-el-Ain and Jerablus. It
is about two hundred miles, and there are many wadis
to cross in the early stages of the journey, but with
luck it may be done in two days. But with December
here the weather is bound to break soon. What will
the Khatūn do?

The Khatūn, ignobly, decides for a Wagon Lit. So
the taxi takes me to a strange little station, and presently a large and important blue sleeping-car comes
along behind a vast puffing engine. A conductor in
chocolate uniform leans out. Madame's baggage is
handed up, Madame herself is hoisted with difficulty
on to the high step from the permanent way.

"I think you're wise," says Max; "it's starting to
rain."

We both cry "See you in Alep!" The train starts! I
follow the conductor along the corridor. He flings open
the door of my compartment. The bed is made.

Here, once more, is civilization. *Le camping* is
ended. The conductor takes my passport, brings me a
bottle of mineral water, says: "We arrive at Alep at
six to-morrow morning. *Bonne nuit, Madame.*"

I might be going from Paris to the Riviera!

It seems strange, somehow, to find a Wagon Lit here
in the middle of nowhere. . . .

Alep!
Shops! A bath! My hair shampooed! Friends to see.
When Max and Mac roll in three days later, plastered with mud and carrying quantities of bustards
shot *en route,* I greet them with the superiority of one
inured once more to the fleshpots.

They have had plenty of adventures on the way—
the weather was bad, and I am satisfied that I chose
the better part.

The cook, it appears, demanded his chit as a driver

when paid off, and Max, before perjuring himself, ordered the cook to drive Mary once round the courtyard.

Jumping into the driving-seat, 'Isa started up, put the gear in reverse, and crashed heavily into the courtyard wall, knocking a large portion of it down. He was deeply injured when Max refused to guarantee him as a chauffeur! The testimonial as finally written announced that 'Isa had been our cook for three months, and had given us useful help with the car!

And so once more to Beyrout and a parting with Mac.

Egypt for us for the winter. Mac is to go to Palestine.

IV

FIRST SEASON AT
CHAGAR BAZAR

IT IS SPRING when we return to Beyrout. The first sight that greets us on the quay is Mac, but a Mac transformed.

He is smiling from ear to ear! No doubt about it—he is pleased to see us! Until now we have never known whether Mac has liked us or not. His feelings have been concealed behind his mask of polite impassiveness. But now it is clear that to him this is a reunion with friends. I cannot tell you how warming this is! From henceforth my nervousness with Mac vanishes. I even ask him whether every day since we last saw him he has sat on his plaid rug writing in his diary.

"Of course," says Mac, looking slightly surprised.

From Beyrout we proceed to Alep, and the usual business of getting in stores, etc., is accomplished. A chauffeur has been engaged for Mary—not this time an "economical" one picked up on the water-front, but a tall, worried-looking Armenian, who has at any rate a certain number of testimonials as to honesty and capacity. He has worked at one time for German engineers, and his principal disadvantage at first appearance is his voice, which is inclined to be a high and irritating whine. There is no doubt, however, that he will be an improvement on the sub-human Abdullah. Inquiries as to Aristide, whom we would have liked to have with us again, elicit the information that Aristide is now proudly in "Government service." He is driving a street watering-cart in Der-ez-zor!

The fateful date arrives, and we advance upon Amuda in two installments. Hamoudi and Mac, with Mary (now deprived of royal honors and known as Blue Mary, since she has received a somewhat lurid coat of blue paint), are to arrive first, and make sure that all is prepared for our reception. Max and I travel grandly by train to Kamichlie, there to spend the day transacting the necessary business with the French military authorities. It is about four o'clock when we leave Kamichlie for Amuda.

It is evident when we arrive that all has not gone according to plan. There is an air of confusion, loud recriminations, and plaints fill the air. Hamoudi has a distracted appearance and Mac a stoical one.

We soon learn the facts.

The house rented by us, which was to have been vacated, cleaned, whitewashed on a certain date now a week old, was found on the arrival of Hamoudi and Mac the day before to be innocent of whitewash, highly unclean, and still containing seven Armenian families!

What could be done in twenty-four hours has been done, but the result is not encouraging!

Hamoudi, by now well trained in the essential doctrine that the comfort of Khatūns comes first, has devoted all his energies to getting one room free of Armenians and live stock, and hastily whitewashing the walls. Two camp-beds have been set up in it for Max and myself. The rest of the house is still in chaos, and I gather that Hamoudi and Mac have spent an uncomfortable night.

But all will now be well, Hamoudi assures us, beaming with his usual irresistible smile.

The litigation and the recriminations that are now proceeding between the Armenian families and the Priest who was their spokesman are fortunately no concern of ours, and they are urged by Max to go and fight it out somewhere else!

Women, children, hens, cats, dogs—all weeping, wailing, screaming, shouting, abusing, praying, laughing, miauing, clucking and barking—depart slowly from the courtyard like some fantastic finale in an opera!

Everybody, we gather, has double-crossed everybody else! The financial chaos is complete, and the angry passions aroused between brothers, sisters, sisters-in-law, cousins, and great-grandparents are far too intricate for comprehension.

In the midst of chaos, however, our cook (a new cook, Dimitri by name) continues calmly to prepare an evening meal. We set to and eat with relish, and after that we retire to bed worn out.

To bed—but not to rest! I have never been one with an exaggerated distaste for mice. An odd mouse or so in a bedroom has left me unmoved, and I have even on one occasion had quite an affection for a persistent intruder named affectionately (though without any real knowledge as to sex) Elsie.

But our first night at Amuda is an experience I shall never forget.

No sooner have the lamps been extinguished than mice in their scores—I really believe in their hundreds —emerge from the holes in the walls and the floor. They run gaily over our beds, squeaking as they run. Mice across one's face, mice tweaking your hair— mice! mice! MICE! . . .

I switch on a torch. Horrible! The walls are covered with strange, pale, crawling cockroach-like creatures! A mouse is sitting on the foot of my bed attending to his whiskers!

Horrible crawling things are everywhere!

Max utters soothing words.

Just go to sleep, he says. Once you are asleep, none of these things will worry you.

Excellent advice, but not easy to act upon! One has first to get to sleep, and with mice taking healthy exercise and having their field sports all over you, that is hardly possible. Or it is not possible to me. Max seems able to do it all right!

I endeavor to subdue the shrinkings of the flesh. I do fall asleep for a short spell, but little feet running across my face wake me up. I flash on the light. The cockroaches have increased, and a large black spider is descending upon me from the ceiling!

So the night goes on, and I am ashamed to say that at two A.M. I become hysterical. When morning comes, I declare, I am going into Kamichlie to wait for the train, and I am going straight back to Alep! And from Alep I shall go straight back to England! I cannot stand this life! I will not stand it! I am going *home!*

In a masterly fashion Max deals with the situation. He rises, opens the door, calls to Hamoudi.

Five minutes later our beds have been dragged out into the courtyard. For a short while I lie gazing up at the peaceful starlit sky above. The air is cool and sweet. I fall asleep. Max, I rather fancy, breathes a sigh of relief before falling asleep himself.

You aren't really going back to Alep? Max inquires anxiously the next morning.

I blush a little over the remembrance of my hysterical outburst. No, I say; I wouldn't really go for the world. But I *am* going to continue to sleep in the courtyard!

Hamoudi explains soothingly that all will soon be well. The holes in the bedroom are being stopped up with plaster. More whitewash will be applied. Moreover, a cat is coming; it has been loaned out. It is a super-cat—a highly professional cat.

What sort of night, I ask Mac, did *he* have when he and Hamoudi arrived? Did things run over him all the time?

"I think so," said Mac, calm as always. "But I was asleep."

Wonderful Mac!

Our cat arrives at dinner-time. I shall never forget that cat! It is, as Hamoudi has announced, a highly professional cat. It knows the job for which it has been engaged, and proceeds to get on with it in a truly specialized manner.

Whilst we dine, it crouches in ambush behind a packing-case. When we talk, or move, or make too much noise, it gives us an impatient look.

"I must request of you," the look says, "to be *quiet*. How can I get on with the job without co-operation?"

So fierce is the cat's expression that we obey at once, speak in whispers, and eat with as little clinking of plates and glasses as possible.

Five times during the meal a mouse emerges and runs across the floor, and five times our cat springs. The sequel is immediate. There is no Western dallying, no playing with the victim. The cat simply bites off the mouse's head, crunches it up, and proceeds to the rest of the body! It is rather horrible and completely businesslike.

The cat stays with us five days. After those five days no mice appear. The cat then leaves us, and the mice never come back. I have never known before or since such a professional cat. It had no interest in us, it never demanded milk or a share of our food. It was cold, scientific, and impersonal. A very accomplished cat!

Now we are settled in. The walls have been whitewashed, the window-sills and door painted, a carpenter and his four sons have established themselves in the courtyard, and are making our furniture to order.

"Tables," says Max, "above all, *tables!* One cannot have too many tables."

I put in a plea for a chest of drawers, and Max kindly allows me a wardrobe with pegs.

Then the carpenters return to making more tables—tables on which to spread our pottery, a drawing-table for Mac, a table off which to dine, a table for my typewriter. . . .

Mac draws out a towel-horse and the carpenters start upon it. The old man brings it proudly to my room on completion. It looks different from Mac's drawing, and when the carpenter sets it down I see why. It has colossal feet, great curved scrolls of feet. They stick out so that, wherever you put it, you invariably trip over them.

Ask him, I say to Max, why he has made these feet instead of sticking to the design he was given?

The old man looks at us with dignity.

"I made them this way," he says, "so that they should be beautiful. I wanted this that I have made to be a thing of beauty!"

To this cry of the artist there could be no response. I bow my head, and resign myself to tripping up over those hideous feet for the rest of the season!

Outside, in the far corner of the courtyard, some masons are making me a mud-brick lavatory.

I ask Mac that evening at dinner what his first architectural job has been.

"This is my first bit of *practical* work," he replies—"your lavatory!"

He sighs gloomily, and I feel very sympathetic. It will not, I fear, look well in Mac's memoirs when he comes to write them.

The budding dreams of a young architect should not find their first expression in a mud-brick lavatory for his patron's wife!

To-day the Capitaine Le Boiteux and two French nuns come to tea. We greet them in the village and bring them back to the house. Set proudly before the front door is the carpenter's latest achievement—my lavatory seat!

The house is now organized The room where we first slept, and which is still cockroach-ridden at night, is the drawing-office. Here Mac can work in solitude, free from human contacts. He is, in any case, quite unmoved by cockroaches!

Next to it is the dining-room. Farther along is the antika-room, where our finds will be stored, where pottery will be mended, and objects sorted and classified and labelled. (It is full of tables!) Then there is a small office-cum-sitting-room, where my typewriter reposes, and where the deck-chairs are set up. In what was the Priest's house are three bedrooms—free from mice (thanks to our cat), free from cockroaches (thanks to the plentiful whitewash?), unfortunately *not* free from fleas!

We are to suffer a good deal from fleas. The flea has abundant vitality, and seems to have a miraculously protected life. It thrives on Keatings and Flit, and every kind of flea-killer. Anointing beds with carbolic merely stimulates fleas to even greater displays of athletics. It is not, I explain to Mac, so much the bites of fleas. It is their tireless energy, their never-ending hopping races round and round one's middle that wears one out. Impossible to drop off to sleep when fleas are holding the nightly sports round and round the waist.

Max suffers from fleas worse than I do. One day I find and kill one hundred and seven in the band of his pyjamas! He finds fleas, he says, enervating. It would appear that I only get the overflow of fleas—the ones, that is, which have not been able to take up their abode on Max. Mine are second-class, inferior fleas, ineligible for the high jumps!

Mac, it seems, has *no* fleas. This seems very unfair. They apparently do not fancy him as a sports ground!

Life now settles down on its accustomed round. Max departs at dawn every morning to the mound.

Most days I go with him, though occasionally I stay at home to deal with other things—*e.g.* mending of the pottery and objects, labelling, and sometimes to ply my own trade on the typewriter. Mac also stays at home two days a week, busy in the drawing-office.

It is a long day on the mound if I go, but not too long if the weather is good. It is cold until the sun is well up, but later it is very lovely. Flowers are springing up everywhere, mostly the little red anemones, as I incorrectly call them (ranunculus is, I believe, the real term).

A nucleus of workers have been brought by Max from Jerablus, Hamoudi's home town. Hamoudi's two sons, after finishing working at Ur for the season, have come to us. Yahya, the elder, is tall, with a wide, cheerful grin. He is like a friendly dog. Alawi, the younger, is good looking, and probably the more intelligent of the two. But he has a quick temper, and quarrels sometimes flare up. An elderly cousin, Abd es Salaam, is also a foreman. Hamoudi, after starting us off, is to return home.

Once the work has been started on by the strangers from Jerablus, workmen from the spot hasten to be enrolled. The men of the Sheikh's village have already begun work. Now men from neighboring villages begin to arrive by ones and twos. There are Kurds, men from over the Turkish border, some Armenians, and a few Yezidis (so-called devil-worshippers)—gentle, melancholy looking men, prone to be victimized by the others.

The system is a simple one. The men are organized into gangs. Men with any previous experience of digging, and men who seem intelligent and quick to learn, are chosen as pickmen. Men, boys, and children are paid the same wage. Over and above that there is (dear to the Eastern heart) bakshish. That is to say, a small cash payment on each object found.

The pickman of each gang has the best chance of finding objects. When his square of ground has been traced out to him, he starts upon it with a pick. After him comes the spademan. With his spade he shovels the earth into baskets, which three or four "basket-boys" then carry away to a spot appointed as dump. As they turn the earth out, they sort through it for any likely object missed by the Qasmagi and the spademan, and since they are often little boys with sharp eyes, not infrequently some small amulet or bead gives them a good reward. Their finds they tie up in a corner of their ragged drapperies to be produced at the end of the day. Occasionally they appeal to Max with an object, and upon his reply, ". . . keep it, or Shiluh, remove it," its fate is decided. This applies to small objects—amulets, fragments of pottery, beads, etc. When a group of pots in position, or the bones of a burial, or traces of mud-brick walls are found, then the foreman in charge calls for Max, and things proceed with due care. Max or Mac scrape carefully round the group of pots—or the dagger, or whatever the find is—with a knife, clearing the earth away, blowing away loose dust. Then the find is photographed before being removed, and roughly drawn in a notebook.

The tracing out of buildings when they appear is also a delicate business needing the specialist. The foreman usually takes the pick himself and follows the mud-brick carefully, but an intelligent, though hitherto inexperienced pickman, soon picks up the art of tracing mud-brick, and before long you will hear him say confidently during his digging: "Hadha libn" (This is mud-brick).

Our Armenian workmen are, on the whole, the most intelligent. Their disadvantage is their provocative attitude—they always manage to inflame the tempers of the Kurds and Arabs. Quarrelling is, in any case, almost continuous. All our workmen have hot tempers, and all carry with them the means of expressing themselves—large knives, bludgeons, and a kind of mace or knobkerry! Heads are cut open, and furious figures are entangled with each other in fierce struggles and torn asunder, whilst Max loudly proclaims the rules of the dig. For all who fight there will be a fine!

"Settle your quarrels in the hours outside the work. On the work there is to be no fighting. On the work I am your father, and what your father says must be done! Nor will I listen to causes of the dispute, or otherwise I should do nothing else! It takes two to fight and all who fight will be fined equally."

The men listen, nod their heads. "It is true. He is our father! There must be no fighting, or something of value and good price might be destroyed."

Fights, however, still break out. For persistent fighting a man is sacked.

This, I may say, doesn't mean permanent dismissal. A man is sometimes sacked for one day, two days; and, even when dismissed altogether, usually reappears after next pay day with a demand to be taken on for the next shift.

Pay-day is fixed, after some experiment, after a period of about ten days. Some of the men come from fairly distant villages, bringing their food with them. This (a sack of flour and a few onions) is usually exhausted in ten days, and the man then asks to go home, since his food is ended. One of the great disadvantages, we find, is that the men do not work regularly. As soon as they are paid they quit work. "I have money now. Why should I continue to work? I will go home." In about a fortnight, the money spent, the man returns and asks to be taken on again. It is annoying from our point of view, as a gang that has got used to working together is far more efficient than a new combination.

The French have their own way of dealing with this habit, which caused them great difficulty when work was in progress on the railway. They used to keep their workmen permanently half-pay in arrear. This ensured their working continuously. The Lieutenant advised Max to adopt this system, but on consultation we decided not to do so, since from Max's point of view it seemed basically unfair. The men had earned their money and were entitled to be paid in full. So we had to put up with the continuous going and coming. It

makes a lot more work with the pay-book, which has
continually to be revised and altered.

Having arrived on the mound at half-past six, a halt
is called for breakfast at eight-thirty. We eat hard-
boiled eggs and flaps of Arab bread, and Michel (the
chauffeur) produces hot tea, which we drink from
enamel mugs, sitting on the top of the mound, the sun
just pleasantly warm, and the morning shadows making
the landscape incredibly lovely, with the blue Turkish
hills to the north, and all around tiny springing flowers
of scarlet and yellow. The air is wonderfully sweet. It
is one of those moments when it is good to be alive.
The foremen are grinning happily; small children driving cows come and gaze at us shyly. They are dressed
in incredible rags, their teeth gleam white as they smile.
I think to myself how happy they look, and what a
pleasant life it is; like the fairy stories of old, wandering about over the hills herding cattle, sometimes sitting
and singing.

At this time of day, the so-called fortunate children
in European lands are setting out for the crowded class-
room, going in out of the soft air, sitting on benches or
at desks, toiling over letters of the alphabet, listening to
a teacher, writing with cramped fingers. I wonder to
myself whether, one day a hundred years or so ahead,
we shall say in shocked accents: "In *those* days they
actually made poor little children go to *school*, sitting
inside buildings at desks for *hours a day!* Isn't it terrible
to think of! Little *children!*"

Bringing myself back from this vision of the future,
I smile at a little girl with a tattooed forehead, and
offer her a hard-boiled egg.

She immediately shakes her head in alarm and hurriedly moves on. I feel I have committed a solecism.

The foremen blow their whistles. Back to work. I
wander slowly round the mound, pausing from time
to time at various parts of the work. One is always
hoping to be on the spot just when an interesting find
turns up. Of course, one never is! After leaning hopefully on my shooting-stick for twenty minutes watching

Mohammed Hassan and his gang, I move on to 'Isa Daoud, to learn later that the find of the day—a lovely pot of incised ware—was found just after I had moved my pitch.

I have another job, too. I keep an observant eye on the basket-boys, for some of the lazier of these, when taking their baskets to the dump, do not return at once. They sit down in the sun to sort through the earth from their basket, and often spend a comfortable quarter of an hour this way! Even more reprehensible, some of them curl up comfortably on the dump and enjoy a good sleep!

Towards the end of the week, in my rôle of master spy, I report my findings.

"That very little basket-boy, the one with the yellow head-dress, is first-class; he never slacks for a minute. I should sack Salah Hassan; he's always asleep on the dump. Abdul Aziz is a bit of a slacker, and so is the one in that ragged blue coat."

Max agrees that Salah Hassan is for it, but says that Abdul Aziz has such sharp eyes that he never misses anything.

Every now and then during the morning, as Max comes round, a spurt of entirely fictitious energy is shown. Everyone shouts "Yallah!" yells, sings, dances. The basket-boys rush panting to and from the dump, tossing their empty baskets in the air and yelling. Then it all dies down again, and things go even more slowly than before.

The foremen keep up a series of encouraging cries of "Yallah!" and a kind of formula of sarcasm, which has presumably become quite meaningless by constant repetition.

"Are you old women, the way you move? Surely you are not men? What slowness! Like broken-down cows!" etc., etc.

I wander away from the work and around the far side of the mound. Here, looking north towards the blue line of hills, I sit down among the flowers and go into a pleasing coma.

A party of women are coming from the distance towards me. By the gaiety of their coloring they are Kurdish women. They are busy digging up roots and picking leaves.

They make a bee-line for me. Presently they are sitting round me in a circle.

Kurdish women are gay and handsome. They wear bright colors. These women have turbans of bright orange round their heads, their clothes are green and purple and yellow. Their heads are carried erect on their shoulders, they are tall, with a backward stance, so that they always look proud. They have bronze faces, with regular features, red cheeks, and usually blue eyes.

The Kurdish men nearly all bear a marked resemblance to a colored picture of Lord Kitchener that used to hang in my nursery as a child. The brick-red face, the big brown moustache, the blue eyes, the fierce and martial appearance!

In this part of the world Kurdish and Arab villages are about equal in number. They lead the same lives and belong to the same religion, but not for a moment could you mistake a Kurdish woman for an Arab woman. Arab women are invariably modest and retiring; they turn their face away when you speak to them; if they look at you, they do so from a distance. If they smile, it is shyly, and with a half-averted face. They wear mostly black or dark colors. And no Arab woman would ever come up and speak to a man! A Kurdish woman has no doubt that she is as good as a man or better! They come out of their houses and make jokes to any man, passing the time of day with the utmost amiability. They make no bones about bullying their husbands. Our Jerablus workmen, unused to Kurds, are profoundly shocked.

"Never," exclaims one, "did I think to hear a respectable woman address her husband in such a way! Truly, I did not know which way to look."

My Kurdish women this morning are examining me with frank interest and exchanging ribald comments with each other. They are very friendly, nod at me, and

laugh, ask questions, then sigh and shake their heads
as they tap their lips.

They are clearly saying: "What a pity we cannot
understand each other!" They take up a fold of my
skirt and examine it with interest; they pinch my
sleeve. They point up at the mound. I am the Khwaja's
woman? I nod. They fire off more questions, then
laugh at the realization that they cannot get answers.
No doubt they want to know all about my children
and my miscarriages!

They try to explain to me what they do with the
herbs and plants they are picking. Ah, but it is no good!

Another great burst of laughter breaks out. They
get up, smile, and nod and drift off, talking and laughing. They are like great gay-colored flowers. . . .

They live in hovels of mud, with perhaps a few
cooking-pots as all their possessions, yet their gaiety
and laughter are unforced. They find life good, with
a Rabelaisian flavor. They are handsome, and full-
blooded and gay.

My little Arab girl passes, driving the cows. She
smiles at me shyly, then quickly averts her eyes.

In the distance I hear the foreman's whistle. Fidos!
It is twelve-thirty—an hour's break for lunch.

I retrace my steps to where Max and Mac are waiting. Michel is setting out the lunch that Dimitri has
packed. We have slices of cold mutton, more hard-
boiled egg, flaps of Arab bread, and cheese—the local
cheese of the country for Max and Mac; goat's cheese,
strong flavored, a pale-grey in color, and slightly
hairy. I have the sophisticated variety of synthetic
gruyère, silver-papered in its round cardboard box.
Max looks at it contemptuously. After the food, there
are oranges and enamel mugs of hot tea.

After lunch we go to look at the site of our house.

It is some hundred yards beyond the village and the
Sheikh's house, to the south-east of the mound. It is
all traced out, and I ask Mac doubtfully if the rooms
aren't very small. He looks amused, and explains that

that is the effect of the open space surrounding it. The house is to be built with a central dome; it will have a big living-and-working-room in the middle, with two rooms off that on each side. The kitchen quarters will be separate. On to the main structure we can add additional rooms if the dig is prolonged and we need them.

A little way from the house we are going to prospect for a new well, so as not to depend on the Sheikh's well. Max selects the spot and then goes back to the work.

I stay for a while, and watch Mac getting things done by means of gestures, head shakings, whistles— everything except the spoken word!

At about four o'clock Max starts going round the gangs and bakshishing the men. As he comes to each one, they stop, line up roughly, and produce the small finds of the day. One of the more enterprising of the basket-boys has cleaned his acquisitions with spit!

Opening his immense book, Max starts operations.

"Qasmagi?" (Pickman.)

"Hassan Mohammed."

What has Hassan Mohammed got? Half a large broken pot, many fragments of pottery, a bone knife, a scrap or two of copper.

Max turns the collection over, flings away ruthlessly what is rubbish—usually those things which have inflamed the pickman's highest hopes—puts bone implements in one of the small boxes that Michel carries, beads in another. Fragments of pottery go in one of the big baskets that a small boy carries.

Max announces the price: twopence ha'penny, or possibly fourpence, and writes it down in the book. Hassan Mohammed repeats the sum, storing it away in his capacious memory.

Terrific arithmetic lies ahead at the end of the week. When each daily sum has been added up and joined to the daily rate of pay the amount is then paid over. The man paid usually knows exactly what he is to receive!

Sometimes he will say: "It is not enough—there should be twopence more." Or just as often: "You have given me too much; fourpence less is what is owing me." They are seldom wrong. Occasional errors arise owing to the similarity of names. There are often three or four Daoud Mohammeds, and they have to be further distinguished by Daoud Mohammed Ibraham, or Daoud Mohammed Suliman.

Max goes on to the next man.

"Your name?"

"Ahmad Mohammed."

Ahmad Mohammed has not very much. Strictly speaking he has nothing at all that we want; but encouragement must be given, however small, so Max selects a few sherds of pottery and throws them into the basket and announces a couple of farthings.

Next come the basket-boys. Ibrahim Daoud has an exciting-looking object, which is only, alas, a fragment of an incised Arab pipe-stem! But now comes little Abdul Jehar, proffering doubtfully some tiny beads, and another object that Max snatches at with approval. A cylinder seal, intact, and of a good period—a really good find. Little Abdul is commended, and five francs is written down to his name. A murmur of excitement breaks out.

There is no doubt that to the workmen, gamblers all by nature, the uncertainty of the business is its principal attraction. And it is astonishing how a run of luck will attend certain gangs. Sometimes when new ground is being broken Max will say: "I shall put Ibrahim and his gang on this outer wall; they've found far too much lately. Now poor old Rainy George has had no luck lately. I'll put him on to a good place."

But lo and behold! In Ibrahim's patch, the houses of the poorest quarter of the old city, straightaway is found a *cache* of an earthenware pot containing a heap of gold earrings—the dowry, perhaps, of a daughter of olden days, and up goes Ibrahim's bakshish; and Rainy George, digging in a promising cemetery area where finds should abound, gets unaccountably sparse burials.

The men who have been bakshished go back to work in desultory fashion. Max goes on till he comes to the last gang.

It is now half an hour before sunset. The whistle blows. Everybody yells "Fidos! Fidos!" They fling baskets in the air, catch them, and run headlong down the hill, yelling and laughing.

Another day's work is over. Those who come from villages two or three miles away start to walk home. Our finds, in their baskets and boxes, are brought down the hill and packed carefully into Mary. A few men whose homes are on our route clamber on to Mary's roof. We set off home. Another day is over.

By a curious coincidence, our well that we have started to dig proves to be at the exact spot where a well has been dug in antiquity. This creates such an effect that a few days later five grave bearded gentlemen wait upon Max as he descends from the mound.

They have come, they explain, from their villages many miles distant. They are in need of more water. The Khwaja knows the places where the wells are hidden—those wells that the Romans had. If he will indicate the places to them they will be eternally grateful.

Max explains that it is pure chance that we have hit upon the spot where a well formerly existed.

The grave gentlemen smile politely but disbelievingly.

"'You have great wisdom, Khwaja; that is known. The secrets of antiquity are to you an open book. Where cities were, where wells were, all these things you know. Therefore, indicate to us the right places to dig and there shall be gifts."

None of Max's protestations are believed. Rather is he regarded as a magician who keeps his secrets. He knows, they murmur, but he will not say.

"I wish to goodness we'd never struck on that beastly Roman well," says Max gloomily. "It's causing me no end of trouble."

Complications arise when the men have to be paid. The official currency of the country is the French franc. But in this part of the world the Turkish mejidi has been in use so long that the conservative inhabitants regard nothing else as satisfactory. The bazaars deal in that currency though the banks do not. Our men refuse persistently to be paid in anything except the mejidi.

Consequently, having got the official currency from the bank, Michel has then to be dispatched to the bazaars to change it into the illegal currency that is the *"effectif"* locally.

The mejidi is a large, heavy coin. Michel staggers in with trays of these—handfuls, bagfuls! He pours them out upon the table. They are all very dirty, and smell of garlic!

We have nightmare evenings before pay-day counting out mejidis, almost asphyxiated with the smell of them!

Michel is invaluable in many ways. He is honest, punctual, and most scrupulous. Unable to read or write, he can carry the most complicated accounts in his head, returning from market with a long string of purchases, sometimes as many as thirty, reciting the price of each accurately, and putting down the exact amount of change. He never makes a single mistake in accountancy.

He is, on the other hand, overbearing in the extreme, extremely quarrelsome with all Mohammedans, very obstinate, and with an unfortunately heavy hand on machinery. *Forca!* he says, his eyes gleaming, and immediately afterwards an ominous snap is heard.

Even more disastrous are his economies. Putrescent bananas and dried-up oranges he is chagrined to find unappreciated. "Were there, then, no good ones?" "Yes, but more expensive. These are more economical."

It is a great word—*Economia!* It costs us a good deal in pure waste.

Michel's third slogan is *"Sawi proba"* (Make trial).

He says it in all kinds of tone of voice—hopefully, coaxingly, eagerly, confidently, sometimes despairingly. The result is usually unfortunate.

Our washerwoman having been unaccountably slow in delivering my cotton frocks, I venture to put on the Empire Builder's wife's shantung coat and skirt, which I have previously not had the courage to wear.

Max takes one look at me.

"What on earth have you got on?"

I say defensively that it is nice and cool.

"You can't wear that," says Max. "Go and take it off."

"I must wear it. I've bought it."

"It's too frightful. You look like the most offensive kind of *memsahib*—straight from Poonah!"

I admit sadly that I have had a suspicion to that effect.

Max says encouragingly: "Put on the greenish buff with the Tell Halaf running lozenge pattern."

"I wish," I say crossly, "that you would not use pottery terms for describing my clothes. It's lime-green! And a running lozenge is a disgusting term—like something half-sucked and left by a child on a village shop counter. How you can think up such disgusting descriptions for pottery patterns I cannot think!"

What an imagination you have, says Max. And the running lozenge is an extremely attractive Tell Halaf pattern.

He draws it for me on a piece of paper, and I say that I know all about it, and that it is a most attractive pattern. It's the description that's so revolting.

Max looks at me sadly and shakes his head.

As we pass through the village of Hanzir we hear the following conversation.

"Who are these?"

"They are the foreigners who dig."

Gravely an old gentleman surveys us.

"How beautiful they are," he sighs. "They are full of money!"

An old woman rushes up to Max.

"Khwaja! Mercy; intercede for my son. They have taken him away to Damascus—to prison. He is a good man, he has done nothing—nothing at all, I swear it!"

"Why, then, did they take him to prison?"

"For nothing. It is an injustice. Save him for me."

"But what has he done, mother?"

"Nothing. I swear it before God. Before God, it is true! He had done nothing but kill a man!"

Now a new anxiety arises. Several of the men from Jerablus fall ill. They are in tents at Chagar Bazar. Three men are laid up, and difficulty arises because the other men will not go near them. They will not take them food or water.

This avoidance of the sick is very strange. But, then, everything seems strange in a community where the value of human life is not accounted as important.

"They will starve if no food is taken to them," says Max.

Their fellow-workmen shrug their shoulders.

"Inshallah, if it is God's will."

The foremen, albeit reluctantly, vindicate their acquaintance with civilization and render some grudging service. Max broaches delicately the question of hospital. He can arrange with the French authorities for the two men who are seriously ill to be admitted to hospital.

Yahya and Alawi shake their heads doubtfully. It will be a disgrace to go to hospital, for in hospital disgraceful things happen. Death is always preferable to disgrace.

I think wildly of mistaken diagnoses, of neglect. "What are these disgraceful things that have occurred?" I asked.

Max goes deeper into the subject. Then, after a

long series of questions and answers which I do not
follow, he turns and explains.

A man was admitted to hospital and there he was
given an enema—

"Yes," I say, waiting for the story to proceed.

Max says that that is all.

"But did the man die?"

"No, but he would have preferred to die."

"What?" I cry incredulously.

Max says that it is so. The man returned to his
village, nursing a deep and bitter grievance. Such an
indignity was too deep! Death would to him have been
preferable.

Accustomed as we are to our Western ideas of the
importance of life, it is difficult to adjust one's thoughts
to a different scale of values. And yet to the Oriental
mind it is simple enough. Death is bound to come—
it is as inevitable as birth, whether it comes early or
late is entirely at the will of Allah. And that belief, that
acquiescence, does away with what has become the
curse of our present-day world—anxiety. There may
not be freedom from want, but there is certainly freedom from fear. And idleness is a blessed and natural
state—work is the unnatural necessity.

I think of an old beggar we came across in Persia.
He had a white beard and a dignified and noble mien.
He spoke proudly, for all his outstretched hand.

"Give me of your munificence a trifle, oh Prince. It
concerns me that I may avoid death."

The problem of the two ill men becomes more acute.
Max goes into Kamichlie and lays his troubles before
the French Commandant. The officers there are always
kind and helpful. Max is introduced to the French
military doctor, and the latter drives out with him to
the mound and examines the patients.

He confirms our fears that the men are really ill. One
man, he says, must have been already in a very serious

state of health when he came to us, and there could never have been much hope of his recovery. He recommends that they should both be brought into hospital. The men are persuaded to agree, and they are driven there forthwith.

The French doctor also very kindly gives us some really powerful aperient medicine, which will, he assures us, move a horse!

This is certainly needed, for the men are constantly coming to Max with graphic accounts of constipation, and ordinary laxatives seem to have no effect whatever.

One of our sick men has died in hospital. The other is well on the way to recovery. Word comes to us of the death two days after it has occurred, and we learn that the man is already buried.

Alawi comes to us with a grave face.

It is a question, he says, of our reputation. . . .

My heart sinks slightly. The word reputation always precedes the expenditure of money.

This man, he goes on, has died far from his home. He has been buried here. That, in Jerablus, will be a great reflection upon us.

But we cannot help the man's dying, says Max. He was already an ill man when he came, and we have done all we can.

Alawi waves death aside. Death is nothing. It is not the man's *death* that matters. It is the *burial*.

For what will be the position of this man's relations—of his family? He has been buried in a strange place. Then they will have to leave home and come to where his grave is. It is a disgrace for a man not to return to be buried in his home town.

Max says that he doesn't see what he can do about it now. The man *is* buried. What does Alawi suggest—a present of money to the sorrowing family?

That will be acceptable, yes. But what Alawi is really suggesting is disinterment.

"What! Dig him up again?"

"Yes, Khwaja. Send the body back to Jerablus. Then all will be done honorably, and your reputation will not suffer."

Max says that he does not know whether such a thing can be managed. It doesn't seem to him practicable.

Finally we go into Kamichlie and have a consultation with the French authorities. They obviously consider that we are mad!

Unexpectedly, this stiffens Max's determination. It is, he agrees, doubtless foolish, but is it *possible?*

The doctor shrugs his shoulders. But yes, it is *possible!* There will be forms—a lot of forms. *"Et des timbres, beaucoup de timbres."* "Naturally," says Max, "that is inevitable!"

Things are set under way. A taxi-driver, shortly making the return journey to Jerablus, enthusiastically accepts the task of conveying the (suitably disinfected) dead body. A workman, cousin of the dead man, will go in charge. All is arranged.

First, disinterment; then the signing of many forms and the attaching of stamps; the attendance of the military doctor armed with a large formalin spray; the bestowing of the body in the coffin; more formalin; the coffin is sealed up, the taxi-driver hoists it cheerfully into position.

"Hola!" he cries. "We shall have a gay journey! We must be careful our brother does not fall off on the way!"

The whole proceedings are now taking on that intense jocularity that can only be paralleled by the spirit of an Irish wake. The taxi drives off, with the driver and the cousin singing songs at the top of their voices. This, you feel, is a wonderful occasion for both of them! They are thoroughly enjoying themselves.

Max breathes a sigh of relief. He has affixed the last stamp and paid the final fees. The necessary forms (a voluminous sheaf) have been entrusted to the taxi-driver.

"Ah, well," says Max, "that is the end of *that!*"

He is wrong. The journey of the dead man, Abdullah Hamid, could be made into a poetical saga. There seems a moment when his body shall never know repose.

The body duly arrives at Jerablus. It is received with the proper lamentations, and with, we gather, a certain pride, so splendid has been its journey. There is a big celebration—a feast, in fact. The taxi-man, calling upon Allah, proceeds on his journey to Alep. It is realized, after he has gone, that the all-important "forms" have gone with him.

Chaos ensues. Without the necessary form the dead man cannot be buried. Is it necessary then, that he shall be returned to Kamichlie? Hot disputes arise on these points. Messages are dispatched—to the French authorities at Kamichlie, to us, to the very problematical address of the taxi-driver in Alep. Everything is done in a leisurely Arab fashion—and in the meantime Abdullah Hamid remains unburied.

How long, I ask Max anxiously, does the effect of formalin last? A fresh set of forms (complete with *les timbres*) are obtained and sent to Jerablus. Word comes that the corpse is about to be sent back by rail to Kamichlie. Urgent wires fly to and fro.

Suddenly all ends well. The taxi-man reappears in Jerablus, flourishing the forms.

"What an oversight!" he exclaims. The funeral proceeds in order and decency. Our reputation, Alawi assures us, is safe! The French authorities still consider we are mad. Our workmen gravely approve. Michel is outraged—what absence of *economia!* To relieve his feelings he hammers *tutti* loudly under the windows in the early hours of the morning until told forcefully to stop.

Tutti is the general name for all construction and usages of petrol tins. What Syria would do without the petrol tin one cannot imagine! Women fetch water from the well in petrol tins. Petrol tins are cut and hammered in strips on roofs and to mend houses.

It is Michel's ambition, he tells us in a burst of confidence, to have a house completely made of *tutti*.

"It will be beautiful," he says wistfully, "very beautiful."

V

FIN DE SAISON

CHAGAR BAZAR IS turning out well, and B. comes out from London as additional help for the last month.

It is interesting to watch B. and Mac together—they are such a complete contrast. B. is definitely a social animal, Mac an unsocial one. They get on very well together, but look at each other in puzzled wonderment.

On a day when we are going into Kamichlie, B. suddenly expresses concern.

"Seems rather bad luck leaving old Mac alone all day? Perhaps I'd better stay with him."

"Mac likes being alone," I assure him.

B. looks incredulous. He goes off to the drawing-office.

"Look here, Mac, like me to stay behind? Rather boring being alone all day."

A look of consternation crosses Mac's face.

"Oh," he says, "I've been looking forward to it."

"Queer chap he is," says B. as we bounce from rut to rut on the way to Kamichlie. "You know that

sunset last night? Beautiful! I was up on the roof
looking at it. Found Mac there. I was a bit enthusiastic,
I admit, but old Mac, he didn't say a word. Didn't
even *answer*. Yet I suppose he went up there to look
at it?"

"Yes, he usually goes up there in the evenings."

"It seems so odd he doesn't *say* anything, then."

I picture Mac on the roof, aloof and silent, B. buzz-
ing enthusiastically beside him.

Later, no doubt, Mac in his scrupulously neat room
will sit upon the plaid rug and write in his diary. . . .

"I mean, you'd think, wouldn't you . . ." B. goes
on perseveringly, but is interrupted as Michel, swerv-
ing across the road with diabolical intentions, steps
heavily on the accelerator and charges a party of Arabs
—two old women and a man with a donkey.

They scatter, screaming, and Max surpasses himself
in swearing angrily at Michel. What the hell does he
think he's doing? He might have killed them!

That apparently, was more or less Michel's intention.

"What would it have mattered?" he asks, flinging
both hands in the air and allowing the car to take its
own course. "They are Mohammedans, are they not?"

After enunciating this, according to his views, highly
Christian sentiment, he relapses into the martyred
silence of one misunderstood. What kind of Christians
are these, he seems to be saying to himself, weak and
irresolute in the faith!

Max lays it down as a positive rule that no at-
tempted murder of Mohammedans is to be permitted.

Michel murmurs sadly under his breath:

"It would be better if *all* Mohammedans were dead!"

Apart from our usual business in Kamichlie of visits
to the Bank, shopping at M. Yannakos', and a polite
call on the French, B. has business of his own—
namely, to collect a parcel sent after him from England
and consisting of two pairs of pajamas.

An official notification has been received by us that

the parcel in question is waiting at the Post Office, and so to the Post Office we go.

The Postmaster is not in evidence, but is summoned to the post of duty by a wall-eyed underling. He arrives yawning, heavily dressed in lurid striped pajamas. Although obviously aroused from heavy slumber, he is polite and amiable, shakes hands all round, inquires as to the progress of our excavations: Have we found any gold? Will we drink a cup of coffee with him? And thus courtesy having been satisfied, we drift to the subject of mail. Our letters now come to the Post Office at Amuda—not a very happy plan, as the elderly Postmaster in Amuda regards them as so precious and valuable that he frequently locks them away in the safe deposit for valuables and forgets to hand them out.

B.'s parcel, however, has been detained in Kamichlie, and we now start negotiations for its delivery.

"Yes, certainly there is such a parcel," says the Postmaster. "It has come from London, England. Ah, what a great city that must be! How much I would like to see it! It is addressed to a Monsieur B." Ah, this is Monsieur B., our new colleague? He shakes hands with B. again and utters some polite compliments. B. replies socially and politely in Arabic.

After this interlude we return to the question of the parcel. Yes, says the Postmaster, it has been here —actually here in the office! But it is here no longer. It has been removed to the custody of the Customs. Monsieur B. must realize that parcels are subject to Custom dues.

B. says that it is personal wearing apparel.

The Postmaster says: "No doubt, no doubt; but that is the affair of the Customs."

"We must, then, go to the Customs office?"

"That will be the proper procedure," agrees the Postmaster. "Not that it will be any use going today. Today is Wednesday, and on Wednesdays the Customs are closed."

"Tomorrow, then?"

"Yes, tomorrow the Customs will be open."

"Sorry," says B. to Max. "I suppose it means I shall have to come in again tomorrow to get my parcel."

The Postmaster says that certainly Monsieur B. will have to come in tomorrow, but that even tomorrow he will not be able to get his parcel.

"Why not?" demands B.

"Because, after the formalities of the Customs have been settled, the parcel must then go through the Post Office."

"You mean, I shall have to come on here?"

"Precisely. And that will not be possible tomorrow, for tomorrow the Post Office will be closed," says the Postmaster triumphantly.

We go into the subject in detail, but officialdom triumphs at every turn. On no day of the week, apparently, are both the Customs and the Post Office open!

We immediately turn and upbraid poor B., and ask him why on earth he can't bring his beastly pajamas with him instead of having them sent on by post!

"Because," says B., defending himself, "they are very special pajamas."

"They should be," says Max, "considering all the trouble they are going to cause! This lorry goes to and from the dig every day; not into Kamichlie as a postal service!"

We try to persuade the Postmaster to let B. sign the P.O. forms now, but he is adamant. P.O. formalities are always undertaken *after* the Customs. Defeated, we go sadly out of the Post Office, and the Postmaster, presumably, returns to bed.

Michel comes up excitedly and says he has made a most advantageous bargain in oranges. He has bought two hundred oranges at a most economical price. As usual, he is sworn at. How does he think we are going to get through two hundred oranges before they go bad—that is to say, if they are not bad already?

Some of them, Michel admits, are perhaps a trifle on the stale side, but they are very cheap, and there is a great reduction for taking the two hundred. Max agrees to inspect them, and on doing so immediately turns them down. Most of them are already covered with green mould!

Michel murmurs sadly: "Economia!" After all, they *are* oranges. He departs, and returns with some economical hens, carried, as is usual, upside down, with their legs tied together. Other economical and uneconomical purchases having been made, we set off for home.

I ask Mac if he has had a nice day, and he says, "Splendid!" with unmistakable enthusiasm.

Gazing uncomprehendingly at Mac, B. sits down on a chair that isn't there, and Mac's perfect day is brought to a delightful finish. I have never seen any one laugh so much! At intervals during dinner he breaks out again. If we had known just what tickled Mac's sense of humor, we could have arranged to give him quite a lot of quiet fun!

B. continues with his uphill task of being sociable. On the days when Max is at the dig and the three of us are in the house, B. roams around like a lost soul. He goes into the drawing-office and talks to Mac, but, meeting with no response, he comes sadly into the office, where I am busy on the typewriter getting down to the gory details of a murder.

"Oh," says B., "you're busy?"

I say "Yes" shortly.

"Writing?" asks B.

"Yes" (more shortly).

"I thought, perhaps," says B. wistfully, "I might bring the labels and the objects in here. I shouldn't be disturbing you should I?"

I have to be firm. I explain clearly that it is quite impossible for me to get on with my dead body if a live body is moving, breathing, and in all probability talking, in the near vicinity!

Poor B. goes sadly away, condemned to work in loneliness and silence. I feel convinced that, if B. ever writes a book, he will do so most easily with a wireless and a gramophone turned on close at hand and a few conversations going on in the same room!

But when visitors arrive, either at the mound or at the house, then B. comes into his own.

Nuns, French officers, visiting archaeologists, tourists —B. is willing and competent to deal with them all.

"Here's a car stopping and some people. Shall I go down and see who they are?"

"Oh, *please* do!"

And presently the party arrives, ably shepherded, with B. chatting in any necessary language. On these occasions, as we tell him, B. is worth his weight in gold.

"Mac's not much good, is he?" says B., grinning at Mac.

"Mac," I say severely, "is no good at all. He won't even *try*."

Mac gives his gentle remote smile. . . .

Mac, we discover, has a weakness. That weakness is The Horse.

The problem of B.'s pajamas is dealt with by his dropping Mac at the mound and continuing to Kamichlie in the car. Mac wants to come home midday, and Alawi suggests that he should ride home. The Sheikh has several horses. At once Mac's face lights up. That gentle aloofness disappears. Eagerness takes its place.

From thence on, whenever there is the least excuse, Mac comes home on horseback.

"The Khwaja Mac," says Alawi, "he never speaks; he whistles. When he wants the pole-boy to go to the left, he whistles; when he wants the mason to come, he whistles; now it is for a horse he whistles!"

The matter of B.'s pajamas is still unsettled. The Customs demand the exorbitant sum of eight pounds! B. points out that the pajamas only cost two pounds a pair and refuses to pay. A most difficult situation is then created. What, the Customs demand, are they to do with the parcel? They return it to the Postmaster. He is not to give it to B., and he is not to let it leave the country! We spend several wasted days and hours going into Kamichlie and arguing the matter. The Bank Manager is called in, and the officers of the Services Spéciaux. Even a high dignitary of the Maronite Church who is visiting the Bank Manager takes a hand, looking very impressive in purple robes, an immense cross, and a large bun of hair! The wretched Postmaster, though still in pajamas, gets hardly any sleep at all! The business is rapidly becoming an International incident.

Suddenly all is settled. The douanier of Amuda arrives at our house with the parcel. The complications have been resolved: thirty shillings for the duty, *douze francs cinquante pour les timbres, et des cigarettes, n'est ce pas?* (Packets of cigarettes are pushed into his hand.) "Voilà, Monsieur!" He beams, B. beams, everybody beams. We all stand round and watch B. open his parcel.

He holds the contents up proudly, explaining, like the White Knight, that this is a special invention of his own.

"Mosquitoes," he explains. "Does away with mosquito nets."

Max says he's never seen a mosquito in these parts.

"Of course there are mosquitoes," B. says. "It is well known. Stagnant water!"

My eyes go immediately to Mac.

"There's no stagnant water here," I say. "If so, Mac would have seen it!"

B. says triumphantly that there is a pond of stagnant water just to the north of Amuda.

Max and I repeat that we have never heard or seen any mosquito. B. pays no attention, but enlarges on his invention.

The pajamas are of white washing silk. They are all in one, with a hood that comes up over the head, and the sleeves end in fingerless gloves. A zip closes up the front, so that the only parts of the wearer exposed to mosquito attack are the eyes and nose.

"And you breathe in and out through your nose, which keeps off the mosquitoes," says B. triumphantly.

Max repeats chillingly that there are no mosquitoes.

B. gives us to understand that when we are all aching and shivering with malaria we shall wish we had adopted his idea.

Mac suddenly begins to laugh. We look at him inquiringly.

"I'm thinking of that time you sat down when the chair wasn't there," says Mac, and goes away happily chuckling.

We are fast asleep that night when a terrific hullabaloo breaks out. We spring up, thinking for the moment that we are being attacked by robbers. We all rush out into the dining-room. A white figure is rushing wildly up and down, yelping and jumping about.

"Good heavens, B., what's the matter?" cries Max.

For a moment we think that B. has gone mad.

But enlightenment comes.

By some means or other a mouse has insinuated itself into the mosquito-proof pajamas. The zip has jammed.

It is daylight before we stop laughing.

Only B. is not really amused. . . .

The weather is growing hotter. All sorts of new flowers come out. I am no botanist, and do not know their names, and, frankly, do not want to know them. (What pleasure does it give you knowing what things are called?) But there are blue and mauve ones, like tiny lupins and little wild tulips; and golden ones, like marigolds and puce-colored delicate spikes of bloom. All the mounds are a riot of color. This is, indeed, the "fertile steppe." I visit the antika-room and borrow some suitably shaped pots. Mac, wishing to draw them, looks for them in vain. They are full of flowers.

Our house is rising now rapidly. The wooden centering is erected and mud-brick is being plastered on it. The effect is going to be very good. I congratulate Mac, standing beside him on the mound.

"This is a great deal better than my lavatory," I say.

The successful architect agrees. He complains, however, bitterly of his workmen, who have no idea at all, he says, of *accuracy*. I say I'm sure they haven't. Mac says bitterly that they just laugh and think it doesn't matter. I turn the talk to horses, and Mac cheers up.

With the hotter weather, our workmen's tempers grow hotter also. Max increases fines for broken heads, and at last comes to a desperate decision. Every morning the men are to hand in their weapons before they start work. It is an unpopular decision, but reluctantly the men agree. Under Max's eye, bludgeons, maces, and long murderous-looking knives are handed over to Michel, who locks them away inside Mary. At sunset they are returned to the owners. It wastes time and is tedious, but at least the workmen escape more serious damage.

A Yezidi workman comes and complains that he is faint for want of water. He cannot work unless he has water to drink.

"But there is water here—why do you not drink?"

"I cannot drink that water. It comes from the well, and this morning the Sheikh's son dropped lettuce into the well."

The Yezidis, by their religion, must never mention lettuce or touch anything contaminated by it, for they believe Shaitan resided in it.

Max says: "Now, I think that lies have been told to you. For this very morning I saw the Sheikh's son in Kamichlie, and he told me he had been there two days. This has been said to you to deceive you."

The Riot Act is then read to the assembled workmen. No one is to tell lies to or to persecute the Yezidi workmen. "On this dig all are to be brothers."

A Mohammedan with a merry eye steps forward.

"You follow Christ, Khwaja, and we follow Mohammed, but both of us are the enemies of Shaitan (the devil). Therefore it is our duty to persecute those who believe that Shaitan shall be restored and who worship him."

"Then to do your duty in future will cost you five francs a time!" says Max.

For some days after this we get no more Yezidi complaints.

The Yezidis are a curious and singularly gentle people, and their worship of Shaitan (Satan) is more in the nature of a propitiation. Moreover, they believe that this world has been placed in the charge of Shaitan by God—and to the age of Shaitan there will succed the age of Jesus, whom they recognize as a Prophet, but one not yet come to power. Shaitan's name must never be mentioned, nor any word that sounds like it.

Their holy shrine, Sheikh 'Adi, is situated in the Kurdish hills near Mosul, and we visited it when we were digging near there. There can be, I think, no spot in the world so beautiful or so peaceful. You wind up far into the hills, through oak trees and pomegranates, following a mountain stream. The air is fresh and clear and pure. You must go on foot or by horse for the last few miles of the way. Human nature is said to be so pure in these parts that the Christian woman can bathe naked in the streams.

And then, suddenly, you come to the white spires of the Shrine. All is calm gentle and peaceful there. There are trees, a courtyard, running water. Gentle-faced custodians bring you refreshments and you sit in perfect peace, sipping tea. In the Inner Court is the entrance to the Temple, on the right of which is carved a great black serpent. The snake is sacred, since the Yezidis believe that the Ark of Noah was grounded on the Jebel Sinjar and that a hole was made in it. The serpent formed itself into a coil and stopped up the hole so that the Ark could proceed.

Presently we removed our shoes and were taken into the Temple, carefully stepping over the threshold, since it is forbidden to step on a threshold. It is also

forbidden to show the soles of the feet, a slightly difficult feat when one is sitting cross-legged on the ground.

The interior is dark and cool and there is trickling
water, the sacred Spring, which is said to communi-
cate with Mecca. In this Temple the Image of the Peacock is brought at festival times. A peacock was chosen
as the representative of Shaitan, some say, because it
was the word most different from the Forbidden name.
At any rate, it is Lucifer, Son of the Morning, who
is the Peacock Angel of the Yezidi faith.

We came out again and sat in the cool silence and
peace of the court. Both of us felt loath to return from
this mountain sanctuary to the turmoil of the world. . . .

Sheikh 'Adi is a place I shall never forget—nor shall
I forget the utter peace and satisfaction that possessed
my spirit there. . . .

The head of the Yezidis, the Mir, came once to our
dig in Iraq. A tall, sad-faced man dressed all in black.
He is the Pope as well as the Chief, though local tradition had it that this particular Mir was entirely "run"
by his aunt, the Khatūn of the Shrine of Sheikh 'Adi
and his mother, a handsome ambitious woman, who
was said to keep her son under drugs so that she could
wield authority.

On a trip through the Jebel Sinjar, we paid a visit to
the Yezidi Sheikh of the Sinjar, Hâmo Shero, a very
old man, said to be ninety years of age. During the
war of 1914-18 hundreds of Armenian refugees fled
from the Turks, and were given shelter in the Sinjar and
their lives saved.

Another furious dissension breaks out over the day
of rest. The day after pay-day is always a holiday.
The Mohammedans claim that since there are more
Mohammedans than Christians on the dig, Friday
should be chosen as the day of rest. The Armenians
refuse, in any case, to work on a Sunday, and say that
as it is a Christian dig, Sunday should be the holiday.
We decree that the holiday shall always be a Tues-

day, which, so far as we know, is the feast-day of no particular religion.

In the evenings the foremen come to the house, drink coffee with us, and report on the difficulties or problems that arise.

Old Abd es Salaam is particularly eloquent this evening. His voice rises in a long impassioned monologue. I cannot get the hang of it, though I listen attentively. It is, however, so very dramatic that my curiosity is aroused. When Abd es Salaam pauses for breath, I ask Max what it is all about.

Max replies in one brief word: "Constipation."

Sensing my interest, Abd es Salaam turns towards me, and pours out further rhetorical details of his condition.

Max says: "He's had Eno's, Beecham's, Vegetable laxatives, and Castor Oil. He's telling you exactly how each one has made him feel, and how none of them has brought about the desired result."

Clearly, the French doctor's horse medicine is indicated.

Max administers a terrific dose! Abd es Salaam goes hopefully away, and we all pray for a happy result!

I am now quite busy. In addition to repairing pottery, there is the photography—a "dark room" has been allotted to me. It somewhat resembles the "Little Ease" of medieval times.

In it, one can neither sit nor stand! Crawling in on all fours, I develop plates, kneeling with bent head. I come out practically asphyxiated with heat and unable to stand upright, and take a good deal of pleasure in detailing my sufferings, though the audience is somewhat inattentive—their entire interest is in the negatives, not in the operator.

Max occasionally remembers to say warmly and tactfully: "I think you're wonderful, dear," in a slightly abstracted manner.

Our house is finished. From the summit of the mound it has a holy appearance, with its great dome rising up white against the sun-baked ground. Inside, it is very pleasant. The dome gives a feeling of spaciousness and it is cool. The two rooms on one side are, first, the Antika-room, and beyond it Max's and my bedroom. On the other side is the drawing-office, and beyond a bedroom shared by B. and Mac. We shall only be here for a week or two this year. Harvest is already come, and the men leave the work every day to go and reap. The flowers are gone, vanished overnight, for the Beduin have come down from the hills, their brown tents are all round, and their cattle at pasturage eat as they go slowly south.

We shall return next year—return to our home, for this domed house in the middle of nowhere already feels like home.

The Sheikh in his snowy robes tours round it appreciatively, his merry little eyes sparkling. This is to be his inheritance eventually, and already he feels an added prestige.

It will be good to see England again. Good to see friends and green grass and tall trees. But it will be good too, to return next year.

Mac is doing a sketch. It is a sketch of the mound —a highly formalised view, but one which I admire very much.

There are no human beings to be seen; just curving lines and patterns. I realize that Mac is not only an architect. He is an artist. I ask him to design a jacket for my new book.

B. comes in, and complains that all the chairs are packed—there is nothing to sit on.

"What do you want to sit down for?" asks Max. "There's a lot of work to be done."

He goes out, and B. says reproachfully to me:

"What an energetic man your husband is!"

I wonder who would believe this if they had only seen Max asleep on a summer afternoon in England . . .?

I begin to think of Devon, of red rocks and blue sea. . . . It is lovely to be going home—my daughter, the dog, bowls of Devonshire cream, apples, bathing. . . . I draw a sigh of ecstasy.

VI

JOURNEY'S END

Our finds have been encouraging, and we are to continue digging for another season.

This year we shall be a different team.

Mac is with another dig in Palestine, but hopes to come to us for the last few weeks of the season.

So we shall have a different architect. There will also be an extra member of the staff—the Colonel. Max hopes to combine a certain amount of digging at Tell Brak with the Chagar dig, and the Colonel can be in charge at one dig whilst Max is at the other.

Max, the Colonel, and our new architect travel out together, and I am to follow a couple of weeks later.

About a fortnight before they start, our architect rings up and asks for Max, who is out. He sounds worried. I ask if it is anything I can do?

He says: "Well, it's just about the journey. I'm at Cook's trying to book my sleeper to the place Max told me, and Cook's say there just isn't any such place."

I reassure him.

"They often say that. Nobody ever goes to the sort

of places we do, and so, naturally, they haven't heard of them."

"They seem to think that what I really mean is Mosul."

"Well," I assure him "you don't."

A light dawns on me. "Did you ask for Kamichlie or Nisibin?"

"Kamichlie! Isn't that the name of the place?"

"It's the name of the *place*, but the station is Nisibin —it's on the Turkish side of the frontier. Kamichlie is the Syrian town."

"That explains it. Max didn't say there was anything else I ought to take, did he?"

"I don't think so. You've got plenty of pencils, haven't you?"

"Pencils?" The voice sounds surprised. "Of course."

"You will need plenty of pencils," I say.

Without fully realizing the sinister significance of this, he rings off.

My progress to Stamboul is peaceful, and I get my quota of shoes safely past the Turkish Customs!

At Haidar Pacha I find I am to share a compartment with a large-sized Turkish lady. She has already six suitcases, two peculiar-shaped baskets, some striped bags, and various parcels of provisions. By the time I have added my two suitcases and a hat-box there is simply no room to put our legs anywhere!

Seeing the large lady off is another slimmer and more lively lady. She addresses me in French, and we converse amiably. I am going to Alep? Ah, her cousin not so far! Do I speak German? Her cousin speaks a little German.

No, alas, I speak no German! And no Turkish? And no Turkish!

How unfortunate! Her cousin speaks no French! What, then, are we to do? How shall we be able to converse?

It seems, I say, that we shall not be able to converse.

"A thousand pities," says the lively cousin. "It would

have been interesting for both of you. But, before the train goes, let us say all we can. You are married— yes?" I admit that I am married. "And children? You have many children, no doubt? My cousin has four children only—but," adds the cousin proudly—"three of them are boys!" I feel that for English prestige I cannot admit to being perfectly contented with one daughter. I add a couple of sons with shameless mendacity.

"Excellent!" says the cousin, beaming. "Now, as to miscarriages? How many miscarriages have you had? My cousin has had five—two at three months, two at five months, and one premature stillborn child at seven months." I am just hesitating whether to invent a miscarriage to enhance the friendly feeling when mercifully a whistle blows, and the lively cousin leaps out of the carriage and along the corridor. "You must tell each other all the details by signs," she screams.

The prospect is alarming, but we get along very well by means of nods, becks, and smiles. My companion offers me generous portions of her immense supplies of highly spiced food, and I bring her back an apple from the dining-car by way of polite rejoinder.

After the unpacking of the food baskets, there is even less room for our feet, and the smell of food and musk is almost overpowering!

When night comes, my travelling companion makes sure that the window is tightly closed. I retire to the upper berth, and wait till gentle and rhythmical snores proceed from the lower bunk.

Very stealthily I slip down and surreptitiously let down the window a fraction. I retire aloft again undiscovered.

Great pantomime of surprise in the morning when the window is discovered to be open. With multitudinous gestures the Turkish lady tries to assure me that it is not her fault. She thought she had closed it. I assure her by gesture that I do not blame her for a moment. It is, I infer, one of those things that happen.

When we reach the Turkish lady's station she parts

from me with great politeness. We smile, nod, bow, and
express regret that the language bar has prevented us
from really getting down to an exchange of the essential facts of life.

At lunch-time I sit opposite a kindly old American
lady. She looks out reflectively at women working in
the fields.

"Poor souls!" she sighs out. "I wonder if they realize
that they are free!"

"Free?" I am slightly at a loss.

"Why, certainly; they don't wear the veil any
longer. Mustapha Kemal has done away with all that.
They're free now."

I look thoughtfully at the laboring women. It does
not seem to me that the point would have any significance for them. Their day is a ceaseless round of toil,
and I doubt very much if they have ever enjoyed the
luxury of veiling their faces. None of our local workmen's wives do.

I do not, however, argue the point.

The American lady calls the attendant and demands
a glass of hot water. *"Je vais Prendre,"* she says, *"des
remèdes."*

The man looks blank. Would she like coffee, he
says, or tea? With difficulty we make him understand
that it is plain hot water that is required.

"You'll take some salts with me?" says my new
friend matily, as one who suggests a cocktail together.
I thank her, but say I don't care for salts. "But they're
good for you," she urges. I have great difficulty in
avoiding having my system drastically purged.

I retire to my carriage, and wonder how Abd es
Salaam's constipation is getting on this year!

I break the journey at Alep, since there are some
things Max wants me to get there. Since I have a day
to spare before the next train to Nisibin, I agree to
make one of a party going to motor out to Kalat Siman.

The party turns out to be a mining engineer and a
very elderly and almost totally deaf clergyman. The

clergyman, for some reason, takes it into his head that the mining engineer, whom I have never seen before in my life, is my husband.

"Your husband speaks Arabic very well, my dear," he remarks, patting my hand benignly as we return from our expedition.

I yell rather confusedly:

"He does, but he isn't . . ."

"Oh, yes, he is," says the clergyman reprovingly. "He is a very fine Arabic scholar."

"He isn't my husband," I shout.

"Your wife doesn't speak Arabic at all,: I gather," says the clergyman, turning to the engineer, who turns brick red.

"She isn't . . ." he begins loudly.

"No," says the clergyman, "I thought she wasn't proficient in Arabic." He smiles. "You must teach her."

In unison we both shout:

"We aren't married!"

The clergyman's expression changes. He looks severe and disapproving.

"Why not?" he demands.

The mining engineer says helplessly to me: "I give it up."

We both laugh, and the clergyman's face relaxes.

"I see," he says, "you've been having your little joke with me."

The car draws up by the hotel, and he gets cautiously out, unwinding a long muffler from his white whiskers. He turns and smiles on us beneficently.

"Bless you both," he says. "I hope you have a long and happy life together!"

Triumphal arrival at Nisibin! As usual, the train halts so that there is a sheer drop of five feet between the step and a surface of sharp, loose stones! A kindly fellow-passenger leaps down and clears the stones, enabling me to jump without turning my ankle. In the distance I see Max approaching, and our chauffeur, Michel. I remember Michel's three Words of Power:

Forca, the applying of brute strength (usually with disastrous results); *Sawi Proba* and *Economia,* the general principle of Economy, which has led before now to break-down in the desert without petrol.

Before we all meet, a uniformed Turk says "Passport" sternly to me, takes it away, and leaps back upon the train.

Greetings then take place. I shake the leathery hand of Michel, who says "Bon Jour. How do you do?" And then adds in Arabic a "God-be-praised" for my safe arrival. Various underlings seize suitcases which the Wagon Lit conductor has been hurling out of the windows. I mention my passport. It and the uniformed Turk have completely disappeared.

Blue Mary—our lorry—is waiting faithfully. Michel opens the back door, and a familiar sight meets the eyes. Several hens, uncomfortably tied together; tins of benzine and heaps of sacking that eventually turn out to be human beings. My luggage is stowed on top of the hens, and the humans and Michel depart to seek my passport. Fearing that Michel may apply *Forca* and create an international complication, Max goes after him. After twenty minutes or so they return triumphant.

We start off—creak, lurch, rattle, bound in and out of potholes. We pass from Turkey into Syria. Five minutes later we are in that rising township of Kamichlie.

There is much business afoot before we can set out for home. We proceed first to "Harrods"—namely, the establishment of M. Yannakos. Here I receive greetings, am offered the chair behind the till, and coffee is brewed for me. Michel is completing the purchase of a horse, which is to be attached to a cart and carry water from the river Jaghjagha to our excavations on Tell Brak. Michel has found, so he says, an excellent horse—a horse extremely *economia.* "How economia is the horse?" Max asks suspiciously. "Is it a good horse? A large horse? A horse of endurance? Better," he says, "a good horse costing a little more money than an inferior horse at a cheap price."

One of the bundles of sacking has left the lorry and turns out to be the ruffian who is to be the waterman —a man with (so he says) a knowledge of horses. He is to go with Michel and report on the horse. Meanwhile we buy tinned fruits, bottles of doubtful wine, macaroni, pots of plum and apple jam, and other delicacies, from M. Yannakos. We then proceed to the Post Office, where we find our old friend the unshaven Postmaster in dirty pajamas. The pajamas do not appear to have been washed or changed since last year. We take our bundles of newspapers and a letter or two, reject three other letters addressed in European handwriting to a Mr. Thompson, which the Postmaster presses anxiously upon us, and go on to the bank.

The Bank is of stone—large, cool, empty, very peaceful. There is a bench in the middle, on which sit two soldiers, an old man in picturesque colored rags with a hennaed beard, and a boy in torn European clothing. They all sit peacefully gazing into space and occasionally spitting. There is a mysterious bed with dingy blankets in a corner. We are received with pleasure by the clerk behind the counter. Max produces a check to be cashed, and we are shown into the office of M. le Directeur. M. le Directeur is large, coffee colored, and voluble. He receives us with the utmost amiability. Coffee is sent for. He has replaced the *directeur* of last year, and is rather sad about it. He has come from Alexandretta, where, as he says, there is a *little* life! But here (his hands fly up), *"On ne peut même pas faire un Bridge!"* "No," he adds, his sense of injury growing, *"pas même un tout petit Bridge."* (Note—what is the difference between *un Bridge* and *un tout petit Bridge?* Presumably both need four players?)

Half an hour passes in conversation on the political situation, and the amenities (or lack of them) in Kamichlie. *"Mais tout de même on fait des belles constructions,"* he admits. He is living, it appears, in one of these new constructions. One has not the electric light, the sanitation, nor any civilized comforts, but the house is at least a *construction*—"*une construction en pierre, vous comprenez!* Madame will see it on her way to Chagar Bazar."

I promise to look out for it.

We discuss the local Sheikhs. They are all alike, he says. "*Des propriétaires—mais qui n'ont pas le sou!*" They are always in debt.

At intervals during the conversation the cashier enters with five or six forms, which Max signs, and also disburses small sums, such as sixty centimes *pour les timbres*.

The coffee comes, and after forty minutes the little cashier arrives with the last three documents, a final request of "*Et deux francs quarante cinq centimes pour les timbres, s'il vous plaît*," and it is intimated that the final ceremonies have been completed, and that the money can now be handed over. "*C'est à dire, si nous avons de l'argent ici!*"

Coldly, Max points out that he has given notice of his intention to draw a check a week previously. The cashier shrugs his shoulders, smiling. "Ah well, we will see!" Fortunately all is well, the money is forthcoming, *les timbres* are affixed, we can leave. The same people are sitting on the benches, still gazing into space and spitting.

We return to Harrods. The Kurdish waterman is waiting for us. He reports that Michel's horse—well, one cannot call it a horse! It is not a horse at all. It is an old woman—just that; an old woman! So much for Michel's *economia*. Max goes to inspect the horse, and I return to the chair behind the till.

M. Yannakos Junior entertains me with halting conversation on the events of the great world. "*Votre roi*," he says. "*Votre roi—vous avez un nouveau roi.*" I agree that we have a new King. M. Yannakos struggles to express thoughts that go beyond his words. "*Le Roi d'angleterre!*" he says. "*Grand roi—Plus grand roi dans tout monde—aller—comme ça.*" He makes an ex-

pressive gesture. *"Pour une femme!"* It is beyond him.
"Pour une femme!" No, such a thing is not believable.
Is it possible that such an extraordinary importance attaches to women in England? *"Le plus grand roi au
monde,"* he repeats in awestruck tones.

Max, the Kurd, and Michel return. Michel, momentarily cast down by the vote of censure on his horse,
has recovered all his aplomb. They are now going to
enter into negotiations for a *mule*. Michel murmurs
that a mule will be very expensive. The Kurd says that
a mule is always valuable. The Kurd and Michel go off
in search of a man whose second cousin's husband
knows a man who has a mule to sell.

Sudden appearance of our idiot houseboy, Mansur.
He beams welcome and shakes me warmly by the hand.
He it is whom it took one whole season to teach to
lay the table—and even now he is apt to break out into
an eruption of forks for tea. Making the beds strains
his mental capacity to the utmost. His movements are
slow, dogged, and everything he does is in the nature
of a trick successfully taught to a dog.

Will we come to the house of his mother (who, incidentally, does our washing) and inspect a collection
of antikas?

We go. The room is much swept and garnished.
For the third time in two hours I drink coffee. The
antikas are brought out—little Roman glass bottles,
fragments of glaze and pottery, odd coins, and a good
deal of complete junk. Max divides it into two groups,
rejecting one, offering his price for the other. A woman
enters, who is clearly an interested party. It seems a
moot point whether she will complete the sale or have
twins first. By the aspect of her it might even be quins.
She listens to Mansur's translations, shakes her head.

We leave and return to the lorry. Negotiations for
the mule having been begun, we go to inspect the
water-barrels, which are to be transported in the cart
the mule is to draw. Once more Michel is in trouble.
He has ordered one water-barrel of such immense
dimensions that it would not fit in the cart, and would

probably kill any horse or mule. "But," wails Michel, "one big water-barrel is more *economia* to make than two small ones, and it holds more water!" Michel is told he is a blasted fool, and that in future he is to do as he is told. He murmurs hopefully: "Sawi proba?" but even that hope is dashed from him.

Next we meet the Sheikh—our own particular Sheikh. He is looking more than ever like Henry the Eighth, with his immense henna-dyed beard. He wears his usual white robes, and an emerald green cloth wound round his head. He is in an extremely jovial mood, as he proposes shortly to visit Baghdad, though, of course, it will take many weeks before his passport is arranged. "Brother," he says to Max, "everything that I have is yours. For your sake, I have not sown any seed in the ground this year that all the land might be at your disposal." My husband replies: "How happy I am that such nobility has also turned out to your own advantage. This year all crops are failing. Those who have sown seed will lose money. You are to be congratulated on your acumen."

Honor thus satisfied, they part on the best of terms.

We climb into Blue Mary. Michel dumps a load of potatoes and oranges on top of my hat-box, completely denting it in; the hens squawk; several Arabs and Kurds beg for conveyance—two are accepted. They get in among the hens and the potatoes and the luggage, and off we go to Chagar Bazar.

VII

LIFE AT CHAGAR BAZAR

WITH AN IMMENSE wave of excitement I catch sight of Our House. There it stands, with its dome, looking like a shrine dedicated to some venerable saint!

The Sheikh, Max tells me, is intensely proud of it. At intervals he and his friends circle round it admiringly, and Max suspects that he is already raising money on it by falsely representing that it belongs to *him,* and is merely rented to us.

Mary draws up with Michel's usual violent application of the brakes *(Forca),* and everyone rushes out of the house to greet us. There are old faces and new ones.

Dimitri, the cook, is the same. His long, gentle face is definitely maternal. He is wearing long trousers of flowered muslin and beaming with pleasure. He seizes my hand and presses it against his forehead, then proudly displays a wooden box with four new-born puppies in it. These, he says, will be our future watchdogs. Ali, the boy, was also with us last year. He is now feeling rather superior, as a second and lesser cook's boy is now employed, by name Ferhid. There is little to say about Ferhid, except that he looks worried about something. But this, Max informs me, is Ferhid's chronic condition.

We have also a new house-boy—Subri. Subri is tall and fierce and looks very intelligent. He grins and shows teeth of assorted white and gold.

The Colonel and Bumps have tea ready for us. The Colonel does things with military precision. Already he has instituted a new custom of lining up the men in military formation at bakshish-time. They think it a great joke. He spends a lot of time tidying up. The days when Max goes into Kamichlie are his great opportunity. The house, he announces proudly, is now as neat as a new pin. Everything that has a place is in its place, and quite a lot of things that have not got a place have been found a place! So much so, that all kinds of inconvenience will arise!

Bumps is our new architect. His nickname has arisen out of an innocent remark made by him to the Colonel on the journey out. In the early dawn, as the train was approaching Nisibin, Bumps pulled up the blind and looked out with interest on the country where the next few months of his life were to be spent.

"Curious place this is," he remarks. "It's all over *bumps!*"

"Bumps, indeed!" cries the Colonel. "Don't you realize, you irreverent fellow, that each of those *bumps* is a buried city dating back thousands of years?"

And from henceforth Bumps is to be our new colleague's name!

There are other new acquisitions for me to see. First, a second-hand Citröen, which the Colonel has christened Poilu.

Poilu turns out to be a very temperamental gentleman. For some reason or other he always chooses the Colonel with whom to misbehave, obstinately refusing to start, or else staging a break-down at some inconvenient spot.

The solution of this mystery dawns on me one day, and I explain to the Colonel that it is his fault.

"How do you mean—*my* fault?"

"You shouldn't have christened him Poilu. After all, if our lorry started as Queen Mary, the least you could do was to christen the Citröen the Empress Josephine. If so, you'd have had no trouble!"

The Colonel, like the disciplinarian he is, says that at any rate it is too late now. Poilu is Poilu, and will have to behave himself. I look sideways at Poilu, who seems to be regarding the Colonel with a rakish air. Poilu, I feel sure, is contemplating that most serious of military crimes—mutiny!

The foremen next come rushing up to greet me. Yahya looks more than ever like a great happy dog. Alawi is looking, as always, very handsome. Old Abd es Salaam is, as usual, full of conversation.

I ask Max how Abd es Salaam's constipation is, and Max replies that most evenings have been devoted to the exhaustive discussion of it!

Then we go to the Antika-room. The first work period of ten days is just concluded, with the bumper result of a find of nearly a hundred tablets, so everyone is very jubilant. In another week we are starting to dig at Tell Brak as well as Chagar.

Back in the house at Chagar, it seems as though I had never been away, though, owing to the Colonel's passion for order, the house is looking a good deal tidier than I have ever seen it. Which brings me to the sad story of the Camembert cheeses.

Six Camembert cheeses had been bought by Max in Alep under the impression that you can treat a Camembert cheese like a Dutch cheese and store it away until wanted. One had been eaten before my arrival, and the Colonel, coming across the other five in his tidying round, had stacked them neatly at the back of a cupboard in the living-room. There they were rapidly overlaid by drawing-paper, typewriting-paper, cigarettes, Turkish delight, etc., and languished in darkness—unremembered, unseen, but not, let it be said, *unsmelt.*

A fortnight later we are all sniffing and hazarding guesses.

"If I didn't know that we'd *got* no drains—" says Max.

"And the nearest gas-pipe must be about two hundred miles away—"

"So I suppose it *must* be a dead mouse."

"A dead rat at least!"

Life indoors becoming unendurable, a determined search is made for the hypothetical disintegrating rat. Then, and only then, is the discovery made of a gluey odorous mass which has once been five Camembert cheeses, and which, passing through the *coulant* stage, are now *coulant* to the *n*th degree.

Accusing eyes are turned on the Colonel, and the horrible remains are entrusted to Mansur for solemn burial at a spot remote from the house. Max explains to the Colonel with feeling how this confirms what he has always known—that the idea of tidiness is a great mistake! The Colonel explains that the tidying away of the cheeses was a good idea; the fault lies in the absent-mindedness of archaeologists who cannot remember that they have Camembert cheeses in the house. I explain that the real mistake lies in buying ripe Camembert cheeses *en bloc* to store for the season! Bumps says, why buy Camembert cheeses, anyway? *He* has never liked them! Mansur takes away the horrible remains and buries them obediently, but he is, as usual, puzzled. Presumably the Khwajas *like* these things, since they pay good money for them? Why, then, destroy them, when their good qualities have become so much more evident than they were before? Obviously it is all a part and parcel of the extraordinary ways of employers!

The servant problem on the Habur is very different from the servant problem in England. You might say that here the servants have an employer problem! Our fancies, prejudices, likes and dislikes are quite fantastic, and follow, to the native mind, no logical pattern whatever!

For instance, various cloths of slightly different texture with different colored borders are issued, and are supposed to be used for different purposes. Why this elaboration?

Why, when Mansur is using a blue-edged teacloth to wipe mud from the car's radiator, does an incensed Khatūn emerge from the house full of condemnation? The cloth has removed the mud most successfully. Again, why unmerited censure when a visit to the kitchen reveals the fact that the breakfast things after washing up are being wiped with a sheet?

"But," protests Mansur, anxious to vindicate his conduct, "it is not a clean sheet we are using. It is a dirty sheet!"

Incomprehensibly this seems to make matters worse.

In the same way civilization's invention of table cutlery presents a perpetual headache to a worried houseboy.

More than once I have watched through an open doorway Mansur nerving himself to the task of laying the table for lunch.

First he adjusts the tablecloth—very seriously trying it both ways, and standing well back to observe which effect is the more pleasing artistically.

Inevitably he plumps for the length of the cloth being placed across the table, so that there is a graceful fall on either side and the ends of the table show an inch of two of bare board. He nods approval, and then, a frown gathering on his forehead, he peers into a somewhat moth-eaten plate basket, bought cheap in Beyrout, in which reposes assorted cutlery.

Here is the real problem. Carefully, and with every sign of mental strain, he places a fork on each cup and saucer and a knife to the left of each plate. He stands back, and studies the effect with his head on one side. He shakes his head and sighs. Something seems to tell him that that is the wrong arrangement. Something also seems to tell him that never, not even at the end of the season, will he really have mastered the principle behind the varied combinations of those three units—knife, fork, and spoon. Even at tea, the simplest meal, his arrangement of a single fork does not meet with favor. For some inscrutable reason we demand, at a time when there is nothing serious to cut, a knife! It simply does not make sense.

With a deep sigh Mansur proceeds with his complicated task. To-day, at least, he is determined to please. He looks again. He lays a couple of forks to the right of every plate, and adds a spoon or knife at alternate places. Breathing heavily, he places plates in position, bends and blows on them ferociously to remove any adherent dust. Tottering slightly with the intense mental strain, he leaves the room to inform the cook that all is in readiness, and that the latter can now remove the omelette from the oven, where it has been keeping hot and getting nice and leathery during the last twenty minutes.

Ferhid, the boy, is then sent out to us. He arrives with a worried look, as though to announce some major catastrophe, so that it is quite a relief when all he has to say is that dinner is ready.

To-night we have all the dishes that Dimitri considers most high class. We start with hors d'oeuvre, hard-boiled eggs smothered in rich mayonnaise, sardines, cold string beans, and anchovies. Then we have Dimitri's specialty—a shoulder (?) of mutton stuffed with rice, raisins, and spice. It is all very mysterious. There is a long stitching of cotton which you have to cut. After that, quantities of the stuffing are easily obtained, but the actual meat eludes one, and only at the close of the course does one, on suddenly turning over the joint, discover the actual mutton! After that we have pears from a tin, as Dimitri is forbidden to make the only sweet he knows, which we all dislike— namely, carmel custard. After this, the Colonel proudly announces that he has taught Dimitri to make a savory.

Plates are handed round. On them is a small strip of Arab bread smothered in hot grease, which tastes faintly of cheese. We tell the Colonel we do not think much of his savory!

Turkish delight and some delicious preserved fruits from Damascus are then placed on the table, and at this moment the Sheikh arrives to pay us an evening call. Our decision to dig at Chagar has changed his position from one of hopeless bankruptcy to that of a man on whom a shower of gold may descend at any minute. According to the foremen, he has acquired a new and handsome Yezidi wife on the strength of this, and has increased his debts enormously as a result of enlarged credit! He is certainly in very good spirits. As always, he is armed to the teeth. Carelessly casting off his rifle and slinging it into a corner, he expatiates on the merits of an automatic pistol he has just acquired.

"See," he says, pointing it full at the Colonel. "The mechanism is like this—excellent and simple. You place your finger on the trigger—so—and bullet after bullet comes out."

In an agonized voice the Colonel asks if the pistol is loaded.

Naturally it is loaded, the Sheikh replies in a surprised voice. What would be the good of a pistol that was not loaded?

The Colonel, who has a proper military horror of loaded weapons being pointed at him, promptly changes his seat, and Max distracts the Sheikh from his new toy by offering him Turkish delight. The Sheikh helps himself lavishly, sucks his fingers in appreciation, and beams round at us all.

"Ah," he says—noting that I am engaged on *The Times* crossword puzzle—"so your Khatūn reads? Does she also write?"

Max says that such is the case.

"A very learned Khatūn," says the Sheikh appreciatively. "And does she give medicine to women? If so, my wives shall come one evening and explain to her all that ails them."

Max replies that the Sheikh's wives will be welcome,

but that his Khatūn, unfortunately, does not understand much Arabic.

"We shall manage—we shall manage," says the Sheikh cheerfully.

Mac inquires about the Sheikh's journey to Baghdad.

"It is not yet arranged," says the Sheikh. "There are difficulties—formalities."

We all have a shrewd suspicion that the difficulties are financial. Rumor has it that the Sheikh has already spent all the money he has received from us, in addition to the rake-off he has obtained from the workmen of his village.

"In the days of El Baron . . ." he begins.

But before an advance in gold can be mentioned, Max quickly circumvents him by asking where is the official receipt for the sixty Syrian pounds that the Sheikh has already received. "The Government will require it."

The Sheikh quickly gives up the idea of a touch, and explains that he has a dear friend and relation outside who has a bad eye. Will we come out and look at it and advise?

We go out into the night and look at the eye by the aid of a torch. It is certainly beyond us, being a mere gory mess. Such an eye must be seen by a doctor, says Max. As soon as possible, he adds.

The Sheikh nods. His friend is going into Alep. Will we give him a letter to Dr. Altounyan there? Max agrees, and starts upon it then and there, looking up to ask; "This man is a relation of yours, you say?"

"Yes."

"And his name?" says Max, still writing.

"His name?" The Sheikh is a little taken aback. "I do not know. I must ask him."

The Sheikh departs into the night once more, returning with the information that his relation's name is Mahmoud Hassan.

"Mahmoud Hassan," says Max, writing it down.

"Or is it," asks the Sheikh, "his *passport* name that you require? His passport name is Daoud Suliman."

Max looks puzzled, and asks what the man's name really *is?*

"Call him what you like," says the Sheikh generously.

The letter is handed over, the Sheikh resumes his warlike accoutrements, blesses us cheerfully, and departs with his mysterious follower into the night.

The Colonel and Bumps start an argument *re* King Edward the Eighth and Mrs. Simpson. This is followed by one on the subject of matrimony generally, which seems to lead quite naturally to the subject of suicide!

At this point I leave them to it and go to bed.

A high wind this morning. It rises, until about midday there is practically a dust-storm. Bumps, who has come up to the mound in a topee, has a good deal of trouble with it in the howling wind, and it finally gets entangled round his neck. Michel, always helpful, comes to the rescue.

"*Forca,*" he says, pulling hard upon a strap.

Bumps turns purple in the face as he is slowly being strangled.

"*Beaucoup forca,*" says Michel cheerfully, pulling harder, and Bumps goes black. He is rescued just in time!

A violent quarrel breaks out after the work between the hot-tempered Alawi and Serkis, our carpenter. It arises, as usual, out of nothing at all, but reaches murderous heights.

Max perforce has to administer one of what he calls his "Prep. school talks." Every day, he says, he becomes more and more fitted to be a headmaster, so easily do nauseatingly moral sentiments pour from him!

The harangue is very impressive.

"Do you imagine," demands Max, "that I and the Khwaja Colonel, and the Khwaja of the Pole, always have but a single thought in our minds? That we never wish to disagree? But do we raise our voices, shout, draw knives? No! All these things we put behind us until we go back to London! Here we put the Work first. Always the Work! We exercise control!"

Alawi and Serkis are deeply affected, the quarrel is made up, and their touching politeness to each other as to who should pass out of the door first is really beautiful to behold!

Purchase has been made of a bicycle—an extremely cheap Japanese bicycle. This is to be the proud possession of the boy Ali, and on it he is to ride into Kamichlie two days a week and collect the post.

He sets out, full of importance and happiness, at daybreak, returning about tea-time.

I say doubtfully to Max that it is a long way to go. Kamichlie is forty kilometers away. I do rather sketchy sums in my head, and murmur: "Twenty-five miles, and twenty-four miles back," and add in consternation: "The boy can't possibly do that. It's far too much for him."

Max says (callously in my opinion): "Oh, I don't think so!"

"He must be exhausted," I murmur. I leave the room, and go in search of the overworked Ali. No sign of him.

Dimitri at last understands what I am talking about.

"Ali? Ali has come back from Kamichlie half an hour ago. Where is he now? He has bicycled to the village of Germayir, eight kilometers away, where he has a friend."

My solicitude on Ali's behalf is abruptly damped, especially when he assists with waiting at table at dinnertime with a radiant face and no signs of fatigue.

Max jeers and murmurs cryptically: "Remember Swiss Miss?"

I fall to thinking of Swiss Miss and her times.

Swiss Miss was one of five mongrel puppies on our first dig at Arpachiyah, near Mosul. They rejoiced (or acquiesced) in the names of Woolly Boy, Boujy, Whitefang, Tomboy, and Swiss Miss. Boujy died young of a surfeit of *klechah* which is a form of exceptionally

heavy pastry eaten by Christian sects at Easter. Some
was brought to us by our Christian foremen and became somewhat of an embarrassment. Having suffered
from its effects ourselves and seriously upset the diges-
tion of an innocent girl guest who partook of it heartily
for tea, we surreptitiously fed the remainder of it to
Boujy. Boujy, unbelievingly crawling out into the sun,
gulped this rich nourishment and promptly died! It
was a death in ecstasy—and much to be envied! Of the
remaining dogs, Swiss Miss was chief, since she was
the Master's Favorite. She would come to Max at sunset when the work was finished, and he would indus-
triously detick her. After that the dogs would line up
by the cookhouse, Swiss Miss at their head, and when
their names were called they would advance one by
one to receive dinner.

Then, in some adventure, Swiss Miss broke a leg
and came limping back a very sick dog. She did not
die, however. When the time came for us to leave, the
fate of Swiss Miss weighed heavily upon me. Lame as
she was, how would she survive once we had gone
away? The only thing to do, I argued, was to have her
put away. We could not leave her to die of starvation.
Max, however, would not hear of this. He assured me
optimistically that Swiss Miss would be all right. The
others—yes, possibly, I said, they could fend for themselves, but Swiss Miss was a cripple.

The argument went on, getting more impassioned
on either side. In the end, Max won and we left, pressing money into the old gardener's hand and bidding
him "look after the dogs, especially Swiss Miss," but
without much hope that he would do so. Fears as to
Swiss Miss's fate haunted me off and on for the next
two years, and I constantly reproached myself for not
standing firm. When we next passed through Mosul
we went out to our old house to look around. It was
empty—there was no sign of life anywhere. I murmured softly to Max: "I wonder what became of Swiss
Miss?"

And then we heard a growl. Sitting on the steps was

a dog—a very hideous dog (even as a puppy Swiss Miss had been no beauty). It got up, and I saw that it walked lame. We called Swiss Miss, and its tail wagged faintly, although it continued to growl under its breath. And then, from the bushes, came a small puppy, that ran to its mother. Swiss Miss must have found a handsome husband, for the puppy was a most attractive little dog. Mother and child regarded us placidly, though without real recognition.

"You see," said Max triumphantly, "I told you she'd be all right. Why, she's quite fat. Swiss Miss has brains, so, of course, she's survived. Think what a good time she'd have missed if we'd had her put away!"

Since then, when I start indulging in anxieties, the words Swiss Miss are used to quell my objections!

The mule has not been purchased after all. Instead, a horse—a real horse, not an old woman, but a grand horse, a prince among horses—has been purchased. And with the horse, inseparable from it, apparently, has come a Circassian.

"What a man!" says Michel, his voice rising in a high whine of admiration. "The Circassians know all about horses. They live for horses. And what care, what forethought this man has for his horse! He worries unceasingly about its comfort. And how polite he is! What good manners he has—to *Me!*"

Max remains unimpressed, remarking that time will show whether the man is any good. He is presented to us. He has a gay air and high boots, and reminds me of something out of a Russsian ballet.

To-day we have a visit from a French colleague—from Mari. With him came his architect. Like many French architects, he looks rather like an inferior saint. He has one of those weak nondescript beards. He says nothing but *"Merci, Madame,"* in polite negatives when offered anything. M. Parrot explains that he is suffering with his stomach.

After a pleasant visit they go off again. We admire their car. M. Parrot says sadly: *"Oui, c'est une bonne*

machine, mais elle va trop vite. Beaucoup trop vite."
He adds: *"L'année dernière elle a tué deux de mes architectes!"*

They then get in, the saintlike architect takes the wheel, and they suddenly depart in a whirl of dust at sixty miles an hour—through potholes, over bumps, twisting through the Kurdish village. It seems quite likely that yet another architect, undeterred by his predecessor's fate, will fall a victim to the determined speed of the machine. Clearly the automobile is always to blame! Never the man whose foot is on the accelerator.

The French Army is now on maneuvers. This is thrilling for the Colonel, whose martial interest is at once awakened. His eager overtures are, however, received extremely coldly by the officers to whom they are addressed. They regard him with suspicion.

I tell him that they think he is a spy.

"A spy? Me?" demands the Colonel, highly indignant. "How could they think such a thing?"

"Well, obviously they do."

"I was just asking them a few simple questions. These things are interesting technically. But their replies are so vague."

It is all very disappointing for the poor Colonel, yearning to talk shop and being firmly rebuffed.

The maneuvers worry our workmen in quite another way. One grave, bearded man comes up to Max.

"Khwaja, will the *'asker* interfere with my trade?"

"No, certainly not; they won't interfere with the dig at all."

"I do not mean the work, Khwaja, but with my own trade."

Max asks him what his trade is, and he replies proudly that it is smuggling cigarettes!

The smuggling of cigarettes over the Iraq border appears to be almost an exact science. The Customs' car arrives at a village one day—and on the next the smugglers. . . . Max asks if the Customs never turn back and visit a village a second time. The man looks reproachful, and says of course not. If they did, everything would go wrong. As it is, the workmen happily smoke cigarettes that have cost them twopence a hundred!

Max questions some of the men as to what exactly it costs them to live. Most of them bring a sack of flour with them if they have come from a distant village. This lasts them about ten days. Someone in the village makes their bread for them, as apparently it is below their dignity to bake their own. They have onions occasionally, sometimes some rice, and they probably get sour milk. After working prices out, we find that it costs each man about twopence a week!

Two workmen who are Turks now come up, and in their turn ask anxiously about the *'asker.*

"Will they make trouble for *us,* Khwaja?"

"Why should they make trouble for you?"

Apparently the Turks have no business to be across the border. One of our pickmen reassures them, however. "It will be all right," he says; "you wear the *kefiyaed."*

A cap on the head is only worn uneasily in this part of the world, and yells of derision come from the *kefiyaed* Arabs and Kurds as they point a scornful finger and yell "Turki! Turki!" at the unfortunate man, who, by order of Mustapha Kemal, is wearing European headgear. "Uneasy lies the head that wears a cap" in these parts.

To-night, as we finish dinner, the anxious Ferhid comes in, and in tones of despair announces that the Sheikh has brought his wives to ask advice of the Khatūn.

I feel slightly nervous. Apparently I have gained quite a reputation for medical wisdom. This is singularly undeserved. Although the Kurdish women make no bones about describing their ailments in detail to Max to pass on to me, the more modest Arab women will only come to me when I am alone. The scene that ensues is mostly pantomime. Headaches are fairly easily

indicated, and an aspirin accepted with reverent awe.
Bad and inflamed eyes can be seen, though to explain
the uses of boracic is more difficult.

"Mai harr," I say (Hot water).

"Mai harr," they repeat.

Then I demonstrate with a pinch of boracic—"Mithl
hadha."

Final pantomime of the bathing of eyes.

The patient then responds by a pantomime of drinking a copious draught. I shake my head. *Outward* application—to the *eyes*. The patient is a little disappointed. However, we hear next day from the foreman
that the wife of Abu Suleiman has been greatly bene-
fited by the Khatūn's medicine. She bathed her eyes
with it, and then drank it all, every drop!

The commonest gesture is an expressive rubbing of
the abdomen.

This has one of two meanings—(*a*) acute indigestion;
(*b*) a complaint of sterility.

Bicarbonate of soda does excellent work in the first
case and has attained a somewhat surprising reputation in the second.

"Your Khatūn's white powder was a worker of mar-
vels last season! I now have two strong sons—twins!"

Reviewing these past triumphs, I nevertheless shrink
a little from the ordeal in front of me. Max encourages
me with his usual optimism. The Sheikh has told him
that his wife suffers from her eyes. It will be a straight-
forward case of boracic.

The Sheikh's wives, of course, unlike the village
women, are veiled. Therefore, a lamp is taken to a
little empty storehouse, where I am to see the patient.

The Colonel and Bumps make several ribald remarks,
and do their best to rattle me as I go apprehensively
to the consulting-room.

Outside in the night about eighteen people are standing. The Sheikh greets Max with a cheerful roar, and
waves his hand towards a tall, veiled figure.

I utter the conventional greetings, and lead the way

into the little storehouse. Not one woman, but five, follow me in. They are all very excited, laughing and talking.

The door is shut upon us. Max and the Sheikh remain outside the door to do what interpretation shall be necessary.

I am a little dazed by seeing so many women. Are they *all* wives? And do they *all* need medical attention?

Off come the veils. One woman is young and tall— very handsome. I imagine that she is the new Yezidi wife just acquired with the advance rent for the land. The principal wife is much older; she looks about forty-five and is probably thirty. All the women are wearing jewelry, and all are the gay handsome Kurdish type.

The middle-aged woman points to her eyes and clasps her face. Alas, it is not a case for boracic! She is suffering, I should say, from some virulent form of blood-poisoning.

I raise my voice and speak to Max. It is a poisoning, I say, of the blood, and she should go to a doctor or a hospital in Der-ez-Zor or Alep, where she would have proper injections.

Max passes this on to the Sheikh, who appears much struck by the diagnosis. Presently Max calls out:

"He is much impressed by your cleverness. This is exactly what he has already been told by a doctor in Baghdad. He, too, said that she should have '*des piqures*.' Now that you, too, say so, the Sheikh is going seriously to consider it. By and by he will certainly take his wife to Alep."

I say that it would be a good thing if he took her soon.

This summer, says the Sheikh, or at any rate in the autumn. There is no hurry. All will be as Allah directs.

The lesser wives or whatnots are now examining my clothing in an ecstasy of delighted merriment. I give the patient some aspirin tablets to relieve pain, and recommend applications of hot water, etc. She is far more interested, however, in my appearance than in her own condition. I offer Turkish delight and we all laugh and smile and pat each other's clothes.

Finally, regretfully, the women resume their veils and take their leave. I return, a nervous wreck, to the living-room.

I ask Max whether he thinks the Sheikh will take her to hospital somewhere and Max says probably not.

Today Michel goes into Kamichlie with the washing, and a long list of shopping to be done. Michel cannot read or write, but he never forgets an item, and can recall its exact price. He is scrupulously honest, which offsets his many annoying qualities. I myself would list the latter in the following order:

1. His high whining voice.
2. His tendency to beat "tutti" under one's window.
3. His hopeful attempts to murder Moslems on the road.
4. His argumentative powers.

A lot of photography to-day, and I am introduced to my "dark room." This is undoubtedly a great improvement on the "Little Ease" at Amuda. I can stand upright, and it has a table and a chair.

But as it is a recent addition, having been added a few days before my arrival, the mud-brick is still damp. Strange fungi grow on the walls, and when one is immured in it on a hot day, one comes out partially asphyxiated!

Max has given the little boy who sits outside and washes the pottery a bar of chocolate, and tonight the little boy waylays him.

"Tell me, I pray you, Khwaja, the name of that sweetmeat? So delicious is it that I no longer care for the sweets of the Bazaar. I must purchase this new sweetmeat, even if it's price should be a mejidi!"

I say to Max that he must feel as though he has created a drug addict. Clearly, chocolate is habit-forming.

Not, Max remarks, like an old man to whom he once offered a piece of chocolate last year. The old man thanked him courteously and folded it away in his robe. The officious Michel asked if he were not going to eat it. "It is good," said Michel. The old man replied simply: "It is *new*. It might be dangerous!"

Today is our day off, and we go over to Brak to make arrangements there. The mound itself is about a mile from Jaghjaga, and the first question to be solved is the water problem. We have had a local well-digger at work, but the water by the mound has proved too brackish for drinking. It will have, therefore, to be brought up from the river—hence the Circassian, the cart, and the water-barrels (and the horse that is not an old woman). We shall also need a watchman to live on the excavations.

For ourselves, we are renting a house in the Armenian village by the river. Most of the houses are deserted there. The settlement began with a considerable expenditure of money, but, so far as one can judge, without the necessary putting of first things first. The houses (miserable mudbrick hovels, though they would probably appear to the Western eye!) were actually over-ambitious, bigger and more elaborate than was needful, whereas the water-wheel on which the irrigation and the whole success of the settlement depended was scamped, since there was not enough money left to build it really well. The settlement was started on a kind of communal basis. Tools, animals, ploughs, etc., were provided, and were to be paid off by the community out of their profits. What actually happened, however, was that one after another tired of life in the wilds, and wished to return to a city, and departed, taking his tools and implements with him. Result: These had continually to be replaced, and the people who remained and worked became, much to their bewilderment, more and more in debt. The water-wheel finally failed to function, and the settlement relapsed into a mere village—and a somewhat disgruntled village at that. The derelict house that we are renting is quite imposing, with a wall round a courtyard, and actually a two-storied "tower" on one side. Facing the tower on the other side is a line of rooms, each opening on to the courtyard. Serkis, the carpenter, is busy now repairing the woodwork of doors and windows, so that a few of the rooms will be habitable to camp in.

Michel is dispatched to collect the new watchman for the mound from a village a couple of miles away, together with a tent.

Serkis reports that the tower-room is the one in the best order. We go up some steps, across a small flat roof, and then into two rooms. We agree that the inner room shall have a couple of camp-beds in it, and that the outer one will do for meals, etc. There are some hinged wooden boards to swing-to across the windows, but Serkis will fit some glass.

Michel now returns, and reports that the watchman he has been sent to transport to the mound has three wives, eight children, many sacks of flour and rice, and a good deal of livestock. Impossible to transport them all in the lorry. What shall he do?

He departs again with three Syrian pounds and instructions to bring what he can, and the surplus can hire themselves passages on donkeys.

The Circassian appears suddenly, driving the water-cart. He is singing and shaking a large whip. The cart is painted a bright blue and yellow, the water-barrels are blue, the Circassian has high boots and gay wrappings. The whole think looks more like the Russian ballet than ever. The Circassian descends, cracks his whip and continues to sing, swaying on his feet. He is clearly very drunk!

Another of Michel's swans!

The Circassian is sacked, and one Abdul Hassan, a serious melancholy man, who says he understands horses, is appointed in his stead.

We start home, and run out of petrol two miles from Chagar. Max turns on Michel with fury and curses him.

Michel raises his hands to heaven and lets out a wail of injured innocence.

It is entirely in our interests that he has acted. He has wished to utilize the very last drop of petrol.

"You fool! Haven't I told you always to fill up *and* carry a spare can?"

"There would have been no room for a spare can, and, besides, it might have been stolen."

"And why didn't you fill up the tank?"

"I wished to see just how far the car would go on what we had."

"Idiot!"

Michel says appeasingly: "Sawi proba," which rouses Max to a howl of fury. We all feel inclined to apply *Forca* to Michel, as he continues to look virtuous—an innocent man unjustly blamed!

Max restrains himself, but says that he sees why Armenians are massacred!

We arrive home at last, to be greeted by Ferhid, stating he wishes to "retire," as he and Ali never stop quarrelling!

VIII

CHAGAR AND BRAK

THERE ARE PENALTIES attached to greatness. Of our two house-boys, Subri is incontestably the better. He is intelligent, quick, adaptable, and always gay. His general appearance of ferocity and the immense knife, carefully sharpened, which he keeps under his pillow at night, are mere irrelevancies! So is the fact that whenever he requests leave of absence it is to visit some relation who is incarcerated at Damascus or elsewhere for murder! The murders, Subri explains seriously, have all been *necessary*. It has been a matter of honor or family prestige. This is borne out, he says, by the fact that none of their sentences are long ones.

Subri, then, is by far the more desirable servant; but Mansur, by right of seniority of service, is the head boy. Mansur, though fulfilling Max's dictum that he is too stupid to be anything but honest, is nevertheless, to put it bluntly, a pain in the neck!

And Mansur, since he is the head boy, attends to the needs of Max and myself, whilst the Colonel and

Bumps, supposedly inferior in rank, have the services of the intelligent and merry Subri.

Sometimes, in the very early morning, a feeling of loathing comes over me for Mansur! He enters the room after knocking about six times, being in doubt as to whether the repeated "Come in" can really be meant for him. He stands inside, breathing laboriously, and holding, precariously balanced, two cups of strong tea.

Slowly, breathing stertorously, and shuffling his feet, he advances across the floor and puts down one cup on the chair beside my bed, slopping most of it into the saucer as he does so. With him comes a strong aroma, at best of onions, at worst of garlic. Neither of these is really appreciated at five A.M.

The spilling of the tea fills Mansur with despair. He stares down at the cup and saucer, shaking his head, and poking at it doubtfully with a finger and thumb.

In a ferocious half-awakened voice I say: "Leave it!"

Mansur starts, breathes hard, and shuffles across the room to Max, where he repeats the performance.

He then turns his attention to the washstand. He picks up the enamel basin, carries it cautiously to the door, and empties it outside. He returns with it, pours about an inch of water in, and goes over it laboriously with one finger. This process takes about ten minutes. He then sighs, goes out, returns with a kerosene tin of hot water, puts it down and slowly shuffles out, shutting the door in such a way that it immediately comes open again!

I then drink off the cold tea, rise, clean the basin myself, throw out the water, latch the door properly, and start the day.

After breakfast, Mansur addresses himself to the task of "doing the bedroom." His first procedure, after slopping a good deal of water about in the neighborhood of the washstand, is to dust very carefully and methodically. This is not bad as a performance, but it occupies an immense amount of time.

Satisfied with the first stage of housework, Mansur goes out, fetches a native broom, returns with it, and begins to sweep furiously. Having raised a terrific dust, so that the air is unbreathable, Mansur makes the beds —either in such a way that your feet are immediately exposed when you get in, or else by his second method, which involves half the length of the bedclothes being tucked under the mattress, the top half reaching only to one's waist. I pass over such minor idiosyncrasies as laying the sheets and blankets in alternate layers and putting both pillow-cases on one pillow. These flights of fancy only occur on clean linen days.

Finally nodding his head in approval, Mansur staggers out of the room, exhausted by nervous strain and hard work. He takes himself and his duties very seriously, and is intensely conscientious. This attitudue of his has made a deep impression on the rest of the staff, and Dimitri, the cook, says quite seriously to Max: "Subri is most willing and industrious, but he has not, of course, the *knowledge* and *experience* of Mansur, who is trained in all the ways of the Khwajas!" Not to subvert discipline, Max perforce makes sounds of agreement, but both he and I look yearningly at Subri as he cheerfully shakes and folds the Colonel's clothes.

I once officiously tried to instill into Mansur my own ideas of the routine of housework, but it was a mistaken move. I merely confused him and roused all his native obstinacy.

"The ideas of the Khatūn are not practical," he said sadly to Max. "She demands that I put tea leaves on the *floor*. But tea leaves are in a *teapot* for *drinking*. And how can I dust the rooms *after* sweeping? I take the dust from the tables and let it fall on the ground, and *then* I sweep it from the ground. That is only reasonable."

Mansur is very strong upon what is reasonable. A demand of the Colonel's for jam to add to his *leben* (sour milk) brought the immediate reproof from Mansur: "No, it is not necessary!"

Some vestiges of military tradition cling around Mansur. His answer to a summons is the immediate reply: *"Présent!"* And he announces lunch and dinner with the simple formula: *"La Soupe!"*

The time of day when Mansur is really in his element is the hour of the bath, just before dinner. Here Mansur presides, and does not have to do anything himself. Under his commanding eye, Ferhid and Ali bring large kerosene tins of boiling water and others of cold water (mostly mud) from the kitchen and set out the baths—which are large, round copper affairs, like immense preserving-pans. Later, still under Mansur's supervision, Ferhid and Ali stagger out with the copper pans and empty them, usually immediately outside the front door, so that if you go out unwarily after dinner you slide on liquid mud and fall headlong.

Ali, since his promotion to postboy and the acquisition of the bicycle, is getting a soul above menial chores. To the worried Ferhid is allotted the endless plucking of fowls and the ritualistic washing up of meals, which involves an immense quantity of soap and hardly any water.

On the rare occasions when I step into the kitchen to "show" Dimitri the preparation of some European dish, the highest standards of hygiene and general purity are at once insisted upon.

If I pick up a perfectly clean looking bowl, it is at once taken from me and handed to Ferhid.

"Ferhid, clean this for the Khatūn to use."

Ferhid seizes the bowl, smears the interior of it painstakingly with yellow soap, applies a brisk polish to the soapy surface, and returns it to me. I have an inner misgiving that a soufflé flavored heavily with soap will not really be nice, but stifle it, and force myself to proceed.

The whole thing is most shattering to the nerves. To begin with, the temperature of the kitchen is usually about 99° F., and to keep it even as cool as that there is only a tiny aperture to admit light, so that the whole effect is a sweltering gloom. Added to that is the disorganizing effect of the complete confidence and rever-

ence expressed in every face surrounding me. There are
a good many faces, for in addition to Dimitri, the slave
Ferhid, and the haughty Ali, there have also come in to
watch in the proceedings: Subri, Mansur, Serkis the carpenter, the waterman, and any odd workmen who may
be doing a job on the house. The kitchen is small, the
crowd is large. They close round me with admiring
and reverent eyes, watching my every action. I begin
to get nervous, and feel that everything is sure to go
wrong. I drop an egg on the floor and break it. So complete is the confidence reposed in me that for quite a
minute, everyone takes this to be part of the ritual!

I proceed, getting hotter and hotter and more and
more unhinged. The pans are different from any I have
ever known, the egg-whisk has an unexpectedly de-
tachable handle, everything I use is a curious shape
or size. . . . I pull myself together, and resolve desperately that, whatever the result may be, I shall pretend
that it is what I have intended!

Actually the results fluctuate. Lemon curd is a great
success; shortbread is so uneatable that we secretly
bury it; a vanila soufflé, for a wonder, goes right;
whereas Chicken Maryland (owing, as I realize later,
to the extreme freshness and incredible age of the
chicken) is so tough that one cannot get one's teeth
through it!

I can say, however, that I know by now what to
impart and what to leave well alone. No dish that needs
to be eaten as soon as it is cooked should ever be at-
tempted in the East. Omelettes, soufflés, chip potatoes,
will inevitably be made a good hour beforehand and
placed in the oven to mature, and no amount of remon-
strance will avail. Anything, on the other hand, however elaborate, that requires long preparation beforehand and which can be kept waiting will turn out successfully. Soufflés and omelettes were regretfully erased
from Dimitri's list. On the other hand, no chef could
turn out regularly, day after day, a more perfect mayonnaise.

One other point may be mentioned in the culinary

line. This is the dish known familiarly to us as "biftek." Again and again the announcement of this delicacy arouses hopes in us, hopes doomed each time to disappointment when a platter containing some frizzled-up little bits of gristly meat is placed before us.

"It doesn't," the Colonel would say sadly, "even *taste* like beef."

And that, of course, is the real explanation—there never is any beef.

The butcher's shop is represented by a very simple proceeding. From time to time Michel departs with the lorry to a neighboring village or tribe. He returns, flings open the back of Mary, and out fall eight sheep!

These sheep are dispatched one at a time as needed, strict orders being given on my account that they should *not* be slaughtered exactly in front of the living-room windows! I also object to seeing Ferhid advancing upon the chickens, a long, sharp knife in hand.

This squeamishness of the Khatûn's is treated indulgently by the staff as another Western peculiarity.

Once, when we were digging near Mosul, our old foreman came to Max in great excitement.

"You must take your Khatûn to Mosul tomorrow. There is a great event. There is to be a *hanging*—a woman! Your Khatûn will enjoy it very much! She must on no account miss it!"

My indifference, and, indeed, repugnance, to this treat stupified him.

"But it is a *woman*," he insisted. "Very seldom do we have the hanging of a woman. It is a Kurdish woman who has poisoned three husbands! Surely—surely the Khatûn would not like to miss *that!*"

My firm refusal to attend lowered me in his eyes a good deal. He left us sadly, to enjoy the hanging by himself.

Even in other ways unexpected squeamishness overtakes one. Though indifferent to the fate of chickens and turkeys (unpleasant gobbling creatures), we once bought a nice fat goose. Unfortunately it turned out to be a companionable goose. It had clearly lived in its village as one of the family. On the very first evening it tried determinedly to share Max's bath. It was always pushing open a door and putting a beak in, in a hopeful "I'm lonely" fashion. As the days passed we got desperate. Nobody could bring themselves to order the goose to be killed.

Eventually the cook took it upon himself. The goose was duly served up, richly stuffed in native fashion, and certainly looking and smelling delicious. Alas, none of us enjoyed a morsel! It was the most depressed meal we ever ate.

Bumps disgraces himself here one day when Dimitri serves up proudly a lamb—head, paws, and all. Bumps takes one look at it and rushes headlong from the room.

But to return to the problem of "biftek." After a sheep has been slaughtered and dismembered it is served in the following order: The shoulder, or some such portion, stuffed with spices and rice and all sewn up (Dimitri's grand dish); then the legs; then a platter of what used to be called in the last war "edible offal"; then a kind of stew with rice; and finally, the last rejected inglorious portions of the sheep, unworthy of inclusion in the better dishes, determinedly fried for a long period until well reduced in size and completely leathery in consistency—the dish known as "biftek"!

Work on the mound has been proceeding satisfactorily—the entire lower half has turned out to be prehistoric. We have been digging on one portion of the mound a "deep cut" from the top to virgin soil. This has given us fifteen layers of successive occupations. Of these the lower ten are prehistoric. After 1500 B.C. the mound was abandoned, presumably because denudation had set in and the levels were no longer good. There are, as always, some Roman and Islamic graves which are purely intrusive. We always call them Roman to the men to spare any Moslem susceptibilities, but the men themselves are an irreverent lot. "It is *your* grandfather we are digging up, Abdul!" "No, it is yours, Daoud!" They laugh and joke freely.

We have found many interesting carved animal amulets, all of a fairly well-known type, but now suddenly some very curious figures begin to be produced. A small blackened bear, a lion's head, and, finally, a queer primitive human figure. Max has had his suspicions of them, but the human figure is too much. We have got a forger at work.

"And he's quite a clever fellow, too," says Max, turning the bear round appreciatively. "Nice bit of work."

Detective work proceeds. The objects turn up in one corner of the dig and are usually found by one or other of two brothers. These men come from a village about ten kilometers away. One day, in quite another part of the dig, a suspicious-looking bitumen "spoon" turns up. It has been "found" by a man from the same village. Bakshish is given as usual and nothing is said.

But on pay-day comes the big exposure! Max displays the exhibits, makes an impassioned speech of condemnation, denounces them as trickery, and publicly destroys them (though he has kept the bear as a curiosity). The men who have produced them are sacked, and depart quite cheerfully, though loudly proclaiming their innocence.

The next day the men are chuckling on the dig.

"The Khwaja knows," they say. "He is very learned in antiquities. You cannot deceive his eyes."

Max is sad, because he would like very much to know exactly how the forgeries were made. Their excellent workmanship arouses his approbation.

One can make to oneself now a picture of Chagar as it must have been five to three thousand years ago. In the prehistoric times it must have been on a much-frequented caravan route, connecting Harran and Tell Halaf and on through the Jebel Sinjar into Iraq and the Tigris, and so to ancient Nineveh. It was one of a network of great trading centers.

Sometimes one feels a personal touch—a potter who has set his mark on the base of his pot, a *cache* in a wall where there is a small pot full of gold earrings, the dowry, perhaps, of the daughter of the house. Then a personal touch nearer our own times—a metal counter, with the name Hans Krauwinkel of Nuremberg, struck in about A.D. 1600, and which lay in an Islamic grave, showing that there was contact between this obscure region and Europe at that time.

In the age roughly perhaps five thousand years ago, there are some very lovely incised pots—to my mind real things of beauty—all made by hand.

There are the Madonnas of that age, too—turbanned figures with big breasts, grotesque and primitive, yet representing, no doubt, help and consolation.

There is also the fascinating development of the "bukranium" *motif* on pottery, starting as a simple ox's head, and becoming less naturalistic and more formal until it has gone so far that you would not recognize it at all if you did not know of the intervening steps. (In fact it is, I realize with dismay, exactly the simple pattern of a printed silk frock I sometimes wear! Oh, well, "bukranium" has a good deal pleasanter sound than a "running lozenge"!)

The day has come when the first spade is to be put into Tell Brak. It is quite a solemn moment.

By the combined efforts of Serkis and Ali one or two rooms are in order. The waterman, the grand horse which is not an old woman, the cart, the barrels—all is in readiness.

The Colonel and Bumps depart to Brak the night before to sleep there and be up on the mound at early dawn.

Max and I arrive there about eight o'clock. The Colonel, alas, has spent a sadly disturbed night wrestling with bats! It sems that the tower-room is literally infested with bats—creatures which the Colonel holds in great aversion.

Bumps reports that every time he awoke during the night the Colonel was barging about the room, lunging wildly at bats with a bath-towel.

We stayed a little while watching the proceedings on the dig.

The gloomy waterman came up to me and poured out a long tale of what seemed to be bitter woe. When Max came up, I asked him to find out what it was all about.

It appeared that the waterman has a wife and ten children somewhere near Jerablus, and that his heart is distracted by absence from them. Could he have an advance of money and send for them to join him?

I plead for a favorable reply. Max is a little dubious. A woman in the house, he says, will lead to trouble.

On our way back to Chagar we meet large quantities of our workmen walking across country to the new dig.

"El hamdu lillah!" they cry. "Will there be work for us tomorrow?"

"Yes, there will be work."

They praise God again and tramp on.

We spend two uneventful days at home, and now it is our turn to do a session at Brak. Nothing of great moment has turned up there yet, but it promises well, and the houses, etc., are of the right period.

A strong wind is blowing to-day from the south— the most detestable of winds. It makes you irritable and nervy. We set out, prepared for the worst, with gum-boots, mackintoshes, and even umbrellas. Serki's assurances that he has mended the roof we do not take too seriously. Tonight will be, as Michel would say, a case of *Sawi Proba*.

The route to Brak is all across country with no track. We are halfway there when we overtake two workmen of ours trudging towards "the work." Since we have room, Max stops Mary and offers them a lift, which causes great jubilation. Walking at their heels, with a small bit of frayed rope round its neck, is a dog.

The men get in and Michel prepares to drive off. Max asks what about the dog? We will take their dog too. It is *not* their dog, they say. It just appeared suddenly out of the desert.

We look more closely at the dog. Though of no known breed, it is clearly a European mixture! In shape it resembles a Skye terrier, with Dandy Dinmont coloring, and a definite touch of Cairn. It is immensely long, has brilliant amber eyes, and a rather common pale-brown nose. It looks neither wretched nor sorry for itself nor timorous—most unlike the average dog of the East. Sitting down comfortably, it surveys us cheerfully, with a slight wag of the tail.

Max says we will take it along with us, and orders Michel to pick it up and put it in.

Michel flinches. "It will bite me," he says dubiously.

"Yes, yes," say the two Arabs. "Assuredly it will have your meat! Better leave it here, Khwaja."

"Pick it up and put it in, you damned fool!" says Max to Michel.

Michel nerves himself and advances on the dog, which turns its head pleasantly towards him.

Michel retreats rapidly. I lose patience, jump out, pick up the dog, and get back into Mary with it. Its ribs are sticking through the skin. We drive on to Brak, where the newcomer is handed over to Ferhid, with instructions that a large meal is to be given to her. We also debate a name, and decide on Miss Ostapenko (since I am just reading *Tobit Transplanted*). Owing mainly to Bumps, however, Miss Ostapenko is never known as anything else but Hiyou. Hiyou turns out to be a dog of amazing character. Avid for life, she is absolutely intrepid, and shows no fear of anything or any one. She is perfectly good-humored and good-tempered, and absolutely determined at all times to do exactly as she likes. She obviously possesses the nine lives usually attributed to cats. If she is shut in, she manages somehow to get out. If shut out, she manages to get in—once by eating a two-foot hole in a mud-brick wall. She attends all meals, and is so insistent that you cannot withstand her. She does not beg—but demands.

I feel convinced that someone took Hiyou out with a stone attached to her neck by a rope and tried to drown her, but that Hiyou, determined to enjoy life, bit through the rope, swam ashore, and started cheerfully across the desert, picking up the two men by her infallible instinct. In confirmation of my theory, Hiyou will come with us when summoned everywhere except down to the Jaghjagha. There she stands firm across the path, more or less shakes her head, and returns to the house. "No, thank you," she says, "I don't like being drowned! Tedious!"

The Colonel, we are glad to hear, has passed a better night. Serkis has ejected most of the bats in repairing the roof, and in addition the Colonel has rigged up a rather Heath Robinsonian device, involving a large bowl of water, into which the bats eventually fall and are drowned. The mechanism, as explained to us by the Colonel, is very complicated, and the preparation of it somewhat cut short his hours of sleep.

We go up to the mound and have lunch in a spot sheltered from the wind. Even then a large proportion of sand and dust is absorbed with every bite. Everybody is looking cheerful, and even the melancholy waterman displays a certain pride as he drives to and from the Jaghjagha, bringing up the men's water. He drives it to the foot of the mound, and there donkeys take it up in water-jars. The whole thing has a Biblical aspect that is rather fascinating.

When Fidos comes, we exchange farewells, the Colonel and Bumps depart in Mary for Chagar, and we take our two days' duty at Brak.

The tower-room looks quite attractive. There is matting on the floor and a couple of rugs. We have a jug and basin, a table, two chairs, two camp-beds, towels, sheets, blankets, and even books. The windows have been insecurely fastened up, and we retire to bed after a rather peculiar meal, served gloomily by Ferhid and cooked by Ali. It is mainly very liquid spinach, with minute islands in it, which we suspect are once again "Biftek!"

We pass a good night. Only one bat materializes, and Max lures it out with a torch. We decide to tell the Colonel that his stories of hundreds of bats are a gross exaggeration and probably due to drink. At four-fifteen Max is called with tea and starts for the mound. I go to sleep again. At six tea is brought in for me. Max returns for breakfast at eight. The meal is served, with a flourish—boiled eggs, tea, Arab bread, two pots of jam, and a tin of custard powder (!). A few minutes later a second course is brought in—scrambled eggs.

Max murmurs: *"Trop de zèle,"* and fearing the imminent arrival of an omelette, sends word to the invisible Ali that what we have had will do nicely. Ferhid sighs and departs with the message. He returns, his forehead corrugated with perplexity and anxiety. We fear a major catastrophe—but no, he merely asks: "Will you require oranges sent up with your luncheon?"

Bumps and the Colonel come over at midday. Bumps has a good deal of trouble with his topee owing to the howling wind. Michel arrives helpfully to apply *Forca,* but remembering last time, Bumps avoids him with dexterity.

Our normal lunch is cold meat and salad, but Ali's ambitious soul has soared to better things, and we eat slices of fried aubergine, tepid and only half-cooked, greasy cold fried potatoes, little discs of "biftek" fried very hard, and a dish of salad complete with dressing applied to it many hours ago, so that the whole thing is an orgy of cold green grease!

Max says he will be sorry to damp Ali's well-meaning efforts, but he will have to curb his imagination.

We find Abd es Salaam employing the lunch-hour by treating the men to a long, moral harangue of a really nauseating character.

"See how fortunate you are!" he shouts, waving his arms. "Is not all done for you? Is not all thought taken for you? You are permitted to bring your food here, to eat it in the courtyard of the house! Immense wages are paid you—yes, whether you find anything or nothing, that money is paid to you! What generosity, what nobility! *And* that is not all! In addition to these big wages, further money is paid to you for everything that you find! Like a father the Khwaja watches over you; he keeps you even from doing each other bodily harm! If you are ill with fever, he gives you medicine! If your bowels are shut, he gives you opening medicine of first-class power! How happy, how fortunate is your lot! And yet further generosity! Does he leave you to work thirsty? Does he make you provide your own water to drink? No! No, indeed! Though under no obligation, freely, in his great generosity, he *brings* water for you to the mound, all the way from the Jaghjagha! Water brought at vast expense in a cart drawn by a *horse!* Think of the expense, of the outlay! What wonderful good fortune is yours to be employed by such a man!"

We steal away, and Max remarks thoughtfully that he wonders some of the workmen don't murder Abd es Salaam. *He* would, he says, if he were one. Bumps says that, on the contrary, the workmen are just lapping it up. It is true. Nods and grunts of appreciation are heard, one man turns to another.

"It is reasonable what he says. Water is brought for us. Yes, there is indeed generosity here. He is right. We are fortunate. He is a wise man, this Abd es Salaam."

Bumps says it beats him how they stick it. But I disagree. I remember with what avidity one lapped up really moral tales as a child! The Arab has something of that direct *naif* approach to life. The sententious Abd es Salaam is preferred to the more modern and less sanctimonious Alawi. Moreover, Abd es Salaam is a great dancer, and in the evenings in the courtyard of the Brak house the men, led by old Abd es Salaam, dance long, intricate measures—or what is really more a *pattern*—sometimes until far into the night. How they can do it and be up on the mound again at five

A.M. is a mystery. But then there is the mystery of how men from villages three, five, and ten kilometers away can arrive exact to the minute at sunrise every day! They have no clocks or watches, and they must start at times varying from twenty minutes to over an hour before sunrise, but there they are. They are neither late nor early. Surprising to see them, too, at Fidos when work is over (half an hour before sunset), throw up their baskets, laugh, shoulder their picks, and *run*— yes, *run* gaily off on the ten-kilometer distance home again! Their only break has been half an hour for breakfast and an hour for lunch, and according to our standards they have always been undernourished. It is true that they work in what may be called leisurely fashion, with only occasional spurts of frenzied digging or running when a wave of gaiety sweeps over them, but it is all really hard manual labor. The pickman, perhaps, has the best of it, for when he has loosened the surface of his area he sits down to enjoy a cigarette whilst the spademan fills the baskets. The basket-boys get no repose except what they snatch for themselves. But they are quite adroit at doing that, moving in slow motion to the dump, or taking a long while to search their baskets through.

On the whole they are a wonderfully healthy lot. There is a good deal of eye soreness, and they are much preoccupied with constipation! There is, I believe, a good deal of tuberculosis nowadays, which has been brought to them by Western civilization. But their recuperative powers are marvelous. One man will cut open another's head, leaving a horrible-looking wound. The man will ask us to treat it and bind it up, but looks amazed at a suggestion that he should knock off work and go home. "What, for *this!* It is hardly a headache!" And within two or three days the whole place is healed up, in spite of the definitely unhygienic treatment which the man himself has doubtless applied to it as soon as he gets home.

One man who had a large and painful boil on

his leg was sent home by Max, since he obviously had fever.

"You shall be paid just the same as if you were here."

The man grunted and went off. But that afternoon Max suddenly caught sight of him working. "What are you doing here? I sent you home."

"I went home, Khwaja (eight kilometers). But when I got home it was dull. No conversation! Only the women. So I walked back. And see, it has been *good*, the swelling has broken!"

Today we return to Chagar and the other two come to Brak. It feels great luxury to get back to our own house. On arrival we find that the Colonel has been busy pasting up notices everywhere, mostly of an insulting character! He has also tidied with such zest that we are quite unable to find anything we need. We meditate reprisals! Finally we cut out pictures of Mrs. Simpson from some old papers and pin them up in the Colonel's room!

There are a lot of photographs to be taken and developed, and, as it is a hot day, I emerge from my darkroom feeling exactly like a bit of wall fungus myself. The staff is kept busy supplying me with comparatively pure water. The grosser mud is first strained off, and it is finally strained through cotton wool into various buckets. By the time it is actually used for the negatives, only stray sand and dust from the air have got in, and the results are quite satisfactory. One of our workmen comes up to Max and asks for five days' leave of absence.

"Why?"

"I have to go to gaol!"

Today has been memorable for a rescue. There was rain in the night, and this morning the ground was still soggy. About twelve o'clock a wild-looking horseman arrived, riding with the wildness and desperation of one who brings the good news from Aix to Ghent, etc. Actually he brings bad news. The Colonel and Bumps have set out to come to us and are bogged halfway. The horseman is sent back at once with two spades, and we fit out a rescue party in Poilu. Five men go with Serkis in charge. They take spades and extra boards and depart very gaily, singing!

Max yells after them not to get bogged themselves. Actually this is exactly what happens, but, fortunately, only a few hundred yards from where Mary is in distress. Her back-axle is buried in mud and her crew are very weary, having been trying to dig her out for five solid hours, and having been exasperated almost to madness by Michel's well-meant exhortations and commands, all uttered in his usual high, whining falsetto, and consisting mainly of *"Forca!"* as he breaks the third jack in succession! With the assistance of the toughs (selected for their heftiness), and under the more able direction of Serkis, Mary consents to come out of the mud, which she does very suddenly, coating everybody from head to foot and leaving a yawning hole behind her, christened by the Colonel "Mary's Grave."

There has been a good deal of rain falling during our latest spell at Brak, and Serkis' roof has not quite stood up to the strain. Moreover, the window boards swing open, and gusts of wind and rain sweep through the room. Fortunately the worst rain falls on our "day off," so that the work is not held up, though our projected excursion to the Kawkab volcano is.

Incidentally, we nearly have a riot over this, as the ten-day period ends on Saturday, and Abd es Salaam, told to announce to the men that there would be no work the next day, like the complete old bungler he is, bleats out: "Tomorrow is Sunday—*therefore,* no work!"

Immediately there is an uproar! What! Are all the good Moslem gentlemen to be insulted and sacrificed to a miserable twenty Armenian Christians? A fiery gentleman called Abbas 'Id tries to organize a strike. Max then makes an oration, stating that if he wants a holiday on Sunday, Monday, Tuesday, Wednesday, Friday, or Saturday, a holiday there will be. As for Abbas 'Id, he is never to show his face on the mound again! The Armenians, who are courting assassination by chuckling in triumph, are told to hold their tongues, after which pay-day begins. Max ensconces himself in Mary, Michel staggers out of the house with sacks of money (no longer mejidis, thank heaven!—they have been made illegal, and Syrian currency is now *de rigueur*), which he disposes in the lorry. Max's face appears at the window of the driving-seat (looking rather like a booking-clerk at a railway station), Michel takes a chair into the lorry and assumes control of the cash, forming the coins up in piles, and sighing deeply as he contemplates how much money is going into Moslem hands!

Max opens an immense ledger and the fun starts. Gang after gang parade as their names are called, and come up and draw what is owing to them. Terrific feats of arithmetic have been performed well into the small hours the night before, as the daily bakshish of each man is checked up and added to his wages.

The inequality of Fate is very marked on pay-day. Some men draw a heavy bonus, some hardly anything. There are a lot of jokes and quips, and everyone, even those passed over by Fortune, are very gay. A tall, handsome Kurdish woman rushes up to her husband, who is counting over what he has received.

"What have you got? Show it to me?" Without scruple she seizes the whole amount and goes off with it.

Two refined-looking Arabs turn their faces gently aside, shocked by such a spectacle of unwomanly (and unmanly) behavior!

The Kurdish woman reappears from her mud-hut and screams abuse at her husband for the way he is untethering a donkey. The Kurd, a big handsome man, sighs sadly. Who would be a Kurdish husband?

There is a saying that if an Arab robs you in the desert, he will beat you but leave you to live, but if a Kurd robs you he will kill you just for the pleasure of it!

Perhaps being henpecked at home stimulates fierceness abroad!

At last, after two hours, everyone is paid. A little misunderstanding between Daoud Suleiman and Daoud Suleiman Mohammed has been adjusted, to everyone's satisfaction. Abdullah has returned smiling, to explain that ten francs fifty has been allotted to him in error. Little Mahmoud expostulates shrilly over forty-five centimes—"two beads, a rim of pottery, and a bit of obsidian, Khwaja, and the day was last Thursday!" All claims, counterclaims, etc., have been examined and adjusted. Information is sought as to who continues work and who is going to leave. Nearly everybody leaves. "But after the next period—who knows, Khwaja?"

"Yes," says Max, "when your money is spent!"

"As you say, Khwaja."

Friendly greetings and farewells are said. That night there is singing and dancing in the courtyard.

Back at Chagar and a lovely hot day. The Colonel has been spluttering with rage over the behavior of Poilu, who has let him down every single day at Brak lately. On each occasion Ferhid has arrived, given assurances that the car is quite all right, nothing wrong with it, and on his demonstration of this fact it immediately starts. The Colonel feels this an additional insult.

Michel comes up and explains in his high voice that all that is needed is to clear the carburetor—it is very simple, he will show the Colonel. Michel then proceeds to do his favorite trick of sucking petrol up into his mouth, gargling freely with it, and finally drinking it. The Colonel looks on with a face of cold disgust. Michel nods his head, smiles happily, says persuasively to the Colonel: "Sawi Proba?" and proceeds to light a cigarette. We hold our breath, waiting to see Michel's throat go up in flames, but nothing happens.

Various minor complications occur. Four men are

sacked for persistent fighting. Alawi and Yahya have a quarrel and will not speak to each other. One of our house-rugs has been stolen. The Sheikh is very indignant, and is holding a court of inquiry into the matter. This we have the pleasure of observing from afar—a circle of white-clad, bearded men are sitting out in the plain with their heads together. "They hold it there," explains Mansur, "so that none can overhear the secret things they say."

The subsequent proceedings are very Eastern. The Sheikh comes to us, assures us that the malefactors are now known to him, that all shall be dealt with, and our rug restored.

What actually happens is, that the Sheikh beats up six of his particular enemies and possibly blackmails a few more. The rug does not materialize, but the Sheikh is in high good humor and seems quite flush of cash again.

Abd es Salaam comes secretively to Max. "*I* will tell you who stole your rug. It is the Sheikh's brother-in-law, the Yezidi Sheikh. He is a very evil man, but his sister is handsome."

Hope of a little pleasant persecution of Yezidis shows in Abd es Salaam's eye, but Max declares that the rug is to be written off as a loss and no more done about it. "In future," says Max, looking severely at Mansur and Subri, "better care is to be taken, and the rugs are not to be left to lie about in the sun outside."

The next sad incident is that the Customs men arrive and pinch two of our workmen for smoking smuggled Iraqi cigarettes. This is very bad luck on the particular two, as in actual fact two hundred and eighty men (our present pay-roll) are all smoking smuggled Iraqi cigarettes! The Customs official seeks an interview with Max. "This is a serious offense," he says. "Out of courtesy to you, Khwaja, we have refrained from arresting these men on your dig. It might not be to your honor."

"I thank you for your kindness and delicacy," Max replies.

"We suggest, however, that *you* should sack them without pay, Khwaja."

"That may hardly be. It is not for *me* to enforce the laws of this country. I am a foreigner. These men have contracted to work for me and I have contracted to pay them. I cannot withhold pay due to them."

The matter is settled at last (with the assent of the guilty parties) by two fines being stopped out of the men's pay and handed to the Customs officer.

"Inshallah!" say the men, shrugging their shoulders, as they return to work. The soft-hearted Max is a little over-generous with the bakshish that week to the two culprits, and pay-day finds them cheerful. They do not suspect Max of beneficence, but ascribe their good fortune to the infinite compassion of Allah.

We have made another excursion to Kamichlie. By now it has all the excitement of a visit to Paris or London. The procedure has been much the same— Harrods, desultory conversation with M. Yannakos, lengthy sessions in the Bank, but enlivened this time by the presence of a supreme dignitary of the Maronite Church, complete with jewelled cross, luxuriant hair, and robes of purple. Max nudges me to offer "Monseigneur" my chair, which I do reluctantly, and feeling rather fiercely Protestant. (Note.—Would I, in similar circumstances, offer the only chair to the Archbishop of York if I happened to be sitting in it? I decide that if I did, he wouldn't take it!) The Archimandrite, or the Grand Mufti or whatever he is, does, sinking down with a sigh of satisfaction and giving me a benignant glance.

Michel, it need hardly be said, tries our tempers to the utmost! He makes ridiculous purchases of a highly economical order. He also goes with Mansur to see about the purchase of a second horse, and Mansur, fired with equine passion, rides the said horse right into the local barber's shop, where Max is having his hair cut!

"Get out, you fool!" yells Max.

"It is a fine horse," shouts Mansur, "and quiet!"

At this moment the horse rears up, and, threatened by two immense front hoofs, everyone in the barber's shop ducks for cover.

Mansur and the horse are ejected, Max returns to finish his haircut, and postpones all that he wishes to say to Mansur until later.

We have a very delicious and recherché lunch with the French Commandant at the Barracks, invite some of the French officers to come out and see us, and return to Harrods to see what Michel's latest enormities are. It is looking like rain, so we decide to start back at once.

The horse has been purchased, and Mansur pleads that he may be allowed to ride it home.

Max says, if so he'll never get home.

I say it is an excellent idea, and please do let Mansur ride the horse home.

"You'll be so stiff you won't be able to move," says Max.

Mansur says he is never stiff when riding a horse.

It is arranged that Mansur is to return on the horse the following day. The mail is a day late, so he will be able to bring that with him.

Rain falls as we drive back (accompanied by the usual uncomfortable hens and derelict humans). We have fantastic skids, but we just get home before the track becomes impassable.

The Colonel has just got back from Brak and has had a lot more trouble with bats. Luring them with an electric torch to the basin has been very successful, only, as he has spent all night doing this, he hasn't had much sleep. We say coldly that *we* never see any bats!

Among our workmen is one who is able to read and write! His name is Yusuf Hassan, and he is quite one of the laziest men on the dig. I never once arrive on the mound to find Yusuf actually working. He has always just finished digging his patch, or is about to begin, or has paused to light a cigarette. He is somewhat proud of his literacy, and one day amuses himself and his friends by writing on an empty cigarette packet: "Saleh Birro has been drowned in the Jaghjagha." Everybody is much amused by this piece of erudition and wit!

The empty packet gets caught up with an empty bread-bag, is crammed into a flour sack, and in due course the sack gets returned to its place of origin—the village of Hanzir. Here somebody notices the inscription. It is taken to a learned man; he reads it. Forthwith the news is sent on to the village of Germayir, Saleh Birro's home-town. Result: On the following Wednesday a great cavalcade of mourners—men, weeping women, wailing children arrive at Tell Brak.

"Alas, alas!" they cry, "Saleh Birro, our loved one, has been drowned in the Jaghjagha! We come for his body!"

The first thing they then see is Saleh Birro himself, happily digging and spitting in his appointed pit of earth. Stupefaction, explanations, and forthwith Saleh Birro, mad with rage, attempts to brain Yusuf Hassan with his pick. A friend on each side joins in, the Colonel comes up and orders them to stop (vain hope!), and tries to find out what it is all about.

Court of inquiry then held by Max and sentence pronounced.

Saleh Birro is sacked for one day—(a) for fighting, (b) for not stopping fighting when told. Yusuf Hassan is commanded to walk to Germayir (forty kilometres), and there explain and apologize for his singularly ill-omened idea. Also to be fined two days' pay.

And the real moral is—Max points out afterwards to his own select circle—what very dangerous things reading and writing are!

Mansur, having been marooned for three days owing to the weather in Kamichlie, suddenly arrives more dead than alive on the horse. Not only is he unable to stand, but he has had the added woe of having purchased a large and delectable fish in Kamichlie, and in the enforced wait it has gone bad on him. For some unappreciated reason he has brought it with him! It is hastily buried, and Mansur retires, groaning to his bed, and is not seen for three days. We meanwhile enjoy the intelligent ministrations of Subri a good deal.

At last the expedition to the Kawkab takes place. Ferhid, his air of concentration greater than ever, volunteers to act as our guide, since he "knows the country." We cross the Jaghjagha by a rather precarious-looking bridge, and abandon ourselves to Ferhid's sad leadership.

Apart from the fact that Ferhid nearly dies of anxiety on the way, we do not do too badly. The Kawkab is always in sight, which is helpful, but the stony ground we have to cross is quite appalling, especially as we draw nearer to the extinct volcano.

Matters in the household were very strained before starting, a passionate quarrel about a small cake of soap having inflamed the whole staff. The foremen says coldly that they prefer not to come on the expedition, but the Colonel forces them to do so. They get into Mary from opposite sides and sit with their backs to each other! Serkis squats down like a hen in the back, and will speak to no one. Exactly who has quarrelled with who it is difficult to find out. However, by the time the ascension of the Kawkab is over all is forgotten. We were expecting a gentle sloping walk up to the top over ground carpeted with flowers, but, when we actually reach the place, the ascent is like the side of a house, and the ground is all slippery black cinders. Michel and Ferhid refuse firmly even to start, but the rest of us make the attempt. I give up soon, and settle down to enjoy the spectacle of the others slipping and panting and scrambling. Abd es Salaam goes up mostly on all fours!

There is a smaller crater, and on the lip of this we have lunch. There are flowers here in quantity, and it is a lovely moment. A marvelous view all round, with the hills of the Jebel Sinjar not far away. The utter peace is wonderful. A great wave of happiness surges over me, and I realize how much I love this country, and how complete and satisfying this life is. . . .

IX

ARRIVAL OF MAC

THE SEASON IS drawing to a close. The time has come for Mac to join us, and we are looking forward to seeing him. Bumps asks many questions about Mac, and displays incredulity at some of my statements. An extra pillow is needed, and we buy one in Kamichlie, the best we can find, but it is indubitably as hard as lead.

"The poor fellow can't sleep on *that*," says Bumps.

I assure him that Mac won't mind what he sleeps on.

"Fleas and bugs don't bite him; he never seems to have any luggage or any personal possessions shed about." I add reminiscently: "Just his plaid rug and his diary."

Bumps looks more incredulous than ever.

The day of Mac's arrival comes. It coincides with our day off and we plan a complicated expedition. The Colonel starts for Kamichlie at five-thirty A.M. in Poilu, and will combine meeting Mac with getting his hair cut. (This has to be done very often, as the Colonel insists on a closely military cut!)

We breakfast at seven and start at eight for Amuda, where we are to *rendezvous* with the others, and all go on to Ras-el-Ain, the idea being to examine a few mounds in that vicinity. (Our holidays are always busmen's holidays!) Subri and the gentle Dimitri also come on this expedition. They are exquisitely dressed, with shining boots and Homburg hats, and are wearing purple suits much too tight for them. Michel, warned by bitter experience, is wearing his working clothes, but he has put on white spats to mark his sense of holiday.

Amuda is as foul as ever, with even more carcasses of decaying sheep displayed than I remember before. Mac and the Colonel have not yet turned up, and I hazard the opinion that Poilu has, as usual, let the Colonel down.

However, they soon arrive, and after greetings and a few purchases (mainly bread; the Amuda bread is very good) we prepare to start, only to find that Poilu has lapsed from his good behavior and has got a flat tire. Michel and Subri attend quickly to this, whilst a crowd gathers round, pressing in closer and closer—always a habit of the Amudaites.

We get under way at last, but after about an hour Poilu repeats his bad behavior, and yet another tire goes. More repairs, and it now appears that none of Poilu's toilet apparatus is any good. His jack is defective and his pump a complete fiasco. Subri and Michel perform miracles by holding on to portions of tubing with their teeth and nails.

Having now lost an hour of valuable time we set off again. We next come to a wadi which is unexpectedly full of water—unusual so early in the season. We halt, and a discussion ensues as to whether we can rush it and get through.

Michel, Subri, and Dimitri are of the opinion that of course we can, if God is willing and merciful. Taking into consideration that if the Almighty is unwilling and disinclined to raise the chassis of Poilu by a miracle, we shall be stuck and probably not get out, we regretfully decide for discretion.

The local village is so much disappointed by our decision that we suspect that they derive a livelihood from pulling out submerged cars. Michel wades in to test the depth of the water, and we are all fascinated by the revelation of his underclothing! Strange white cotton garments tied with tapes round the ankles make their appearance—something like a Victorian Miss's pantalets!

We decide to lunch here by the wadi. After lunch, Max and I paddle our feet in it—delicious, till a snake suddenly darts out and quite puts us off paddling.

An old man comes and sits down beside us. There is the usual long silence after greetings have been given.

Then he inquires courteously if we are French? German? English?

English!

He nods his head. "Is it the English this country belongs to now? I cannot remember. I know it is no longer the Turks."

"No," we say; "the Turks have not been here since the war."

"A war?" says the old man, puzzled.

"The war that was fought twenty years ago."

He reflects. "I do not remember a war . . . Ah yes, about the time you mention, many 'asker went to and fro over the railway. That, then, was the war? We did not realize it was a war. It did not touch us here."

Presently, after another long silence, he rises, bids us farewell politely, and is gone.

We return by way of Tell Baindar, where what seems like thousands of black tents are pitched. It is the Beduin coming south for pasturage as the spring advances. There is water in the Wadi Wajh, and the whole scene is vibrant with life. In another two weeks, probably, it will be empty and silent once more.

I pick up one find on the slopes of Tell Baindar. It appears to be a small shell, but on examining it I see

that it is actually made of clay and has traces of paint
on it. It intrigues me, and I speculate vainly on who
made it and why. Did it adorn a building, or a cosmetic
box, or a dish? It is a *sea* shell. Who thought or knew
of the sea here so far inland all those thousands of
years ago? What pride of imagination and craftsman-
ship went to the making of it? I invite Max to speculate
with me, but he says cautiously we have not got any
data; but adds obligingly that he will look up parallels
for me and see if the same type of thing has been found
elsewhere. I do not even expect Mac to speculate—
it is not in his constitution, and he is quite uninterested.
Bumps is much more obliging, and consents willingly
to play games with me on the subject. "Variations on
the find of a pottery shell" continue for some time, but
we end by uniting all together to fall upon the
Colonel, who has gone all Roman on us (terrible
solecism on a dig such as ours). I relent sufficiently to
agree to take special trouble to photograph a Roman
fibula brooch which has been among our (despised)
finds, and even to allot it a plate all to itself!

We all arrive home in merry spirits and the Sheikh
rushes out to greet Mac. "Ha, the Khwaja engineer!"
He embraces him warmly on both cheeks.

Many chuckles from the Colonel, and Max warns
him:

"Next year *you*'ll be treated that way."

"Allow myself to be kissed by that disgusting old
man?"

We all lay bets on the subject, the Colonel remaining very stiff and dignified. Max, he informs us, was
greeted as Brother, and submitted to a very hearty
embrace; "but it is not going to happen to *me*," says the
Colonel firmly.

Rapturous greeting of Mac by the foremen. They
pour out Arabic, and Mac, as usual, responds in
English.

"Ah, the Khwaja Mac!" sighs Alawi. "Still will it
be necessary for him to whistle for all he wants!"

An immense dinner materializes in next to no time,

and after it, tired and comfortable, with special delicacies in honor of holiday and Mac's arrival (Turkish Delight, preserved aubergines, bars of chocolate and cigars), we sit and talk, for once, of subjects other than archaeology.

We come to the question of religions generally—a very vexed question in this particular part of the world, for Syria is full of fiercely fanatical sects of all kinds, all willing to cut each other's throats for the good cause! From there we fall to discussing the story of the Good Samaritan. All the Bible and New Testament stories take on a particular reality and interest out here. They are couched in the language and ideology which we hear daily all around us, and I am often struck by the way the emphasis sometimes shifts from what one has commonly accepted. As a small instance, it come to me quite suddenly that in the story of Jezebel, it is the painting of her face and the tiring of her hair that emphasizes in puritanical Protestant surroundings what exactly a "Jezebel" stands for. But out here it is not the painting and tiring—for all virtuous women paint their faces (or tattoo them), and apply henna to their hair—it is the fact that Jezebel *looked out of the window*—a definitely immodest action!

The New Testament comes very near when I ask Max to repeat to me the gist of long conversations that he has with the Sheikh, for their exchanges consist almost entirely of parables—to illustrate your wishes or your demands, you tell a story with a point to it, the other counters with another story which turns the tables, and so on. Nothing is ever couched in direct language.

The Good Samaritan story has a reality here which it cannot have in an atmosphere of crowded streets, police, ambulances, hospitals, and public assistance. If a man fell by the wayside on the broad desert track from Hasetshe to Der-ez-Zor, the story could easily happen today, and it illustrates the enormous virtue compassion has in the eyes of all desert folk.

How many of us, Max asks suddenly, would really

succor another human being in conditions where there were no witnesses, no force of public opinion, no knowledge or censure of a failure to extend aid?

"Everyone, of course," says the Colonel firmly.

"No, but would they?" persists Max. "A man is lying dying. Death, remember, is not very important here. You are in a hurry. You have business to do. You do not want delay or bother. The man is nothing whatever to you. And nobody will ever know if you just hurry on, saying that, after all, it isn't your business, and somebody else will come along presently," etc., etc.

We all sit back and think, and we are all, I think, a little shattered. . . . Are we so sure, after all, of our essential humanity?

After a long pause Bumps says slowly: "I *think* I would. . . . Yes, I think I would. I might go on, and then, perhaps, feel ashamed and come back."

The Colonel agrees.

"Just so; one wouldn't feel *comfortable*."

Max says he thinks *he* would, too, but he isn't nearly so sure about himself as he would like to be, and I concur with him.

We all sit silent for a while, and then I realize that, as usual, Mac has made no contribution.

"What would you do, Mac?"

Mac starts slightly, coming out of a pleasant abstraction.

"Me?" His tone is slightly surprised. "Oh, I would go on. I wouldn't stop."

"You wouldn't? Definitely?"

We all look interestedly at Mac, who shakes his gentle head.

"People die so much out here. One feels that a little sooner or later doesn't matter. I really wouldn't expect any one to stop for *me*."

No, that is true, Mac wouldn't.

His gentle voice goes on.

"It is much better, I think, to go straight on with

what one is doing, without being continually deflected by outside people and happenings."

Our interested gaze persists. Suddenly an idea strikes me.

"But, suppose, Mac," I say, "that it was a *horse?*"

"Oh, a horse!" says Mac, becoming suddenly quite human and alive and not remote at all. "That would be *quite* different! Of course, I'd do everything I possibly could for a horse."

We all roar with laughter and he looks surprised.

Today has definitely been Constipation Day. Abd es Salaam's health has been for some days the burning topic. Every kind of aperient has been administered to him. As a result he is now, he says, "much weakened." "I should like to go into Kamichlie, Khwaja, and be pricked with a needle to restore my strength."

Even more parlous is the condition of one Saleh Hassan, whose inside has resisted all treatment, from a mild beginning with Eno's to a half-bottle of castor oil.

Max has recourse to the Kamichlie doctor's horse medicine. An enormous dose is administered, and Max then addresses the patient, telling him that if his inside "moves before sunset" a large bakshish will be given him.

His friends and relations forthwith rally round him. The afternoon is spent by them walking him round and round the mound, uttering encouraging cries and exhortations, whilst they keep an anxious eye fixed on the declining sun.

It is a near thing; but a quarter of an hour after Fidos we hear cheers and cries. The news goes round like wildfire! The floodgates have opened! Surrounded by an enthusiastic crowd, the pale sufferer is escorted to the house to receive his promised reward!

Subri, who is assuming more and more control, has taken the Brak establishment severely in hand, considering it is not nearly grand enough! He, like everyone else, is zealous for our "reputation." He persuades

Michel to forswear *economia* and buy soup-bowls in the
Bazaar at Kamichlie. They and an enormous soup
tureen make their appearance every evening, and take
up far too much room on the one small table, so that
everything else has to be balanced precariously on the
bed! Ferhid's idea that you can help every dish and
eat it with a knife has also been overruled, and a
bewildering assortment of cutlery makes its appearance.
Subri also gives Hiyou a bath, and combs out the
knots in her hair with an immense comb (grudgingly
bought by Michel), and even ties a bow of cheap
pink satin round her neck. Hiyou is devoted to him!

The waterman's wife and three out of his ten children
have arrived. ("Your doing," says Max to me reproachfully.) She is a whining and rather unpleasant woman,
and the children are singularly unprepossessing. Their
noses are, frankly, in a disgusting condition. Why should
it be only the human young whose noses run when left
in a state of nature? Young kittens, puppies, and
donkeys do not seem to suffer from this affliction!

The grateful parents instruct their young to kiss the
sleeves of their benefactors on every possible occasion,
which they dutifully do, evading all efforts on our part
to escape the ceremony! Their noses look much better
afterwards, and I see Max looking down at his sleeve
with a definite lack of confidence!

We hand out a fair amount of aspirin for headaches
these days. It is very hot now and thundery. The men
take advantage of both Eastern and Western science.
Having swallowed our aspirins, they hurry off to the
Sheikh, who obligingly places discs of red-hot metal on
their foreheads "to drive out the evil spirit." I don't
know who gets the credit of the cure!

A snake is discovered in our bedroom this morning by Mansur when he comes in to do his *"service."*
It is coiled up in the basket under the washstand. Great
excitement. All run and join in the kill. For the next
three nights I listen apprehensively to rustlings before
going to sleep. After that I forget.

I ask Mac at breakfast one morning if he would like a softer pillow, glancing at Bumps as I do so.

"I don't think so," says Mac, looking rather surprised. "Is anything wrong with mine?"

I throw Bumps a glance of triumph and he grins.

"I didn't believe you," he confesses afterwards. "I thought you were just making up a story about Mac, but he is incredible. Nothing he has or wears ever seems to get dirty or torn or untidy. And as you say, he's *nothing* in his room except his rug and his diary, not even a book. I don't know how he manages it."

I look round Bumps' half of the room he shares with the Colonel, which is strewn with the signs of his exuberant and overflowing personality. Only strenuous effort on the part of the Colonel avoids an overlap on to *his* side.

Michel suddenly begins hitting Mary with a large hammer just outside the window, and Bumps flies out like a rocket to tell him to stop!

Max and Bumps present a great contrast in costume now that the heat has come. Bumps has taken off everything that he can take off. Max, following Arab custom, has put on everything available. He is heavily dressed, with a very thick tweed coat pulled up round his neck, and does not seem to notice the sun at all.

Mac, we observe, is not even sunburnt!

The burning moment of "The Division" is now drawing very near. At the close of the season the Director of the Services des Antiquités comes up or sends a representative to divide all the season's finds.

In Iraq this used to be done object by object, and used to take several days.

In Syria, however, the system is much simpler. It is left to Max to arrange everything found in two parts exactly as he pleases. The Syrian representative then comes, examines the two collections, and selects which of them he will have for Syria. The other is then packed up for dispatch to the British Museum. Any particularly

interesting objects, or anything unique, that may be in
the Syrian half, is usually loaned by them, so that it can
be studied, exhibited, photographed, etc., in London.

The real agony lies in making the two collections.
You are bound to lose certain things you want desperately. Very well, then you must balance them on
the other side. We all get called in to help Max as he
deals with each class of object in turn. Two lots of
celts, two lots of amulets, and so on. Pots, beads, bone
objects, obsidian. Then, one by one, the rest of us are
called in.

"Now, which lot of these two would you take? A
or B."

Pause whilst I study the two.

"I'd take B."

"You would? All right. Send in Bumps."

"Bumps, A or B?"

"B."

"Colonel?"

"A, definitely."

"Mac?"

"I think B."

"Hm," says Max, "B's evidently too strong."

He removes a delightful little stone amulet of a
horse's head from B to A, replaces it with a rather
shapeless sheep, and makes a few more alterations.

We re-enter. This time we all plump for A.

Max tears his hair.

In the end we lose all sense of value and appearance.

Meanwhile all is feverish activity. Bumps and Mac
are drawing like mad, and dashing to the mound to
plan houses and buildings. The Colonel sits up into the
night classifying and labelling those objects not yet
done. I come and assist, and we disagree violently over
nomenclature.

"Horse's head—steatite, 3 cms."

Me: "It's a *ram*."

"No, no, look at the *bridle*."

"That's the *horn*."

"Hi, Mac, what's this?"

Mac: "It's a gazelle."

Col.: "Bumps—what would you call this?"

Me: "A ram."

Bumps: "Looks like a *camel*."

Max: "There weren't any camels. Camels are quite modern animals."

Col.: "Well, what do *you* say it is?"

Max: "Stylized bukranium!"

So it goes on, passing through various puzzling small amulets representing kidneys, and various obscure and ambiguous ones which are labelled discreetly by the convenient name of "cult object."

I am developing and printing and trying to keep the water cool. I do most of it early about six A.M. It is very hot now in the middle of the day.

Our workmen trickle away day after day.

"It is harvest now, Khwaja. We must go."

The flowers have long since disappeared, eaten by the pasturing cattle. All is now an even dim yellow on the mound. Round it, on the plain, are the corn and the barley. The crops this year are good.

At last the fateful day arrives. M. Dunand and his wife are arriving this evening. They are old friends of ours, whom we saw at Byblos when we were at Beyrout.

Evening comes; a superb (or what we think is superb) dinner is ready. Hiyou has been washed. Max is taking one last agonized look at the two shares spread out for display on long tables.

"I think that balances up. If we lose that lovely little horse's head amulet and that very uncommon cylinder seal (jolly interesting!), well, we shall get the best Chagar Mother Goddess and the double axe amulet, and that very fine incised pot. . . . But, of course, there's that early painted pot on the other side. Oh, hell, it will have to do now! Which would *you* choose!"

In common humanity we refuse to play further. We say we simply couldn't decide. Max murmurs sadly that Dunand is a very shrewd judge. "He'll have the better half all right."

We lead him away firmly.

The hours go on. Night falls. No sign of the Dunands.

"I wonder what can have happened to them," Max muses. "Of course, like everyone else out here, they drive at about ninety miles an hour. Hope there isn't an accident."

Ten o'clock, eleven o'clock. No Dunands.

Max queries whether they can possibly have gone to Brak instead of to Chagar.

"No, surely not. They know we're living here."

At midnight we give it up and go to bed. People do not motor much after dark in this part of the world.

Two hours later sounds of a car are heard. The boys run out and call us excitedly. We tumble out of bed, slip on something, and come out into the living-room.

It is the Dunands, and they have gone to Brak by an error. On leaving Hasetshe, they asked for a direction to "the digging of antiquities," and a man who had himself always worked at Brak directed them there. They lost their way, and were some time finding it. Once there, a guide came with them across country to show them the way to Chagar.

They have been motoring all day, but are quite cheerful and unruffled.

"You must have something to eat," says Max.

Madame Dunand says politely there is no need. A glass of wine and a biscuit—it will be quite sufficient.

At that moment Mansur enters, followed by Subri, and a whole four-course dinner makes its appearance! How the servants out here do that sort of thing I don't know. It seems a kind of miracle. We discover the Dunands have had nothing to eat and are really

very hungry. We eat and drink far into the night, with
Mansur and Subri standing beaming by.

As we are going to sleep Max says dreamily that
he'd rather like to take Subri and Mansur to England.
"They're so useful." I say I, too, would like to have
Subri.

In the pause that follows I envisage the impact of
Subri upon an English domestic household—his large
knife, his oil-stained pullover and unshaven chin, his
big echoing laugh. The fantastic uses to which he puts
glasscloths!

Servants in the East are rather like *Jinns*. They appear from nowhere, and are there waiting for you when
you arrive.

We never send word to tell of our coming, but sure
enough, when we arrive, there is Dimitri. He has come
all the way from the coast to be ready for us.

"How did you know we were coming?"

"It is known that there is to be digging again this
year."

He adds gently: "It is very welcome. I have now the
family of two of my brothers to support; there are
eight children in one and ten in the other. They eat
much. It is good to earn money. 'See,' I said to my
brother's wife, 'God is good. We shall not starve this
year—we are saved—the Khwajas are coming to dig!' "

Dimitri pads gently away, displaying his flower-pat-
terned muslin trousers. His gentle meditative face beats
the maternity of the Chagar Madonna to a frazzle. He
loves puppies, kittens, and children. He alone of the
servants never quarrels. He doesn't even *own* a knife
except for culinary purposes.

All is over! The Division has taken place. M. and
Madame Dunand have examined, handled, reflected.
We have stood looking on in the usual agony. It takes
M. Dunand about an hour to make up his mind. Then
he flings a hand out in a quick Gallic gesture.

"Eh bien, I will take *this* one."

True to human nature, whichever half is chosen, we immediately wish it had been the other.

However, the suspense over, the atmosphere lifts. We are gay and the thing becomes a party. We go over the dig, examine the architects' plans and drawings, drive over to Brak, discuss work to be done the next season, and so on. Max and M. Dunand argue as to exact dates and sequences. Madame Dunand amuses us all by her dry witty remarks. We talk in French, though I fancy that she speaks English quite well. She is intensely amused by Mac and his stubborn limitation of conversation to *"Oui"* and *"Non."*

"Ah, votre petit architecte, il ne sait pas parler? Il a tout de même l'air intelligent!"

We repeat this to Mac, who is unperturbed.

On the next day the Dunands prepare for departure. Not that there is much preparation; they refuse food or drink to take with them.

"Surely you'll take *water!*" Max exclaims, brought up in the principle never to travel in these parts with no water.

They shake their heads carelessly.

"Suppose you had a breakdown?"

M. Dunand laughs and shakes his head.

"Oh, that will not happen!"

He lets in the clutch, and the car departs in the usual French desert style. Sixty miles an hour!

We no longer wonder at the high death rate for over-turned archaeologists in these parts!

And now, packing up once more—days of it! Crate after crate filled and fastened down and stencilled.

Then come the preparations for our own departure. We are going from Hasetshe by a little-used track through complete wilderness to the city of Raqqa on the Euphrates, and crossing the Euphrates there.

"And we shall be able," says Max, "to have a look at the Balikh!"

He says the word Balikh in the way he used to say Jaghjagha, and I perceive that he is forming plans to have just a little fun in the Balikh region before he finally leaves off digging in Syria.

"The Balikh?" I say innocently.

"Whacking great Tells all along it," says Max reverently.

X

THE TRAIL TO RAQQA

HERE WE GO! We are *off!*

The house is all boarded up, and Serkis is nailing the last planks across the windows and doors. The Sheikh stands by swelling with importance. All shall be secure until we return! The most trusted man of the village is to be our watchman! He shall guard it, says the Sheikh, night and day!

"Have no fear, brother!" he cries. "Even should I have to pay the man out of my own pocket, the house shall be guarded."

Max smiles, knowing quite well that the handsome remuneration already arranged with the watchman will probably go mostly into the Sheikh's pocket by way of rake-off.

"Everything will, indeed, be safe under your eye, we know," he replies. "The contents of the house will not easily deteriorate; and as for the outside, what pleasure it will be to us to hand it over to you in good condition when the day comes."

"May that day be long distant!" says the Sheikh.

"For when it comes, you will return no more, and that will be a sadness to me. You will perhaps dig only one more season?" he adds hopefully.

"One or two—who knows? It depends upon the work."

"It is regrettable that you have found no gold—only stones and pots," says the Sheikh.

"These things are of equal interest to us."

"Yet gold is always gold." The Sheikh's eyes glitter covetously. "In the days of El Baron——"

Max deftly interrupts:

"And when we return next season, what personal gift may I bring you from the city of London?"

"Nothing—nothing at all. I want nothing. A watch of gold is a pleasant thing to have."

"I shall remember."

"Let there be no talk of gifts between brothers! My only wish is to serve you and the Government. If I am out of pocket by so doing—well, to lose money in such a way is honorable."

"We should know no peace of heart unless we were quite sure that gain and not loss will be the result to you of our work here."

Michel comes up at this moment from where he has been nagging at everybody and shouting orders to say that all is in order and we can start.

Max checks up on the petrol and oil, and makes sure that Michel has with him the spare cans he has been told to have, and that no sudden qualms of *economia* have triumphed. Provisions, a supply of water, our luggage, the servants' luggage—yes, everything is there. Mary is loaded to bulging point both on the roof and inside, and perched amidst all are Mansur, Ali, and Dimitri. Subri and Ferhid return to Kamichlie, which is their home, and the foremen are going by train to Jerablus.

"Farewell, brother," cries the Sheikh, suddenly clasping the Colonel in his arms and embracing him on both cheeks.

Enormous joy of the whole Expedition!

The Colonel turns plum color.

The Sheikh repeats his salutation to Max and shakes the "Engineers" warmly by the hand.

Max, the Colonel, Mac, and myself get into Poilu. Bumps goes with Michel in Mary to curb any "good idea" Michel might have *en route*. Max reiterates his instructions to Michel. He is to follow us, but *not* at a distance of only three feet. If Michel tries to run down any parties of donkeys and old women on the road, half his salary will be stopped.

Michel murmurs "Mohammedans!" under his breath, but salutes and says in French: *"Très bien."*

"All right, off we go. Are we all here?"

Dimitri has two puppies with him. Hiyou is accompanying Subri.

"I will have her in splendid condition for you next year," Subri shouts.

"Where's Mansur?" shouts Max. "Where's that damned fool? We shall start without him if he doesn't come. Mansur!"

"Présent!" cries Mansur breathlessly, running into view. He is trailing two immense and horrible smelling sheepskins.

"You can't take those. Phew!"

"They will be worth money to me in Damascus!"

"What a reek!"

"The sun will dry them if they are spread on the top of Mary, and then they will not smell."

"They're disgusting. Leave 'em behind."

"He is right. They are worth money," says Michel. He climbs up on top of the lorry, and the skins are precariously lashed up with string.

"As the lorry is behind us we shan't smell them," says Max resignedly; "and anyway, they'll fall off before we get to Raqqa. Mansur tied one of those knots himself!"

"Ha, ha!" laughs Subri, throwing back his head, and showing his white and gold teeth. "Perhaps Mansur wants to make the trip on a horse!"

Mansur hangs his head. The staff have never stopped ragging him about his ride back from Kamichlie.

"Two gold watches," says the Sheikh in a meditative voice, "are a good thing to have. One can then lend one to a friend."

Max hurriedly gives the signal for departure.

We drive slowly through the cluster of houses and out on to the Kamichlie Hasetshe track. Crowds of small boys yell and wave.

As we drive through the next village of Hanzir, men run out from the houses and wave and shout. They are our old workmen.

"Come back next year," they yell.

"Inshallah!" Max yells back.

We drive along the track to Hasetshe, and look back for one last look at the mound of Chagar Bazar.

At Hasetshe we stop, buy bread and fruit, and go and wish the French officers good-bye. A young officer who has just come up from Der-ez-Zor interests himself in our journey.

"You go to Raqqa then? I will tell you. Do not follow the signpost when you come to it. Instead, take the track to the right of it and then the one that forks left. So you will have a straight track easy to follow. But the other way is most confusing."

The Capitaine, who has been listening, cuts in to say he strongly advises us to go north to Ras-el-Ain, then to Tell Abyadh, and take the well-frequented track from Tell Abyadh to Raqqa. Then there will be no mistake.

"But it is much longer, an immense way round."

"It may come shorter in the end."

We thank him, but persist in our original design.

Michel has made the necessary purchases and we start off, taking the bridge across the Habur.

We follow the young officer's advice when we come to a meeting-place of tracks with a signpost or two. One says Tell Abyadh, one Raqqa, and between them is one unmarked. That must be the one.

After a little distance along it the track divides into three.

"Left, I suppose," says Max, "or did he mean the middle one?"

We take the left-hand track, and after a little way it divides into four.

The country is now full of scrub and boulders. One has definitely to follow a track.

Max takes the left one again. "We should have taken the one to the extreme right," says Michel.

No one pays any attention to Michel, who has led us on more wrong tracks than we can possibly count.

I draw a veil over the next five hours. We are lost—lost in a part of the world where there are no villages, no cultivation, no Beduin pasturing—nothing.

The tracks deteriorate until they are hardly distinguishable. Max tries to take those leading roughly in the right direction—namely, a little west of south-west, but the tracks are perverse in the extreme. They twist and turn, and usually obstinately return due north.

We halt for a while and eat lunch and drink tea, which Michel makes. The heat is suffocating, the going is very bad. The jolting, the heat, and intense glare give me an excruciating headache. We all feel a little worried.

"Well," says Max, "we've got plenty of water at any rate. *What's that damned fool doing?*"

We turn. Mansur—the idiotic—is happily pouring out our precious water and sluicing it over his face and hands!

I pass over Max's language! Mansur looks surprised and a little aggrieved. He sighs. How difficult, he seems to be thinking, these people are to please. One's simplest action may annoy them.

We take the road again. The tracks turn and twist worse than ever. Sometimes they peter out altogether.

With a worried frown, Max mutters that we are going far too far north.

When the tracks divide now, they seem to run north and north-east. Shall we turn back altogether?

It is getting towards evening. Suddenly the quality of the ground improves, the scrub peters out, the stones are less plentiful.

"We've got to get somewhere," says Max. "I think we can go straight across country now."

"Where are you heading for?" asks the Colonel.

Max says due west for the Balikh. If we once strike the Balikh we shall find the main Tell Abyadh-Raqqa track and can go down it.

We drive on. Mary has a puncture and we lost precious time. The sun is setting.

Suddenly we see a welcome sight—men trudging ahead. Max lets out a whoop. He draws up beside them, giving greetings, asking questions.

The Balikh? The Balikh is just ahead of us. In ten minutes, in a machine like ours, we shall be there. Raqqa? We are nearer to Tell Abyadh than Raqqa.

Five minutes later we see a streak of green ahead—it is the vegetation bordering the river. A vast Tell looms up.

Max says ecstatically: "The Balikh—look at it! Tells everywhere!"

The Tells are indeed imposing—large, formidable, and very solid looking.

"Whacking great Tells," says Max.

I say disagreeably, because my head and eyes have reached an almost unbearable degree of pain: "Min Ziman er Rum."

"You're about right," says Max. "That *is* the snag. That solidity means Roman masonry—a chain of forts. The right stuff farther down, I've no doubt, but too long and expensive to get down to it."

I feel completely uninterested in archaeology. I want somewhere to lie down, and a great deal of aspirin and a cup of tea.

We come to a broad track running north and south, and turn South to Raqqa.

We are a long way out of our way, and it takes us an hour and a half before we see the city sprawling ahead of us. It is dark now. We drive into the outskirts.

It is an entirely native city—no European structures. We ask for the Services Spéciaux. The officer there is kind, but troubled for our comfort. There is no accommodation for travellers here. If we were to drive north to Tell Abyadh? In two hours, if we drove fast, there we should be really comfortable.

But nobody, least of all my suffering self, can bear the thought of two more hours jolting and bouncing. The kindly officer says there are two rooms—very meagre, though, nothing European—but if we have our own bedding? And our servants?

We arrive at the house in pitch-black darkness. Mansur and Ali run about with torches and light the primus and spread out blankets and get in each other's way. I long for the quick and efficient Subri. Mansur is incredibly slow and clumsy. Presently Michel comes in and criticizes what Mansur is doing. Mansur stops and they argue. I hurl all the Arabic I know at them. Mansur looks scared and resumes operations.

A roll of bedding and blankets is brought and I sink down. Suddenly Max is beside me with the longed-for cup of tea. He asks cheerfully if I feel bad. I say yes, seize the tea, and swallow four aspirins. The tea tastes like nectar. Never, never, *never* have I enjoyed anything so much! I sink back, my eyes close.

"Madame Jacquot," I murmur.

"Eh?" Max looks startled. He bends down. "What did you say?"

"Madame Jacquot," I repeat.

The association is there—*I* know what I mean—but the phrase has escaped me. Max has a kind of hospital nurse's expression on his face—on no account contradict the patient!

"Madame Jacquot's not here just now," he says in a soothing tone.

I throw him an exasperated glance. My eyes are gently closing. There is still a lot of bustle. A meal is being prepared. Who cares? I am going to sleep— sleep. . . .

Just as I am going off—the phrase comes. Of course!

"*Complètement knock out!*" I say with satisfaction.
"What?" says Max.
"Madame Jacquot," I say, and fall asleep.

The best of going to sleep utterly weary and pain-racked is the marvelous surprise you feel when you wake up well and energetic next morning.

I feel full of vigor and ferociously hungry.

"You know, Agatha," says Max, "I think you must have had fever last night. You were delirious. You kept talking about Madame Jacquot."

I throw him a scornful look and speak as soon as I can, my mouth being full of hard-fried egg.

"Nonsense!" I say at last. "If you'd only taken the trouble to *listen* you'd have known exactly what I meant! But I suppose your mind was so full of the Tells on the Balikh——"

"It would be interesting, you know," says Max, eager at once, "just to run a trial trench or two in some of those Tells. . . ."

Mansur comes up, beaming all over his stupid, honest face, and asks how the Khatūn is this morning.

I say I am very well. Mansur, it seems, is distressed because I was so fast asleep when supper was ready that nobody liked to wake me. Will I have another egg now?

"Yes," I say, having already eaten four. And this time, if Mansur fries it for about five minutes, it will be quite enough!

We start for the Euphrates about eleven. The river is very wide here, the country is pale and flat and shining, and the air is hazy. It is a kind of symphony in what Max would describe as "pinkish buff," if he were describing pottery.

To cross the Euphrates at Raqqa is a matter of a very primitive ferry. We join some other cars and settle down happily for an hour or two's wait until the ferry comes.

Some women come down to fill kerosene tins of water. Others are washing clothes. It is like a pattern on a frieze—the tall, black-clad figures, the lower half of the face covered, the heads very erect, the great dripping tins of water. The women move up and down, slow and unhurried.

I reflect enviously that it must be nice to have your face veiled. It must make you feel very private, very secret. . . . Only your eyes look out on the world—you see it, but it does not see you. . . .

I take out the glass from my hand-bag and open my powder compact. "Yes," I think, "it would be very nice to veil *your* face!"

Approaching civilization stirs within me. I begin to think of things. . . . A shampoo, a luxurious drier. Manicure . . . A porcelain bath with taps. Bath salts. Electric light . . . . More shoes!

"What's the matter with you?" says Max. "I've asked you twice whether you noticed that second Tell we passed on the road down from Tell Abyadh last night."

"I didn't."

"You didn't?"

"No. I wasn't noticing *anything* last night."

"It wasn't as solid a Tell as the others. Denudation on the east side of it. I wonder perhaps——"

I say clearly and firmly: "I'm tired of Tells!"

"What?" Max looks at me with the horror a medieval inquisitor might have felt on hearing a particularly flagrant bit of blasphemy.

He says: "You can't be!"

"I'm thinking of other things." I reel off a list of them, starting with electric light, and Max passes his hand over the back of his head and says he wouldn't mind having a decent haircut at last.

We all agree what a pity it is one can't go straight from Chagar to, say, the Savoy! As it is, the sharp pleasure of contrast is always lost. We go through a stage of indifferent meals and partial comfort so that the pleasure of switching on electric light or turning a tap is dulled.

Now the ferry is here. Mary is driven carefully up the inclined boards. Poilu follows.

We are out now on the broad Euphrates. Raqqa recedes. It looks beautiful, with its mud-brick and its Oriental shapes.

"Pinkish buff," I say softly.

"That striped pot, do you mean?"

"No," I say, "Raqqa. . . ."

And I repeat the name softly, like a good-bye, before I get back to the world where the electric light switch rules. . . .

Raqqa. . . .

XI

GOOD-BYE TO BRAK

NEW FACES AND old faces!

This is our last season in Syria. We are digging now at Tell Brak, having finally closed down at Chagar.

Our house, Mac's house, has been handed over (with immense ceremony) to the Sheikh. The Sheikh has already borrowed money on the house about three times over; nevertheless he displays distinct pride of ownership. To own the house will be good, we feel, for his "reputation."

"Though it will probably break his neck," says Max thoughtfully. He has explained to the Sheikh at length and with emphasis that the roof of the house must be seen to every year and duly repaired.

"Naturally, naturally!" says the Sheikh. "Inshallah, nothing will go wrong!"

"A bit too much Inshallah about it," says Max. "All Inshallah and no repairs! That's what will happen."

The house, a gaudy gold watch, and a horse have been presented to the Sheikh as gifts, exclusive of the rental due and compensation for crops.

Whether the Sheikh is a satisfied or a disappointed man we are not quite sure. He is all smiles and extravagant professions of affection, but he has a good try at getting extra compensation for "spoiling of the garden."

"What, then, is this garden?" asks the French officer, amused.

What indeed? Asked to produce any trace of ever having had a garden, and indeed of knowing what a garden *is*, the Sheikh climbs down. "I intended to produce a garden," he says austerely; "but by the digging my intention was foiled."

The "Sheikh's garden" is a subject of jest among us for some time.

This year we have at Brak with us the inevitable Michel; the gay Subri; Hiyou, with a litter of four hideous puppies; Dimitri, yearning tenderly over the puppies; and Ali. Mansur, the No. 1, the head boy, the servant skilled in European service, has, El hamdu lillah, joined the police force! He comes to see us one day, resplendent in uniform and grinning from ear to ear.

Guilford came out with us this spring as architect, and is with us again now. He has aroused enormous respect in me by being able to cut a horse's toe-nails.

Guilford has a long, fair, serious face, and was once, at the beginning of his first season, very particular about the careful sterilizing and application of dressings to the local cuts and wounds. Having seen, however, what happens to the dressings once the men get home, and having observed one Yusuf Abdullah remove a neat bandage and lie under the dirtiest corner of the dig letting sand trickle into his wound, Guilford now dabs on a good deal of permanganate solution (appreciated because of its rich hue!) and confines himself to emphasizing what is to be applied to the outside and what can safely be drunk.

The son of a local Sheikh, exercising a car after the manner of breaking-in a young horse, and having been overturned into a wadi, comes to Guilford for treatment with an immense hole in his head. Horrified, Guilford more or less fills it up with iodine, and the young man staggers about, reeling with pain.

"Ah!" he gasps when he can speak. "That is fire indeed! It is wonderful. In future I will always come to you—never to a doctor. Yes—fire, fire, indeed!"

Guilford urges Max to tell him to go to a doctor, as the wound is really serious.

"What—*this?*" demands the Sheikh's son scornfully. "A headache, that is all! It is interesting, though," he adds thoughtfully. "If I hold my nose and blow—so—spittle comes out through the wound!"

Guilford turns green, and the Sheikh's son goes away laughing.

He comes back four days later for further treatment. The wound is healing with incredible rapidity. He is deeply chagrined that no more iodine is applied; only a cleansing solution.

"This does not burn at all," he says discontentedly.

A woman comes to Guilford with a pot-bellied child, and whatever the real trouble, she is delighted at the results of the mild medicaments given her. She returns to bless Guilford "for saving the life of my son," and adds that he shall have her eldest daughter as soon as she is old enough; whereat Guilford blushes, and the woman goes away, laughing heartily and making a few final unprintable remarks. Needless to say she is a Kurd, and not an Arab woman!

This is an autumn dig we are doing now to complete our work. This spring we finished Chagar and concentrated on Brak, where many interesting things were found. Now we are finishing up Brak, and are going to end the season by a month or six weeks' digging at Tell Jidle, a mound on the Balikh!

A local Sheikh, whose camp is pitched near the Jaghjagha, invites us to a ceremonial feast, and we accept. When the day comes, Subri appears in all the glory of his tight plum suit, polished shoes, and Homburg hat. He has been invited as our retainer, and he acts as a go-between, reporting to us how the cooking of the feast is proceeding and the exact moment at which our arrival should occur.

The Sheikh greets us with dignity under the wide, brown canopy of his open tent. There is a large following of friends, relations, and general hangers-on with him.

After courteous greetings, the great ones (ourselves, the foremen, Alawi and Yahya, the Sheikh and his chief friends) all sit down in a circle. An old man, handsomely apparelled, approaches us, bearing a coffee-pot and three little cups. A tiny drop of intensely black coffee is poured into each. The first one is handed to *me*—proof that the Sheikh is acquainted with the (extraordinary!) European custom of serving women first. Max and the Sheikh have the next two. We sit and sip. In due course another tiny drop is poured into our cups and we continue to sip. Then the cups are taken back, refilled, and Guilford and the foreman drink in their turn. So it goes on round the circle. A little distance away stands a considerable crowd of those of the second rank. From behind the partition of the tent close beside me come muffled giggles and rustlings. The Sheikh's womenfolk are peeping and listening to what goes on.

The Sheikh gives an order, and a follower goes out and returns with a perch, on which is a handsome falcon. This is set in the middle of the tent. Max congratulates the Sheikh upon the magnificent bird.

Then three men appear, carrying a large copper cauldron, which is set down in the middle of the circle. It is full of rice, on which is laid pieces of lamb. All is spiced and smoking hot and smelling delicious. Courteously we are invited to eat. We have flaps of Arab bread, with which and our fingers we help ourselves from the dish.

In due course (which is not for some time, let me say) hunger and politeness are satisfied. The vast platter, with its choicest morsels gone but still more than half-full, is lifted up and set down a little farther along, where a second circle (including Subri) sit down to eat.

Sweetmeats are handed to us and more coffee is served.

After the secondary folk have satisfied their hunger, the platter is set down in yet a third place. Its contents now are mainly rice and bones. The complete inferiors sit down to this, and those who, destitute, have come to "sit in the shadow of the Sheikh." They fling themselves upon the food, and when the platter is lifted it is quite empty.

We sit a little longer, Max and the Sheikh exchanging grave comments at intervals. Then we rise, thank the Sheikh for his hospitality, and depart. The coffee-server is handsomely remunerated by Max, and the foremen single out certain mysterious individuals as those to whom *largesse* is due.

It is hot, and we walk home, feeling quite dazed with rice and mutton. Subri is highly satisfied with the entertainment. All, he considers, has been conducted with strict propriety.

Today, a week later, we in our turn have entertained a visitor. This is none other than a Sheikh of the Shammar tribe—a very great man indeed. Local Sheikhs were in attendance on him and he arrived in a beautiful grey car. A very handsome and sophisticated person, with a dark thin face and beautiful hands.

Our European meal was the best we could make it, and the excitement of the staff at the consequence of our visitor was immense!

When he finally drove away, we felt as though we had been entertaining the royal family at least.

Today has been a day of catastrophe.

Max goes in to Kamichlie with Subri for shopping and to transact business with the Bank, leaving Guilford planning buildings on the mound and the foremen in charge of the men.

Guilford comes home to lunch, and he and I have just finished, and he is about to take Poilu back again to the work when we notice that the foremen are running towards the house as fast as they can come with every sign of agitation and distress.

They burst into the courtyard and pour out a flood of excited Arabic.

Guilford is completely blank, and I understand about one word in seven.

"Somebody's dead," I say to Guilford.

Alawi repeats his story with emphasis. Four people, I gather, are dead. I think at first that this has been a quarrel and the men have killed each other, but Yahya shakes his head emphatically at my halting questions.

I curse myself for not having learnt to understand the language! My Arabic consists almost entirely of phrases like "This is not clean. Do it like this. Do not use that cloth. Bring in tea," and such domestic orders. This recital of violent death is quite beyond me. Dimitri and the boy and Serkis come out and listen. They understand what has happened, but since they can speak no European language, Guilford and I are still no wiser.

Guilford says: "I'd better go up and see," and moves towards Poilu.

Alawi grabs him by the sleeve and speaks vehemently, evidently dissuading him. He points dramatically. Down the sides of Brak, a mile away, a mob of motley and white-robed figures are pouring, and there is somehow an ugly and purposeful look about them. The foremen, I see, are looking frightened.

"These fellows have run away," says Guilford sternly. "I wish we could understand what the trouble is."

Has Alawi (hot tempered) or Yahya killed a workman with a pick? It seems wildly unlikely, and certainly they could not have killed *four*.

I suggest again haltingly that there has been a fight, and illustrate in dumb show. But the response is emphatically negative. Yahya gestures to something coming down from above his head.

I look up at the sky. Have the victims been struck down by a thunderbolt?

Guilford opens the door of Poilu. "I'm going up to see, and these fellows must come with me."

He beckons them in authoritatively. Their refusal is prompt and decisive. They are not coming.

Guilford sticks an aggressive Australian chin out. "They've *got* to come!"

Dimitri is shaking his large gentle head.

"No, no," he says. "It is very bad."

"*What* is very bad?"

"There's some kind of trouble up there," says Guilford. He jumps into the car. Then, as he looks at the rapidly approaching mob, his head turns sharply. He stares at me in consternation, and I see what may be described as the "women-and-children-first" look come into his eyes.

He descends from the car, taking care to make the movement leisurely, and says in a careful holiday tone:

"How about taking a spin along the road to meet Max? Might as well, as there is no work going on. You get your hat or whatever you want."

Dear Guilford, he is doing it beautifully! So careful not to alarm me.

I say slowly that we might as well, and shall I bring the money? The expedition money is kept in a cash-box under Max's bed. If we really have an infuriated mob coming to attack the house, it will be a pity if they find money to steal.

Guilford, still trying not to "alarm me," pretends that this is quite an everyday suggestion.

"Could you," he says, "be rather *quick?*"

I go into the bedroom, pick up my felt hat, drag out the cash-box, and we lift it into the car. Guilford and I get in, and we beckon to Dimitri and Serkis and the boy to get in at the back.

"We'll take them and not the foremen," says Guilford, still condemnatory of the latter's attitude in "running away."

I am sorry for Guilford, who is obviously longing

to go and face the mob, and has instead to care for my safety. But I am very glad that he is not going to the men. He has very little authority with them, and will, in any case, not understand a word they say, and he may easily make matters very much worse. What we need is to get Max on to the matter and find out what has really *happened*.

Guilford's plan for saving Dimitri and Serkis and leaving the foremen to deal with their responsibilities is at once circumvented by Alawi and Yahya, who push aside Dimitri and climb into the car. Guilford is furious and tries to eject them. They refuse to budge.

Dimitri nods his head placidly and gestures to the kitchen. He walks back and Serkis goes with him, looking a little unhappy about it.

"I don't see why these fellows——" begins Guilford.

I interrupt.

"We can only take four in the car—and actually it seems to be Alawi and Yahya whom the men want to kill if anybody, so I think we'd better take them. I don't think the men will have anything against Dimitri and Serkis."

Guilford looks up and sees that the running mob is getting too near for more argument. He scowls at Yahya and Alawi and drives rapidly out through the courtyard gate and round by the village to the track which leads to the Kamichlie road.

Max must have started back by now since he intended to be on the work early this afternoon, so we ought to meet him before long.

Guilford draws a sigh of relief and I tell him that that was very nicely done.

"What was?"

"Your casual suggestion of a pleasant drive to meet Max, and the way you avoided alarming me."

"Oh," says Guilford; "so you realized I wanted to get you away?"

I look at him pityingly.

We drive at full speed and in about a quarter of an hour we meet Max returning with Subri in Mary. Very surprised to see us, he pulls up. Alawi and Yahya pour themselves out of Poilu and rush towards him, and an excited spate of Arabic fills the air as Max asks sharp staccato questions.

Now at last we learn what it is all about!

For some days past we have been finding a large number of very beautifully carved small animal amulets in stone and ivory in a certain part of the dig. The men have been getting high bakshish for these, and in order to find as many as they can they have been undercutting in the pit where they are, since the amulets are at a level some way down.

Yesterday Max stopped this, since it was getting dangerous, and put the gangs to work on top again to cut down from there. The men grumbled, since it meant that they would have a day or two's digging of uninteresting levels before they came to the amulet level once more.

The foremen were put on guard to see that they obeyed orders, and actually, although they were sulky about it, they did what they were told, and started working from the top as vigorously as possible.

This was the position when work was knocked off for lunch. And now comes a tale of base treachery and greed. The men were all stretched out on the hillside near the water jars. A gang of men who had been working on the other side crept away, sneaked round the mound to the rich spot, and began furiously digging in at the already undercut spot. They were going to rob the other men's pitch, and pretend to produce the filched objects from their own patch of ground.

And then Nemesis overcame them. They undercut too far, and down came the higher levels on top of them!

The yells of the one man who escaped brought the whole crowd running to the spot. At once they and the foremen realized what had occurred, and three pickmen began hurriedly to dig their comrades out. One man was alive, but four others were dead.

Wild excitement rose at once. Cries, lamentations to

Heaven, and a desire to blame someone. Whether the foremen lost their nerve and decided to run away, or whether they were actually attacked, is hard to make out. But the result was, that the men poured after them in a suddenly nasty mood.

Max inclines to the view that the foremen lost their nerve and put the idea of attacking them into the men's heads, but he wastes no time in recrimination. He turns the cars, and we both drive for all we are worth towards Kamichlie, where Max lays the matter at once before the officer at the Services Spéciaux who is in charge of security.

The Lieutenant is quick to comprehend and act. He collects four soldiers and his car and we all drive back to Brak. The men are on the mound now, seething and swaying rather like a swarm of bees. They subside when they see authority approaching. We walk up the mound in a procession. The Lieutenant sends his car off with one of the soldiers, and he himself goes to the scene of the tragedy.

Here he inquires into the facts, and the men whose place it properly is explain that it was not they but a rival gang who were trying to steal a march on them. The survivor is then interrogated, and confirms this story. Are these all the men of the gang? One unhurt, one injured and four dead? There is no possibility of any one still being buried? No.

At this point the Lieutenant's car returns with the local Sheikh of the tribe to which the dead workmen belong. He and the Lieutenant take charge together. Question and answer goes on.

Finally the Sheikh raises his voice and addresses the crowd. He absolves the Expedition of all blame. The men were digging out of work hours in their own time, and were, moreover, endeavoring to steal from their comrades. Theirs has been the reward of disobedience and greed. Everyone is now to go home.

The sun has set by this time and night is falling.

The Sheikh, the Lieutenant, and Max drive down to

the house (where we are relieved to find Dimitri placidly cooking dinner and Serkis grinning).

Consultations proceed for about an hour. The incident is regrettable. The Lieutenant says that the men have families, and although there is no obligation, doubtless a donation would be appreciated. The Sheikh says that generosity is the hallmark of a noble nature, and will much enhance our reputation in the countryside.

Max says that he would like to make a gift to the families, if it is clearly understood that it *is* a gift, and not in any sense compensation. The Sheikh grunts earnest agreement. That shall be set down in writing by the French officer, he says. Moreover, he will himself make it known on his word. The question remains of how much. When that has been adjusted and refreshments have been served, the Sheikh and the Lieutenant depart. Two soldiers are left on the mound to guard the fatal spot.

"And mind," says Max as we go very tired to bed, "someone's got to watch that spot to-morrow at lunchtime or we'll have the same thing happening again."

Guilford is incredulous.

"Not after they know the danger and have seen what happened!"

Max says grimly: "Wait and see!"

On the next day he himself waits inconspicuously behind a mud-brick wall. Sure enough, whilst lunch is in progress, three men come stealing round the slope of the mound and start furious scrabbling at the adjoining portion of the excavation not two feet from where their comrades were killed!

Max strides forth and delivers a terrific harangue. Do they not realize that what they are doing will bring death?

One of the men murmurs "Inshallah!"

They are then formally sacked for attempting to steal from their companions.

After that the spot is guarded after Fidos until the

moment when, on the following afternoon, the top levels have been cut down.

Guilford says in a horrified voice:

"These fellows don't seem to have any care for their lives at all. And they are extraordinarily callous. They were laughing about the deaths and making dumb show of the whole thing this morning during the work!"

Max says death isn't really important out here.

The foremen's whistle blows for Fidos, and the men run down the mound past us singing: *"Yusuf Daoud was with us yesterday—today he is dead! He will not fill his belly any more. Ha, ha, ha!"*

Guilford is profoundly shocked.

XII

AIN EL ARUS

HOUSE-MOVING FROM Brak to the Balikh.

We walk down to the Jaghjagha on our last evening and feel a gentle melancholy. I have come to have a great affection for the Jaghjagha, that narrow stream of muddy brown water.

Still, Brak has never had the hold on my affections that Chagar has. The village of Brak is melancholy, half deserted and tumbling down, and the Armenians in their seedy European clothes look out of tune with the surroundings. Their voices rise scoldingly, and there is none of the rich Kurdish and Arabic joy of life. I miss the Kurdish women strolling across the countryside—those great gay flowers, with their white teeth and their laughing faces, and their proud, handsome carriage.

We have hired a ramshackle lorry to take what furniture we shall need. It is the kind of lorry where everything has to be tied on with string! I have an idea that nearly everything will have dropped off by the time we get to Ras-el-Ain.

212

All is loaded up at last and we start off, Max Guilford and I in Mary, and Michel and the servants in Poilu with Hiyou.

Halfway to Ras-el-Ain we halt for a picnic lunch, and find Subri and Dimitri in roars of laughter. "Hiyou," they say, "has been sick all the way, and Subri has been holding her head!" The inside of Poilu bears eloquent testimony to this story! It is fortunate, I reflect, that it strikes them as funny.

Hiyou, for the first time I have known her, looks defeated. "I can face," she seems to say, "a hostile world to dogs, the enmity of the Moslem people, death by drowning, semi-starvation, blows, kicks, stones. I fear nothing. I am friendly to all but love nobody. But what is this strange new affliction that takes from me all my self-respect?" Her amber eyes go mournfully from one to the other of us. Her faith in her ability to meet the worst the world can do is shattered.

Happily, five minutes later, Hiyou is restored to her normal self, and is devouring immense quantities of Subri's and Dimitri's lunch. I ask if this is really wise, pointing out that the car journey will soon be resumed.

"Ha," cries Subri, "then Hiyou will be sick a great deal more!"

Well, if it amuses them. . . .

We arrive at our house early in the afternoon. It is in one of the main streets of Tell Abyadh. It is an almost urban dwelling; what the Bank Manager calls a "construction en pierre." There are trees all down the street, and their leaves are brilliant now in autumn coloring. The house, alas, is very damp, being below street level, and the village has streams everywhere. In the morning one's top blanket is quite wet, and everything you touch feels damp and clammy. I get so stiff I can hardly move.

There is a pleasant little garden behind the house, and it is much more sophisticated than anywhere we have lived for a long time.

We have lost three chairs, a table, and my lavatory seat from the lorry when it arrives! A good deal less than I thought we should!

Tell Jidle itself is set by a big pool of azure-blue water formed by the spring which feeds the Balikh. It has trees round the pool and is really a lovely spot and is the traditional meeting-place of Isaac and Rebecca. This is all very different from where we have been before. It has a lovely but melancholy charm, but none of the untouched freshness of Chagar and the rolling country round it.

There is a lot of prosperity here, well-dressed Armenians and others walk along the streets, and there are houses and gardens.

We have been there a week when Hiyou disgraces us. All the dogs of Ain el Arus arrive to woo her, and since none of the doors shut properly it is impossible to keep them out or her shut up! There is howling, barking, and fighting. Hiyou, a pensive amber-eyed belle, does everything to encourage the pandemonium!

The scene is exactly like that of an old-fashioned pantomime when demons pop out from windows and trap-doors. As we sit at supper a window flies open and a large dog leaps in, another leaps after it in pursuit—crash! The bedroom door flies open and another dog appears. All three rush madly round the table, charge Guilford's door, burst it open, and disappear, to reappear like magic through the door from the kitchen with a frying-pan hurled after them by Subri.

Guilford spends a sleepless night, with dogs bursting in at the door, over his bed, and out through the window. At intervals Guilford gets up and flings things after them. There are howls, yelps, and general dog saturnalia!

Hiyou, herself, we discover, is a snob. She favors the only dog in Ain el Arus who wears a collar! "Here," she seems to say, "is real *class!*" He is a black dog, snub-nosed, and with an immense tail rather like a funeral horse.

Subri, after spending sleepless nights with tooth-ache, demands leave of absence to go to Aleppo by train and visit the dentist. He returns two days later beaming.

His account of the proceedings is as follows:

"I go to the dentist. I sit in his chair. I show him the tooth. Yes, he says, it must come out. How much, I say? Twenty francs, he says. It is absurd, I say, and I leave the house. I come again in the afternoon. How much? Eighteen francs. Again I say absurd. All the time the pain is increasing, but one cannot allow one-self to be robbed. I come the next morning. How much? Still eighteen francs. Again at midday? Eighteen francs. He thinks that the pain will beat me, but I continue to bargain! In the end, Khwaja, I *win*."

"He comes down?"

Subri shakes his head.

"No, he will not come down, but I make a very good bargain. Very well, I say. Eighteen francs. But for that you must take out not one tooth but four!"

Subri laughs with enormous gusto, displaying sundry gaps.

"But did the other teeth ache?"

"No, of course not. But they will begin to some day. Now they cannot. They have been taken out, and for the price of one."

Michel, who has been standing in the doorway listen-ing, now nods his head approvingly. "Beaucoup econo-mia," he says.

Subri has kindly brought back a string of red beads, which he ties round Hiyou's neck. "It is what the girls put on to show they are married," he says. "And Hiyou, she has lately been married."

She certainly has! To every dog in Ain el Arus, I should say!

This morning, which is a Sunday and our day off, I am sitting labelling finds, and Max is writing up the pay-book, when a woman is shown in by Ali. She is a most respectable-looking woman, dressed neatly in black, with an enormous gold cross on her bosom. Her lips are tightly pressed together and she looks very upset.

Max greets her politely, and she begins at once to pour out a long tale, evidently of woe. Now and then Subri's name enters the narrative. Max frowns and looks grave. The tale goes on, getting even more impassioned.

I surmise that this is the old and well-known tale of betrayal of the village maiden. This woman is the mother, and our gay Subri is the base deceiver.

The woman's voice rises in righteous indignation. She clasps the cross on her breast with one hand and holds it up, and appears to be swearing something on it.

Max calls for Subri to be sent in. I think that perhaps it would be more delicate if I withdrew, and I am just about to edge out unobtrusively when Max tells me to stay where I am. I sit down again, and since I am presumably required to give the effect of a witness, look as though I understand what it is all about.

The woman, a grave, dignified figure, stands silent until Subri appears. Then she flings out a hand of denunciation, and evidently repeats her accusation against him.

Subri does not defend himself with any vigor. He shrugs his shoulders, raises his hands, appears to admit the truth of the indictment.

The drama goes on—argument, recrimination, the adoption of a more and more judicial attitude by Max. Subri is being defeated. Very well, he seems to be saying, do as you like!

Suddenly Max pulls a sheet of paper towards him and writes. He puts the written words in front of the woman. She puts a mark—a cross—on the paper, and, holding up the gold cross once more, swears some solemn oath. Max then signs, and Subri also makes his mark, and swears apparently some oath of his own.

Max then counts out some money and gives it to the woman. She takes it, thanks Max with a dignified inclination of the head, and goes out. Max addresses some biting reproaches to Subri, who goes out looking very much deflated.

Max leans back in his chair, passes a handkerchief over his face, and says "Whoof!"

I burst into speech.

"What was it all about? A girl? Was it the woman's daughter?"

"Not exactly. That was the local brothel-keeper."

"What?"

Max gives me as nearly as possible the woman's own words.

She has come to him, she says, so that he can redress a grievous wrong done to her by his servant Subri.

"What has Subri done?" Max asks.

"I am a woman of character and honor. I am respected throughout the district! All speak well of me. My house is conducted in a God-fearing manner. Now comes this fellow, this Subri, and he finds in my house a girl whom he has known in Kamichlie. Does he renew his acquaintance with her in a pleasant and decorous manner? No, he acts lawlessly, violently—in a way to bring disrepute on me! He flings down the stairs and out of the house a Turkish gentleman—a rich Turkish gentleman, one of my best patrons. All this he does violently and in an unseemly fashion! Moreover, he persuades the girl, who owes me money and has received much kindness from me, to leave my house. He buys a ticket for her and sends her away on the train. Moreover, she takes with her one hundred and ten francs that belong to me, which is robbery! Now, Khwaja, it is not right that such abuses should be done. I have been an upright and virtuous woman always, a God-fearing widow, against whom none can speak. I have struggled long and hard against poverty, and have raised myself in the world by my own honest efforts. It cannot be that you will take the side of violence and wrong. I ask for retribution, and I swear to you (this was the point where the gold cross came into play) that all I have said is true, and I will repeat it to your servant Subri's face. You can ask of the Magistrate, of the Priest, of the French officers of the garrison—all will tell you that I am an honest and a respectable woman!"

Subri, summoned, denies nothing. Yes, he had known the girl in Kamichlie. She was a friend of his. He had got annoyed with the Turk and pushed him downstairs. And he had suggested to the girl that she should go back to Kamichlie. She preferred Kamichlie to Ain el Arus. The girl had borrowed a little money to take with her, but doubtless all would be repaid some day.

It was then left to Max to pronounce judgment.

"Really, the things one has to do in this country. You never know what is coming next," he groans.

I ask him what his judgment has been.

Max clears his throat and goes on with his recital.

"I am surprised and displeased that a servant of mine should have entered your house, for that does not accord with our honor, the honor of the Expedition, and it is my command that none of my servants shall enter your house in future, so let this be clearly understood!"

Subri says gloomily it is understood.

"As to the matter of the girl leaving your house, I will take no action, for it is not any concern of mine. For the money that she took with her—that, I consider, should be repaid to you, and I will repay it to you now, for the honor of the servants of the Expedition. The sum shall be stopped out of Subri's wages. I will write a paper, which I will read you, acknowledging the payment of this money and repudiating any other claim upon us. You shall make your mark upon it, and you shall swear that this is the end of the matter."

I recall the dignity and Biblical fervor with which the woman had held up the cross.

"Did she say anything more?"

"I thank you, Khwaja. Justice and truth have prevailed as they always do, and evil has not been allowed to triumph."

"*Well,*" I say, rather overcome. "*Well . . .*"

I hear light footsteps tripping past the window.

It is our late guest. She carries a large missal or prayerbook and is just going to church. Her face is grave and decorous. The large cross bobs up and down on her breast.

Presently I get up, take the Bible from the shelf, and turn to the story of Rahab the harlot. I feel I know—a little—what Rahab the harlot was like. I can see this woman playing that part—zealous, fanatical, courageous; deeply religious, and nevertheless—Rahab the harlot.

December is upon us; the end of the season has come. Perhaps because it is autumn and we are used to spring, perhaps because already rumors and warnings of European unrest are in the air, there has been a touch of sadness. There is the feeling, this time, that we may not come back. . . .

Yet the Brak house is still rented—our furniture will be stored there, and there is still plenty to be found in the mound. Our lease runs for two years. Surely we shall come back. . . .

Mary and Poilu take the road through Jerablus to Alep. From Alep we go to Ras Shamra, and spend Christmas with our friends, Professor and Madame Schaeffer, and their very delightful children. There is no spot in the world more charming than Ras Shamra, a lovely little bay of deep-blue water framed in white sand and low white rocks. They give us a wonderful Christmas. We talk of next year—some year. But the feeling of uncertainty grows. We say good-bye to them. "We shall meet again in Paris."

Alas, Paris!

We leave Beyrout by boat this time.

I stand looking over the rail. How lovely it is, this coast with the mountains of the Lebanon standing up dim and blue against the sky! There is nothing to mar the romance of the scene. One feels poetical, almost sentimental. . . .

A familiar hubbub breaks out—excited cries from a cargo boat we are passing. The crane has dropped a load into the sea, the crate has burst open. . . .

The surface of the sea is dotted with lavatory seats. . . .

Max comes up and asks what the row is about? I point, and explain that my mood of romantic farewell to Syria is now quite shattered!

Max says he had no idea we exported them in such quantities! And he shouldn't have thought there was enough plumbing in the country to connect them up to!

I fall silent, and he asks me what I am thinking of?

I am remembering how the carpenter at Amuda set up my lavatory seat proudly by the front door when the nuns and the French Lieutenant came to tea. I am remembering my towel-horse with its "beautiful feet"! And the professional cat! And Mac walking up and down the roof at sunset with a happy remote face. . . .

I am remembering the Kurdish women at Chagar like gay striped tulips. And the vast henna red beard of the Sheikh. I am remembering the Colonel, kneeling with his little black bag to attend at the uncovering of a burial, and a wag among the workmen saying: "Here is the doctor come to attend the case," so that ever afterwards "M. le docteur" becomes the Colonel's nickname. I am remembering Bumps and his recalcitrant topee, and Michel crying *"Forca"* as he pulls on the straps. I am remembering a little hill all covered with golden marigolds where we had a picnic lunch on one of our holidays; and closing my eyes, I can smell, all round me, the lovely scent of flowers and of the fertile steppe. . . .

"I am thinking," I say to Max, "that it was a very happy way to live. . . ."

EPILOGUE

THIS INCONSEQUENT CHRONICLE was begun before the war, and was started for the reasons I have stated.

Then it was laid aside. But now, after four years of war, I have found my thoughts turning more and more to those days spent in Syria, and at last I have felt impelled to get out my notes and rough diaries and complete what I had begun and laid aside. For it seems to me that it is good to remember that there were such days and such places, and that at this very minute my little hill of marigolds is in bloom, and old men with white beards trudging behind their donkeys may not even know there is a war. *"It does not touch us here. . . ."*

For after four years spent in London in war-time, I know what a very good life that was, and it has been a joy and refreshment to me to live those days again. . . . Writing this simple record has been not a task, but a labor of love. Not an escape to something that was, but the bringing into the hard work and sorrow of today of something imperishable that one not only *had* but still *has!*

For I love that gentle fertile country and its simple people, who know how to laugh and how to enjoy life; who are idle and gay, and who have dignity, good manners, and a great sense of humor, and to whom death is not terrible.

Inshallah, I shall go there again, and the things that I love shall not have perished from this earth. . . .

Spring, 1944.

FINIS
EL HAMDU LILLAH

Agatha Christie